SPARKS OF LIGHT

SPARKS OF LIGHT

JANET B. TAYLOR

HOUGHTON MIFFLIN HARCOURT
BOSTON   NEW YORK

For information about permission to reproduce selections from this book,
write to trade.permissions@hmhco.com or to Permissions,
Houghton Mifflin Harcourt Publishing Company,
3 Park Avenue, 19th Floor, New York, New York 10016.

hmhco.com

The text was set in Adobe Caslon Pro.

Library of Congress Cataloging-in-Publication data is available.

ISBN: 978-0-544-60957-0 hardcover
ISBN: 978-1-328-91526-9 paperback

Printed in the United States of America
DOC 10 9 8 7 6 5 4 3 2 1
4500722249

This book is dedicated to my mom, Nena Butler, who gifted me with her love of reading, and taught me that with a book in your hands, the journey never ends.

CHAPTER 1

Decapitation.

Decapitate, *verb. From the Latin,* decapitatus. *To remove the head from the rest of the body.*

It happened in the bedroom. In *my* bedroom to be specific, though it still seemed bizarre to think of it as mine, this once-sumptuous chamber of velvet and marble and antique furniture that was so massive and solid it would likely survive the apocalypse. As with a prom queen at the end of a long night of debauchery, only touches of the room's original glamour remained.

Not that I had firsthand prom knowledge per se. But one does read about these things.

After another excruciating day, which had included three muddy hours of stabbing practice, my muscles were in full-on noodle mode, and I was already mentally sinking into my comfy, if craterous, feather mattress. So when I pushed open the door, it took me a second to get it. Though I froze before the utter and complete annihilation scattered across the scuffed floorboards, my brain, Old Reliable, began to catalogue the horror.

Splayed, crooked limbs. Clothing ripped to shreds. Matted clumps of hair strewn about a slim, fragile neck that was now nothing but a ragged stump.

I did not see a head.

Yes, my life had become decidedly weird in the last few months. And though it hadn't been what most folks would call apple-pie normal in the first place, at least there'd been no brain-twisty flights through time and space, no assault, no mutilation or bloodshed.

That was no longer the case.

Since arriving at my aunt's manor in the Scottish Highlands, I'd seen medieval soldiers battle with blood and sword. I'd befriended a legendary queen. I'd been pursued by a vengeful saint. I'd engineered a prison escape and helped bring my mother back from the dead.

I'd killed a guy.

Maybe. Probably. The temporal jury was still out on that one. The fact that he'd been a very *bad* guy didn't temper the horrible nightmares.

But this victim had been an innocent. Her destruction a direct result of my own negligence. I took in a breath and stepped inside. As I picked my way through torn lace and body parts, my heart tried to crumble into minuscule, crackling bits.

No, I thought as I faced off with the murderess herself. *This I will never forgive. This was assassination. For this I will forever swear vengeance upon your head.*

With a smirk playing around her unrepentant mouth, the killer sat down on the floor amid the carnage she had wrought and—without the slightest hint of remorse— began to lick her own butt.

"Oh, that's real nice."

My best friend's new calico kitten interrupted her bath, one leg raised in that peculiar contortion only cats can perform, and blinked at me with wide, oh-so-innocent eyes.

"Oh, don't you dare look at me like that," I snarled at the little puff-head. "I know you did it."

The fur-ball stood on three stubby legs and glared at me for daring to chastise her. The right rear leg dangled, nothing but a nub, though it didn't slow her even the slightest.

Mac, Collum and Phoebe's grandfather, had found her outside the barn. Wet, bloodied, one of her legs mangled beyond repair. After returning from the vet, the feline had quickly usurped control of the manor.

She stretched languidly, back arching as she gave a yippy little yawn. I frowned and reached down to snatch a hunk of blond hair caught in her whiskers.

"This." I waved it before her. "Is evidence. See it? Red. Freaking. Handed."

With a little hiss, she raised a minute paw and batted at the blond curl. I jerked back just in time to avoid having my finger ripped open by needle-sharp claws.

The kitten had evil in her, I was sure of it. She despised anyone with two X-chromosomes, though for some reason, she adored the guys. Mac, in particular, was smitten, toting her around, the little whiskered face peeking out from the pocket of his down vest. Her only redeeming feature was how utterly uncomfortable she made Collum, as she continually appeared out of nowhere and yowled at him to pick her up.

"Why?" I whispered as I surveyed the destruction. "What did I ever do to you?"

She'd been delicate, beautiful. Ancient. Much, much older than the eighteenth-century house itself. The beheaded doll that now lay in scattered ruin across my bedroom floor was the only evidence of my true origins. The only reminder of the child I had once been.

That is, the only *tangible* reminder. In a way that hurts my brain to think on, just twelve years had passed since someone had plucked her from an icy forest, keeping her safe until he could return her to me.

Twelve years, give or take a few hundred.

"Hey, Hope, have you seen Hec . . ."

Phoebe MacPherson skidded to a halt in the doorway. Her hair, previously spiky and the color of blue-raspberry soda, now bore a sleek, chin-length bob, and was dyed what could only be described as shrieking purple. Freckled, barely five feet, and sporting her favorite panda-print jammies, my friend would've looked closer to twelve than sixteen if it hadn't been for her rather abundant chest.

Phoebe gasped as she took in the shredded, headless body. "Oh-h-h," she moaned. "No-o-o. No no no! Tell me she didn't."

I shrugged. "She did." I turned away before she could notice my lips trembling. "My fault. I must've left the door open."

Phoebe knelt, and carefully scooped up the fragile carcass. Bits of yellow silk floated to the ground. We both looked around for the head. I spotted it first, half-buried beneath a pillow.

"Got it." I climbed up the three wooden steps and stretched out full-length across the mattress. As my fingers closed around the round shape, the cat jumped up on the bed to claim her prize.

Avoiding her, I sat up and stared at the delicate painted face in my cupped palm. I sniffed. Stupid to get upset about a dumb doll. Still.

Soft fur rubbed against my elbow. I glanced down as Sister Hectare "Hecty" MacPherson gave a sympathetic meow and nestled against my side.

"Oh, no. I do *not* accept your apology, you furry little butt-head."

Hecty nudged me.

"Don't you get all purry with me, missy," I said. "You are a bad, bad kitty."

Phoebe climbed the steps and settled in on my other side, holding the carcass's torso in her lap. I tried to maintain my ire, but when the kitten put her paws on my leg and looked up at me again in that melty, Puss-in-Boots way, I groaned. Conceding defeat, I reached down to scratch the velvety spot just behind her ears.

She hissed, and tried to rip the head from my hands with her tiny teeth. I snatched it away just in time. Disgusted, the cat hopped down and—tail high—stalked out the door.

"Doesn't really match the name, does she?" I said. "Sister Hectare was nice. *That* thing is a nightmare."

"Well, the good sister did have sharp claws, aye?"

I huffed. "That's true enough."

The stud through Phoebe's eyebrow glinted as we shared wobbly smiles, both of us thinking of the decrepit little nun who'd used up the last bit of her strength to save our lives. To us, Hectare had died only a few weeks before. Not a thousand years in the past. Her image, and that of the incomparable Queen Eleanor of Aquitaine, remained sharp in both our minds.

Though the history books chronicled many details of Eleanor's life, Sister Hectare's story had disappeared into the mists of time.

"So." Phoebe sniffed and swiped at her eyes. "Is it broken, then?"

I examined the head in my palm. The carved wooden features were blessedly intact. But the paint was scratched, and there was a bald patch on one side where the kitty had snacked on the brittle golden strands of real hair imbedded in the skull.

"No," I said. "I don't think so."

I should have known better than to leave it lying right there on the bed, with full-on feline access.

But I'd taken to sleeping with the doll. Stupid, I knew. Childish. Still, it was all I had left of that murky "time before." And . . . the only thing I had left of him. Of Bran Cameron. The only physical evidence that we—as a *we*—had really existed. That what had happened between us was real.

Every morning when I woke, there were always a few sleepy seconds before it hit me. A hammer blow to the chest.

Not one word in all this time. Not since he'd gone back. To *her*. To his mother, Celia Alvarez, the woman who'd trapped my mother in the past, then left us all there to die. And though she'd allowed Bran to return to the Timeslippers, I didn't want to think what kind of torments she'd inflicted on him for his betrayal.

"Oi." Phoebe reached out and took my hand, squeezing hard enough to pull me back from the dark place. "He *does* love you, you know."

"Oh, really?" I jerked away and rubbed my bloodless fingers. "Then why not one word in all this time, huh? It's been nearly two months. Two bloody months."

I scowled when her pointed nose crinkled and one side of her wide mouth curled up.

"What?"

"It's just funny to hear you say 'bloody.'" She grinned. "It's all like . . . *bluudee.*"

"Shut up." I jabbed her with an elbow. But a reluctant smile began to tug at my lips.

We sat in silence for moment. None of us had any idea what Celia was planning. Where or *when* she might decide to travel next. The only thing we knew for sure was that she would never give up, not until she found the Nonius Stone, the infamous opal she believed would allow her to better control the entity we knew as "the Dim."

This we could not allow.

And the thing that knotted my stomach the most was that I knew Bran. He'd take crazy risks. To protect us. To protect *me.* And if Celia caught him thwarting her plans, adopted son or not . . . I had no doubt what she'd do.

As if she'd read my mind yet again, Phoebe said, "He's okay, you know. I mean, it's Bran. If anyone can talk themselves out of a tough situation, it's him."

I sat up straighter at that. "Well, that's the truth. He does have a kind of knack for getting out of trouble, huh?"

When Phoebe beamed that grin at me, the one that lit up an entire room, I couldn't help but return it.

"That's my girl."

She gave my leg a pat and launched herself off the bed, clearing the steps in one acrobatic leap. Despite her petite size, my best friend was freakishly strong. I followed, easing down the steps in my own distinctly unathletic manner.

"Gram can fix her, you know." Phoebe plucked the doll's head from my hand and stuck it in the pocket of her jammies. Cradling the battered torso in one hand, she said, "I'll drop her off in the sewing room, then I'm for bed." She gave a huge yawn. "It's late and you could use some beauty sleep yourself. You look like something the dog dragged in."

"Thanks a lot," I said. "But I think I might—"

"To bed. No excuses," she ordered, giving me her sternest —no use arguing—face.

In that moment, she looked and sounded so much like Moira, I raised my hands in submission. "Okay, okay."

"Good girl." At the doorway she turned. "Actually," she mused, "think I'll drop off our mangled friend here, then scoot downstairs and see if I can't entice my Doug away from that damn computer of his. Lad's been working around the clock, and it's not good for his condition."

"Good luck," I said. "But you'd better watch out. I swear he and that thing have something going on the side."

She gave a lewd wink. "Oh . . . I'm not worried. I've a few moves I doubt that blasted computer can match."

She sashayed out the door, hips swaying. I shook my head, grinning because I knew she was right. Our resident genius might be deep down his computer rabbit hole. But I'd seen Phoebe bring it before, and I had no doubt that in the end ... she'd have him—probably literally—eating out of her hand.

CHAPTER 2

THE GIRL'S GRANDFATHER, GANGLY AND STOOPED IN HIS scholar's robes, held tight to her hand as they hurried through the huge, ornate chamber. She was feeling very important indeed as they followed the Lord Chamberlain through room after room, moving past all the handsome lords in their doublets and ruffs. Past ladies in their silks, their hair piled high and strung with pearls as they waited for an audience with the queen. Though she'd been instructed to stare directly ahead, back straight, chin high, she couldn't help gawping at the ladies' white-painted faces.

Her mother claimed painting one's face was nothing but vanity, and silly besides. Though the girl wondered sometimes had her mother been a great lady, instead of the wife of a cloth merchant, if she might feel differently.

As they passed through the last pair of green and white doors, the girl saw her. The red-haired queen sat behind a small desk, eating orange slices. She felt a little stab of disappointment not to find Her Majesty seated on her great throne, beneath a canopy of state. But the queen's jewel-encrusted gown sparkled prettily in the light that slanted down through the mullioned windows, and the girl thought that was very nice.

A tall, handsome man in a velvet cape the color of grass leaned against the queen's chair, speaking quietly to her.

"That is Robert Dudley, the Earl of Leicester," her grandfather told her in a whisper. "A great friend to the queen and to myself."

When they entered, the earl straightened and came around the desk to greet them.

"Good morrow, John," he said to the girl's grandfather. "'Tis been some time. I've missed our games. No one else beats me at chess quite as soundly as do you."

"It has been a while, Your Grace," her grandfather agreed. "And if I recall correctly, you very nearly won the last time we played."

Grinning down at the girl, Robert Dudley doffed his feathered cap and pressed it to his chest. "Oh Glorious Majesty. Queen of my heart." He turned and gave the queen a theatrical wink. "I do believe this beautiful maiden might have just stolen my love clean away."

"Oh, do get out, Robin." The queen waved him away with a ringed hand. "And don't come back for two days. I tire of your jokes." Her voice sounded severe. But the girl saw the queen's lips quirk, and observed that her gaze never strayed as she watched the earl sweep into a deep reverence, then saunter out the door.

They approached the desk. The queen's face turned terribly stern, though there was a sadness around her eyes as they flicked again toward the closed door.

The queen swallowed hard, and the girl thought maybe Her Majesty hated wearing the high, frilly collar as much as she herself did. When the girl's fingers rose to tug at the thing—starched into submission by her mother that very morning—her grandfather whispered for her to stop fidgeting.

As I lay curled beneath the quilts in a half doze, I knew the scene filling my mind was no dream. It happened like that now. The once-cloaked memories of my strange early childhood bubbled up from the shadowy part of my brain, returning at odd times. When I was distracted, or my brain logy with sleep.

Unlike the memories of so-called normal people, mine emerged crystal clear. Every detail as sharp and crisp as if it had happened only days earlier. Before I'd come to Scotland, my photographic memory had been yet another thing that singled me out. Made me different. Made me a joke with my father's family. Add to this that I was the only home-schooled kid in our entire infinitesimal town and it's not hard to deduce that my social calendar was rarely full.

And yet, as the memories emerged full-bodied and complete, I felt removed from them. As if I were watching a beloved character from one of my favorite books come to life.

A few feet from the desk, the girl's grandfather bent low in a respectful bow. She followed with her best curtsy, proud that she

held it without tipping over. Back at home, before her grandfather had hoisted her onto his huge horse, her sister had leaned down to hiss into her ear, "Do be careful, sister. You know how clumsy you are. I'd hate for you to fall flat on your face when you meet Her Majesty."

One winter day, as the girl wept in her mother's arms, her mother had explained that it was envy that caused her sister's occasional cruelty. She resented their grandfather's special affection for the girl, her mother had said. Though he visited their house often, eating at their table and spending long hours teaching all three of them — her brother, sister, and herself — to read and write, he took only the younger girl with him when he went to visit his mother's home at Mortlake.

After he informed the girl's mother he was taking her to meet his great friend, the queen, the girl's sister had yanked on her braid and would have pinched her had their older brother, Willie, not warned her away.

Her small legs trembled as she held the curtsy. When, finally, the queen's rich, husky voice ordered her grandfather and her to rise, the girl dared a look. The queen's lips, painted in a red cupid's bow, stretched as she smiled fondly at the girl's grandfather. When he returned a slow grin, the girl knew something special existed between them, this magnificent queen and her own ratty old Poppy with his ink-stained fingers and scruffy gray beard. Her chest and cheeks glowed with pride. She wondered, though, why the queen's own mother hadn't taught her to use a willow twig to clean her teeth, as they looked very dark against her white face.

After a moment, her grandfather made the introductions. "Your Majesty," he said. "This is the child I've mentioned to you."

Queen Elizabeth Tudor's painted eyebrows arched into a high, plucked forehead. "Ah," she said, smile dimming. "Yes. I seem to recall. You did *help support a poor orphaned child once long ago, did you not? A girl, I believe? Grown now, with children of her own. How very . . . philanthropic you are, John.*"

The girl's grandfather went very, very still as the queen picked up a tiny golden spoon and began to tap the end of a boiled egg. It cracked, and she peeled the shell off in one long coil.

"But." She reached out to pinch some salt from the silver salt cellar, sprinkling the egg before stabbing the spoon into the tender white flesh.

A dripping bit of yolk made its way to the queen's painted lips. And when she looked back at the girl's grandfather, her black eyes had gone cold.

"In truth," Queen Elizabeth said. "This child is your granddaughter. Her mother a bastard, a by-blow from your younger days. A fact which you did not deign to share with me."

The girl's back stiffened at that, though her grandfather's hand squeezed hers in warning.

How dare you, *thought the little girl, her small body almost vibrating as she seethed with outrage.* How dare you call my mother a bastard!

Even at four and one-half years, the girl knew what that meant. A scurrilous lie, *she thought, crossing her arms over her thin chest as she waited for her grandfather's no doubt furious rebuttal.*

She waited and waited. And when her grandfather only stared down at his feet, the girl's heart sank. She determined then to demand the truth from her grandfather the moment they set out from Windsor Castle.

"Did you think I would not hear, John?" The queen stood, anger cracking the smooth white paint. "Nothing happens in my kingdom that I do not learn of it!"

Queen Elizabeth threw the spoon hard against the near-by window. It clattered to the ground. A trail of yellow slime dripped down the glass. Silence reined for a long moment. The girl watched sunlight glint off diamonds and emeralds as the queen paced back and forth, a hand pressed to her flat abdomen. The girl may've been young but everyone in the kingdom whispered of it. How the great Virgin Queen would not choose a husband. How she had no child, no heir, to call her own. How she was beginning to age.

Her grandfather spoke softly. "Your Gracious Majesty," he began. "In my youth, I made many mistakes." His grip on the girl's hand loosened, though he did not let go as he looked the queen in the eye. "My only regret in this matter is that I did not share it with you. But the deed itself I cannot lament. Not for one moment. Not when this child is the outcome. She is like me. She holds my gift of memory. And I believe with the right training, she could one day be very useful to you and to England."

Finally, seeming to come to some decision, Queen Elizabeth gave a short, sharp nod. Her grandfather's shoulders relaxed as he let go of the young girl's hand. The girl held tight to the poppet he'd bought for her in the market only that morning, squeezing her as the queen's sharp black eyes roved over her face.

Opening pursed lips, Elizabeth the Virgin Queen, Gloriana, Queen of all England, Scotland, Ireland, and Wales, began to scream.

Wait, that's not right, I thought. *What happened next was that the queen had taken her grandfather aside to speak privately while the girl . . . while I . . . looked out the window at the garden. Then—*

My eyes popped open as the scream came again, faint and lingering, followed by a high-pitched wail. A glance at the digital clock on my bedside table told me it was 11:43 p.m., meaning I'd been in bed a total of twenty-seven minutes.

I threw off the covers and stumbled down the wooden steps. I dashed across the room and threw open the door.

Illuminated only by antique wall sconces, converted in the last century from their original gas, the darkly paneled hallway seemed to stretch out to nightmarish lengths. My bare feet slid on the faded carpet runner as I skidded to a halt before the last door on the left.

From inside came two distinct cries.

I wasn't the only one who'd heard. Moira MacPherson, plump cheeks flushed from sleep, appeared seconds later, and I allowed myself an inward sigh of relief that I wouldn't have to face this alone. In her fluffy bathrobe and pink sponge curlers, Moira nodded at me solemnly.

Down the hall, Mac, Moira's balding husband, was wrapping a flannel robe around his gangly form.

"Happening again, is it?" Yawning, Mac scrubbed at small blue eyes, identical to his granddaughter Phoebe's. "I thought Greta had prescribed something to help our Sarah rest?"

In the last month, Dr. Greta Lund, Aunt Lucinda's Danish doctor friend, had spent hours with my mom, helping her learn to cope with the aftereffects of her traumatic ordeal. Afterward, Greta and Lucinda often spent time together, sharing a cup of tea or a glass of wine.

That the good doctor also knew all the family secrets came as something of a surprise.

"Thick as thieves, those two were," Moira had told Phoebe and me one evening after Aunt Lucinda had escorted Greta through the back door to her car. "Greta spent all her holidays and summers here, her own family being a bit of a mess, you see? When she chose medicine over staying on with the Viators, it nearly broke Lu."

Taken aback, Phoebe and I looked at each other. The idea of anything "breaking" my imposing aunt was beyond both of our imaginations.

The hell? Phoebe mouthed.

I shrugged. But as Moira ambled off to clear the dinner table, Phoebe and I scrambled to the kitchen window to watch Lucinda and the pretty, gentle-voiced Dr. Lund. They were standing very close together. And when Greta laid a hand on Lucinda's cheek, my aunt smiled down at her with such devastating emotion, I could only gawp.

"Whoa," Phoebe whispered, eyes going round as marbles as she turned to look at me.

"Yeah," I agreed. "Whoa."

Phoebe beamed. "But that's brilliant! I always felt sorry for Lu, you know? No matter how strong she is or how she claims to be 'married to the Viators,' she has to be lonely. And especially now, with the illness and all. Gram claims the blood transfusions are helping. But I heard Greta tell her that without a sample of the disease, there's no real way to cure it."

I turned away from the window, giving the two women their privacy. Whatever was killing my aunt's red blood cells was a complete mystery to her doctors. Of course, what they did not know—could never know—was that the disease rampaging through my aunt's bone marrow had been acquired during a trip to thirteenth-century Romania.

From behind my mother's closed door, the baby mewled.

"Mom won't take the sedatives, 'cause of the nursing," I told Mac.

"I offered to wean the babe to the bottle," Moira put in. "But Sarah wouldn't have it."

As Mac started down the hall, Moira waved him back.

"No need, mo ghràdh," she said quietly. "Get to yer bed. Hope and I can handle this. It won't be the first time, aye?"

Mac paused, then stifled a yawn as he nodded. "A'right then. But call if you have need of some warm milk. Or a tot o' whiskey. I can fetch either."

As the door to their bedroom closed, Moira turned back to me. "Scotsmen," she tsked. "Always thinking life's ills can be cured with a bit o' spirits."

Moira and I faced the door together. For the moment all was silent.

Maybe they went back to sleep.

The staccato tinkle of shattering glass sounded through the thick wood. Moira gave a cry and grabbed the crystal knob. It turned, but the door wouldn't open. Cursing in Gaelic under her breath, Moira reached into the pocket of her robe and pulled out a skeleton key.

"Learned my lesson last time," she told me as she twisted the brass key in the lock.

Though every lamp was lit, so that the room blazed with light, I didn't see my mom. The wicker bassinet in the corner was empty, but the room was filled with the sound of my two-month-old sister's squalls.

The bedroom smelled of baby powder and furniture polish, underlaid with a metallic tinge. Light from the small chandelier glinted off shards of glass that lay strewn across the wooden floor and braided rug. On the bedside table, strands of purple heather tangled in a puddle of water where a vase of Waterford crystal had stood earlier that evening.

While Moira dashed to the bed and rifled through the rumpled quilts, hoping to find the baby there, my gaze flicked around the room. In the shadowed space beneath the four-poster bed, I thought I saw something shift.

"Mom?"

Moira, back at my side, pointed a shaking finger. "Hope," she murmured. But I'd already seen it. A small scarlet stream that flowed from beneath the bed.

I dropped to my hands and knees. "Mom," I choked out. "It's me, Hope. Mom, are you hurt? Is Ellie okay? There's blood, Mom. Why is there blood? Please come out, you're scaring me."

"Hope?" My mother's voice sounded scratchy and hoarse, as if she'd been shrieking for hours. "Is it really you? She . . . she didn't take you?"

"Wh-what?" Stifling the sob that was trying to wrench itself from my throat, I croaked, "No one took me, Mom. I'm right here. Just . . . come out, okay?"

Moira eased down, knees cracking as she knelt.

"Sarah," she called softly. "It's me, darling girl. It's your Moira. Hope's fine. Come on out, now. We're sore worried about you. And the babe."

For a time, my sister's wails quieted and all we could hear was my mother's uneven breathing. I glanced down as something warm touched my fingertips. The blood had reached the spot where my hand pressed against the floor. It began to pool up around my fingers. Shuddering, I jerked away.

"Mom!" My voice cracked. "Mama. Plea—"

"Sarah Elizabeth Carlyle!" A stern voice cut me off. "Stop this nonsense and come out of there this instant!"

My arms wobbled, and I nearly wilted in relief as my Aunt Lucinda marched across the room, towering over me. "L-Lu?"

"Of course it's me, Sarah," my aunt snapped. "Now come out from under that bed. Your child is in distress."

With a sharp gesture, my aunt waved me back as my mom began to shuffle out from beneath the bed, her left arm squeezing my red, flailing sister tight against her side.

Over the last few weeks, my mother's strawberry blond hair had developed a large streak of white. Marie Antoinette syndrome, Dr. Lund had explained. A condition that occurs when a terrible shock causes the hair follicles to stop producing pigment. Aunt Lucinda, eight years my mother's senior, had always looked so much older than Mom.

But now, seeing her ragged face beneath the unforgiving lights, I realized my mother had aged a decade in the last year.

Dr. Sarah Carlyle had been one of the world's most sought-after and respected historians. An author of bestselling biographies, once a year my mom had crisscrossed the world on her sold-out lecture tours. Later, of course, I learned the true reason a renowned critic once wrote, "Dr. Carlyle's descriptions are so clever and so damn realistic, one would swear she had been there to witness the events for herself."

My mother was clever, no doubt. But she'd also put her trust in the wrong person, and it had almost killed her.

For eight long months, she had been trapped in the twelfth century. Tricked, then abandoned in medieval England by a woman who'd once been her very best friend. Celia Alvarez had sold her out, and the abuse my mother had endured at the hands of the brutal man she was forced to marry was unimaginable. Alone and heavily pregnant, by the time Collum, Phoebe, and I arrived in that distant era to save her, my strong, brilliant mother had been so badly broken, I'd barely recognized her.

Lucinda helped Mom to her feet, gently pried my squalling sister from her arms, and handed the squirming bundle off to Moira.

My heart twisted itself into a hard, pulsing knot when I saw blood smeared across the tiny ducks on Ellie's onesie. Moira laid my sister on the bed and gave her a quick, practiced once-over.

"The babe isn't hurt," Moira whispered. "Only scared and likely hungry."

Lucinda's broad shoulders sagged just a bit as she gave Moira a brisk nod. Mom flung her arms around her sister's neck, clinging as she trembled and muttered to herself.

When I saw the large shard of crystal jutting from my mother's clenched fist, all the breath left me in a whoosh. Blood poured down her wrist to stain the back of Lucinda's peach bathrobe as my mother held on.

"Aunt Lucinda." My voice vibrated. "Her hand—"

"I'm aware," she said, without moving. "Moira? The child?"

"I'll take her downstairs," Moira said. "If you've got this?"

"She's coming for us," my mother whispered in a voice that felt like spiders marching down my spine. "Celia's coming. She swore it, Lu. She came to me and said she'd take us all back there if it was the last thing she ever did. I had to protect my daughters."

A silence fell, as if the name had poisoned the very air around us.

The back of Lucinda's neck flushed. Cheek pressed against my mom's lank, sweaty hair, she said quietly, "Moira, please fetch the first aid kit before you go. Hope and I will tend to Sarah."

As Moira bustled out, Lucinda slowly eased my mother's arms from around her neck.

"Hope, a clean cloth, if you please." Though she aimed to speak in her normal, stolid manner I could hear my aunt's voice quaver as I snatched a cloth diaper from a nearby laundered stack. Holding on to my mom's other side, I helped

Lucinda ease her down into the wooden rocker next to the bed.

"Sarah." Lucinda knelt before the chair. "Remember what Greta told you. They are only nightmares. Dreams. Nothing more. You know we have eyes on Celia. She cannot hurt any of us."

I flinched, knowing full well who was keeping an eye on Celia. Who supposedly reported her dealings to my aunt, commander general of the Viators. I shoved away thoughts of Bran, refusing to dwell on how much danger he was in, or what would happen if Celia ever found out he was spying for us.

As Lucinda gently opened my mother's fist, I swallowed hard at the damage. Only one person was to blame for this.

One day I would make her pay.

Tutting, Lucinda carefully withdrew the vicious shard. I took it from her outstretched fingers, then dropped it into the nearby metal waste bin with a heavy plink as my aunt pressed the cloth into the jagged wound.

"Oh, Sarah," she said under her breath. "What have you done?"

My aunt snatched up a thick, folded sheaf of papers from the floor beside the bed and passed them to me. "Take this away, please."

Nodding, I turned my back and unfolded the pages.

The stark, black words at the top read: *DIVORCE DECREE: Petition for Dissolution of Marriage.*

I closed my eyes as rage flared inside me.

I shouldn't have been surprised. When Dad had arrived weeks earlier, responding to my aunt's urgent summons, he hadn't taken the news well. Not only was his wife back from the dead . . . he also had a newborn daughter. A scientist, my adoptive father refused to accept the truth, even after my aunt, Mac, and I had explained everything. That his wife had been trapped in the past. That she'd been tricked by an evil woman. That—after being told for years it was impossible—the baby she bore was his.

He'd begged me to go with him. As if I would even consider leaving my mom alone.

"This is my home now," I told him, realizing the truth of the words even as they left my lips.

Later, of course, we learned that he and Stella had become engaged on their vacation. That while we were fighting for our lives in the brutal medieval world, my father had been kneeling on a beach in Mexico, proposing to a nice librarian.

I'd hated him for it at first. His cowardice. His disloyalty. But Mom convinced me that in the long run, it was best for everyone. My dad's world was algae and test tubes. Fourth of July parades and iced tea on front porch swings. She'd said she'd known that about him, and had thought it was the life she wanted as well. It was why she'd never told him the truth about who she really was. About who I am, and where I came from. For years, she'd tried to stuff herself—and me

—into a world that was always going to be too small for people like us.

Apparently, Dad had made his decision. And it was just one more thing to pile on. One more punch to the gut, along with everything else Mom had suffered. Well, maybe I couldn't protect her from this, but I sure as hell would protect her from Celia Alvarez.

I crumpled the pages in my fist as I turned back around.

"Mom?" I said, my voice fierce and low as she raised her bloodshot eyes to mine. "I—I love you, Mom."

CHAPTER 3

"BLADE!"

By the time I managed to snatch my dagger from its hidden sheath in my boot and bring it up, it was far too late. My attacker's sword whipped down, so close I felt the breeze on my cheek and heard the weapon slice the air next to my ear. A few dark curls floated to the muddy ground and disappeared into the muck.

Heart slamming, I tried to dance away. But the tight waist of the practice gown had long ago stolen what little breath I had. The full skirts tripped me up, and I went down hard. In seconds the cold, boggy ground seeped through the thick layers of wool and muslin.

I scuttled back on my butt, boot heels making divots in the mud.

"Stop. Can't brea—" The sword tip nudged my throat. Cold, sharp, stinging.

Ignoring the raindrops that pattered my cheeks and eyelashes, I glowered up at the grin spreading across my opponent's broad, freckled face.

"Better." Collum MacPherson sheathed the short gladiator sword that had once belonged to his father. "You drew quick enough that time." He offered me a hand up. All pride gone, I took it.

"But you paused," Collum went on. "And you can't hesitate, Hope. Not for an instant. Not when you're under attack."

"But," I said, my voice just south of a whine. "I could've cut you."

Collum's blond eyebrows quirked puppy-like over his eyes, though he was kind enough to hide the smile. "Unlikely."

That was true enough, though it irked me to no end that he had to look so damn smug about it. Despite weeks of endless training, I was still clunky and awkward with any and every type of weapon. Besides, I'd never seen anyone faster with a sword than Collum MacPherson.

Well . . . that part wasn't exactly true. But before the image of a dark-haired figure whipping two curved blades like they were extensions of his own body could fully form, I pushed it away.

"What?" Collum's hazel eyes narrowed on me.

"Nothing. Just cold." I shivered for effect.

"Cold?" he queried. "In July?"

"It's a Scottish Highland July. What is it, like sixty-eight, seventy degrees? It's ninety-eight in Arkansas right now. In the shade. Plus," I added, gesturing to the mud that was congealing on the back of my skirts. "Ick."

"Ick?" Collum closed his eyes and pinched the creased skin between his sandy brows. "So what you're saying is that when you get into trouble on a mission, you'll simply . . . what? Call a time-out?" His voice went high-pitched in the worst American accent I'd ever heard. "'Excuse me! Hello, all you murderers. Could you stop swinging at me for a moment, please? I've a muddy bum.'"

"Well, I—"

"No." He picked up my blade and handed it to me, hilt first. "Again. And again and again. And never mind the 'ick.'"

In the two months since my abrupt return from the past, Collum had been relentless. Two hours. Every day. Tired or exhausted. Rain or . . . well, less rain, I was dragged outdoors to defend myself—in costume, no less—against an opponent of his choosing.

With Phoebe, a much more patient and gentle teacher, I learned how to use my opponent's larger size against them. Only for me, that happened about one out of every hundred times, and usually because my feet got accidentally tangled with theirs.

Phoebe had trained almost since she'd left the womb, in an insane regimen and with a variety of martial arts. With a body weight of a hundred pounds dripping wet, my petite "bestie" could put down any attacker. Usually in less than five moves. Watching her send Collum crashing to the mud was one of the joys of my life.

I wasn't any better at knife throwing, Phoebe's other exquisitely honed skill. As Mac often said, "My granddaughter can peel the wings off a fly at thirty paces, she can."

After days, weeks, two *months* of kicks and punches, knife chunks and bow twangs. After countless nicks from steel objects—mostly self-inflicted. After hours in Moira's Epsom salt baths, trying to soak the feeling back into my numb muscles, you'd think I'd have become at least *somewhat* less pathetic.

You would be wrong.

"Argh! I can't do this!"

I threw the light practice sword away in disgust. It twirled through the air, hit the mud point first, and stuck there.

"Hey!" I called to Collum as I watched the part that wasn't sunk in the mud sway back and forth. "Kinda stuck the landing, didn't I? I mean, sure, it was an accident and all. But you gotta admit, it was kinda cool, was—"

From twenty yards away, Collum rushed me. Like his woad-painted ancestors before him, he raised his sword and shrieked an ancient battle cry as his large feet pounded across the stable yard.

It happened without conscious thought. A translucent film, tinged neon green, overlaid my vision. Multiple arcs drew themselves from every angle, tracing out possible escape routes and countermeasures. Instantaneously, my mind filtered through every lesson, every bit of training, calculating each possible outcome of this scenario.

As two hundred pounds of bellowing Celtic warrior descended on me, my mind discarded one idea after another after another until . . .

I stepped aside and stuck out my foot.

Collum's speed was such that he couldn't veer off in time. His trajectory took him straight into my path, where he tumbled over my outstretched leg and splatted, face first, into the mud.

"Ow!" I hopped on one foot, trying to rub the already bruising flesh where the toe of his boot had cracked against my ankle.

He rose slowly while hunks of slimy earth slid down to glop back onto the ground. Collum MacPherson swiped at his eyes, flinging mud from his fingers as he glared at me for a long moment. All I could see of his face were two clear hazel eyes amid the brown gunk.

"Um." I grimaced. "Sorry?"

White flashed amid the rich ocher as he grinned. Grinned and began to laugh.

And then I was laughing too because well, it was all so utterly, utterly ridiculous. All of it.

"You . . ." I wheezed. "Covered in . . . And holy crap, we . . . freaking time travelers." I bent, breathless as I let it all go in a long, soundless spasm that I was sure would burst every blood vessel in my brain. "How . . . st-stupid is that?"

"Aye." Collum hiccupped. "And damn my eyes if you

don't look like a wee barbarian yerself with yer hair all stuck to one side of yer head!"

We laughed. We laughed until we couldn't laugh anymore. Until tears tracked through the mud on our faces and the sun peeked through the clouds to infiltrate the raindrops.

"They say when the sun shines through the rain it's the devil beating his wife," Collum said as we headed toward the house.

"Well, that is so not cool." I climbed the steps to the screened porch. "Mrs. Satan should file a restraining order against that ass-hat."

He snorted and reached out to pluck something from my hair. Turning his palm over, I saw it was a solid clump of stable yard mud or . . . what I sincerely hoped was mud. Above us, the mountaintop had disappeared behind a cloak of white mist. The air around us had turned an odd peachy plum, as if each droplet emitted its own tiny rainbow.

Collum sighed. "Oh, but I do love this time of day," he said. "When the day rests her bones beneath night's soft cloak."

"Why, Collum MacPherson," I said. "Were you just being poetic? Hang on, I need a pencil and paper. *Someone* has to notate this auspicious occasion."

Collum's always-windburned cheeks went neon as he bumped me with his shoulder. And despite the mud and the rain and the sore muscles . . . as we both smiled, I felt something peaceful and comforting settle around me, a warm blanket to chase away the chill.

"Might be that a shower is in order." He gave the dark clump a dubious look.

"Right back atcha," I threw over my shoulder as we headed inside. "'Cause you look like a golem."

We were still laughing as we went upstairs.

CHAPTER 4

EVEN IN OUR MODERN AGE OF SMARTPHONES, DELIVERY by drone, and social media addiction, there is apparently nothing more sacred to the average Scottish Highlander than the Gathering.

"Here. Put this on."

I eyed the teensy scrap of red and green tartan Phoebe was holding out to me.

"What, uh . . . What is it, exactly?"

Phoebe just shook her head and tossed the fabric in my direction so that I had no choice but to catch it. Wrinkling my nose, I shook out the scant folds of soft wool, holding them tight with two fingers as if some errant breeze might —at any moment—come along and blow them away.

I gave her a look like, *You have got to be kidding*.

"But," I tried to argue, as I looked down at the knee-length skirt Moira had altered for me the day before. "I already have a skirt."

Phoebe raised a hand to silence my protests as she

stepped back to give the modest, loose-hanging plaid I currently wore a scathing once-over. "You're having one over on me, aren't you?" she said. "You can't really be planning on wearing that old thing? You're sixteen, Hope, not fifty."

When I only looked at her, she rolled her eyes to the ceiling. "No," she said. "No way I'm letting you out of the house in that ... that horrible granny garment. You'll wear this one, and you'll look brilliant." She marched to my closet and rummaged through, snorting at the selection. Finally, she emerged with a cropped ivory top with cap sleeves and a low neckline. "This'll do. And you can just quit shaking your bloody head at me, missy. Trust Auntie Phoebe. You've got great legs. It's time to show them off."

My friend had no issue whatsoever with the amount of skin *she* displayed. Her own skirt—patterned in the red, blue, and yellow tartan that had clothed generations of MacPhersons—barely covered the necessities.

I cringed as her critical gaze roamed me up and down. My hair, though freshly washed, was pulled up in its usual tight pony. And my face hadn't seen more than a lick of mascara in weeks.

I hadn't seen the need. Not when most of my day was filled with endless hours in the library, broken up only by the occasional mud-soaked farce that was my so-called weapons training.

"You know what it's time for, don't you?" she said, her blue eyes narrowing as she stalked toward me.

"No-o." I backed up, stepping on poor Hecty's tail in my fruitless attempt at escape.

Yowling, the tiny cat shot under the bed and turned to glare at me from the shadows.

"Oh, aye. It's makeover time." With a firm grip on my arm, Phoebe marched me toward the bathroom. "Let's be on with it, then. We're running out of time and you—my darlin' girl—are sadly in need of an expert hand."

In the passenger seat of the battered old Range Rover, I spent most of the hour-long drive yanking at the soft, loose curls that whipped about in the wind, and tugging on the short skirt that seemed determined to ride up.

Thing was, I hadn't really felt like doing much of anything lately. Even racing across the moors on Ethel's back had done little to penetrate the gray film that seemed to coat my senses like a dirty shroud.

As Phoebe and Doug chattered and giggled in the back seat, the yeasty, savory scent of Moira's meat pies rose from the neatly packed boxes in the floorboard. With this batch, Moira had sworn she'd at last beat out "that braggart Catriona MacLean," for the blue ribbon.

I folded and refolded the square of crinkled wax paper that had held a sample of her entry for Scottish tablet, a buttery, sugary confection I'd scarfed down within five minutes of getting in the car.

Even Collum was in rare form.

"Sure, and there are bigger fairs around," he said, eyes pinned on the winding road ahead as he followed Mac's truck up into the glory of the Highlands. "Braeburn and Atholl, for instance. But they've become so damn commercial. Food trucks that sell junk like corn dogs and burgers and chicken on a stick, for God's sake. None of which can match Archie Gordon's bannock and bangers, mind. And they bring in ringers from other countries, so locals have little chance to place in any of the competitions."

Traffic had come to an abrupt halt as we joined the line of cars attempting to crawl through the tiny, quaint village that had played host to the ancestral gathering for a thousand years or more. An enormous ruin loomed atop a nearby hill. Only the ghosts of its noble occupants now watched over town and fields and glassy loch. Even smaller and older than the village near Christopher Manor, the sidewalks before the homes and businesses that lined the town's only street now bustled with strolling Highlanders.

When we eventually reached the grassy field that served as a parking lot, the sun was just peeping over the mist-cloaked mountains to the east. As the guys moved off with a roll of striped canvas and poles, to set the Carlyle tent among the other clans, I reveled in the fragrance of the cool early air that sieved around us.

Deep water. Highland pine. Ancient mysteries that would remain forever unsolved.

I'd never seen any of the guys in a kilt. But as they greeted old friends on the way to our assigned spot, they looked oddly natural among all the other kilted lads. Collum's back muscles bulged beneath the blue and white rugby jersey as he pounded tent stakes in the ground. By the time they'd pulled the canvas taut, Doug's gold-framed glasses were opaque with steam, and beads of sweat dripped from his finger-length dreads to trail down his face.

Collum swiped a handkerchief over his face. "Think that's it, then. If you're done with us, Gran, we'll be off."

If Collum and Doug blended the ancient with the modern in their T-shirts, tartans, and plain sporrans ... when Mac MacPherson stepped into the newly erected tent, he looked like something out of a storybook.

"Whoa, Mac!" I gaped at his intricate attire. "You look magnificent!"

"As well he should." Moira playfully bumped her husband with a hip on her way to rearranging the last of the food. "Representin' our house in the march, what with Lu feeling peaky, now isn't he?"

"And judging the sheepdog trials again," Phoebe said, scrunching her nose at her grinning grandfather. "Though I still think that darling one-eyed bloke should've won last year."

"Aw, go on w' you now." Mac, in kilt, furred sporran, and military-style black cap, waved his wife away when she fussed with the silver broach that fastened the formal plaid at his shoulder. It draped over one side of the formal blue jacket, just skirting Mac's knobby knees. "You kids better get on with it, 'fore Moira here finds more chores that need doing."

"Now you mention it ..." Moira tapped her fingers thoughtfully against her lips as she eyed the stacked jars of jam and strategically arranged baskets of baked goods.

"Go. Go. Go." Collum, one eye on his grandmother, shooed the rest of us out before Moira could come up with any more tasks.

"Wise of ye to get while the gettin's good." Mac chuckled as he followed us out the open tent flap. "No daft children did I raise, even if I say so myself." He turned to the boys. "And which heavies will you lads compete in today?"

"The caber, of course," Doug replied, slinging an arm around Phoebe's shoulders. "I'll likely sign for the sheaf toss as well. And Coll's for the hammer, I think?"

"Aye," Collum agreed. "And we'd best go or we'll be so far down on the list we won't compete till sunset. See you, Mac."

"Good luck to ye, son." When Mac clapped Collum on the shoulder, I saw the glow of pride in the older man's care-worn face as he grinned at his grandson. "And don't forget what your da and I taught ye. With the caber, 'tis not distance that matters, but accuracy, aye?"

Collum's windburned cheeks flushed an even deeper red as he bestowed one of his rare and lovely smiles on his grandfather. "Aye, Mac," he said, his voice so gruff he had to clear it. "I remember."

As I watched the two of them, my own throat tightened

a bit. I'd seen the photos. Little Collum—all big teeth and chipmunk cheeks—crushed between his dad and grandfather. Scattered all over the manor were snapshots of the three of them, the two men hoisting the freckled little boy on their shoulders. Grinning, sporting poles and matching fishing hats, the three of them setting off on manly fishing trips.

According to Moira, Collum and Phoebe's mom had been a silly, selfish woman who'd run off with another man shortly after Phoebe's birth. "And better off we are without *that* one," she'd declared more than once.

But their dad, Michael MacPherson, was another story. Even after twelve long years, his absence was a painful, palpable thing.

And whose fault was that?

If—twelve years ago—they'd simply left me to freeze to death in that forest, Michael would be here now, filling this gaping hole in their lives.

Their family would be intact. Happy and whole.

I was the reason it all went to crap. Me . . . and no one else.

"Hope?"

I jerked my chin up to find Mac gone and Collum standing only a foot away, hazel eyes narrowed as they peered into mine. "What's the matter, then? You're awfully far away."

"N-nothing." My voice cracked and I had to swallow back the part of me that wanted to fall to my knees and beg them all to forgive me for ruining their lives. "Must be something I ate. I'm okay now."

"Come on, you gadabouts!" Phoebe called. "Daylight's wasting and if I miss out on Mollie Nichols's famous scones and raspberry preserves you'll be dealing with one surly ginger, that's for certain."

For a moment, Collum didn't respond as he examined my face. I forced a smile and brushed past him with a breezy "Better get going before she whips out those knives of hers and starts chucking them at us."

In the grassy strip between rowdy tents labeled Mac-Gregor and Fraser, MacLaine and Buchanan, Doug paused to pull his phone from his sporran. He glanced at the screen, then at Phoebe.

He answered her questioning look with a thumbs-up. A grin split her face nearly in two.

"What was that all about?" I asked as Doug and Collum split off from the two of us and disappeared between two tents.

"Oh, nothing." Without another word, she hurried after the boys, leaving me staring suspiciously at her twitching skirt.

"Oi," she said, when I caught up. "I hate it when Doug throws that damn pole. I mean, God knows watching him gets me going. But, well . . . I worry that kind of strain isn't good for him. What if it brings on a seizure, you know?"

"I'm sure he'll be fine," I said. "Doug knows his limits, and he's been feeling pretty good lately, hasn't he?"

Phoebe gave a noncommittal shrug as we emerged from Clan Row into the central field. I'd done a little flash research the night before so I'd have some idea what to expect from a true Highland Gathering and wouldn't look like a *complete* novice. The articles I'd dredged up slipped into place as we stopped for a moment to observe brawny males of just about every age practice the ancient art of hurling heavy objects through the air.

The first official mention of the Scottish "tossing of ye barr" had been recorded during a military muster in the year 1574.

The Tossing o' the Caber—a large tapered pole or tree that has one end wider than the other—is now the highlight of the Heavy Athletic Competition for most Highland games.

Ranging from 15 to 23 feet long, and weighing between 70 and 150 lbs, the caber toss is the only event where the competitor is not striving for distance or height, but is a show of strength, timing, balance, and momentum.

In other words, the caber, as the text streaming through my mind explained, was a competition where strong men (and now women too) picked up what amounted to a sawed-off telephone pole. Then, cradling the end like a baby in a snuggie, toss it into the air while trying to maintain a straight trajectory.

As I watched the judges dodge the weighty missiles, I

couldn't imagine that the caber had been a very effective warfare accessory. Seemed to me, to avoid getting your head bashed in, one could simply take a little step to the side.

Across the field Collum was bent over a table, signing up for another event that appeared to consist of throwing gigantic, iron-headed hammers from a standing position. I cringed as a premature release very nearly bludgeoned the first row of spectators.

"So." Phoebe's blue eyes flicked past me to skim the clearing. "I'll go sign up for the knife toss, and meet you by the stage, yeah?"

I glanced over at a raised wooden platform where several little girls in brightly colored kilts were dancing around and over a pair of crossed swords.

"Nah. I'll just go with—"

"No." I stumbled as she basically shoved me toward the stage. "Go on with you, now. You'll want to see the bairns dance. It's adorable."

Without another word, she scuttled off to join the group of men and women gathered around a different table.

"Okay." I frowned, huffing as I stomped off toward the edge of a sparse knot of people who were watching the baby dancers. "Guess I can take a hint."

I was still grumbling under my breath when someone tugged at my skirt. I glanced down to find a little girl in red and white Highland dancer's plaid blinking up at me through too-long bangs.

"That man thaid to give you thith."

No more than five or six, the girl pulled a hand from behind her back and thrust out a dimpled fist. In her chubby palm lay a shiny red apple.

She giggled when I took it, revealing a gap where two baby teeth had disappeared into fairyland. I tried to thank her as she raced off to join her friends near the stage, but my voice too had apparently absconded.

Lids closing, I raised the round, fragrant fruit to my nose and breathed in the scent of ice and memory. The apple's cool skin brushed against my lips as I smiled and opened my eyes.

And there he was, leaning against the side of the nearby ale stand, arms and ankles casually crossed, as if he'd been waiting there since dawn.

Grinning, he pushed away from the weathered wood and took three long-limbed strides toward me.

I'm dreaming, I thought. *Gotta be.*

The dreams came often now, leaving me gasping and sweaty, filled with a new kind of nameless ache. But the boy standing before me did not disappear, or dissolve into mist that filtered through my fingers.

CHAPTER 5

FROM RUMPLED BLACK HAIR TO HIGH-TOP SNEAKERS, Bran Cameron looked perfectly at ease draped in the odd dichotomy of ancient kilt and vintage Lord of the Rings tee. Bran was a person comfortable in his own skin, a reality I couldn't really comprehend. I wondered idly if he'd meant the plaid to match the startling blue and green of his heterochromatic eyes.

"Madainn mhath."

As he spoke, I realized two things simultaneously.

One ... that I was staring like a starveling at a pretty piece of cake.

And two ... that the air, so rich in oxygen only seconds earlier, had gone suddenly and woefully thin.

"W-what?"

"Madainn mhath. It's Gaelic for good morning." He flicked a hand at his attire. "Seemed appropriate, considering."

"I know what it means."

"Well, of course you do," he said. "You *are* a superhero, after all. Though I must say, I believe I prefer that skirt to a cape and tights." A slim dark eyebrow cocked as his gaze tracked down my bare legs. "You know," he mused, "we never gave you a proper superhero name. Personally, I prefer Brain Girl, but we can open the floor for discussion if you—"

"Bran." His name tasted of mountains and heather and caramelized sugar. "How ..." I had to stop, swallow. And then I couldn't stop the questions that had built inside me for weeks.

"What are you doing here? Is it safe? Are you all right? What about Tony? Oh God, I can't believe you're really —Does Celia know? I mean, don't get me wrong, I'm glad you're here. I'm really, *really* glad you're here. It's just ..."

As I continued to babble incoherently, he took my hand and towed me toward a shady spot behind the ale stand. As I followed, my gaze slipped down past back muscles that moved under a snug T-shirt, slim waist encircled by a wide leather belt, and narrow hips concealed by yards of tartan wool.

He stopped, turned, and caught me staring. He was smiling when I looked up into a face I'd known since I was four years old.

"I did warn you the sight of my bare knees might drive you mad with lust." His voice sounded scratchy, strained. "Do you remember?"

I did. Of course I did. I was the girl who remembered everything, wasn't I?

Up close I could see the changes in his features. Jaw sharper than I remembered. Cheeks leaner under rough stubble, making the slightly too-long nose more pronounced. The injury he'd sustained and the corresponding blood infection had taken their toll. But his eyes—one blue, one green—strangely hypnotic and indescribably beautiful, looked the same as they had when we were little more than babies.

"What are you doing here?"

"It's something of a long story," he said.

"What happened? Is it Celia? Did she kick you out? Is it your—"

He placed two fingers lightly against my lips, stopping the flow of words. A grin, sweet and slow as maple syrup, curved one side of his mouth as he leaned in and whispered, "Forgive me. But for God's sake, Hope, just . . . stop talking."

And then his arms were around me and he was burying his face in my hair. I couldn't breathe, yet somehow my mouth and nose and lungs filled with the scent and taste of him. Fabric softener and fresh-cut wood and, *always,* the tang of ripe apples that lingered just for me.

I couldn't get close enough.

His mouth skimmed up the side of my neck, along my jaw, across my cheek. Achingly soft, his lips touched my brow and closed lids. When his mouth finally . . . finally pressed against mine, I arched against him. My fists clenched in the warm fabric of his shirt. My lips opened under his, and I felt the groan rumble through his chest.

His fingers tangled in my hair, roamed down my back. When I nipped at his bottom lip, he gripped my hips to pull me hard against him. A pressure was singing inside me as he lifted me off my feet and we spun, my back slamming against the rear wall of the ale stand.

I thought I heard . . . something . . . but when he swallowed the air that whooshed from my lungs, I didn't care . . . I didn't care . . . I didn't care. Not about anything but being here with him and doing this forever. Short skirt be damned, I wanted to wrap my legs around his waist and kiss him and kiss him until the stars died out. I wanted . . .

"Um, guys?" Someone cleared her throat. "So sorry to interrupt, but you might want to know you have something of an audience."

Bran stilled. His regretful sigh brushed against my neck, rippling shivers across my skin. His grip loosened and I slid down until my toes once again touched the earth.

Breathing hard, he stared down at me. His blue and green eyes drilled into mine with such raw need, I felt it in the marrow of my bones.

"Damn," he whispered as he rested his forehead against mine.

My reply came out high and oddly squeaky. "Y-yeah."

We turned to find Phoebe grinning at us like a Miss America contestant. Behind her, Doug was being all honorable, trying to shoo away the clutch of giggling tween dancers who'd gathered to watch.

"Told you that outfit was the right call." Phoebe winked sagely. "Just proves one should always listen to ole Auntie Phoebe when snogging's on the menu."

Before I could reply she greeted Bran with a hearty punch to the shoulder. "Good to see *you* again, Romeo. How's your mad bitch of a mum, eh?"

"Phoebe!" Doug cried. "That's an awful thing to say to the lad."

Doug reached out, his huge hand engulfing Bran's finer bones. "Damn good to see you again, man. You look a sight better than you did last I saw you, to be sure."

I knew the two had met only briefly, when the Dim had violently disgorged Bran and me from its midst. Fortunately for us, it had chosen to take us back where we marginally belonged.

We'd been whisked off to the hospital. Me with a concussion. Bran only half-conscious from an infection that had entered his bloodstream to ravage his body, courtesy of a knife wound inflicted by his own mother.

"Glad this worked out," Doug said. "I tried everything to open that file you sent last week, but the encryption was too damn good."

"Last week?" I mouthed the words mostly to myself, certain I'd heard wrong.

I shot a look at Phoebe. She was watching me. But at the look on my face, she quickly ducked her violet head, and began tugging at her thigh-high socks. "Damn things always creeping down."

I turned to Doug—who was basically incapable of lying. "Doug?"

"W-well, you see, Hope." Whisking off gold-framed specs, Doug pinched sweat from between his eyes. "It's only that—"

"It was me." Bran jumped to the traitorous pair's defense. "I swore them to secrecy. But only because I wanted to surprise you."

"Yeah, well. Mission accomplished, I guess."

Bran's grin faded. "We've only been conversing a few weeks, you see, and—"

"Wait." Voice deathly quiet, I held up a hand to stave off the rest of his words. "Did you say *weeks?*"

Phoebe cast a scathing look upon both boys, moving to my side in a show of girl unity.

"Doug didn't tell me until last night, Hope. They've been keeping their little bromance to themselves, it seems. No one else knew of it." Hands on hips, she glared at Doug. "And I told you she wouldn't like it. Hope hates secrets."

Bran's brow creased. "You're angry?"

"Oh, no," I said. "Not at all. I lo-o-o-ve being left out in the dark. My mom did it to me my whole life. Why should you be any different?"

Maybe I was being petty. Having him here was a wonderful—no, a stupendously wonderful—surprise. But I had a feeling our impromptu little reunion was only part of the story.

"If this was all about *surprising* me, then what's all this about a file?"

Doug's face filled with regret. "I'm sorry, Hope. I should've told you. I — I know what it feels like to be excluded, aye?"

We locked eyes, and I realized that of everyone in my new family, Doug was the only person who truly understood what it feels like to be left out in the cold.

Doug's dad had been one of Mom and Aunt Lucinda's closest relatives. Which — leaving aside my bizarre bloodlines — made him my cousin. When his parents died in a car accident, the seven-year-old had come to live with Lucinda as her ward. Though he survived the tragedy that killed his folks, the head injury he'd sustained carried long-term effects. Doug now suffered from a dangerous case of epilepsy. A few weeks earlier I'd witnessed one of the violent seizures that came upon him suddenly, this time at the dinner table. It had been one of the most terrifying things I'd ever seen. Because of the instability of Doug's condition, Lucinda had long ago decreed that he'd never be able to travel with the rest of the Viators. Though the brilliant boy accepted his supporting role with an astonishing amount of grace, it had to hurt.

Douglas Carlyle, the smartest person I'd ever known, was the only one of us permanently bound to this time.

It wasn't fair.

I reached up to pat his broad shoulder. "It's okay."

He dipped his head in a nod and I turned back to Bran. "But you," I said. "Get talking."

"You've no idea how much I've yearned to hear you snap at me," he said, trying — and failing — to look contrite. "You see," he said, "there were some things I needed to work out first. Things I knew Doug was uniquely qualified to help with. Then, once I learned you lot would be coming here, I fabricated a false lead on the Nonius in Inverness. Naturally, Celia didn't want to send me, but I withheld the pertinent information until she had no choice. After that, it was simply a matter of drugging Flint's lager — so that I could slip the leash, so to speak. Then, I, um . . . borrowed a set of keys from the valet station, located a car in the hotel's long-term parking, and drove like a demon so I could see you." Slender, elegant hands danced through the air, punctuating the story as he finished. "There's more, of course. But that is it in a nutshell."

As he looked down at me, I saw an oddly shy expression peek out from behind the cocksure curve of his mouth. A warmth spread through my chest as I thought to myself, *He's gone to so much trouble. Taken so many risks. He drugged a guy for God's sake.*

Just to see me.

His eyes closed as I rested my palm against his stubbly cheek. "I guess I forgive you," I told him. "Just this once."

"Well," he scoffed as he brushed windblown curls back from my face. "I must say that is a huge relief."

Bran and I shared a smile. A blaze of heat and tenderness and something else I couldn't yet name began to flood through me. The rest of the world faded away into a distant thrum. What existed between us had survived through time and space. I thought ... maybe ... we could become something extraordinary. Something legendary.

But the thing about legends is that they rarely have a happy ending. Romeo and Juliet? Antony and Cleopatra? The prince of Troy and his Helen? Every one of those fateful couples was doomed, what drew them together burning too hot and too bright to last for very long.

I let my hand drop.

Bran looked at me quizzically. "What?"

"Nothing." I stepped back, deliberately puncturing the bubble that had pushed the rest of the world away. "You, uh ... You said there was more you needed to tell us?"

Bran's gaze searched my face before he nodded, and turned to include Doug and Phoebe.

"Yes," he said. "Well, back to Phoebe's initial query about my mother. I'm afraid she's quite correct. Celia is worse than ever these days. I fear the woman has gone completely off her nut."

"Why does that scare me more than anything I've ever heard?" I muttered.

Bran chuckled, a pallid sound that dissipated as he gestured for the others to come closer.

"Which brings me to the other reason I came," he said, taking care that his voice wouldn't carry beyond our small huddle. "Which is to inform you of the newest scheme my dear, demented mater has hatched."

"Jesus, Mary, and St. Bride," Phoebe groaned. "What kind of heinous plan does the Mistress of Bloody Darkness have on tap for us today?"

"That," a gruff voice spoke up, "is something I'd be sore interested in hearing."

CHAPTER 6

"Cameron."

As Collum strode over and wedged himself between Doug and Phoebe, the two boys sized each other up.

"Nice tartan," he said. "Rent that at the costume shop, did you?"

Bran ignored the jibe. "Well, if it isn't Collum MacPherson in the flesh. You know, I was wondering when you'd grace us with your presence. Off playing with sticks, were you? Tossing them in the air and whatnot?"

"Didn't see your name on any of the entry sheets," Collum replied. "Course, most of the competitions here require big arms, not a big mouth."

Bran laughed. "Got me there, MacPherson. But it's a shame, isn't it? Maintaining all those bulging muscles must route so much blood away from the brain."

Collum's cheeks turned a mottled fuchsia. His large, freckled hands fisted.

Phoebe stepped inside our loose circle. Reaching into her

tiny, furry sporran, she removed a small bottle of perfume. Her skirt flew around her as she whirled, pumping squirts of the flowery essence into the air and coughing theatrically.

"So, uh," I said as the others stared. "Whatcha doing there, Pheebs?"

"Just trying to clear some of this bloody testosterone from the air so we can get down to business," she said. "Wanna help? We'll never get anything done with this lot if we don't."

Everyone but Collum burst into laughter. And even his tense features relaxed by a margin.

"As an evolved member of the male species," Doug said, "I agree with my woman. We may be dressed like savages, but we're modern men, are we not? So shake hands or punch each other in the face and let's get on with it, aye?"

With that, Phoebe and Doug hurried away to fetch Mac and Moira, who also needed to hear what Bran had to say. Collum's turn at the hammer toss was coming up, so he veered off, leaving Bran and me to stroll across the grassy field alone.

Contestants shouted or grunted as they hoisted enormous poles and sensationally long hammers into the air. Announcers extolled the various feats of the athletes while spectators cheered. The smells of summer, of roasting meat and the yeasty scent of beer, all mingled as the mild Scottish sun beamed down upon our shoulders.

Bran took my hand in his. And I was happy.

We reconvened around one of several massive wooden tables that edged the performance field. Very wide and solid, with their split tree trunk benches, they were gray with age, as though they'd been here since Sir William Wallace was a boy. The hard wood of the table's surface was worn smooth as glass, and scored with hundreds of initials, each pair encased inside a roughly hewn heart.

"Look, D. Here's ours." Phoebe's fingertip traced the letters *P.M. + D.C.* near the right corner of the table. "How old were we when we did this?"

"Nine," he replied, pulling her down to perch on his generous lap. "And if I recall correctly, you dragged me over here, ordered me to do it, or you'd put a snake in my bed."

I smiled at the thought of the fierce little girl, fiery braids swinging as she dragged a tall, awkward boy toward the very same table we sat at now. I could see them still, as they passed a gentle look between them. They'd been a couple even before that day, when Phoebe had rescued the newly orphaned Doug from a pack of schoolyard bullies who hadn't cared for the color of his skin.

I'd seen pictures of Doug's beautiful Senegalese mother and round-faced, freckled dad. With her high cheekbones and intelligent eyes, and his father's kind expression, Doug was a superb representation of two remarkable people.

"Mac carved ours over on the table near the big tree, the year before we married," Moira said as she settled in next to her granddaughter. "'Tis said any couple carved into the wood here shall never part. Even my grandda's and grandma's are here somewhere."

Mac stood behind his wife, both gnarled hands on her shoulders. He leaned down and whispered something in her ear that made her jump.

"John MacPherson!"

"Well," he said, "'tis true. And it was after that, I knew I wanted to marry ye."

Moira's plump face flushed as red as the second-place ribbon pinned to her shirt.

She caught me looking at it. Wrinkling her nose, she flicked it. "I swear that Catriona MacLean pays off those damn judges," she scoffed.

"Well, let's hear it then, Cameron." Collum spoke over the laughter that followed. "What brought you all the way here from that spider's lair? And what have you been doing that we haven't heard a word in all this time?"

Seated beside Bran, I pivoted to better see his expression as he answered a question I'd asked myself every moment since we'd parted.

"Oh, you know me." Bran shrugged. "Cricket. Pub crawls. Playing double agent amid a gang of murderous time-traveling thugs. It's exhausting."

"For Christ's sake." Collum's hands shot up in disgust.

"Bran," I said quietly. "Just tell us, okay?"

He followed my gaze as I glanced up at the sun, climbing

ever higher overhead. The morning was passing too fast, and I knew we didn't have much time before he'd have to leave me. Again.

His eyes met mine and he nodded. Beneath the table, I felt his graceful fingers entwine with mine.

"It was Doug's idea, really," Bran said. "The man's a genius."

"No genius," Doug replied, humble as always. "It's just that I remembered something Bran said while he was in hospital. Before his moth—before Celia—had him transferred out, that is. He mentioned that he and his brother, Tony, secretly communicated through online video games."

"I'd been going mad trying to find a way to contact all of you," Bran said. "Naturally, since my return, my every move is monitored. Gaming is the only contact I have with the outside world. And that only because *she* has no idea the level of sophistication some of these games possess. She believes them nothing but mindless diversion. Which they basically are, at least until Doug created this program."

"I'd been tinkering with a new game design for a while, actually," Doug said. "I contacted some gamers at his brother's school and asked them if they'd like to beta-test. I had to be careful not to ask for Bran's brother specifically, so it took some time . . ."

"It's an amazing construct. A role-playing game, but one of the most interactive and realistic I've ever seen. If you ever decide to leave the Viators, Doug, you could make a fortune as a game designer. Tony and his mates are obsessed. He sent me an invite," Bran continued. "Then, Doug contacted me within the game . . . and here we are."

"And where is that exactly, lad?" Mac asked.

Bran released my hand to reach into the sporran at his waist and removed several folded sheets of paper. He laid the first one down and smoothed it out over the silvered wood. Moonlight made the pale brick of the hulking façade in the printout practically glow against the shadowy mountain behind it.

Collum slapped a hand down on the paper. "What the devil is this, Cameron?"

I leaned forward, squinting at the image. "It's the front of our house. I mean, the manor. But . . ."

"Where's the portico? And what's that building?" Phoebe tapped the left edge of the photo, indicating a lofty stone structure I'd never seen before.

"That's the old carriage house." Voice gone flat, Mac studied the picture. "Lu and Sarah's grandda, old Henry Carlyle, had it brought down just after the Second War. Used the stone to build a new shearing shed."

"Yes, well," Bran said, fidgeting a bit beneath Mac's level gaze. "This is, as you've observed, Christopher Manor. Circa 1895. As you can see by the date and time stamp, however, this image was captured only three weeks ago."

When we all began speaking at once, Bran raised his

hands in a request for quiet. "I promise to explain the whens, whys, and wherefores—at least what I know of them—in a moment. But first, take a look at the others."

When he laid the second image down, there was no question.

The full-color photo had been snapped at 11:23 the morning after the first photo. The lighting on this one was perfect, the image crisp and clear. From the partial obstruction and steep tilt of the camera angle, it was obvious the four figures, embroiled in conversation several feet away, were unaware of being photographed. The scene behind them was unmistakable. But it wasn't the bookshelves or marble fireplace or the portrait above the mantel that sent shock waves through me.

Mac grunted. "Well, damn my eyes."

"Is that . . . ?" asked Moira in a hushed tone. "Is that who I think it is?"

The crease between Bran's eyes deepened. "Yes, ma'am, it is," he said. "Jonathan and Julia Carlyle, Archie MacPherson, and Luis Alvarez as they appeared in February of 1895."

"Who took this?" I asked, though I was pretty sure I already knew the answer.

Bran took in a deep breath through his nose before slapping down the last and final printout onto the very center of the table. Everyone leaned in to get a closer look. I could feel Bran's gaze on me as my hand covered my mouth.

"Holy crap on a bleeding cracker," Phoebe gasped.

"Phoebe Marie MacPherson, what have I said time and

again about using vulgarities?" Moira's admonishment came by rote, lacking its usual heat.

"Aye, I know, I know. 'Tis cheap and all that. But Gram!"

"I don't know, darlin'." Hands white-knuckled now on Moira's shoulders, Mac peered down at the picture. "I'm thinking this particular occasion might call for a bit o' language."

Though somewhat pixilated, there was no mistaking the identity of the woman now standing between the Edwardian-clad versions of a young Jonathan Carlyle and his wife. With her dark eyes and haughty features, she even resembled her several-times-great Aunt Julia. In the shot, Celia Alvarez was the only one looking directly at the camera. Her smile, as she faced the clandestine photographer, was unmistakably triumphant.

Mac straightened and let out a long breath. His wise, hooded eyes rose to meet Bran's. "Do you yet know the meaning of this, lad?"

"First," Bran said, "I want you to know that I knew nothing of this until a few days ago."

Collum snorted but said nothing as he glared at Celia's smug expression.

When Bran faltered, Moira reached out to him. "Go on then, Bran. We're listening."

Bran glanced down at Moira's age-spotted hand as she patted his arm. When I saw the shy, almost awkward way in which Bran looked at her, I realized that such a simple maternal gesture was utterly foreign to him.

And I added yet another mark to the tally of reasons I despised Celia Alvarez.

"The Timeslippers have been recruiting heavily. Though most are little more than mercenaries, thieves, forgers, what have you . . . one of my mother's newer 'acquisitions' is a Swiss physicist. A man named Dr. Gunnar Blasi."

"Blasi?" Doug nodded slowly as he spoke. "I've heard of the man. I remember seeing a lot of chatter about him in some of the science forums a year ago or so. Worked for CERN, the international nuclear research facility in Geneva, right? Some hotshot working with Higgs boson particles in their Large Hadron Collider. But he got the boot and there was all kinds of crazy speculation about it, because he was supposed to be some kind of wunderkind. No one knew for sure; I just remember reading that he'd done something unsavory."

"Yes," Bran said. "'Unsavory' sums up Blasi's character quite nicely. And though I haven't a clue what happened at CERN, I can tell you he's a nasty character who's only fueled my mother's obsession with finding a way to gain control over the Dim and ultimately . . . over time and space themselves." Bran's lip curled. "Yes, you heard right. The man's ego is monstrous. Blasi had been working on a way to harness the lodestones to the current machine, in preparation for when they 'locate the Nonius.' Recently, however, the focus of his research has changed."

"What happened?" I asked when Bran's shoulders slumped.

Bran's gaze fixed on the tabletop. He swallowed hard. The shouts and cheers from the festival grounds became muted, as though something as simple as joy could not penetrate the invisible barrier around us.

"*I* happened," he muttered. "It's my fault."

CHAPTER 7

"The wheres and whys aren't important." Bran didn't look up from the table as he spoke. "Suffice it to say that during the course of a recent discovery mission to gain some of Tesla's more obscure papers, I happened upon a box. Nothing of substance, or so I thought, though I'd hoped to mislead Celia and Blasi into wasting time with it. The box's contents were eroded. They were moldy, and at some point mice had been at them. It wasn't until we returned and began to sort through that I realized my mistake. Hidden among bundles of receipts and formulas scribbled on cloth napkins was a letter, written by a man named Emil Stefanovic, one of Tesla's assistants. The note was addressed to Emil's friend, or—based on the letter's tone—his lover. In any case, Blasi noticed my interest and took the letter from me. But not before I'd made several copies." Bran looked across the table at me, his face carefully neutral as he removed a creased sheet of paper from his sporran. He unfolded it and pressed it smooth over the table's surface.

"Here."

January 15th of the year 1895

My dearest companion,

I hope this letter finds you well. And that your family has recovered from the terrible loss of your father. I know your mother and sisters must find great comfort in your return. Yet I pray that you soon find your way back to me. There is great excitement in the professor's lab these days. Yet I feel little of it, for the days have turned gray without you by my side and in my bed. Sell the land. Return to New York. Bring your family if you must. But come back, my sweet friend. As you yourself have said many times, you would make a terrible farmer.

Now, the news I promised in my last letter. Oh, if only you'd been here to share in the wonder. For the first trial, Tesla chose that bootlicker Jacobo. A wise choice in my eyes, as there would be no loss if the man never returned, yes? Though he has not yet revealed our secret relationship to anyone, he still looks upon me with disgust and uses every opportunity to discredit me with Tesla.

But back to the tale. It has been two weeks since Jacobo returned, after being "away" for three days! Bedraggled and filthy he was, but very much alive. Hard to fathom, I know. But believe that I speak nothing but truth. The device the good professor has created! It is genuine. It. Is. Real.

I write you now to let you know this... The professor has finally agreed that I shall be next ..."

Bran shrugged. "The next few sentences were too damaged to make out. Only the signature remained."

"Tesla?" Moira whispered. "That can't be right. This would indicate that Tesla . . ."

"Built his own device in New York City." Bran slapped a hand on the table. "Exactly. The moment my . . . Celia . . . learned this, she became obsessed with contacting the man himself. It will come as no surprise that I am not exactly in my mother's inner circle these days. So it took a while to tease out a few details. But from what I can ascertain, Gunnar Blasi has come up with an idea for an enhancement, which—for all intents and purposes—would mask the bearer's genetic signature, giving the traveler more time in the past."

Collum straightened abruptly. "More time? How much more time?"

Bran shrugged. "Several days more, according to my source. Blasi claims he must dismantle and rework the original Tesla device to know if his sketches for the enhancement are truly plausible. The good news is that Celia does not trust him enough to allow this. So, for weeks she's been searching for a timeline that would allow them to meet up with Nikola Tesla so they could take Blasi's sketches to the inventor himself. She finally became impatient when the Dim would not cooperate. And now . . ."

"Now," I finished for him, "she's contacted Jonathan Carlyle and convinced him to do her dirty work for her."

Bran looked suddenly exhausted as he nodded. "Just so."

"And," Doug mused, "since we know that once the past has been penetrated time moves in a linear fashion in both timelines, by now Jonathan would've had time to sail to New York."

Bran's eyes skipped from face to face, turning last to me. "You cannot begin to imagine my mother's frustration when —only days ago—she received word that the time and location she'd been hoping for would soon open."

Oh, and I bet she's royally pissed about that. I smiled a little at the thought. *Since poor little Celia already entered that stream, and the mean old Dim won't allow anyone to travel twice to the same timeline, her butt is stuck here. Aww. Guess she'll have to sit this one out.*

My head shot up. The question emerged from my lips, though I already knew the answer. Of course I did.

"She's sending you, isn't she?" I said. "That's what you came here to tell us. She's sending you back."

Bran's lips were pressed into a tight line, but he raised his chin to look straight into my eyes. "Yes."

"And you agreed?"

Bran's blue and green eyes sparked with fury, and when he spoke, it was with such bone-deep resentment, I felt it ignite my own hatred of the woman all over again. "She has withdrawn my little brother from the school he's called home since he was six years old, and is withholding his current location from me. She has further informed me that should I ever wish to see or speak to Tony again, I will obey her." Bran rose, the tips of his fingers whitening as they pressed hard into the tabletop. "My loving mother has grown increasingly suspicious of Blasi and most of the others, you see. Recently, she learned that he tried to circumvent her by going directly to Doña Maria. The demented old bat being the one who holds all the money cards, Blasi thought to cut out the middleman."

When Bran looked at me, I could see the bewilderment hiding behind the anger. "It has come to this. Aside from Jasper Flint, *I* am now the only person my mother trusts. And isn't *that* just a sad state of affairs?"

Mac broke the silence that followed. "Do you believe this enhancement will actually work, lad?"

"Blasi is convinced."

Collum stood up and scrubbed both hands back over his bristly hair. Like a great cat sensing prey, he paced back and forth. "If this thing does what Cameron claims, do you realize what it could mean?" His voice rose, his gestures growing animated. "Think what we could do with even three more days. How often have we seen the Dim open to England in the right time but not the right location? With extra days, we could do a proper search and still get back in time." I jumped as he slammed his palms down on the tabletop. "My God! We could find him. We could finally bring Da home."

"Bran." Moira spoke in a quiet voice. Her eyes were shut, as though in pain. "If Celia were to get this device . . . this enhancement . . . what do you think she'd do?"

"Mrs. MacPherson," Bran replied, "for once, my mother's actions are not the most concerning. I came to speak with you today because of how badly Gunnar Blasi wants this. I don't know why, and *that* is what scares me more than anything."

"Well, that settles it then," Phoebe said. "We have to go."

"Hang on a tic." Doug reached down to pull his phone from his sporran. After jabbing at the screen a few times, he looked up. "I, ah, I've built an app that links into the computer and displays the upcoming passages." He swallowed. "It appears that when you factor in the —"

Phoebe grabbed his large wrist and tilted the phone toward her. "Longitude and latitude, blah blah," she read, scrolling down. "Numbers, numbers, numbers. Hey!" Her blue eyes widened as they skimmed down the page. "Well, Bran. Looks like your lot won't be all alone in the Big Apple."

Collum made a grab for the phone but Phoebe was quicker. Doug put an arm around her and squeezed her to him as she scrolled again. She stopped, head tilting. "Hmm," she said. "Better warm up your sewing machine, Gran. We've got less than four days to prepare." She was squirming now, practically dancing with excitement. "I've always wanted to do the Victorian era. I only wish it were Christmastime and not March. No one did Christmas like the Vickies."

Caught up in her own excitement, Phoebe didn't notice the way Doug's shoulders fell. I tried to catch her eye, but she had already passed the phone back to him, mumbling to herself about which gowns could be altered.

Doug hesitated before punching a few numbers into the phone. "Actually," he said, "it is three days, sixteen hours, and twenty-two minutes. Tuesday, at 8:23 a.m., the Dim will open."

"And to which exact date, Douglas?" Moira asked.

Doug held out the phone but Collum took it first. Sitting next to his grandmother, he tilted it so that he, Moira, and Mac could all view it at once. As Moira slipped a pair of readers from their usual spot on top of her graying black hair, Mac's head tilted against his wife's as all three read the words together.

Mac read it aloud to the rest of us. "March eleventh, 1895." His head rose to level a look at Bran. "That concur with your dates, Bran?"

Bran hesitated. "Yes. The same. Though I believe our arrival is some two hours earlier. Looks like we'll get to do a bit of sightseeing before you all arrive."

My brain began to pound, to fill with every political, social, and civil event that had occurred in and around the New York area on the three days following March 11, 1895.

I forced most of it back. I already knew there was only one sentinel event — one historical occurrence too well known to ever be revocable — that really mattered. One reason and one reason alone that the Dim would open to that specific date and time and location.

"The thirteenth," I spoke up. "It's all about the thirteenth."

Doug was already nodding as Mac said, "March thirteenthth,1895?" A million wrinkles formed around his eyes as he squinted, head cocked. "The date does ring a bell. Why is that?"

"March thirteenth, 1895," I said as I turned back to the others, "was the night Nikola Tesla's Fifth Avenue lab burned to the ground. It's the night he lost everything."

CHAPTER 8

Mac straightened. "We need to relay all this to Lucinda and I don't want to do it over the phone. We'll have little enough time to prepare, and so must leave at once."

My stomach sank into my feet. *We're leaving? But . . . but that's not fair.*

Bran got up when Moira stood. Mac gripped his shoulder in thanks. Moira gave him a hearty embrace, speaking loudly over Phoebe's groans of protest.

"Thank you for coming to us, Brandon. And we won't be forgetting it. But Mac's right. Lu has to know, and we've decisions to make. Hope, you stay, but say your goodbyes quickly." With a wave, she motioned for the others to rise. "The rest of you, no more bellyaching. You heard your grandfather. Get to the tent and get everything packed up. We leave in ten."

Collum was the only one who lingered at the picnic table while Bran and I stayed put, staring remorsefully down at the hundreds of carved initials.

"I think you're holding out on us." Collum rose slowly, gaze narrowed on Bran. "There's more to this than you're saying, Cameron. You know it. I know it."

Knuckles pressed to the tabletop, Collum loomed over us. Behind him, the mist-shrouded Highland peaks rolled on and on, as unchanged and unyielding as the people who lived there.

"Make no mistake: If *anyone* gets hurt because of something you concealed, you'll answer to me."

With that, Collum wheeled about and stomped away, kilt swinging, broad shoulders rigid with tension.

"Never thought I'd miss the dear lad." Bran's natural good humor was trying to return. His grin flashed, revealing that one crooked eyetooth. "But damn if he doesn't grow on you."

"Bran."

As he turned on the bench toward me, the grin slowly faded.

"There's never enough time, is there?" he said. "For us, I mean. It seems to have become something of a pattern."

"No," I said. "Never enough. And we're time travelers, no less. Seems like that ought to afford us some kind of privilege."

He huffed a chuckle. "You know, things have been ... difficult at home. Worse than you could imagine."

I watched as his fingertip traced the carved hearts on the table. He had such graceful hands, though they were scarred, callused from riding and swordplay. And as he went on all I could think about was having those hands on my skin.

"I wanted to leave, you know? Started to run a hundred different times. But then, I'd think of that day when my stupid horse tossed me into the river. And there you were, standing in the freezing water and glaring down at me, shivering but so fierce. Or I'd remember how you looked with the snow falling all around you as you melted iron bars to save a friend. And I would tell myself that if you could possess that kind of courage," he said, "then I could stand it a little longer."

My breath caught as his hands moved to glide over my shoulders, down my arms. The warmth of his palms heated every inch of me they touched. His arm slid around my waist and held tight as we watched the Highland games.

If I squinted, I could almost pretend we were in a place set apart from time. A world where mighty Highlanders from every clan had come together on this ancient field to practice their form of warfare. To ready themselves against British attack.

Babies cried from their mothers' hips. Men slapped each other on the back as they tipped steins of beer. Children ran and called to one another, their eyes wide with wonder as they watched their parents compete. Happy, hearty smells of heather and clean water and the mouth-watering aroma of steaming meat pasties suffused the air. Beneath our feet, the earth trembled with the *thunk*s of heavy objects striking the ground.

"Are you safe?" I asked, not looking at him. "Will you be all right?"

"Of course," he said. "I am a very clever lad, after all."

We turned to each other, then. He raised my hands to his lips. One after the other, he placed a soft kiss in the center of each palm. I shivered as I squeezed my fists shut, trying to hold on to those kisses.

"You know," he said in a musing tone, "if you weren't leaving in six minutes and twenty-two seconds, and if we lived in the age where all this"—he waved a hand at the field of contestants and spectators—"was real. Back when men were men and all that. I'd simply heave you over my shoulder and carry you off into yonder meadow over there."

"Ha! I'd just kick you in the kilt and run away." I was grinning, though my face went red at the images his statement produced.

He threw his head back and laughed up at the blue, blue sky. "Yes. You would, wouldn't you?"

"So, um, six minutes and twenty-two seconds, huh?"

He nodded. "Six minutes, eight seconds now. But who's counting?"

Our faces were very close. My lips tingled as they remembered the feel of his mouth on mine. I think I must've sighed, or groaned, or made some other kind of embarrassing noise. Because his eyes went all smoky, and he chuckled low in his throat. The sound went through my chest and settled shivery and low in my belly. All my attention sharpened on his mouth as his hands came up to cradle my face. He held me there, so close I could feel the heat of his sun-warmed skin on my lips. My eyes closed as I leaned in to close that minuscule distance.

Collum coughed loudly as he and Doug passed by, canvas-wrapped tent poles suspended between them.

Bran broke away and pulled me to my feet. His voice low, urgent, he said, "I know I can't talk you into staying, but please, please be careful. Promise me?"

"You too." As he let go of my hand and backed away, my chest constricted. And it felt as though some giant vacuum had suddenly appeared in the sky to suck away all the oxygen in the open field around me.

Bran called to Mac. "Thank you for listening to me, sir."

Mac waved in acknowledgment, then got into the driver's seat. He and Moira pulled away, back tires spinning up gravel.

"Well," I said, "I'd better go."

Bran nodded, wordless. We began to walk away in opposite directions. We did that a lot, it seemed.

Suddenly I heard the crunch of footsteps on the gravel behind me. "Wait!" Bran called. "Wait . . . just wait one second."

He towed me quickly back toward the long, stout table that had been in place since Moira's grandmother was a girl. Reaching down, he withdrew his sgian dhub, the tiny but lethal knife all proper Highlanders wore, stuffed into the top of their right sock.

"Nearly forgot," he said. "Can't have that, now can we?"

His long neck bent to the task. Muscles in his lean shoulders flexed. Sun flashed on polished steel. It took only a moment. He straightened and drew me to his side as he brushed away the pale shavings that littered the top of the ancient table.

There we were. Our initials looked so new, so fragile, amid all the others that had weathered the years and decades together. But staring down at them, I also realized how bright we glowed against the aged wood.

BC + HW.

Instead of enclosed in a heart like all the others, Bran had wrapped us up together inside the shape of a small and perfect apple.

"You heard what Moira said." His hand smoothed over my hair as he smiled down at me. "Now it's forever."

CHAPTER 9

"BRANDON!"

Bran jolted back, his body going as stiff and still as if he'd just been struck in the head by one of the flying cabers.

A girl stood next to the table, head cocked as she watched us. Amusement played over her features as Bran's eyebrows lowered and his mouth went tight. I realized I'd seen her, though only briefly, in the group of people watching the preschool dancers.

"Gabi," Bran said through clenched teeth. "What are you doing here? You promised you would wait in the car."

She shrugged. "Me aburrí, mi primo."

"Bored?" Bran huffed in agitation. "We had an agreement."

Did that ... Did she ... just call him cousin?

The girl dimpled when she smiled, and I suddenly understood the expression "murderous impulse" much better.

"I am sorry, Brandon." R's rolling, her tongue slipped over the English with exotic flair. "When you were so long away, I became worried."

Bran seemed to deflate. His head bowed for a few seconds before he straightened his shoulders and turned to me.

"Hope," he said, "this is—"

"Gabi." I stood. When I felt my bottom lip split a little, I realized my mouth had stretched into something approximating a smile. "Yes, I heard."

It wasn't that she was beautiful. Well, she was. She was also tall, tan, and fashionable in a way I could never be. *Lissome.* That word slunk up from my mental thesaurus. Sunglasses that probably cost more than my entire wardrobe pushed back the girl's honey-colored hair. Her ensemble of linen and raw silk had undoubtedly been created for her by people with singular names like Gucci and Prada.

Long-limbed and graceful, or so I thought until she moved toward me and I saw the pronounced limp. And then she was grabbing my hands, squeezing them and smiling down at me with such fervency I could only blink up at her.

"I am Gabriella de Roca," she said. "And I know who you are, of course."

"Do you?"

"Oh, yes, and I am so very happy to meet you at last, Hope Walton."

"Gab-ri-ella." Bran stumbled over the name, obviously more accustomed to his little nickname for her. "Is—in a manner of speaking—a relative of mine. Her grandfather, the Duke of Martelleña, was married to Celia's grandmother, Doña Maria." He moved close to me. I edged away until his arm was no longer pressed against mine. "We, uh

... we've known each other since we were children, though she spends most of the year away at school. Until recently, that is."

So. An aristocrat. Well, of course she is. If that isn't the product of generations of wealth and beauty intermarrying, I don't know what is.

"Brandon is much too courteous," Gabriella said. "What he does not say is that when dear Abuelo passed, my mamá took his money and some of her pretty boys and left me all alone. Doña Maria was kind enough to take me in. Though I was not much in attendance, at least I had a place to go during the holidays. Now ..."

She let go of my hands and spread hers in a uniquely European manner that I thought was supposed to convey something like, "You get it."

But I most certainly did *not* get it. Not at all.

"Gabriella is a dancer," Bran hurried to explain. "Studying at the Institut del Teatre in Barcelona."

Well, naturally. What else could she possibly be?

"Ah, mi primo." Gabriella wagged a finger. An ironic and sad smile tugged at the dimples. "Gabriella *era* una bailarina. Ahora, ella no es nada."

"This again," Bran muttered. He half turned to me. "Gabriella tore the ligaments in her knee and has had several surgeries to repair them. The doctors are not yet certain if she will be able to dance on a professional level." He clucked at her. "But, you will dance again. You'll see. In any regard," he told her, "you are *not* nothing."

No, I thought. *No, you most certainly aren't.*

The rational part of my brain was telling me to stop being ridiculous. The girl was his cousin, for God's sake. But some primitive instinct had begun to creep up the DNA chain. Some predisposition left from cavewomen ancestors who —when faced with a rival—simply knocked her brains in with a rock.

"Hope," Bran said. "I—"

"Oi!" I swiveled at a shout from behind us. Collum was strolling over, loaded up with gear. Phoebe was right behind him, hoisting a box of Moira's jam.

My friend's eyes narrowed as she took in the three of us. When her gaze landed on Gabriella, her nostrils flared. She set the box on the table, then sauntered over, taking a position at my left flank.

"And just who might you be, then?"

Gabriella started to answer but Bran stopped her, waiting until Collum had joined our happy little entourage.

Collum, I noted, had not stopped staring at Gabriella since he'd spotted us.

Bran pinched the skin between his brows and quickly made the intros. "But before you haul off and punch me, mate," he said to Collum, "you need to know that Gabi . . . Gabriella is no friend to Celia."

Gabriella snorted as if that was the understatement of the year. For a second I hated her a tiny . . . tiny bit less.

"Ah!" She clapped her hands, white teeth flashing. "But it

is a great honor to meet the famous MacPhersons en persona. I have heard much of your heroics."

Phoebe's expression resembled that of her Celtic shield-maiden ancestors. "Interesting. Since we've never heard of you."

"Please, do not blame Brandon," Gabriella hurried to put in. "This was my wish. Though I have always known the ways of the family, I believe Celia to have no honor. For years, I wanted only to continue my studies, to have nothing to do with this viaje en el tiempo. Only recently have my choices become more limited. But know that I will never reveal your alliance. This I swear on the grave of my grandfather."

Gabriella wobbled when she stepped back onto her unstable left leg. Mr. Proper Gentleman, Collum, steadied her. She beamed up at him. "Gracias."

"Aye, n-no problem." Collum's cheeks blazed as he stepped back.

"For God's sake," Phoebe muttered under her breath.

"You should go, Gabi," Bran said. "I'll—I'll be right behind you."

Gabriella nodded. Her green eyes met each of ours in turn. And though part of me wanted to rip her pretty face off, there was something about her. Something that made me want to trust her.

She limped away. Collum spun on Bran. "What. Was. That?"

Bran's eyes squeezed shut. "That," he said, "was nothing. Gabriella won't say a word." When his eyes opened, he was looking straight at me, ignoring Collum's grumbling agitation. "Hope. Please understand. I never mentioned her before because—up until now—she has been a nonentity in all this."

"Didn't look like a bloody nonentity," Phoebe snapped.

Bran slid past Collum and Phoebe to take my limp hand in his. "Please, listen," he said. "Gabi can help us. She already has, in fact. She agreed to be my alibi so I could come here to see you. And she has a better chance of finding out where my brother is, since they don't monitor her every move as they do mine. She could be valuable to what we're trying to accomplish."

"So," I said, "she's not going, then? She's not part of this new team of yours?"

Bran's shoulders rose. Dropped. "Actually, Doña Maria has insisted that she accompany us, though it irks Celia no end."

I looked away, my thoughts returning to the girl. Her delight at meeting us seemed genuine. Still.

Doug rambled up, holding the last of the boxes. "Mac's already left. I told him we were right behind him, so we better . . ." He paused, sharp eyes roaming over our faces. "What's wrong?"

"Nothing."

But as I caught sight of Gabriella's retreating figure, I mentally tacked a word onto that statement, amending it to *Hopefully, nothing.*

CHAPTER 10

"Wait till you see the gowns," Phoebe gushed around a mouthful of eggs. "Gah! All that silk. They're a dream. And hey, maybe no one will try to kill us this time, yeah?"

As I'd discovered on my very first morning in Scotland, my best friend was one of those annoyingly perky morning people. As she yammered on about bustles and petticoats, I nodded at the appropriate times, tried to avoid looking at the congealing mass of baked beans she'd piled on her eggs and toast, and did my best not to think about Bran and his BFF cousin.

After my breakfast of champions—coffee and a bite of toast—we rinsed off our plates and headed for the library. The smell of aged wood and lemon polish, mothballs and damp ash surrounded us as we tromped through the dining room and past sporadic groupings of antique furniture lining the long, interconnecting rooms of Christopher Manor's first floor.

When I'd first arrived at my aunt's house—an immense, blocky affair of white Highland stone, built in the mid-seventeen hundreds by one of the sour-faced ancestors whose images lined the main staircase—I admit I'd been intimidated. But I now knew it as a place of warm hearths and cozy nooks. Of knitted afghans and ancestral shields. A place for family. A home.

The view from my second-story bedroom displayed a pastoral scene of sheep and river and valley so lovely it made my heart hurt. Beyond the small village's ocher roofs, the Highland moor spread out in an explosion of purple heather and yellow gorse.

It was a travel agent's dream come true.

But no tourist bus had ever disgorged its camera-wielding cargo at Christopher Manor. Butting up against the base of an enormous bald mountain, the house held its secrets close.

As Phoebe and I entered the library, bright beams of morning light slanted in through the tall multipaned windows. I smiled as Moira's mortal enemy—billions of golden dust motes she battled with singular hatred—swirled up to settle on the floor-to-ceiling bookshelves and burrow into the crevices of buttery leather chairs. Tiny tea tables were laden with framed photos displaying generations of manor residents. And in the central place of honor, the long oak table where I spent the vast majority of my days, eyeball-deep in research.

Out of habit, I glanced up at the portrait above the marble

fireplace. Lord and Lady Hubert Carlyle glared down with the prim, constipated expression common to portraiture of the eighteen hundreds. But I'd always loved the mischievous slant the artist had captured in their young son Jonathan's hazel eyes.

Jonathan was grown in the next portrait, though you could still see that spark as he gazed down at his stunningly beautiful wife, Julia. Looking at them, you'd never guess at the horrible tragedy that would soon befall the two sweet-faced little girls kneeling at their mother's feet. As I stared up at the doomed family, something struck me.

"Crap!" I bolted over to a shelf and snatched up the leather-bound journals I'd left there two days earlier. "Why didn't I think of this last night?"

I plopped down at the table and scanned the gilt-inlaid covers. Setting aside the one for the last quarter of 1894, I opened the diary labeled *January–March, 1895.*

Jonathan's scrawl filled every page. The entries were meticulous and straightforward, and yet revealed his wry sense of humor. In January, there'd been a wildly unsuccessful, if colorful, voyage to Verona in the late sixteenth century. This, on flimsy evidence they'd uncovered, proved that William Shakespeare had—in fact—visited the Italian city.

They were sorely disappointed to learn that the Bard had likely never been anywhere near that most famous story's location.

But I quickly flipped past all that to the latter part of

February. And there it was, a short, somewhat vague notation.

An interesting visitor arrived today with news of great import. This charming lady knew much of us and more. Though Julia took to her at once, I felt some measure of reluctance, especially when viewing the countenance of her companion. Still, as her proof is sound, we have no reason to doubt her. And so I have booked passage on the RMS Campania. Soon, I take ship to New York, there to visit my very dear friend.

"Balls," Phoebe groaned, reading over my shoulder. "Well, that's it, then, isn't it?"

I nodded. "I guess."

"Could we not find out from the later journals exactly what happened?"

"No. The rest are stored down in the Dim chamber. They won't have changed, no matter if there has been a shift. I just happened to leave these up here the other day. Stupid."

"Nah," she said, nudging me. "How could you know? And anyway, since time is moving at the same pace there and here now, won't young Johnny still be on the boat?"

I did a quick calculation of the dates. "Maybe. But he's probably close by now."

"Well," she said, pulling me to my feet. "Nothing for it but to soldier on, is there? Let's go."

"You know," I told Phoebe as we squeezed through the fake broom closet and down a flight of hidden stairs to the manor's vast cellar, "I can think of one thing that scares me way more than shifts in the timeline."

Phoebe quirked a pierced, russet eyebrow. "What?"

"Corsets."

Most people claim if they could travel back in time, they'd take out people like Hitler or John Wilkes Booth.

And sure, I'd join those crusades any day. But my personal list for time-travel assassination includes, in no particular order:

Hungarian aristocrat Countess Elizabeth Báthory (1560–1614). Obsessed with staying young, this "first female vampire" exsanguinated hundreds of peasant girls, then drank and bathed in their blood, all to keep her own skin looking dewy fresh.

Marie Delphine LaLaurie (1775–1849). Notorious for throwing lavish dinner parties in her French Quarter home, the New Orleans socialite secretly carried out macabre medical experiments on the dozens of helpless slaves chained in her attic.

And finally, there was the dude—for surely it was a man—who originally invented the corset. I thought hell surely had a very special room for that guy.

The manor's dank undercroft lay buried deep inside the granite mountain. Mighty brick pillars marched off into the shadows, bearing the house upon their shoulders. If even one of them crumbled while we were down here . . .

My mouth dried up. *Stop it. This place has stood for nearly four hundred years. It's fine. You're fine.*

I even believed it. In theory.

But no matter how many times I wove through the narrow, deliberately labyrinthine path, no matter how often I passed the towering heaps of dusty, spider-infested clutter, my chest would start to cave in. The historian in me longed to dig, to discover the undoubted treasures buried within the piles of castoffs built up over the centuries.

The claustrophobic in me ran. Every. Time.

I shoved past Phoebe and bolted down the path. As I burst through the Watch Room door, the positive-air barrier blasted my hair back in a powerful stream that kept out every speck of dirt.

I bent double, heaving for breath.

"Again?" I heard Collum mutter. But he hurried over, voice gentle as he patted my back. "It's all right, Hope. You got this, lass. Slow down. Count like your mum taught you. In . . . two, three. Out . . . two, three. There you are. Good as new."

My lungs began to re-inflate. Spots receded from the edge of my vision and I blinked down at the sight of Collum's sock-covered feet. His grandmother's order no doubt. No mud-crusted work boots would ever set foot on Moira's immaculate white-tiled floor.

"You've got a hole in the left one."

The hand on my back stilled. "That so, is it?"

With a final inhale, I straightened to grin up at him. "Pretty big one, too. Your toe's sticking out."

Collum "Everything in Life Is So Serious" MacPherson tried to glare, but I saw his lips twitch. "That's the thanks I get, then? I help you and you ridicule my clothing?"

"Just your sock," Phoebe put in helpfully. "But if you like, I can think up plenty about that clatty old flannel shirt you wear every other day."

"This I get from someone whose hair's the color of a bloody dino—"

"Enough!" Moira's single clap echoed off the tile walls. "If you're going to act like bairns, then I'll treat you as such. Collum." She held out an imperious hand. "Give me that sock. I'll darn it for ye while the girls are changing."

"Gram," he started to protest, but Moira marched over to him, glaring up from her four-foot-eleven-inch height.

"You may be a foot taller and outweigh me again by half—"

"Don't know about *that*," Phoebe whispered.

Moira wheeled, smirking as she patted her admittedly ample rump. "I wouldn't be talking out o' turn, girl-o," she said. "Just so ye know, I was as spritely as yourself when I was a lass."

Phoebe's eyes widened as she gave her grandmother's round figure a quick once-over. She raced to the mirror, twisting to see her backside.

"Oh, gads." My friend shook her head sadly. "You're right, Gram. It's going to be enormous."

"More to love," Doug—wisely never turning from his spot at the computer terminal—called out.

Slipping inside one of the wide, curtained changing booths to strip down to gym shorts and tee, I listened to the playful bickering.

This, I thought. *This is family. Real family.*

Oh, my parents loved me. I never doubted it. But our house had been more academic than homey. My world revolved around study and learning. There had never been much . . . any . . . room in my mother's ironclad schedule for play.

As I stepped out and over to the triple dressing mirror, Moira's gaze met mine in the glass. The dear laugh lines radiating from her eyes deepened as we exchanged a grin. She'd seen it in me from the start, I think. My loneliness. The desperation to belong. I had to look away, my throat going suddenly tight. Not with claustrophobia, this time. But with the overwhelming realization that I was finally home.

CHAPTER 11

As with the capable way she did everything, Moira attacked the issue of preparing our historically accurate costumes.

"All right, lamb," she said, after lacing up the despised whalebone and canvas contraption. "Hold tight to the pole and suck in."

Gripping the metallic pole installed for just this purpose, I felt the corset curve my spine and rearrange my organs as Moira yanked ruthlessly on the laces.

"Can't . . . breathe . . ." I wheezed. "Lungs . . . in . . . throat . . ."

"Now, now," Moira replied, neatly tying off the torture device. "That just means it fits proper. All the women of this era had the hourglass figure. Ye'd stick out like a banged thumb without it." She gave me a satisfied pat on the shoulder. "Aw, ye'll be fine, lamb. Women wore corsets for centuries and very few died of it."

"Only a few, huh?" I rasped. "That's comforting. Killed by corset. Yeah, that would be my luck."

"Your turn, darlin' girl." Moira had an unmistakable glint in her eye as she crooked a finger at Phoebe. "Let's just see how small we can get that wee waist of yours, aye?"

"Um, Gram." Phoebe paled. "I—I'm right sorry about—"

"Shh," Moira said. "Come on, now. You're wasting daylight."

Unable to sit in the horrible garment, I watched Doug and Collum study the enormous computer screen that filled the entire back wall. A dozen computers calculated the complicated and ever-shifting spider web of green and red. While hundreds of feet below us, the ley lines the display represented buzzed and hummed with their own strange power.

Though I wanted to burn the corset, I knew they were a necessary evil for us to pass as nineteenth-century ladies. All the Viators' costumes were era-appropriate, down to the last thread.

I should know. Since arriving home from the Highland games, Aunt Lucinda had ordered me to bone up on all things related to the late-Victorian world of 1895 New York.

"Hey, Hope," Phoebe said. "Why again—do they call it —the Gilded Age?" Puffs of air punctuated her speech as Moira yanked ever harder on the strings.

"Mark Twain actually coined the phrase," I told them, as the black and white text marched across my vision. "He and Charles Dudley Warner wrote a book called *The Gilded Age: A Tale of Today,* first published in 1873. It was a series of allegorical tales about the terrible social problems of the time that were covered over by a thin veneer of gold."

I recited Twain's words without conscious thought. "'The external glitter of wealth conceals a corrupt political core that reflects the growing gap between the very few rich and the very many poor.'"

I went on for a while, trailing off only when I noticed them all looking at me. From one blink to the next, a memory —cold as a shard of lethal ice—stabbed into me.

"You."

My paternal grandmother, Beatrice "Mother Bea" Walton, feared . . . or worshiped . . . by everyone in our tiny town, had pointed a manicured finger down at the skittish six-year-old me, as I knelt on her living room floor.

Confused by her acrid tone, I tried to smile.

Around my new cousins and me, the carpet was littered with the detritus of a Christmas morning frenzy. Shiny, crumpled paper. Ripped cardboard. Twinkling lights. Christmas music played from hidden speakers, mixed with the comforting murmur of adults around the dining table. Cinnamon cider and roasting turkey wafted from the kitchen of Mother Bea's stately house. I'd been so excited to attend my very first Christmas with my new American family, I'd barely been able to sleep.

It should have been glorious. But then my twelve-year-old

cousin, RJ, had unwrapped a book on dinosaurs. When he'd scoffed and tossed it aside, I'd picked it up to thumb through. A girl cousin had snatched it away, calling me a baby and claiming I'd rip the pages. To prove her wrong, I began to recite every word I'd read in the short hardcover.

They called me a liar. Said I memorized it beforehand to impress them. RJ's face reddened with fury as he tried to follow along, one finger running across the pages. Standing, he'd shrieked at me and in a tantrum, tossed the book into the nearby fireplace.

Mother Bea had witnessed the whole event. She snatched me up by the arm, fury in her expression as she spat the words. "Oddities like you should not exist in God's world. I told your father, but would he listen? No. But I say you have no business being among decent Christian folk." She shook me until my head snapped back. "Go outside until I call you. I won't have you ruining Christmas for any more of these precious children."

The memory slunk back where I'd hidden it. Head bowed, I listened to the heavy silence from the room around me and I felt my skin shrink. My shoulders tried to curl in, but the accursed corset held them erect.

"That," Phoebe said, "was bloody amazing, Hope!"

My head shot up as she started clapping. Moira beamed at me. "You're a treasure, girl, and no mistake."

Doug, standing near the door now, called out, "Hey, I've got to run upstairs for a bit. But when I get back, will you tell us about the expansion of the railroads? I've always been fascinated by the American West."

I locked eyes with Collum. He nodded. "We'll need all that and more where we're going," he said. "Keep up the good work, aye?"

A warm flush rolled through me as I cast off that six-year-old's shame. I didn't have to hide my abilities anymore. These people genuinely cared about me. They valued me. They . . . they *needed* me.

After Moira deftly fastened the endless buttons that roved up the back of the tailored wool traveling gown, I hustled to the mirror. Phoebe scooched in to stand beside me.

Weeks of Moira's sumptuous cooking had filled in most of the hollow spaces in my own figure, areas carved off during the eight months I'd mourned my "dead" mother. I no longer looked quite as ghoulish as when I'd arrived, and I realized I kind of liked the new curves.

Phoebe flounced off to plop down in the chair left empty by Doug. I watched Moira in the mirror as, pins in her mouth, she fussed with my hem. Above the plump cheeks, her small gray eyes looked unusually worried.

"What's wrong, Moira?"

She glanced up, her eyes meeting mine in the glass. "I don't like it," she muttered after a few seconds. "Feels off to me. Like something . . ."

Lips pinched, she shook her head. Hating the stricken look on her face, I tried to joke.

"Personally I'd bet on my spleen. Of course, it could be my liver. Either way, one of them will definitely explode if we don't loosen these laces. Maybe—"

"Hold your water, lass." Moira twitched the folds of fine wool. "That's no' what I meant and well ye know it. It's just that it's all so rushed." She took a breath and quoted, "'By failing to prepare, you are preparing to fail.'"

"Ben Franklin?"

"Aye." She nodded. "Though I first heard it said by Oprah."

A laugh bubbled out. "Oprah?"

"What can I say? The woman is wise." She winked, sighing. "Ah. Go on w' ye then and try on the silk. And don't worry about me, 'tis nothing I'm sure. Just nerves."

Moira seemed better as she finished the final touches to the delectable ball gown in a shade Phoebe called Sea Storm Blue.

Afterward, Moira ordered me to select matching accessories. "Anything within the fourth through the sixth doors should do."

The tall, climate-controlled cabinet that housed the Viators' costume collection hissed as I pressed in the frosted glass to release the magnetic latch. Inside each compartment, historically accurate costumes were labeled with three-by-five cards pinned to the sleeves.

Beneath the gowns and suits, sectioned bins held shoes, accessories, and currency for each time period. After burrowing a bit, I found a gorgeous pair of ankle boots in a creamy ivory leather.

While I tried to figure out how to work the conveniently provided buttonhook, Moira briskly secured Phoebe into a black gown with frilly white apron and cap.

A low whistle sounded from the doorway. Doug Carlyle's large form filled the space as he gaped at her. "Brilliant," he said in a husky voice. "It's. Wow."

With a deliberate sway to her hips, Phoebe slunk toward Doug. Rising on tiptoe, she planted a kiss on his wide mouth. "You like?"

"A bit more than 'like,' I'd say."

"*Must* I remind you two that I'm standing right here?" Moira put in, primly.

"And me," I called.

Collum only groaned.

Phoebe hustled back over to the dressing booth and snapped a saucy wink at us as she pulled the curtain shut. Doug's smile dropped away. His eyes closed on a deep exhale, as though preparing to cannonball into ice water.

His face oddly tense, he moved to the mirror and slipped off his jacket. "Ready when you are, Moira."

"Ready for what, babe?" Phoebe stepped out, back in jeans and bright pink sweater.

Moira peered up at Doug. "You've cleared it with Lu, then?"

At Doug's hesitant nod, Moira frowned. "Douglas Eugene Carlyle, you know I won't be goin' behind Lu's back. It can wait till she's made her decision."

"Lu's still thinking on it," Doug said. "I thought it couldn't hurt to be prepared."

Static caused strands of Phoebe's vivid purple hair to float away from her head. A gold ring winked in her left brow as she frowned. "Be prepared for what?"

When neither Doug nor Moira answered, Phoebe stomped a bare foot. "Someone better start talkin' or I'm going to flip my—"

"I'm going with you," Doug blurted. "To 1895. That is . . . well . . . I might be."

I felt as though my jaw had hit the floor.

All the color drained from behind Phoebe's freckles, until her face looked like a sun-bleached sheet splattered with rust. Her mouth opened. It snapped shut. She began blinking too fast.

I'd only seen that look once, back in 1153, when one of Thomas Becket's guards had tried to kill her brother. It hadn't ended well for the thug.

Collum took a step toward them. "Phee. Listen to what he—"

She stopped him with one upraised palm. "Don't."

Unnerved, I glanced at Collum, who looked back at me as he raked his hands back through his hair. *We should go,* he mouthed.

I nodded in utter and complete agreement.

Silence roared in the room, broken only by the whirring of the computers. Phoebe rounded on her grandmother. "You knew?" she asked. "You knew he was planning this and you didn't tell me?"

"Wasn't my tale to tell, now was it?"

I'd never seen Moira intimidated. Not by anything. But as her granddaughter's face flamed to the color of a ripe tomato, the small woman slowly backed away.

"This is gonna be bad, huh?" I whispered as the door closed on the ominous silence.

Moira let out a deep sigh. "Aye," she said. "Oh aye, I'm afraid so."

CHAPTER 12

I was wrong. It wasn't bad.

It was war.

The next day, you could've cut the tension inside Christopher Manor with a Nerf sword. Over a strained dinner of shepherd's pie, Aunt Lucinda announced her decision. When Phoebe leapt up in protest, Lucinda held up a quelling hand. "I understand your concerns," she said. "And I assure you, I share them. When Douglas made his case, my first inclination was to decline. However — upon further consideration — as he is our best resource when it comes to Tesla's machine, I believe Douglas has earned the right to make his own decision here."

As the arguments ratcheted up to volcanic proportions, I kept my head down and my big trap shut.

I adored Doug. He was a gigantic, lovable teddy bear. The kindest person I'd ever met and the smartest by a wide, *wide* margin. But he'd never gone on a mission. And though Moira assured us she knew how to run the device well enough to bring us back, I knew that wasn't what was bringing furious tears to Phoebe's eyes.

"What if you seize?" she shouted across the table at a stormy-eyed Doug. "What if you get sick and we can't get help? What then?"

"I'm not some bleeding invalid," Doug snapped back. "Much as you like to think so."

Collum spoke up through a mouthful of food. "It actually makes a lot of sense, Phee." He studied the potato on his fork, carefully not looking at his sister. "It's not as if any of the rest of us understands all the technical mumbo jumbo. Doug is our best chance to truly understand exactly how the enhancement works."

Angry interruptions flew hard and fast across the table. Sickened by the discord brewing within this tight-knit clan, I shrunk in my chair, becoming as small a target as possible.

From her place at the head of the group, Aunt Lucinda rose. She didn't speak until the table quieted. "Douglas," she said, "*will* join you. It has been decided. Now that we've to contend with Gunnar Blasi, it is even more imperative that we have on hand someone with Doug's abilities and knowledge to counter. And I will hear no more on the subject."

The gentle glow from the massive elk-antler chandelier glittered in Phoebe's eyes as she, too, stood and glared back at Lucinda. "So it's been *decided*, has it?"

Ignoring her, Aunt Lucinda pinned Collum with a look. "And you misunderstand me. Under no circumstance are you to bring anything whatsoever back upon your return. The enhancement must be destroyed. And Tesla must be convinced of the danger of ever creating another. I believe our best chance of that would be to make contact with Jonathan Carlyle. Reveal as little of yourselves as possible. But do what you must to ensure that this is the end of Tesla's experimentation with the device."

Without a word, Phoebe snatched up her still-full plate and shoved through the swinging kitchen door. Dishes crashed in the sink. When the back door slammed, Doug rose and stomped off in the opposite direction.

Collum hadn't taken his eyes from Lucinda. "Why ..." He paused, jaw flexing as he tried to control the rage I saw rise up. "*Why* would we not bring back the enhancement? Why would we not utilize the one thing that might help us find my father? Or have you forgotten all about him?"

When Moira made a strangled noise, Mac wrapped an arm about her shoulders, but his eyes were on his grandson. "We canna take the chance, son. Much as it pains me, it is too risky to introduce something we don't understand into this time period. Your gram and I agree with Lu on this."

Watching the look of betrayal creep over Collum's face, I thought maybe — in this instance — the adults were being too cautious.

What if the enhancement really works? What if this is the Viators' one chance to change the parameters of the game but fear makes them pass it by?

"Um," I said into the dead silence, "I think—"

A faint cry echoed from the baby monitor on the nearby buffet.

"Hope," Moira muttered. "Go up and see to your sister."

Her tone left no room for argument. The protest building inside me faded as Aunt Lucinda echoed her friend. "Go," Aunt Lucinda said. "Please."

By the time I made it upstairs, the crying had stopped. In the small nursery, the ancient crib that had housed generations of Carlyles and MacPhersons held nothing but a tumble of tiny soft blankets. Fear made my pulse speed up. Then I heard a quiet hum filtering down the hall.

"Mom?" I knocked quietly on the half-open door, relief rushing through me when I saw the bundle in her arms. I tiptoed to the wooden rocker and knelt beside her. "What are you doing up? You know the doctor said you need rest."

I traced a finger over the soft down that covered my little sister's head. Her mouth puckered and her minuscule nose crinkled, as if my touch tickled.

"I think she was just lonely," Mom said. "The minute I picked her up, she went right back to sleep."

"You know Moira says we're spoiling her, holding her all the time."

Mom and I exchanged a smile at that, aware that Moira was the worst culprit of all, often wearing Ellie in a sling cradled against her chest as she cooked and cleaned.

My mom still looked terrible. Even nearly two months after the rescue, her freckles stood out like pebbles strewn across a snowbank. She adjusted the baby's blanket, and in the golden glow of the bedside lamp, I saw spots of blood staining the bandage that covered her wounded palm.

I scooted close, and leaned my head against her shoulder.

"Based on all the shouting," she said, patting my arm, "I assume Lu broke the news that she's agreed to let Doug come with you?"

"You know about that, huh?"

"Lu asked my opinion. I told her it was a good idea."

Surprised that my aunt still consulted Mom on anything, I asked, "You really think he should go?"

She stood, still a bit wobbly as she cradled the baby to her. I jumped up in case she needed support. But she walked tall and straight as she settled the warm bundle into the yellowed wicker bassinet near the foot of the bed.

Perching on the mattress, she patted the patchwork quilt next to her.

I settled in beside her. "Hope." Turning slightly so she could look at me, she said, "I made a terrible mistake, keeping the truth from you all this time. But I want you to know that I did it to protect you, not because I believed you couldn't handle it."

The scents of baby powder and floor wax filled my nose as I inhaled sharply. My fists squeezed the rumpled bedclothes. In the weeks since our return from the twelfth century, Mom and I had skirted around the truth of my . . . origins. She'd been so ill, so fragile, that I'd had to tuck away the anger and confusion that had eaten away at me all this time.

I glanced at the divorce papers on her bedside table. Before Lucinda had returned them to Mom, she'd let me read through the document. One phrase had burned itself into my brain. *"Parental Rights hearing will be scheduled for Minors #1 and #2 pending DNA test of Minor #2."*

Dad wasn't letting go completely, then. It was something we'd eventually have to face. Mom, Ellie, and I.

For now, Mom took my hand in hers and squeezed. I was amazed to see her looking almost peaceful. Her shoulders were straighter, as if a heavy blanket had been lifted from them.

"We're going to be fine." Mom glanced past me to where tiny fists waved above the edge of the bassinet. "The three of us. We have each other, and the rest of our family, after all." My sister grunted as if in affirmation, and I couldn't help but smile.

"You've been worried." It wasn't a question, but I answered it.

"Yes. You scared us, Mom. You scared me."

She pulled me into her arms as she whispered, "I—I know. And I am so very sorry, sweetheart. And though we've had to put Ellie on the bottle, I must admit that with the medication, I feel . . . lighter, somehow."

She released me, but held on to my hands. "The Viators. Believe me when I say that it is a dangerous path to walk, Hope. You've earned the right to make your own choice.

But please, *please* make absolutely certain that it is what you want."

I looked up. My heart flopped as—for the first time in over a year—I saw *her* behind the blue eyes. My mother. Peering out from behind the ghost who'd been inhabiting her skin. I nodded. "I do, Mom. I really do. I think it's what I'm supposed to do. Does that make sense?"

She squeezed my hands tight. "Then I must insist upon one thing," she said. "Come home. Promise me that you'll always come home."

I smiled. "I will. I promise."

She let go and took a deep, deep breath. When she exhaled, I could almost see the darkness fading. And maybe that was enough for now.

CHAPTER 13

CURTAINS CLOSED AGAINST THE NIGHT, PHOEBE, MOIRA, and I clustered at one end of the library table, picking through boxes of newspapers, old letters, and telegrams from the Viators' extensive archives.

Though mismatched lamps and the remains of a fire cast a cheery glow over the room, it did little to dispel the friction that had electrified the house since dinner. At this late hour, everyone looked exhausted. Empty, ink-smudged teacups sat before us, though no one had touched Moira's famous lemon squares.

Stifling a groan, I lifted yet another stack of old newspapers from the cardboard box and began to sort through for anything relating to March of 1895.

I'd just suffered my fiftieth paper cut when something caught my eye. "Hey."

No one looked up.

"Hey!" I said louder. "I think I've got something." I folded the yellowed newsprint carefully, then slapped it down in the center of the table. "Voilá!"

"Is that . . . ?" Phoebe leaned over the library table to look at the aged newspaper photo.

"Aye." Moira peered through her readers. "Good lass, Hope. That's old Nikola himself, cutting quite the dashing figure in white tie and tails, if I might add."

"Yeah," I said. "And it takes place on the very night his lab burns. Look, says here he was attending a soiree at the Vanderbilt mansion. That's William Kissam Vanderbilt beside him." In his tuxedo, the trim, neat Tesla stood next to the slightly blurred image of a shorter man. A pin attached to Vanderbilt's jacket had caught the camera's flash, blurring it and creating a smear of light across the picture. Tesla's face was clearer as he frowned at the photographer. I squinted, trying to make out the smudged edge. "Is that a woman's arm tucked into his?"

"Could be," Moira mused. "Though Tesla never married or had any female involvements that we know of, he was quite popular. Of course, people talked as people do. Called him unnatural. Whispers often circulated. That he was homosexual or deviant. And this in a time when that was a criminal offense. Why, poor Oscar Wilde was arrested and sentenced to two years of hard labor for his relationship with the son of a marquis."

Phoebe spoke for the first time since dinner. "We learned about Oscar Wilde in school, but I'd quite forgotten. It's bloody awful, punishing a person simply because of who they love. One can't help that, can they?"

"No," Moira agreed. "No, they can't. But what we can do is support those we love, whether we agree or no. We protect them, aye. While also allowing them the freedom to become the person they're meant to be. Do you take my meaning?"

Phoebe's gaze dropped to the table. She knew exactly what—or who—Moira meant. And though stubbornness pressed her lips together, she didn't argue the point.

Later, in front of the computer in my bedroom, I hesitated.

"If you don't do it, I will," Phoebe said. "We need to find out more about this Gabriella chippy."

Phoebe tugged my hand from my lips. Blood was smeared on the thumbnail where I'd been nipping at the cuticle. "Do it."

I heaved a sigh and hit Enter next to the search box beside her name.

Gabriella's full name popped up first.

Gabriella de Roca y Fonseca de Villena.

"Well, that's a mouthful," Phoebe snorted.

Though a very old and noble name, the current family was nothing compared to what it had once been. From what we could find, Gabriella had been telling the truth. After her grandfather's death, she'd pretty much had to fend for herself.

She'd done well. Full scholarship to Barcelona's Institut del Teatre. Accolades aplenty. Competition wins. She'd been an up-and-comer in the classical dance world until—a year earlier —her career had been cut short by the injury to her knee.

There were so, so many photos. Captured mid-leap, a pale and mournful Gabriella dancing the Black Swan in *Swan Lake*. A pensive Gabriella, poised on the ends of her toes and dressed in full Spanish regalia as she performed the flamenco before an enormous crowd.

Then, there were the paparazzi shots of her, smiling and glamorous, wheat-gold hair loosed from its tight bun in a variety of photos with members of posh European party sets.

The last photo was a year old, and looked to be the final taken before injury had sidelined the girl forever. In it, a group of young elites was being ushered past a waiting crowd into some nightclub or chic event. Dressed in a slinky silver number that revealed nearly every inch of her long and perfectly sculpted thigh muscles, Gabriella gleamed at the camera over one bare shoulder. The boy beside her had shed his black jacket and rolled up the sleeves of a white tuxedo shirt. One of those tanned arms was wrapped loosely around Gabriella's tiny waist. Though we couldn't see his face, I didn't need to read the tabloid caption.

Phoebe paused to squint at the monitor. "Wait. Is that...?"

"Yep," I said. "It sure as hell is."

In bed, I tried to convince myself. *She's his cousin. Okay, not technically a blood relative but still. He would've told me about*

her, eventually. I know he would've. But I couldn't shake that image of his arm around her waist.

After exhaustion and . . . yeah, okay . . . jealousy and *fear* dragged me under like a relentless tide, I woke exhausted, sweaty from nightmares of careening through a black abyss. I finally gave up and spent the predawn hours huddled in one of Moira's comfy afghans as I stared out over the dark and enigmatic world outside my window.

CHAPTER 14

THE FIRST TIME I ENTERED THE IMMENSE HIGH-TECH vault beneath my aunt's home I'd inadvertently locked myself inside, and for a while—until I found the light switch that revealed a collection worthy of any museum—I had lost my mind. Now, as I stepped past the five-inch-thick reinforced steel door that housed the Viators' extensive treasure trove, I stopped short. Collum cursed as he bumped into my back.

"Watch it," he muttered, sliding around me.

Moving out of the doorway, I edged over to stand before one of two hermitically sealed cases that flanked the round entry. Inside the smoked glass cubicle, two wires dangled from the ceiling, empty and useless.

"Aunt Lucinda?" My voice pinged off the stone. "Where is it? Where's the tapestry?"

"The hanging was donated to the Museum of Edinburgh two weeks ago," Aunt Lucinda said as she passed by.

"Thanks for telling *me*."

She stopped, one eyebrow raised beneath her blond wig as she pivoted toward me. "I wasn't aware that I needed your approval to run this business, Hope," my aunt replied crisply. "I shall endeavor to do so from now on." Without another word, she walked away.

Nostrils flaring, I choked back a reply. For reasons I couldn't exactly explain, every time I passed through here, it had comforted me to glance over and see my mother's face woven into the ancient tapestry. It meant we'd won. That my mom was safe. Alive.

"Oi," Phoebe said, giving my corseted waist a quick squeeze. "Don't worry, aye? We'll go see it at the museum soon as we return. I promise."

One glance at my friend's sympathetic expression and I felt like the world's biggest ass. Was I really standing here fretting over a stupid piece of cloth while she worried herself sick over what might happen to Doug? Not to mention that my mom had made it back. Her dad was still out there.

Good going, Hope. Could you be *any more selfish?*

Since Doug's announcement, a worry line had made a permanent home across Phoebe's forehead. I smiled as I tugged at a curl of her auburn wig.

"Listen, we're going to watch out for him," I promised. "Make sure he takes his medicine. Doesn't overdo it. All that. We'll keep him safe, Pheebs."

When she shrugged and tried to pull away, I held on. "Doug wants this so much. He wants to prove he's not some invalid that you have to take care of," I said. "I think . . . I think you should let him do that."

Her eyes cut away, but not before I saw the gloss of tears. "If something happens to him," she rasped, "I don't know what I'll do."

"I know," I said. "Which is why I am prepared to be on him like white on rice."

She looked at me askance. "What in all blazing hells does that mean?"

"No idea, but my great-grandma used to say it all the time when anyone in our family acted like a douche to me." I humped my shoulders, quoting in my best Southern old lady voice. " 'You little hellions leave my sweet girl alone or I'll be on you like white on rice.' "

Her laugh burst out on a snort. "Jesus, that was terrible."

"Are you two going to stand there laughing like a couple of lunatics?" Collum called out. "Or are we doing this?"

"Yeah, yeah," I said. "We're coming."

As we hurried to catch up, I grinned, gratified to see that the wrinkle over my friend's eyes had vanished.

We followed Aunt Lucinda's tall frame past crates bristling with swords, chests packed with bags of gold and silver coin, glass-topped cases brimming with ornate jewels. Warm, dry air gusted from multiple vents to keep the contents of the room free of rust or mold. The glare of fluorescent lights exposed thousands of not-quite-legal acquisitions, gathered by previous generations of Viators. Against the far walls, marble forms of half-naked Greeks and ebony statues with creepy jackal heads stood at attention. As we reached the door inset into the back wall of the stone vault, Lucinda called a halt.

"This is where we say farewell," she said as we gathered around her. "As you are aware, the stairs are a bit taxing for me at the moment."

The overhead light wasn't kind to my aunt. Shadows the color of an old bruise ringed her eyes, and her face held a sallow tinge. Even the trek through the cellar and vault had caused sweat to bead at her hairline and on her upper lip.

She looked over each one of us in turn. A final inspection.

I'd only ever seen Mac in jeans and flannels, but the tweed suit with bow tie and vest he now wore looked strangely right on his lanky frame. Lucinda gave Phoebe's dark housemaid gown and gray cape a nod, while Collum bore her scrutiny of his rough wool pants and suspenders with his usual stoic calm. With a flat newsboy's cap in hand and pistol holstered beneath one arm, he stared coolly back.

Only I fidgeted under my aunt's attention. Moira had been kind when tightening the corset, only squeezing half my organs out of shape in deference to the journey ahead. Still, beneath the layers of shift, stockings, corset, and petticoats, all topped with a fashionable plum wool traveling gown and cape, I was already sweating.

Aunt Lucinda's eyes, the tired color of overwashed denim, scanned me from head to toe. "A lady's posture is one of her best features. No slumping, Hope."

"As if I could," I muttered.

"I realize we've discussed all this ad infinitum; however, I shall go over a few key points again, as they do bear repeating," Aunt Lucinda said. "As always, keep your interactions with the locals to a minimum. Use every caution when dealing with Nikola Tesla. No matter what happens, he must be thoroughly convinced to destroy both the enhancement and the duplicate device, and to never attempt to rebuild either. Since it appears Celia has already broken the proverbial ice with Jonathan Carlyle . . ." Her already thin lips pinched in annoyance. "Use your best judgment where he is concerned. But offer no additional information beyond the specific mission." I bristled when her sharp-eyed gaze snapped to Phoebe and me. "You are prohibited from making any mention of the unfortunate events that will directly affect Jonathan's family. Do I make myself perfectly clear?"

We had brought it up to her only once, two days earlier, as she sat sipping tea in her office.

"Can't we at least warn the man?" Phoebe had asked insistently. "We could simply explain that they should never mess with any existing trees when they're back in their past. We don't have to go into specifics."

"Please," I pleaded. "What could be wrong with that? It would give those poor little girls a fighting chance, at least."

Unwilling to even discuss the matter, Lucinda had shut us down in seconds.

"It may seem hard of me, even uncaring," Lucinda went on now. "But I assure you that is not the case. The incident with Jonathan and Julia's daughters has already occurred. It is in our past, regardless of the inevitability that the two timelines will—temporarily—touch. To tell him anything would be breaking the Viators' cardinal rule—a rule, may I remind you, that Jonathan Carlyle himself set down.

"This will not be easy," she went on. "Buy Tesla's cooperation, if you must. Our accounts at the 1895 Bank of New York have more credit than you will ever need. In addition, Mac carries with him enough currency and gold to cover any additional expense. Guard it—and yourselves—well. You all know your roles. Do well and come home safely."

Not an emotional person by nature, my aunt's chin still wobbled as she turned on her heel to sweep back through the vault. As the others filed through the narrow security door I watched her go, shooting up a quick prayer that she'd be all right. That they'd find a cure soon. I didn't always agree with her, but I could not bear thinking what might happen to the Viators without her rock-steady leadership.

By the time we descended the many, many flights of stairs carved into the heart of the mountain, my thighs were screaming.

Though I'd been inside the strange cavern several times

before, I couldn't help but hesitate on the last step. The first time I stepped down onto the mosaic floor and felt that strange, prickling power of the intersecting ley lines surge over my feet, I almost bolted.

Only two things stopped me. A wisp of optimism that my mom might still be alive. And the two man-size towers on either end of the chamber. The instant I'd seen them, I knew their creator. Nikola Tesla. I'd always been fascinated with the man, and seeing miniaturized versions of his famous Wardenclyffe Tower kept me from running.

Hewn out of black rock, the cavern was roughly oval, the walls covered with carvings of ancient symbols and languages no one now alive could read. The closest translation —"the Dim Road"—seemed pretty accurate to me.

"Cutting it a bit close," Doug, in his sober black valet suit, called. "We only have about seven minutes."

Phoebe sucked in a breath as Doug's fingers rose to his hair in a nervous habit.

I realized there was no longer anything left for him to tug. Doug's finger-length dreadlocks had been chopped away, the remaining hair smoothed down and parted in the middle. With round, steel spectacles having replaced his normal frames, Doug Carlyle looked like a different person. He knew his mixed heritage and height would make him stand out. To make this journey with us, he had endured the most drastic transformation.

Phoebe's hands were fisted at her sides as she stared. If I was startled, I couldn't even imagine how Phoebe felt.

"What do you think, then?" he asked Phoebe in voice so soft I barely heard it.

"I—you could've told me," she said.

"You weren't speaking to me."

Her left eye twitched. The frown line reappeared. "And I'm still not," she snapped, and stomped off to a corner to wait.

Though I'd never say it, I would have felt better with Doug running the show. I knew he'd taught Moira all he could about the mushroom-topped devices. And he'd assured us that he had preset the devices to bring us back in precisely seventy-two hours, the exact length of time the Dim ever allowed. All Moira would have to do is act as monitor. Still, Doug knew those machines better than anyone except maybe Tesla himself. So it was more than a bit disconcerting that he'd be powerless to help if something in this time went wrong.

Didn't help my nerves to dwell on it, though. So I joined Phoebe in her corner, huddling next to her when the cavern's chill bled through the layers and burrowed into my bones.

"Here you are, lamb." Moira stood before me, holding out the ancient doll. Invisible stitching had repaired the ripped dress. The spots of new paint were barely noticeable. And the missing hunks of hair had been painstakingly reinserted. She looked good as new. Well, as good as a doll with twelve (or—depending on how you looked at it—more than four hundred and fifty) years under her belt *could* look.

"Wanted you to see how well we'd fixed her up before you . . . well." Moira swallowed. "And when you return, you can thank your mum for replacing that missing chunk o' hair. Stayed up all night, she did."

Her papery hand rested on my cheek before pulling me into a smooshy, grandmotherly embrace that made my eyes sting. With her other arm, she brought Phoebe in for a three-person hug. After a few seconds, Phoebe's stiff posture melted and she squeezed us both with a strangling ferocity.

Before I could give the doll back for safekeeping, Moira abruptly released us and hurried over to Mac. They held a short private conversation, then Mac's gnarled hands rose to cup Moira's round face. He leaned down and touched his forehead to hers as he whispered softly to her in Gaelic. Moira pulled back, smiling up at her husband of forty years as she said something back.

I couldn't quite make it out, but next to me, Phoebe sighed.

"What did they say?"

My friend turned to glance at Doug, who was doing last-minute checks on the machines. "Well," she began, her voice thick. "'Tis from a poem by Rabbie Burns, see? Mac said, 'As fair art thou, my bonie lass, So deep in luve am I; And I will luve thee still, my Dear, Till a' the seas gang dry.'"

Inside my chest, my heart contracted into a painful knot

as Phoebe went on. "And then Gram, she ... she answered, 'And fare thee weel, my only Luve. And fare thee weel, a while. And I will come again, my Luve, Tho' it were ten thousand mile.'"

"Ohh," was all I could manage.

"All right, everyone," Moira exclaimed, voice cracking only a bit. "You'll be arriving just after dawn on March eleventh at 0721. That's seven twenty-one a.m., a' right? I expect to see all of you back, safe and ..." She trailed off and took a deep breath. "Oh, let's just get this damn thing over with."

Phoebe—anger at Doug not *quite* gone—leapt up, and without hesitation picked up her carpeted bag and marched over to take her place in the exact center of the chamber. I followed at a more reluctant pace. Moira checked us over, confirming that each person's opal lodestone was secure. Tucked safely inside the high-necked gown, my pendant twitched and warmed against my skin.

Mac and Doug flashed thick men's rings. Collum plucked at the plain silver chain that ran beneath his white shirt. Moira grimaced as Phoebe patted her belly.

All hell had broken loose when Phoebe and Doug had returned from a trip to Edinburgh a few weeks earlier, Phoebe gleefully sporting a new bellybutton piercing complete with fire-opal stick pin.

"But, Gram," Phoebe had explained. "At least you won't have to worry that I'll lose it."

Trying to keep myself from running like hell for the stairwell, I focused on the black and white mosaic beneath my buttoned boots.

The same ancients who carved out this chamber had also imbedded tens of thousands of black and white stone chips into the floor. The design—a sideways figure eight that represented infinity, crossed over with three wavy lines —indicated the spot where the portal to the Dim would appear. Lucinda and those before her believed that the long-lost people who had created the chamber had done so out of worship, and that they'd recognized it as a place of immense power.

But it had been the combination of technology and the ethereal that had—accidentally—helped the early Viators discover the place's true potential.

With a loud, finite pop, the buzz and whine from the Tesla devices amped up until the sound drilled into my ear-drums. Purple jolts of electricity began to crackle around the silvery metal of the twin mushroom tops. Building. Building.

The first time I stood here, waiting for the Dim to take me to some great unknown, I'd at least had ignorance on my side. Dressed in a furred cape and long gown of the medieval period, I'd had no idea what I was facing.

I think that was better.

Between them, Doug and Collum hoisted the period-appropriate leather trunk that housed our spare costumes and supplies. One hand gripping each handle, they braced themselves while Mac gave us all one last comforting nod.

Clutching my own carpetbag so hard the wooden grips dug into my palm, I looked at Collum. Some of my growing terror must have shown because he edged a bit closer, taking my free hand in his.

"Be at peace, lass," he said. "All is well."

Squeezing his hand so hard I was sure his bones would break, I clustered close with the other four as the surges of electricity built higher and higher above our heads.

Shaking all over now, I willed myself to breathe. In— two, three. Out—two, three. It wasn't working. My breaths were coming too quick. The bones in my legs were turning to rubber as everything that could possibly go wrong flashed before my eyes. I locked my knees to keep from crumpling to the cold floor.

"John MacPherson," Moira cried from her place next to the screaming machines. "You bring yerself and those bairns back to me safe and sound, you hear me?"

"Aye!" Mac called back. "Always. *Mo chridhe!*"

With a shriek of power, the electrical pulses clashed together high above our heads. The force they created interrupted the flow of the ley lines, forming a vacuum. From every direction, the natural power tried to force its way through the interruption, causing a hurricane wind to build around us. Something dug into my side and I realized I still clutched the doll in my hand. It was too late to hand her off, and I clenched her under one arm as the two forces—man's and nature's—battled each other. A translucent cylinder began to rise, rise up around us, enclosing us within its protective shield.

"Time!" Moira shouted, voice hoarse. "Go with God's blessing and with mine, dear ones!"

The five of us inhaled a collective breath as Moira clasped the upraised switch with both hands and slammed it down.

CHAPTER 15

I'D TRIED TO PREPARE MYSELF FOR A REPEAT PERFORMANCE of the experience I had the first time the Dim had taken me. Then, I'd careened helplessly through an infinite darkness broken only by the images of a thousand decaying faces. But this time, as my body and mind exploded into millions of individual particles, a memory slammed into me with the force of a sledgehammer. I could only watch, as if the small child I'd been was a character in a beloved movie, seen through a faraway lens.

There was nothing the girl loved more than visiting her Poppy. He told the most marvelous stories. And, unlike her mother, he did not send her to bed with the sun. They stayed up late before the fire, taking tiny sips of a substance called choc-o-late. A gift from the queen herself, the dark, creamy liquid was new and very dear. And though it smelled wonderful, the taste was so bit-

ter on her tongue it made her mouth pucker. Still, the girl adored her grandfather and so pretended to like it.

During the day they read together or took long walks in the garden, where she memorized the names of all the plants and flowers. At night, they stood beneath the clear sky and he pointed out the magical beings that made up the stars.

Riding in front of her grandfather on his great horse, the girl was sad their visit was over, though she had missed Mother and Papa. The veered off the rutted forest road and trotted down a sun-dappled lane that wove through the trees. As the last leaves of blazing autumn drifted down to crunch beneath the gelding's hooves, the girl breathed the brisk morning air and blew it out in a pleasing cloud of white.

"I like the way the forest tastes today, Poppy," she told him.

"Tastes?" She felt his chuckle rumble against her narrow back. "You can taste the forest?"

"Of course I can." She giggled. "Can't you?"

Her grandfather filled his lungs as the girl instructed, holding his breath until she gave him leave to release it.

"Ah," he said. "I believe I understand. But tell me what you taste, so that we may compare."

"Well," she said. "I taste oak leaves and green moss. Rose hips and hazelnuts that the squirrels have hidden away." She sniffed at the air, smacking her lips to make her grandfather laugh again. "There are juniper berries and holly, and ice that hides in the shady spots. Now you go."

"Hmm," her grandfather mused, smacking his own lips,

hidden as they were beneath gray whiskers. "Why, I believe you're right, child. There is all that, along with a sweet bouquet of white ash and beech, and mulch that covers the forest floor. That thick layer will protect tender seeds as they sleep away the cruel winter. This part of the forest is old. Very old, though it shrinks each day as more and more people rob its precious bounty." Her grandfather leaned down. His beard tickled her cheek as he whispered, "I smell snow coming, and if I don't get you home before it arrives, your mother shall take a strap to the both of us."

They laughed together at the thought of her mother with her quiet voice and soft hands, chasing her own father around with a shaving strop.

The girl's grandfather pulled in a huge breath. "Ah," he said. "And if I'm not mistaken, I believe there is a hint of venison stew with turnips, new-baked bread with butter and strawberry preserves on the air today."

The girl giggled again. "That is silly, Poppy. How can you taste stew when we are so far into the . . ."

The tiny cottage appeared out of nowhere, as though it had sprouted like a mushroom from the crackling forest floor. The house was seated a ways back from the trampled path, and blended so cleverly among the huge trees and massive, moss-covered stones the girl had to squint to make out the walls of speckled river rock and the slant of its thatched roof.

"It's a fairy cottage," the girl breathed.

Her grandfather chuckled again. "No, child, though I will grant that the lady who lives here was once as lovely as the fair folk themselves."

He slid from the horse and helped her to the ground. He tied the bay's lead to a branch, then took her hand in his, whistling a tune as they followed the narrow path of flat stones that led to the cottage.

At the edge of the clearing that surrounded the home, the girl smiled, charmed by the neat little structure with its tidy herb garden and green shutters. "Who lives here, Pop—?"

Her grandfather's hand clamped over her mouth. He yanked her back into the trees. "Hush," he whispered, as he shoved her behind him.

Kneeling, he peered around a large trunk and scanned the clearing.

"Is something amiss?" the girl whispered. She did not care for the look on her grandfather's wrinkled face. And when he only put a finger to his lips in reply, she pressed her doll harder to her chest.

She did not laugh this time when her grandfather sniffed at the air.

The sweet, nutty breath of the deep woods carried a scent of smoke. Nothing strange in that, *she thought.* The day is cold. The owner likely lit a fire to ward off the chill.

But why was her grandfather frowning so? And why had the forest gone so suddenly silent? Even the birds had stilled their chatter.

A horse whinnied, the sound rolling out from somewhere behind the cottage. A sudden crash from inside made her jump. Her grandfather went rigid. The girl edged over so she could peek around the tree. The door of the sweet cottage hung ajar and at an odd angle, half ripped from its hinges. Through the open door-way, she saw an orange light as flames bloomed inside. Shadows moved against the wall. Several rough-looking men stepped out, followed by a broad man clad in the Spanish manner.

The girl's grandfather stiffened as he muttered, "The Spaniard."

Fire began to eat through the thatched roof, spreading quickly to send a plume of white smoke into the sky.

"Poppy?" she whispered, but he was already tugging her back through the trees.

"We must leave," he said. "Now."

He tossed her onto the saddle and pulled himself up behind her. The gelding raced down the rutted path, faster and faster, until the wind stole the girl's breath and she had to duck her head to keep from swallowing air. Her grandfather's urgency as he commanded the horse to hurry, hurry, hurry twisted her stomach into knots.

Her fists tightened in the coarse mane when she heard a faint shout behind them. The gelding's powerful muscles strained, and her grandfather's long beard brushed against her cheek as he leaned low, shielding her body with his own. "Hear me well, child. A village lies just ahead. I am known there and I believe its people will shelter us. When we stop, do exactly as I say. Do you understand?"

The girl nodded. She wanted to ask who they were running from, but fear had frozen her tongue to the roof of her mouth.

One, two bends in the path and they were racing through a collection of several dozen thatched huts set around a stone well.

A group of young boys played a game with sticks and a rock on the dirt-packed village square. Near the well, apron-covered women gossiped over a large community trough as they scrubbed wads of soiled clothing. Others teamed up to twist out the excess water and drop the damp cloth into buckets for hanging. An old woman, in the same colorless dun of the rest, plucked a beheaded fowl on a leveled stump. She chuckled to herself as she watched three little girls skitter about, trying to catch the blowing feathers.

As the girl and her grandfather skidded to a halt, a bloody feather floated down to land on the back of her clenched fist.

"Madeleine!" her grandfather cried, breathless. "Madeleine the Healer?"

At their approach, the boys stopped their game to gape at them. One, a thin, black-haired lad only slightly older than the girl, took a few steps in their direction, shading his eyes as they fixed on her face.

Aided by a tall staff, an elder with a crooked back had begun hobbling toward them. He called up to her grandfather. "Good day to you, Doctor. Our healer is not here just the now. Called away to tend an injured man in the next village, she was. I know not when she will return. Are you ill?"

Before answering, the girl's grandfather muttered a quiet prayer of thanks. "We are not," he said. "What of Madeleine's daughter, Margery?"

The elder squinted at them for a moment, then angled his long stick at the black-haired boy. "Lad, go and fetch your mother. Quick-like."

The boy tore his eyes from the girl and disappeared among the cluster of cottages. The girl's grandfather surveyed the villagers who had begun to gather around them. Women. Babes. Small children, none older than five or six years. The elderly and infirm.

"Where are your men? Your older lads?"

"Out cutting wood, same as every day," one of the washer-women said.

As her affable grandfather slid from the horse's back, the girl was appalled to hear him snarl a word used only by the rough drivers who delivered wagonloads of her father's cloth.

He took in a deep breath, then raised his voice as he addressed the murmuring group. "Heed my words, all of you. You know me. I've visited your healer and her family for many years. Just now my granddaughter and I witnessed a group of men ransacking Madeleine's home. When they do not find what they are looking for, they will come here next. You must hide. Now. Take the children and flee into the forest."

Gasps and confusion erupted from the gathered villagers. "What mean you by this, Doctor?" called the elder. "Why harm us? As you see, we have little enough to steal."

Before her grandfather could answer, the black-haired boy flew around the corner of a nearby cottage with a pretty woman on his heels. Their breath steamed up into the chilly air. The woman's long dark braid bounced against her back as she lifted the hem of her brown homespun and raced toward them.

"Doctor," she gasped, breathless. "What is amiss?"

Her grandfather explained what they'd witnessed back at the fairy cottage. When he leaned in, whispering urgently, the woman drew back in dismay.

In a voice gone hoarse with horror, she replied, "But my mother is not here. And in any case, she has not seen nor touched that cursed jewel since the day she fled the sisterhood. She—"

"Margery," her grandfather interrupted gently. "This I know. But it matters not, for they believe she knows its location. When they do not find it or her, they will come for her here. These men will not give credence when you say you know nothing of the jewel. The only option is to run. Now."

The boy moved to his mother's side and took her hand as she tugged on a leather thong strung about her neck. Weak sunlight glinted off the round silver medallion as Margery worried it against her lips.

"How many men?" the elder asked.

The girl's grandfather shrugged. "I saw eight men at the cottage."

"Nine," the girl reminded him. "There were nine men, Poppy."

Margery and the elder exchanged a long look.

"No, Doctor," she said, finally. "We shall not hide. This village is our home and we have defended it before when our menfolk were away. We are many and they are few, and though we may be but women and the old, helpless we are not."

The girl's grandfather tried to protest, but Margery stood her ground. With rapid-fire efficiency, she ordered the able-bodied to arm themselves as they had done in the past. The older children *were commanded to take the small ones and hide in the forest root cellar.*

"Your granddaughter may go down into the cellar with the others. My son will see her safely there," said Margery, turning her face up to the girl's grandfather. "But what of you, John Dee? Will you stay with us? Will you fight?"

CHAPTER 16

IN A SPACE OF TIME BOTH INSTANTANEOUS AND INFINITE, the memory pierced my heart in a dozen bloody places, threading barbed hooks through every vein and artery. Then, like dust whipped through a screen door, even that memory scattered as each individual molecule that had ripped apart was shoved through the barrier that separated past and present.

I'd somehow allowed myself to forget the part that came just before: the gray lassitude that whispered, *"Give up. Give in. Let go and rest a while."*

And wasn't it easy to float, serene and quiet, in that great shroud of oblivion? Wouldn't I give anything to avoid what came next: bone and nerve and flesh knit together by a force greater than any that had ever existed?

Oh God, the pain. Hurts. Please. Help. Pain. No-o-o . . .

Stomach roiling, eyes shut, I felt the scratch of grit beneath my cheek as it pressed against the cold earth.

Nearby, someone heaved up their guts. Someone else groaned and muttered, "What—"

"Get up!" Mac's urgent shout penetrated my fuzzy hearing. "All of you, get up! We have to run! Run!"

I was hauled upright, and I began to stumble along on numb feet. As my lungs recalled how to inflate, I sucked in a great draft of musky, fetid air. Then I felt it, the earth shuddering beneath me.

"Hope!" A shout near my ear. "Open your eyes, for God's sake! The cattle are stampeding! We have to run!"

Shoved from behind, I tripped as I forced open sticky lids. Just ahead, Phoebe and Doug bolted side by side down a long tunnel that was lined at intervals by swaying oil lanterns. Dirt rained down on them from the wooden support beams that kept the shaft's low, earthen ceiling from collapse.

Collum's hold on my sleeve propelled me onward as the rumbling grew intense. "Cattle in the tunnel behind us," he panted over the racket of moos. "Heard it just as we arrived. Something spooked them."

"Us, most like," Mac shouted from just behind. "Don't stop. They're out of control. Go!"

The tunnel. Cattle.

"Here!" Doug thrust Phoebe hard into the wall. She cried out, but as we darted past, I saw it was but one of several man-size declivities built into the sides of the tunnel.

"There's more ahead! Hurry!" Doug waved us on frantically as we hurtled toward the other indentations we'd spotted.

The cattle were upon us now. Hot breath raked across the backs of our necks. With a whip of his arm, Collum pitched me face first into the nearest bolthole, slammed his grandfather into the next, and waved Doug into the last spot on that side. With a leap, Collum cleared the tunnel and burrowed into the empty space opposite, a millisecond before the horns and tawny backs of the herd thundered past.

Dirt and dust and wood particles shivered down. The musk of dozens of animals enveloped me as I pressed myself harder into the tiny space. Behind me, I felt my skirts billow out on the breeze created by the cattles' passage. I tried to snatch them back, but a hoof or horn snagged in the thick wool. Pain as my fingernails dug into rough planks. Splinters burrowing beneath my nail beds. An inexorable force pulling me, pulling . . .

With a final rip, the material gave. My face slammed hard into the wall as I gagged with relief.

The shouts of angry men followed the hoofbeats. I didn't look, didn't turn as the cattle drovers raced past, apparently too engaged in chasing the animals to even glance our way.

After what felt like an eternity, Mac spoke. "All right. I think it's safe to come out."

Badly shaken, the five of us emerged from our hidey-holes, Mac blessing the engineer who'd thoughtfully provided the emergency escapes. After a quick jog back to see what was left of the belongings we'd abandoned when the stampede began, a dejected-looking Collum and Doug returned with one tattered carpetbag and a handful of stomped-on and ragged clothing.

"Oh no-o-o," Phoebe mourned. "Not the watered silk."

Taking the remnants of the smoky blue ball gown from her brother's arms, she squeezed it to her. She and Moira had worked long into the night, fitting it to my measurements, embroidering the bodice and neckline with whorls of shimmering silver thread.

The dress was ruined, along with nearly every article of clothing we'd brought and . . . I gasped as I realized the doll was no longer tucked beneath my arm. "Oh, no. No. No. No." Relief spiked through me when I saw her crumpled on the ground, safe inside the bolthole where I'd hidden. I snatched her up and brushed dirt and wood particles from the yellow silk.

"So your wee dolly survives, but not my spare boots?" Collum eyed the toy with distaste. "Aye, that seems fair."

Phoebe quickly inventoried the rest, which had been shredded by hundreds of sharp hooves and ground into the dirt-packed floor. There wasn't much left.

"Think we can salvage this," she said.

This was a huge-brimmed hat of mauve velvet with clots of garish yellow flowers sewn around the crown.

"Of course we can," I groaned.

Mac's shaving kit had been pulverized. Hats and coats and shoes all trashed beyond repair. The only things that made it were in the carpetbag. Hairpins, a diamond hair clip. A silver-backed brush-and-comb set, though the matching mirror was shattered—an ominous sign.

Only one real bit of good news. Mac had managed to hold on to the black leather case that contained all the bank notes and gold.

"Well, Phee," Collum said as he clapped a hand onto his dejected sister's shoulder. "One good thing came of this, aye?"

Grumpy, she snapped, "Oh, yeah? What's that then?"

"You get to go shopping."

A few hundred yards down the tunnel, ramps branched off from either side. Filtered sunlight and mooing sounds drifted down, so we deduced that the ramps led up to the cattle pens and instead chose a set of narrow stairs set into the very end of the dark, smelly passageway.

Coated in grime and dust, we ascended into a very different sort of nightmare.

"Holy crap." I slapped a hand over my mouth and nose as we crowded through the small door. "What is that?"

The smell that met us at the top of the stairs was unspeakable. An entity that inundated the senses, saturating our pores with the stink of blood and death. A cavernous space stretched out before us, lit by skylights that pocked the ceiling two stories above. As far as the eye could see, a riotous assembly line of horror spread out across the straw-covered brick floor.

Through a wide double door set into the left-hand wall, we could see men in gore-spattered aprons heave now-headless bovine corpses onto gleaming metal hooks that swung from overhead wires. A pulley system brought them here, into the massive main processing area. At the first station, hides were stripped away and piled into bins. Hooves like those that had nearly run us down only moments before were chopped off and dropped into buckets. Coiled entrails plopped onto wooden tables and were sorted by grim-faced workers. Blood spattered or dripped or gushed into troughs that ran with a congealing, clotting mess.

"Abattoir," Doug choked from behind his hand. "Guess we might've thought this through a little better, huh?"

"That's it," Phoebe muttered. "I am now a vegetarian."

"Me too," I agreed.

"There's the door to the street," Collum snapped. "Move it, aye?"

Since no one in their right mind would spend one second more than was absolutely necessary amid this disgusting display, we hurried after him.

Sweating men in gore-encrusted aprons eyed us as we passed. Young boys no older than seven or eight rushed by toting buckets of something I knew I didn't want to see. I tried to keep my gaze locked on the back of Mac's tweed coat, but when a cloud of noxious steam rolled over me, I cut my eyes away just in time to see a heavyset man hoist a net full of boiled cow skulls from an enormous iron vat.

Behind me, I heard Phoebe gag.

Don't do it, I begged silently on behalf of my lurching gut.

On a platform high above the abattoir floor, four men in rough suits tracked our movements as we wove our way toward the door. They conferred for a moment before three of them cut away and began to descend the steps, clearly intent on cutting us off.

"Hurry," Mac mumbled over his shoulder. "This could be difficult to explain, aye?"

I nodded and picked up the pace. He didn't have to tell me twice.

We almost made it. Only feet away, pedestrians strolled by an open doorway to what looked like an ordinary street, though I noticed each person who passed held a handkerchief pressed to his or her face.

"Help ya?"

"Why no, my good man," Mac told the sweating, stocky fellow who stepped into our path. "Bit lost, is all. We'll just be on our way."

With two smaller men flanking him, the speaker frowned. Heavy jowls drooped as if the bushy red sideburns were trying to shove them off his face. The three spread out in a bid to block our exit as he looked us over.

"And just where in blazes did *ye* come from?"

For a split second, no one spoke. Then Mac gave a hearty chuckle and clapped the man on the shoulder.

"Och, ye wouldna believe me if I told ye, man." Mac deepened his already thick Scot's brogue to match the supervisor's. "Scoundrel of a steamboat captain went and got himself in his cups. Dumped milady and the rest o' us off at the wrong landing. Can ye believe it? What a numpty! Nearly got ourselves killed when the cattle ran, we did."

The man's squinty eyes narrowed, suspicious. Mac was quicker, though.

He held out a hand. "Mac MacPherson, newly from Edinburgh," he said, laying the burr on thick. "And from yer speech, ye're a Glasgow man, or my name's Tom Thumb."

The man reluctantly took Mac's proffered hand. "Aye," he said. "Come over these twelve years past, but—"

"I'm a barrister, ye see," Mac interrupted. "Sent by milord the Earl of Airth to escort this good lady to our lovely isle where she is to wed his son, the Viscount Allardice."

"I don't give a rat's furry arse what no bleeding rich bastard—"

"Well, that's the thing." Mac cut the man off, slick as egg white as he turned his back on the rest of us to lean in and whisper conspiratorially. "See, I'm with you. Bunch of no-good fancy boys with their fox hunts and their silver-plated ballocks. Got no idea how life is for us hard-working blokes, do they now?

"I'll tell ye a secret," he went on, gesturing for the three leaders to come closer. Mac's expression was mild, though he eyed the largest man up and down as if assessing the quality of his suit. "I'm of a mind to hold that captain ... and anyone else with a stake in those cattle ... responsible for our lost luggage." Still gripping the man's hand, he pulled him close. "O' course if I get the lady and her servants out o' here quick-like, with no trouble, my mind might change on that score."

The man's piggish eyes roved from me, in a ruined though clearly expensive dress, to Phoebe, in her dusty maid's garb. He darted a quick glance at Doug and Collum, braced on either side of us, then nodded.

"Guess ye'd best be on yer way then."

He jerked his hand from Mac's. I noticed him massaging the blood back into his whitened fingers as he edged out of our way.

"For your trouble." Mac flicked a silver coin into the air and motioned us out the door.

CHAPTER 17

NEW YORK IN THE LATE EIGHTEEN HUNDREDS WAS A CITY in flux. The old-world charm rapidly being overtaken by industry and the birth of commerce. Greasy black smoke belched from a hundred smokestacks, coating the city with a layer of smeary grime. Though we passed a few odd, ramshackle wooden buildings, most had been ripped out to make way for the dense, brick high-rises of six and seven stories that had begun to crowd the sky.

Once out of that horrifying blood-house, we hadn't waited long for the boys to hail a halfway decent carriage to take us to our first destination, the famed Waldorf Hotel, current residence of one Nikola Tesla. From there, we'd clean up and split into teams. One team would keep an eye out for the physicist—or, we hoped, his good friend Jonathan Carlyle. The other would reconnoiter Tesla's Fifth Avenue lab for the same purpose. Our backup plan was to find a way to attend the March 13 Vanderbilt soiree, where firm photographic evidence had placed Tesla.

Even though the sun had not yet risen enough to banish the previous night's shadows, as our carriage squelched between the tenements of the immigrant district, people were already mobbing the streets.

It was astonishingly . . . painfully . . . loud.

"What?" I shouted to Phoebe over the rumble of carts; the jangle of miles of leather harness; the combined cries of vendors, patrons, and newsboys; and the shouts of irritated wagon drivers in a variety of languages.

"I said," Phoebe practically yelled, cupping her hands around her mouth, "think I prefer the stink of medieval London to this cacophony."

My eyebrows shot up. "Nice word choice."

"Aye, been waiting to use that one."

I snorted. Phoebe returned my smile, but it didn't reach her eyes.

"Hey," I said, "how long is this gonna go on?"

"Not sure. How far away are we from the —?"

"That's not what I mean and you know it."

She turned toward the window, where we could see the edge of Doug's fingertips trailing down from his seat next to the carriage driver. "I don't know."

I touched the back of her hand. As quietly as was possible over the roar outside I said, "How many times have you told me how it hurts you to watch Doug get left behind time and again?"

One slim shoulder lifted. A hand swiped at her freckled cheek. "Aye," she said. "But he lied to me, Hope. He — he's *never* done that before, you know? And if something happens to him, I can't. I just can't." She turned. Looked me in the eyes. Hers were full. There was hurt there, yes, and anger. But mostly what I saw . . . was fear.

"I get it," I told her. "I really do. I—" I snipped off that thread, because this wasn't about Bran and me, or my worries for him. *Or how I can't stop thinking about him and that impossibly elegant cousin of his.* But I understood that sick, helpless feeling so well. How you wanted to protect them. Keep them safe. And the powerlessness that ate at you when you couldn't.

"But don't you see?" I said. "Doug is *here.* There's nothing you can do about that. And can you imagine seeing his face light up when he meets Tesla for the first time? You've been dying to share this with him for so long." I squeezed her hand. "And you're missing it, Pheebs. Because of stubbornness."

She pulled her hand away and dropped her gaze to the dingy carriage floor. She didn't speak, but I thought I saw the tension in her shoulders lessen. Beneath my skirts, I crossed my fingers that they'd work this out soon.

Doug's dream of traveling with the rest of us had finally come true. They loved each other so much, and I was eager for Phoebe to share in his joy.

Seated across from us in the carriage, Mac tilted his head toward Phoebe and gave me a quick wink that said we'd set this to rights. I grinned back as I realized that we'd made it. Another trip through the Dim. We were alive and no one was hurt. We'd lost most of our belongings, sure. But those were only *things*.

On my first voyage, I'd been sick with fear. Fear that we'd never find my lost mother. Fear that even if we did, we'd be too late to save her.

Today, as we passed through each dingy yet colorful neighborhood, I began to relax. Soon I was hanging half out the window in my excitement as I tried to take it all in. Smaller, older structures of graying wood huddled between their larger brick cousins — the tenements that were sprouting up everywhere, replacing single-family homes. Though here, even these new constructions were beginning to appear fatigued. Faces in every skin tone peeked out of grimy windows, making me grin as the historian in me fizzed to life.

Whoa, I thought. *This. This is the true birth of our nation.*

My brain whirred into action, offering up facts and figures on the immigrants who had just begun to turn the country into the melting pot it would one day become. The terrible injustice of slavery was only thirty years abolished. But as we passed through a largely African-American neighborhood, I watched men kiss their wives as they headed off to work. Women gathered around wagons to peruse the vendors' morning wares. Two little girls in braids and spotless white dresses held hands as they skipped down the sidewalk. Pride gleamed from their mother's face as she watched her little ones at play. I felt an upsurge of joy, knowing that horrific era was finally over. It would be a long road, but I knew that we were, at least, witnessing the infancy of a new age of freedom.

A mélange of scents wafted through the carriage window, changing at each cross street. Frying onions and garlic. Stewed cabbage. Exotic, unidentifiable spices that battled the overall stench of rotting garbage and crowded humanity.

With each block, however, the evidence of indescribable poverty grew more and more heartbreaking. Workers trudged by, heads bowed, lunch pails clasped tightly as they headed off to work in factories or mills. Packs of ragged children roamed sidewalks or huddled over metal grates in the ground to take advantage of the warm steam that billowed up.

During a brief traffic snarl, I watched a rouged woman haggle with three sailors. After counting and stuffing the bills into her low-cut bodice, she sighed and turned to follow the swaggering trio into the shadowed alley behind her. Her gaze snagged with mine. When I saw cheeks still rounded with baby fat, I realized the "woman" was a girl. A girl even younger than I was.

"God, she's just a kid," I whispered.

"What?" Phoebe leaned in, but I only shook my head as the girl tossed me an obscene gesture and disappeared into the alley.

When I looked out again, I realized we'd passed most of the worst of the destitution. The sidewalks here were choked with kerchiefed women in colorful skirts. I waved at a black-eyed baby propped on his mother's hip as she gossiped with her neighbor in melodic Italian. When the baby graced me with a beaming, toothless grin, I laughed out loud.

"What?" Phoebe asked. "What's funny?"

"I—it's just so incredible," I said. "Look at them out there."

Open carts piled with root vegetables or stacked with crates of squawking chickens took up half the street. A myriad of dialects twined into the air beneath a steady *plink, plunk* that bounced off the carriage roof.

Is that rain?

Sticking my head out, I peered up. Then jerked back just in time, as a piece of cloth came unmoored from the vast spider web of laundry lines strung between buildings and plopped wetly onto the road.

Before I could blink, two old women began scrabbling and shoving over the sad scrap.

We'd traveled only a few more blocks, when a cry came. "Hold!"

Mac, Phoebe, and I jolted as the carriage shuddered to a stop. Out the window, buildings crowded in. A worn-looking mother sat on a nearby stoop, nursing a fretful baby.

From the door behind her, a girl with the big teeth, braids, and gawky build of preadolescence emerged and dashed down the steps. She stooped to kiss the woman's cheek and tickle the baby under its chin. She straightened as a large group of kids trekked down the street toward them.

"Witaj, Anika." One of the older girls hurried forward, speaking in the consonant-heavy accent of Poland. "Are you ready? We must not be late, or Mister Johansen will dock us."

As the girl, Anika, went to meet her friend, the older girl called up to Anika's mother, "Is the baby feeling better today, Pani Wadisavka?"

I examined the thin, pale faces. None looked older than twelve or so. The boys in baggy overalls, flat caps shoved down over protruding ears. The girls in braids, work boots, and faded calico. All trudged past without once looking up from the cracked sidewalk. The group was eerily hushed, with little of the jollity that normally surrounds school-age kids.

As Anika joined her friend, an older woman wearing a babushka bustled out the front door toting a tin, cloth-covered pail.

The grandmother hobbled down the steps to pass Anika the lunch bucket. She paused for a moment to straighten the girl's collar and fuss with her braids. Anika murmured something in Polish, then reached up to quickly buss her grandmother on her withered cheek before darting off.

When they'd disappeared around the corner, the old woman's rounded shoulders slumped. She limped back toward the stairs.

"Wonder how far they have to walk to get to school?" Phoebe asked.

"I don't think they're going to school."

Mac nodded. "In this age, children like those have to work to help support their families," he said. "Mostly in the factories or sewing mills. They start young. Often as young as five or six."

My excitement dimmed once more at the image of the cheery-faced Anika trapped inside a dank space with dozens of others just like her, laboring over the foot pedals of a sewing machine.

"But that's awful," Phoebe said.

"Aye," Mac said. "Life here is hard for new immigrants, though it's likely better than what they left. 'Tis especially difficult for the young ones. But they have to eat. Their fathers make little to nothing and their mums are usually nursing all the new babes that keep coming. So it's left to the older children to bring in extra."

"That's just ..." Phoebe trailed off, shaking her head. "The poor, wee things."

"What's the holdup, Douglas?" Mac called to where Doug was perched beside the driver.

The carriage began to inch forward. Half a block down, Doug yelled out to Collum. The springs bounced as Collum hopped down off the rear brace and tugged the newsboy cap over his eyes.

"Dead horse in the road," he called with a grimace. "Looks like it's been there a while. Still tied to the ice wagon. They're moving it now."

Phoebe gagged and turned pale as skim milk when the scent wafted in. The pervasive odor of death reminded me of Roadkill Alley, the stretch of curving two-lane highway near our house where possums and raccoons—making a bid for freedom to one side or the other—littered the surface of the county road.

When I was seven years old, after witnessing an injured raccoon drag itself off the blacktop, I decided to start a Save the Hurt Animals club. Who knew how many of those poor creatures might need my help, I reasoned. I'd gather them all up, take them to the vet, and once they were healed they'd become my pets.

Half a mile and two mangled corpses later, I realized that when starting a club, it really helped if you had more than one member.

Gravel crunched behind me when Dad pulled up on the side of the road and emerged from the car, carrying a shovel and a garbage bag. When he knelt next to me on the grassy verge and wiped my wet cheeks with the back of his sleeve, the clean scent of washing detergent muffled the other, awful odors.

His smile was warm as the sun emerging from a cloudbank. "Got room for one more member?"

Later, after sending me off for a long bath, he'd made us each one of his famous grilled cheese sandwiches and gently explained how maybe it wasn't the best idea for me to go scraping animal guts off the highway.

Wiping my nose with the handkerchief Moira always thoughtfully tucked into our sleeves, I wondered if Dad was standing in our kitchen right now, wearing one of those same goofy aprons.

Or . . . I guess it's Dad and Stella's kitchen now.

The thought stung. I tried to tuck it back, but the truth was that the dissolution of my parents' marriage had left me shaky, as if the ground beneath my feet had suddenly turned to thin glass.

If the obstacles between my mom and dad were insurmountable, what kind of chance did Bran and I have with all that stood in our way?

The carriage rocked as Doug hopped down to help Collum and several other men unhook the dead bony horse from its flat, hay-covered wagon. With grunts and a squeak of ropes, the road cleared enough for us to pull forward.

Blocks of ice melted in the warming air as we creaked past. Water flowed down the street in rivulets as the men heaved the animal's corpse up onto the sidewalk. The boys reboarded, and with a snap of our driver's whip, the carriage jolted forward. I turned away and swiped at my eyes, determined to look only forward. To survive whatever lay ahead and stop mourning for those things that were behind me now.

CHAPTER 18

A FEW BLOCKS LATER WE EMERGED ONTO THE WIDE, FLAT surface of Fifth Avenue, and the nineteenth-century New York City of my imagination spread out before us.

My fists loosened as the street opened up and the sky once again appeared. Despite the cold, small, scattered parks sprouted with the first hints of spring. The air, though hazy with smoke and other forms of pollution, became breathable. As poverty gave way to affluence, the mud and rough cobbles morphed into a smooth, concrete-like roadway.

"That there is macadam," Mac said proudly, pointing out the window to the flat surface. "Invented by a Scotsman, you know."

The green tint behind Phoebe's freckles lessened as the coach's horrible juddering smoothed and we cruised serenely down the wide, paved avenue. There was less traffic on the street. But along the swept sidewalks, hundreds of mostly well-dressed people meandered past. Women in sober day dresses walked arm in arm, gazing in shop windows. Men in tweed suits and bowler hats strolled by, newspapers tucked under their arms.

"Well, this is better, aye?" Mac took a deep breath, his grip on the coach's open window loosening.

Doug's upside-down face appeared in the window as he leaned down. "Everyone all right, then?" he asked, gaze locked on Phoebe.

When it became clear she still wasn't speaking to him, I answered instead.

"We're good. How much farther?"

Doug disappeared. Seconds later his voice drifted down, informing us we'd be pulling up in less than a minute.

Even though the journey had improved immensely, I breathed a sigh of relief. Between a dead horse and having the flesh shaken from our bones by the rough ride, I was ready for this part to be done.

"Waldorf Hotel!"

"Better put this on." Phoebe brushed flakes of dust from the huge flower-laden hat. "A lady mustn't be outdoors without a hat, you know. You'd take on too much notice."

"Yeah," I said, cramming the monstrosity on my head. "Thanks."

The wheels ground to a halt. Outside, harnesses creaked as the horses stamped, likely as ready for a break as we were.

Collum leaned in, his serious face coated in dust as he murmured, "Everyone clear on their roles? Should we refresh one last time?"

When Doug and I nodded, Phoebe groaned.

"None of that, now," Mac chided. "The lad's right. I know 'tis old hat to you, m' darlin', but Hope and Doug here, they're new at this. Only fair to go over it once more. To be safe, aye?" He gestured at me. "Hope?"

I had only met my father's great-aunt Abagail once. His great-uncle's wealthy widow had been gracious and lovely, and I'd fallen madly for her when I noticed how very much she intimidated my horrible grandmother. While introducing the rest of her blond, simpering brood, Mother Bea had pointedly ignored my presence. A true Southern lady from a very old and distinguished New Orleans family, the poised, soft-spoken Abagail Randolph Walton had put the bitter Mother Bea in her place with one raised finger.

"But, Beatrice," she said in that honeyed drawl. "You failed to mention this lovely brunette flower in your garden. Matthew's daughter, isn't she? And what might your name be, ma chère?"

The rest of that day, Abagail kept me by her side, enthralling me with stories about her Garden Street home and some of her more eccentric neighbors. When we'd begun formulating our backstories for this journey, I dug into Abagail's family history.

I channeled her now, ending my sentences on an up tilt as if each statement were a question.

"Why good sir, I am but poor lil' old Hope Battiste Randolph? Of the Lafayette Parish Randolphs? My daddy's too busy running for district judge to take me over the big water to be married? To the second son of the Earl of

Airth over in Scotland? Of course, he's nothing but a big ole douchebag who's marrying me for my money. Didn't even come himself. Sent his *lawyer* to get me?" I gestured at Mac in his tweeds. "How romantic."

Phoebe snorted. "What a wank."

Mac grinned. "Agreed. A common enough occurrence for this time though, even if our earl is fictional. Not likely to be an issue, and safer than naming a real man who someone might've met."

"And you're sure this Randolph has come and gone?" Collum asked. "This could go south fast if the fellow happens to be tucked away in his wee bed upstairs when we go waltzing in, claiming kin."

I tamped down my irritation. I knew Collum was only being cautious. And unlike our previous sojourn into 1154, I was much less sure of myself in this particular place and era. Though I had, of course, studied American history, it'd never fascinated me the way European history did.

It took only an instant before the image of the Waldorf's yellowed register, conjured by Moira's research wizardry, pinged open inside my mind. *There.* Dated less than a year previously, the June 1894 signature of wealthy Louisiana sugar cane magnate Waldo T. Randolph—Abagail's great-great-grandfather—glowed from the page.

"I'm positive," I said. "And the man had eleven kids, so this should be perfect."

Collum glanced at Phoebe, then Doug. "You two?"

"Gah, Coll," Phoebe snipped. "We've got it, aye? I'm the

new Lady Airth's lady's maid, sent by her git of a betrothed to serve on her journey." She flicked a finger in Doug's direction, though I noticed she still wouldn't look at him. "*He* is valet to his Lordship's barrister. And you ..." She poked a finger hard into Collum's vest-covered chest. "Are nothing but a boot-scraping serving lad, so get to work and leave us to do ours."

The sting in Phoebe's tone, so unlike her usual, cheery demeanor, took everyone aback, even Collum. To my astonishment, he nodded and stepped back, raising his voice only to be heard over the sidewalk clamor as he stooped to unlatch the folded steps attached to the side of the carriage.

"We'll just be getting your luggage down then, sir, miss."

Mac got out first, then helped me alight. As I wobbled to the sidewalk, Phoebe scurried after, straightening my gown and tucking stray hairs back beneath the massive hat, fussing around me, playing her role to perfection.

Doug's entire demeanor changed as he took the bag from Mac and stepped back, head bowed as he assumed his part as Mac's valet.

"Remember," Mac murmured quietly to me as he straightened the bowler hat over his balding pate and jerked the wrinkles out of his coat. "If I have any trouble with the manager, you act the Southern belle. The staff won't be able to resist helping a spoiled little rich girl."

"Let me fix that for you, miss," Phoebe said loudly, readjusting a pin where one of my curls had sprung loose.

"Ow," I grumbled as pointed metal scraped across my

scalp. "Spoiled brat, huh?" I said under my breath. "I don't see that being a huge problem."

Mac winked, and turned toward the bellhops lined up beneath the canopy that sheltered the ornate entrance. They exchanged glances before hurrying forward, likely bewildered at our lack of luggage. Most were probably used to guests who brought half their household rather than two sad-looking bags.

"My good man." Mac addressed the oldest bellhop, a graying man with the most gold braid adorning his burgundy uniform. "If you could see us to your manager at once. The young miss here has had a horrific experience and is in sore need of rest and refreshment."

That was my cue. Fluttering a hand at my throat, I tried to look petulant and pitiful all at once. After what we'd just been through, it wasn't a big stretch.

"Right away, sir." The bellhop bowed. "This way, sir. Miss."

Mac tapped his gold-headed cane on the sidewalk and offered me an arm. As Doug and Phoebe took their assigned spots behind us, I half turned to Collum. "Oh, and get our bags, won't you, boy?"

He tipped his flat cap and picked up the small — the only — leather traveling case we'd managed to save. Though he kept up the blank servant's façade, I saw his eyes tighten at the corners just a bit. Turning the snort that followed into a delicate, ladylike cough, I flipped a curl over one shoulder and sauntered through the double doors into the Waldorf Hotel.

CHAPTER 19

AN OLDER MAN IN A CUTAWAY BLACK SUIT MET THE senior bellhop at the door and gave our bedraggled lot a sly inspection. After a quick conference, the new man turned to us and bowed.

"I'll fetch Mr. Oscar, shall I?" he said. "If you'd kindly have a seat for just one moment."

From the instant we'd stepped through the heavy brass doors into the elegant lobby, I'd been trying not to gawp. It was hard. Soaring frescoed ceilings. Marble floors. Enormous mirrors that reflected golden light from ornate chandeliers. Everything was gilded and exquisite and perfect. Even the air smelled gorgeous, perfumed by massive floral arrangements tucked into golden vases.

"Cheese 'n crackers," Phoebe whispered in an awed tone as she nervously smoothed down the front of her black maidservant's gown.

"Easy now," Mac muttered under his breath. "This should be the easy part."

At this early hour, the expansive lobby was relatively empty, though guests—mostly men in tweeds or black suits—occasionally descended the curving double staircase. Some exited. But most crossed to a pair of walnut doors labeled with a brass sign that read MEN'S CAFÉ. Each time the uniformed attendant opened the doors for a guest, I caught a glimpse of dark paneling, leather chairs, and cast-iron chandeliers strung from stout chains. As the doors closed behind each gentleman, the scents of coffee, alcohol, and cigars wafted our way.

Rarely, the men escorted a corseted wife or daughter. Invariably, the women split off to disappear behind a set of white and gilt doors on the opposite side of the lobby. The plaque beside that segregated area read LADIES' RE-CEPTION.

"Nice." Phoebe scowled at the darkly paneled doors. "Hey, Hope, what do you say we hold a protest? Just march into that man cave over there and demand a brandy and cigar?"

"I like it. Let's go freak 'em the hell out."

"Don't even think about it," Collum growled.

"Jeez, relax, Coll," Phoebe said. "We're joking ... and besides, it's early yet for brandy. Wonder if they'd make us bloody marys instead." Her mouth pursed. "Um, has the bloody mary been invented yet, Hope?"

"Nope. Not till 1921, by a Parisian bartender named Fernand Petiot. But we could show them how—"

Mac wheeled on us, though I saw him hide a grin

beneath the fake walrus mustache Moira had glued into place. "Enough, girls. You'll make poor Collum's head explode. And must I remind you—ah ..."

A young man with the posture and perfectly pressed suit of an authority figure approached our group and bowed. "Good morning, sir. Miss. Welcome to the Waldorf Hotel. I am Oscar. And how may I be of service?"

The hard *v*'s and *k*'s of the man's accent hinted at eastern Europe, and as I nodded a greeting, I realized we were meeting none other than Oscar Tschirky. Also known as Oscar of the Waldorf, the man who served brilliantly as maître d'hôtel of the Waldorf—and then the Waldorf-Astoria—for fifty years and was credited with inventing the famous Waldorf salad, along with other culinary masterpieces.

As with any exclusive hotel in our own time, most guests would have made reservations weeks in advance. Step one was to convince this dapper dude that despite appearances, we were bona fide rich folks.

"Oh, Mr. Oscar," I said. "I am so grateful to see you. I cannot tell you the trials we have suffered. Before I left home, my dear papa told me, 'Now, my darlin' daughter. Soon as you get yourself to New York, you make Mr. Oscar's acquaintance, you hear? Oscar's a good man. He'll take care of all your needs.'"

Oscar Tschirky didn't bat an eyelash. "And so we shall, Miss ... ?"

"Randolph." I made a little curtsy. "Of the Lafayette Parish Randolphs, naturally," I hurried to add. "Papa would've come himself, but he's been *so* busy of late. The judgeship, you know."

"Of course, Miss Randolph." Oscar gave a sage nod. "Let us see what we can do to accommodate you, yes? I don't recall the hotel taking a reservation under the name Randolph."

"Well, of course we arranged one. One simply doesn't just walk in off the street at a fine establishment such as the Waldorf, does one?"

"A good morning to you," Mac cut in quickly. "I am John MacPherson, sent by His Lordship the Earl of Airth to escort this lovely young lady to wed his second son, Charles. Known the lad since he was in knee-britches, I have. They grow up so fast, don't they?"

"I'm mighty tuckered out, Mr. Oscar," I pressed. "This journey has been such a trial." I batted my lashes at the man, though it probably just looked like I had gook in my eyes.

In my peripheral vision, I saw Collum's eyes roll up to the high, sculpted ceiling. Doug swiped at the corners of his mouth. Phoebe didn't even try to hide her grin as Mac put in quickly, "His Lordship had a telegram sent here not three weeks ago. I assume all arrangements are in order? I would sure hate to have to tell the earl his new daughter-in-law was not taken care of in the manner befitting her station."

Oscar didn't miss a beat. "And we shall of course extend every courtesy to the young miss. If you shall but follow me?" Oscar bowed once more, then led Mac over to the glossy reception desk.

"Nice flirting," Phoebe murmured as she eased up beside me.

"Learned from the master."

My whining, along with Mac's letters of credit linked to a very real fortune in the Bank of New York, must have impressed. The eighth-floor suite of rooms that spread out before us dripped with decadence.

"Wow," Phoebe gasped. "This is . . ."

"Yeah," I agreed. "It is."

After riding up the man-operated elevator to the eighth floor, Oscar—bolstered by a train of hotel servants—took us through the enormous suite. By the time the maître d'hôtel had completed his tour of living spaces, parlor, exquisite private dining and morning rooms, library, four bedrooms, and two private baths, all I wanted was to kick off my boots and let my aching feet sink into one of the dozen Turkish carpets. I saw Doug eying a delicate, gilt-inlaid Louis XIV chair and knew he was trying to calculate the chance it would hold up under his weight.

Though each space was more magnificent than the one before, after ten minutes of admiring the no-doubt priceless bric-a-brac that covered every surface . . . the garishly painted silk wallpaper had started to close in on me.

When Oscar opened the balcony doors, a brisk March

wind sliced through the room, bringing with it the scent of factory smoke and newly cut wood. Yards of lace and scarlet silk that had probably cost more than my dad's car tried to unmoor themselves as they gusted upward on the breeze. Oscar tutted and started to shut the doors.

Phoebe, noting my flinch, spoke up. "Leave it be, please, Mr. Tschirky. Her, um . . . Ladyship prefers the fresh air."

Oscar nodded. Pride glazed his voice as he clicked his heels together. "Although I'm certain this shan't compare to your new home at the earl's estate, here at the Waldorf we strive to ensure our guests receive every comfort."

We followed the manager to the walnut-paneled dining room area. "As I assume Miss Randolph wishes to refresh herself in some privacy, I've taken the liberty of ordering luncheon. It shall be brought up at once. Someone will guide your servants to their dining hall, belowstairs. As is customary, staff meals are served promptly at five, a.m. and p.m." Oscar's gaze skimmed over Doug's large form. "Mr. MacPherson's valet may come to the back door of the kitchen at four thirty to receive his meals. The dining area for colored staff is located just off the stable. He may—"

"What?" Phoebe's voice severed Tschirky's speech as neatly as a surgeon's blade slicing off a diseased mole. "What did you just say?"

Oscar frowned, confused. "I don't . . ."

Doug jerked discreetly on Phoebe's skirt. He gave a graceful bow. "Thank you, sir. I will do just that."

I could hear Phoebe's teeth grinding. My own hands

fisted at my sides as Oscar motioned two maids forward. "Emma and Lila will serve as Miss Randolph's first and second housemaids during your stay. And will, of course, answer to her lady's maid."

As the two maids curtsied, Oscar went on. "Lastly, I've also taken the liberty of sending for the best dressmaker in town to come at once. She shall begin replacing the trousseau Miss Randolph so tragically lost in the steamboat accident."

"Yes," I muttered. "The steamboat accident *was* truly awful."

Oscar headed for the door, where he paused to point out a series of bell pulls, each labeled with a different function.

CONCIERGE. DINING. PORTER. 1ST MAID. 2ND MAID. VALET. KITCHEN. STABLE.

"Please ring if you have need of anything at all," Oscar said. "Miss Randolph's personal maid shall take the small area just off her mistress's bedchamber." He jerked a nod at Doug. "And while the usual custom is for a valet to take the room set aside for him off the gentleman's quarters . . ." He trailed off again, gesturing helplessly at Doug. "It seems we must make other arrangements in this case."

Phoebe vibrated with fury. My breath hissed out. And even Collum's face began to redden with anger. Doug only nodded. "Of course, Mr. Tschirky."

"We thank you for your hospitality." Mac hustled Oscar out the door before anyone went ballistic. "I'm sure Miss Randolph is eternally grateful. As is my employer, the earl."

With a snap of the maître d'hôtel's fingers, the staff filtered out and shut the door behind them.

"Racist bastard," Phoebe snarled at the door. "How dare he?"

"Babe." Doug's voice was gentle, though I heard the underlying note of steel. "It's 1895. The American Civil War ended only thirty years past. It's shameful the way most people of color are treated during this time, yes. Awful. But coming here was *my* choice. And I am willing to face it."

She threw up her hands and dropped down onto a tapestried love seat. "Oh, great. How very noble of you. Well, you might be '*willing to face it,*' but that doesn't mean *I* have to. Not a damn, bleeding bit of it."

"Phee," Collum began, but she wheeled around on him and he backed off, palms raised.

Phoebe leapt up at a soft knock on the door. She stomped over and jerked it open.

"Yeah?" she snapped at the two housemaids who stood outside, each carrying a stack of cream-colored towels.

They bobbed in tandem and entered as Phoebe stepped back.

"Mr. Tschirky sent us for to draw bath on Miss Randolph," the blonde—an older girl with light blue eyes and sturdy, Nordic bone structure—said. "It is through door there. All inside plumbing at Waldorf, miss. Water comes hot as summer day straight from pipes. We scrub back and wash hair."

Phoebe groaned, though I saw her features lighten just a

bit. "Thank you. But Miss Randolph won't need you at the moment. Take a break. But please show the dressmaker up the moment she arrives, aye?"

The smaller, mousy one bobbed again and skirted out. The blonde nodded, though she cut an uneasy glance my way. "You are to be bathing the mistress yourself, then?"

"Aye. I'll manage." After practically closing the door in the girl's face, my friend plopped down next to me.

"Aw, Phee," I said. "That's so sweet of you. I mean, a bath sounds *awesome* right about now." I flashed a wicked smile. "Remember, I'm allergic to lavender. And hey, can I see a loofah menu before you bathe me?"

"You," she shot back, fighting a grin, "can go bathe my fat butt."

Doug gave a low whistle as he turned from the fire. "Now *that* is something I'd like to see."

"Douglas Eugene Carlyle," Mac snapped.

"Jesus, man," Collum groaned. "That's my sister."

Doug and Phoebe locked eyes. Phoebe stood and marched over to him. For a moment, no one breathed.

Finally, she shook her head. "You just keep dreamin', big boy," she said, jumping up to wrap her arms around his neck, practically strangling him. "You just keep right on dreamin'."

Behind the round wire-framed glasses Doug's brown eyes closed as his arms came around her and held her close. His voice very quiet in the silence of the room, he said, "I never stop dreaming of you, mo chridhe."

Collum's tawny eyebrows shot up at the pair's first real exchange in nearly a week. The back of my throat ached as I recalled Mac calling out the same Gaelic endearment to Moira in the cavern.

Mo chridhe. My heart.

CHAPTER 20

WE BENT THE RULES, OF COURSE. SHORTLY AFTER OSCAR'S departure, men in red jackets had shown up to whisk away ten of the rosewood dining table's twelve chairs, and to set two places with more crystal, china, and silver than I'd ever seen in my entire life. Collectively.

A stream of tuxedo-clad waiters wheeled in carts laden with trays. Wisps of steam escaped from the sides of their embellished silver domes, filing the air with a delicious mélange of scents. Bread and meat, fish and cream and berry-laden sauces. As the smells coalesced, my stomach gurgled. I thought the head waiter would blow a gasket when Mac bustled the whole lot of them out the door, insisting, "Thank you, but the lady and I prefer to serve ourselves."

"I never," we heard one of them mutter as Mac shut the door behind him. "Most irregular," argued another.

We pulled up random chairs, split out the dishes and silver, and attacked. I bit into a roll, watching Collum slurp down a thin, brownish soup from a silver tureen.

"You, uh, know that's turtle, right?"

He looked up, heavy spoon halfway to his mouth. "Pardon?"

My mouth curved up. "I just had no idea you were so into turtle soup. It's one of this era's most popular delicacies."

Steam wreathed Collum's broad face as he glanced down into the murky liquid. Bits of greenish meat floated to the surface. Phoebe snorted and Doug wiped his grin away with a napkin as Collum pushed the bowl aside.

I dug into a creamy, earthy mushroom soup, followed by tiny soft-shell crabs sautéed in drawn butter. We all oohed and aahed over beef tenderloins in a red wine sauce that disintegrated in our mouths. Phoebe was entranced by a cold, gel-like meat dish that quivered when she poked it with a fork. By the time delicate slices of almond cake went around, I could barely pick at it.

As Mac rang for the servants to clear, we disguised the evidence of our diverse dining group. In moments the scraps were scuttled away, and we had a new visitor.

Oscar was, at the least, a man of his word. And obviously influential. Soon I found myself standing on a low table in the elaborate, over-decorated Francis I bedroom that was the mistress's chamber, being fitted for a new wardrobe. I longed to skip the whole dress thing, but thanks to the cattle, my only options were the tattered, filthy traveling gown I was currently wearing, or nothing.

Madame Belisle—forties, waspish, and supremely arrogant—glanced up from a kneeling position, a pained expression souring her narrow face.

"Non," she spluttered, after forcing me to strip down to corset and bloomers. Wasting no time on pleasantries, she rounded on one of her cowed assistants. "You see? Thick through ze waist. And ze bosom is nonexistent. Tighten that corset at once!"

Thick through the . . . Oh, you can just bite me.

Phoebe snorted behind her hand. Of course, she'd had it easy. When I'd insisted that my lady's maid would be accompanying me to every event, Madame Belisle had muttered in French and absolutely refused to have anything to do with the "peasantry." The poor overburdened assistant had done a quick—and poke-free—job of taking Phoebe's measurements, leaving me to glare at everyone and dream up ways to murder Madame Snarly.

Still no word from Bran, though I'd yanked on the bell pull marked CONCIERGE three times in the past hour. The last time, there was no mistaking the irritation in the bellhop's breathless "And once again, miss. There are no messages."

I was starting to worry. Bran had promised to meet up with us as soon as he could. At the very least, he would have arranged to leave a message at the front desk.

Where the hell are you?

I twitched as an image of Gabriella de Roca popped up

in my head like an oil-slicked bubble from grimy bath water. I was promptly rewarded with a pin jab to the left thigh.

An hour later, the fashion nazi and her browbeaten team
were being bundled out with an order for two more gowns
to be delivered on the morrow. More than anything I wanted to give the hateful snob a swift kick in the rear on her way
out. But the truth was, you couldn't argue with results. Aside
from the promised ball gown, underthings, and a variety
of travel wear, I'd been left with a quick-fitted, velvet day
gown in shades of teal, with muted silver piping that Phoebe
couldn't quit cooing over.

The last of the lunch crowd having filtered in and out
downstairs, Collum rejoined us in the suite for one of
his tiresome *Just-because-Mac-is-here-doesn't-mean-I'm-not-
still-in-charge-of-you-two* speeches. Scrubbing his face with
a thick white towel, he laid down the orders.

"No sign of Carlyle or Tesla yet. Mac sent Doug to stake
out the front of the hotel, since none of the people Celia
would've sent know his face. He'll watch from across the
street, and keep an eye out for anyone suspicious looking.
I'm joining Mac at the lab and from there, we'll hit up a
few more places the absent professor's known to frequent.
Phoebe, you should already be down in the servants' area. If
you two are done playing dress-up—"

"Dress-up?" Phoebe stormed up to her brother, hands on
hips. "I'll give you dress-up, you misogynistic prat!"

While the two raged at each other in what I could only assume was a prequel to double-sibling homicide, I snatched up the matching smoke-colored reticule Madame Belisle had left for me, and backed toward the door.

"So, yeah," I called over the cursing. "I'll just be down in Ladies' Reception, trying to suss out info on that soiree Tesla attended. Attends . . . will attend . . . whatever."

Phoebe, from her new spot atop the ironbound steamer trunk Oscar Tschirky had so thoughtfully provided, raged at her brother. "I'll remind you I am not a *child* anymore, Collum Michael MacPherson! I've nearly as much experience as you, and . . ."

I let the door click shut behind me. When those two reached the point of calling each other by their full names, things tended to get a little dicey.

The inside of Ladies' Reception looked as if someone had picked up a room in one of Marie Antoinette's Versailles apartments and plunked it down smack in the middle of New York City.

Everything in the oval-shaped room was white, gold, or pink. An inset ceiling soothed in a pastel mural of chubby angels and fluffy lambs, uplit by crystal chandeliers. As I was escorted inside, I eyed pieces of dainty furniture that looked as though they might collapse under the weight of a chunky cat.

In small groupings around the room, upper-crust women in high-necked day gowns gossiped over tiny sandwiches and tea in paper-thin china. High hair on swan necks pivoted my way as I entered. Having decided I was no one of consequence, they returned to their shark smiles and polite verbal eviscerations.

"Look, Jemima," I heard one croon as I passed by. "Carlotta is wearing that lovely rose gown of hers ... yet again."

"Why, Letitia, dear," said another between sips of tea. "That extra weight you're carrying fills your face out so nicely."

"Here you are, miss." The maid spoke up, directing me to a seat next to a marble pillar. "I'll see to it that tea is brought right away."

As I perched on the edge of the tapestried chair, the corset dug into my rib cage. My spleen or pancreas or some other solid organ shifted into a space it was decidedly *not* meant to enter.

Least I don't have to worry about slumping.

When the maid, bowing, brought my tea tray, I tried my best to appear haughty and bored, not nauseated and sweaty. The glances I kept getting from the little gossip groups, however, suggested that my attempt to fit in wasn't working all that well. Or maybe they did that to every newcomer.

While I pretended to ignore the whispered conjectures about who on earth I was supposed to be, and where I'd gotten my "*most* interesting" gown, the middle-aged woman seated next to me resumed her hushed conversation with the pretty young girl seated stiffly on her other side.

"Don't you dare swallow that." The older woman thrust out a large linen napkin. "You know what Mr. Fletcher says. 'Chew each bite one hundred times, and then spit it out. Never swallow.'"

"But." The girl's light eyes skittered around the room. "It's only that I am so very hungry, Mother."

"I see," the mother said. "Well, if you *wish* for your ingratitude and disobedience to cause me another arrhythmia . . . If you want me to take to my bed again . . . Or . . ." Her plain features gone cunning, she looked straight at the girl. "Or perhaps you prefer to send me straight to my grave, Consuelo . . ."

The woman—whose features bore an uncanny resemblance to a potato, and whose sturdy proportions beneath her expensive, pea-soup velvet suggested more than a few bites had made their way down *her* esophagus—clutched at her heart. The girl's face went white. "No, Mother. Oh, please, Mother, forgive me."

As the stricken girl fluttered around her mom, the name pinged something in my memory files. *Consuelo.*

"How is it," Phoebe had asked me once, around a mouthful of Moira's famous jam sandwiches we'd carried out to the stables, "that you aren't completely nutters?"

She didn't elaborate, but I knew what she meant. Feet shuffling across the straw-strewn floor, I'd breathed in the homey scents. Hay and horse. Leather and wet stone and mud. Before following my best friend up the wooden ladder to the hayloft, I removed an apple from my pocket, held it to my nose. When my mare, Ethel, whuffed an impatient horsy breath into my hair, I let my forehead rest against her homely face. "I know," I whispered. "I miss him too."

In a liquid twilight, with the rain pounding outside, the cozy stable at Christopher Manor had felt like peace. Like safety and solidity. Protected by the overhang, Phoebe and I had settled in the hayloft door to peer out past silver sheets of rain that drained off the slanted slate roof. Far below, lambs cavorted across the Highland valley, bleating and getting very, very wet. Our feet dangled, heels kicking weathered stone.

Phoebe plucked a piece of straw from her mouth and let it drop to the churned-up mud below. "I mean, I can barely hold enough in this barmy noggin . . ." Tapping a fingertip to her forehead, she left behind a sticky red dot, a strawberry jam version of an Indian bindi. "To make it through exams. And once they're done, I just let it go. But you. To think of all that's rolling around beneath those gorgeous black curls of yours. It's pure amazing. But I don't get how your head doesn't simply explode."

Sometimes it felt like that. An explosion. When the vast information contained inside the flesh and blood and neurons of my brain expanded too quickly. When I lost control

of it. When—instead of teasing out one or two tidy threads
—a whole skein of it blew out at once in a massive, knotted
tangle. Those were bad days.

Not this time, though. Fortunately for me, I'd never developed the same fascination with American history as I had
with British or European. My mother taught me plenty
about the land where we lived, of course.

But this was manageable. Green-tinged portraits of
wealthy young girls with elaborate hair and gorgeous gowns
flickered by. My fingers twitched as my mind flew through
the data I'd collected on the notable people of New York
City in the late eighteen hundreds.

Too old. Too young. Wart.

An image slowed, cleared. My eyes snapped open. I
smiled into my teacup.

Gotcha.

"Had it from Mrs. Paget herself," potato mama was saying, the napkin's scalloped edges still dangling from her outstretched fingers. "The duke abhors plumpness in women.
Several of his set will be in attendance. And what will His
Grace say when he learns you appeared at your own mother's soiree looking like a stuffed Christmas goose? We shall
all be shamed."

The exquisite girl blinked, one hand reaching to touch
her insanely tiny waist. I could all but see the wheels spinning beneath the poof of brown hair, anchored in place by

a pale pink ribbon that matched the lacy layers of her day gown.

She sighed and took the proffered fabric. She brought it to her lips, balled it up, then set it on a silver tray at her side. "Yes, Mother."

I wanted to scream. *Stand up to her! Don't let her treat you that way!*

Then a thought hit me. *Who am I to give that kind of advice?* Hadn't I been just like this girl until very recently? My mother had always been kind, of course. But she had regimented each and every moment of my day. She'd kept me apart. *Alone.* I understood her reasoning now, but back then, I never argued. Never once said, *"Enough. This is my life, not yours."*

Seated next to me in the ladies' salon were none other than Alva and Consuelo Vanderbilt. Wife and only daughter of the astronomically wealthy William K. Vanderbilt. Details tried to flood in, but I tamped them down to a bare minimum. March 11 of 1895. Okay, so Alva would—later this month, actually—send shock waves through her upper-crust society when she divorced her cheating tycoon hubby. And in November, Consuelo would marry the ninth Duke of Marlborough.

Old chubby hater himself. *Ick.*

The admittedly shallow research I'd filed away on Consuelo Vanderbilt threaded up. And it made me want to cry. At eighteen, Consuelo was in love with (and secretly engaged to) another man. She'd initially refused to marry the duke. But Alva Vanderbilt was intent on the match, and she ruled her daughter with an iron fist. After months of unsuccessful coercion, Alva had used psychological warfare. She convinced her daughter of her own impending death, saying her last wish was that Consuelo marry the duke. Of course, Mama made a remarkable recovery after Consuelo eventually acquiesced. She and the duke were married for twenty-six years. And though she would produce two sons —the requisite "heir and a spare," a phrase she is credited with having coined—husband and wife would live most of those years apart. There would be rumors of affairs on both sides, until they finally divorced in 1921.

As Consuelo Vanderbilt's entire life flashed through my mind, my stomach ached. She was sitting right here, and yet, there was nothing I could do to help her.

I swallowed hard. *Stick to the mission, Walton. That's what matters. You can't go fixing everyone, so just stop.*

One thing and one thing only was important right now. Alva Vanderbilt was throwing the party that Tesla would attend. If we couldn't get to the physicist any other way, the soiree, at least, was a sure thing. My duty was clear. Fingers crossed . . . she would be our way in.

CHAPTER 21

"Mother, might we not at least discuss—?"

"No." Alva cut her daughter off. "Do you have any notion of how difficult this marriage was to arrange? And I hear Mrs. Astor *herself* is impressed with the match. So much so," she said, leaning closer, "that she is practically green with envy."

Consuelo ducked her head. "It is only that I shall hate to leave your side. And, well, England is so very far away."

Alva harrumphed, her face softening only a little as she looked at her only daughter. When she snapped pudgy fingers for a hovering maid to refill her teacup, I saw Consuelo's eyes flash with momentary triumph.

Ooh . . . she's smart! Pandering to Mama's soft spot. It's a good strategy. But now I need to talk to her. Alone. So how to get rid of Mommy Dearest?

Ideas flickered on the edge of my vision. An accidental tripping and falling into Alva's stout lap. Or, hey, keep it simple with a hearty slap on the rump. "Did someone say soiree?"

At the very thought, my hands and feet went cold. Of course, I *ought* to be totally used to embarrassing myself by now. Yet the thought of all those haughty eyes turned my way . . .

Rescue came in the guise of a petite ginger that skimmed through the room toward me.

Phoebe bobbed a low curtsy, whispering, "I got nothing from the servant's quarter on Jonathan or Nikola. Any luck here?"

"Maybe." I slanted a sideways look toward the sour-faced Alva. "If I could talk to the daughter. Alone."

Phoebe's blue eyes narrowed as she nodded in understanding.

"More tea you say, Miss Wal—Randolph?" she asked in an excessively loud voice. "Certainly. I'll see it's brought right away. And I'll make sure it's hot. *Scalding*, if you take my meaning?"

"Okay. If you're sure?"

"Oh, I am."

She was back in a moment, a servant pushing a rolling tea tray in her wake. With practiced movements, the server whisked away my cup and replaced it with another. When she went to pick up the steaming kettle, however, Phoebe plucked it from the affronted girl's hand.

"No," my friend said as she maneuvered herself into position. "I'll serve Miss Randolph myself. She prefers it that —Oh!"

Phoebe stumbled, allowing the contents of the teakettle to slosh out and splash across the bottom of Alva Vanderbilt's ugly, voluminous skirts. Though the multiple layers beneath Alva's gown minimized the chance of second-degree burns, the results were spectacular.

"You bumbling fool!" She surged from her chair like a breaching manatee. "You've ruined my gown!"

Phoebe began babbling apologies. "Oh, madame! I'm that sorry, I am. Here, let me help you."

I jerked my chin at the door and mouthed, *Get rid of her.*

Alva, her pudding face now an alarming shade of plum, screeched at the line of ladies' maids waiting behind the marble columns. "Margót!"

A pale brunette, who looked as though she made a habit of sucking on lemons, materialized at Alva's side. "Mon Dieu, madame!" she tutted over her mistress. "We shall feex thees right away. You—" When she tried to shoo Phoebe away, I stood.

"No, no. Phoebe will help you. Especially since this will take at *least* ten or fifteen minutes . . ."

"Oh, aye." Phoebe nodded. "At least."

Margót began to bustle the furious aristocrat away, wet skirts trailing on the patterned carpet.

"Shall I come too, Mother?" Consuelo asked, though I noticed she didn't rise from her seat.

Alva, too flustered to think straight, only waved her daughter off. "Stay. Stay. I shall return momentarily. But you—" She whirled on me, one trembling, beringed finger pointing in my face. "If that incompetent worked for me, she'd be out on her ear with no reference."

"Thank you," I replied. "I will definitely give your advice much consideration."

Phoebe made a face at me behind Alva's swishing skirts as they hustled off.

The efficient wait staff had already scrubbed the stains from the carpet and replaced Alva's dampened chair with a dry one. With what I hoped was a proper degree of ennui, I balanced on the edge of the new chair and turned to Consuelo Vanderbilt.

"My apologies for my maid," I said. "She's new."

The girl covered her mouth. It was a graceful move, but I'd already seen the grin. "Not to worry," she said in a breathy voice. "At least Mother will have something new to complain about. Something other than me, that is."

Her stifled giggle sounded rusty, like wind chimes hanging too long beneath the summer rain.

"Forgive me," I said. "I couldn't help overhearing. You said you were betrothed?"

All the merriment vanished from the girl's light eyes. "Yes. I—I am to wed in the autumn."

"And you are not happy about it," I said, faking a theatrical sigh. "Well, I understand *that* all too well."

I watched her face as she puzzled over my words. The

wealthy socialite was probably used to girls squealing in delight over how she'd landed a duke. My empathy intrigued her. I could see it. Still, her upbringing came to the fore and made her cautious. She held out a slim white hand.

"I'm Consuelo," she said, omitting the powerful surname. "Connie. And you are?"

"Hope Randolph," I said, taking her fingertips in mine. "Of the Lafayette Parish Randolphs. Pleasure to make your acquaintance."

I drew a handkerchief from my sleeve and dabbed my eyes, attempting an Oscar-worthy performance. "I'm to take ship for England soon." I raised my eyes to Connie's and let her witness my faux misery as I whispered, "To be married."

Connie's slender throat bobbed as she swallowed in sympathy. Quickly, I laid my ace on the table. "He's a Scottish earl," I choked. "I have only met him once. Daddy made all the arrangements, and though I am grateful . . ." I let my voice fade, so that she had to lean close as I dropped my head. "The truth is that I feel so desperately alone."

A few seconds of silence passed while I stared into my lap, gritting my teeth and wondering if I'd overplayed it.

This has to work. Has to—

Connie reached for my hand and squeezed until I thought it would crumple into a bag of bone fragments. For a fragile-looking little thing, she was strong as an ox.

I looked up to find that her lovely blue eyes were wet.

Her lips trembled as she leaned toward me and whispered, "You poor thing."

I smiled, trying to emulate her little wobbly lip. She sniffed and reached for her own lace handkerchief. "And yet, has it not always been this way for girls of our station? We are sold off to the highest bidder for money or power or titles. We pay the price while our families reap the rewards. But are *they* sent far from home? Far from all they have ever known?" Her voice dropped into a fierce whisper. "Are *they* forced to bring someone they barely know and care nothing for into their bed? Are *they* ripped away from the one they truly . . ."

Connie bit back the rest of the statement, but in my head I filled in the blanks: *the one they truly love.*

When the sour tang of sympathy coated the back of my throat, I forced myself to swallow it down.

Keep on task, Walton. Sure, it's sad and all, but you can't help her. You can't.

I met her miserable gaze with one of my own. "I understand completely. I only wish I did not have to spend my last few days alone. It is only that I am so new in town, and do not know anyone. I suppose I shall simply stay in my room and bear it all alone until my ship sets sail."

Come on. Come on. Take the hint.

Connie snapped upright in her chair and turned to me. "Oh, but you must attend my parents' soiree the night after tomorrow," she said, eyes widening as the idea took hold.

"Oh, say you will come. You are the only one who under-stands."

From just outside the salon door came a commotion. Alva's maid was weaving toward us. I didn't see Phoebe, but I could tell from the way Connie stiffened that our time was up.

Perfect white teeth clamped down on her full lower lip as she leaned closer. "Please," she said. "Say you will come."

"I would love to," I told her, taking a chance. "But I couldn't possibly attend without my guardians. My father would be scandalized."

"Name them," she said, "and it is done."

As I quickly whispered the names of all my friends, Consuelo pulled a tiny book from her drawstring bag and wrote each one down with a miniature gold-plated pencil.

"Miss Vanderbilt," the maid pressed. "Your mother awaits you een the carriage. Eet is time. You know she will not like thees delay."

Consuelo nodded again. Standing, she smoothed her skirts, all impeccable manners and propriety. As the maid turned to lead her out, the sad-faced girl looked at me once more.

"I shall have the invitations sent over right away," she said in a hushed tone. "I hope to see you there. I — I should very much like to have someone to talk to."

CHAPTER 22

Seated on the edge of a glossy padded chair in the Waldorf's grand lobby, I had a good view of both the front entrance and the discreet service door Phoebe had disappeared through a half hour earlier, following a lead whispered by one of the chambermaids.

As I waited for everyone else to return from their assignments, the corset dug relentlessly into my rib cage. *You did good,* I told myself, partly to pull my thoughts away from the pain. *You accomplished your mission, and you didn't get personally involved. Aunt Lucinda would be proud.*

So why did I feel like I'd just kicked a kitten?

A shout bled through from the street outside the main entrance, snatching me from that line of thought. The brass doors swung open.

"You! Come back here! I say . . . Boy! You don't—"

The rest of the doorman's harangue faded when I saw

Doug shamble inside. Clothes rumpled. Steel specs askew on his broad cheekbones. Collar loose and a pocket on his tweed coat ripped away. His panicked gaze scraped the room.

"H-Hope?"

Before I knew it, I was on my feet and hurtling across the shiny expanse toward him.

"Doug, what's wrong?" My heart rate ratcheted up at his odd, unfocused look. "Do you need your meds? Tell me."

"Attacked," he managed. "Someone s-stuck me with a . . . with a . . ."

His hand went to his throat. A line of drool spilled from one side of his mouth. His eyes locked with mine. Then they rolled to white as he fell forward and collapsed against me.

My friend outweighed me by at least a hundred pounds. I tried to keep him upright, but his bulk took us both down hard. We crashed to the floor in a heap.

"Doug!" I screamed as I wrenched myself from beneath him and shoved him over onto his back. "Can you hear me?"

Think, Hope. Think. What do you do for a seizure? What?

Doug's large hands clenched into fists. Every muscle in his body had gone as rigid as the floor beneath him. The tendons in his neck strained and stretched against the high collar. His chin wrenched up and the back of his head began slamming against the unforgiving marble again and again.

When I'd first learned of Doug's condition, I'd done my

research. Just in case. An article for family members of epileptic patients rushed through my head.

Ensure the patient is lying on a hard, flat surface. If no neck injury is suspected, turn patient to the side to reduce choking hazard. Do not put anything in patient's mouth. Place soft object under patient's head to avoid further injury.

Panting, I snatched the silken wrap from my shoulders and jammed the material beneath his shorn hair, cushioning his head before he could bash his brains out. I ripped his tie off and loosened his collar. Dimly, I realized that hotel guests had begun to gather around us, their faces shocked at the sight of me tearing at my friend's clothes.

Remain calm. Seizures rarely last longer than sixty to ninety seconds.

I prayed that was true, though it seemed like hours, not minutes, as Doug wrenched and juddered. I tried to turn him to his side but he was too heavy, the muscle contractions too strong. His arm flailed up. When his fist glanced off my jaw, snapping my head back, someone in the crowd cried, "Notify the authorities at once! That colored boy just struck this girl!"

"No, he didn't, you idiot." I snarled as I swiped away the warmth that trickled from my split lip. "And he doesn't need police! He needs a doctor! He's having a seiz . . . a—a fit!"

Oh God. Collum. Mac. Phoebe. Where are you?

Time after time, Doug's head banged against the wadded

cloak. His breaths were torn, ragged things that made fear curl into a hard ball in the pit of my stomach.

As long as proper measures are taken, seizures rarely cause any permanent damage.

Doug's neck stretched so far back I thought his head would pop off. As ropy ligaments strained, a small red dot caught my eye. I frowned and peered closer at the single bead of drying blood. When I swiped at it, another filled in and trickled down the side of his neck.

Is that . . . Is that a puncture wound?

I thought back to the wild look in Doug's eyes as he had entered the lobby. The pinprick pupils. The vein thudding frantically in his neck. He'd been trying to tell me something.

Someone s-stuck me with a . . . with a . . .

Laying a hand on his chest, I could feel a heartbeat, but it was erratic. And way, way too fast.

Does this happen during a seizure? I don't know. I don't know. I don't—

His breath stuttered. The hammering beneath my hand paused.

No.

Another shallow rasp. *Thump-thump.*

And then . . . it all just stopped.

I blinked, two, three, ten times. My palms felt numb as I pressed them harder to his deep chest, waiting to feel the next heartbeat. The next ragged inhalation.

Nothing. Nothing. Nothing.

"But . . ." In the silence that choked the expansive marble and gilt lobby, my voice sounded so small.

Though difficult to watch, the article had promised, *a seizure can often be more traumatic to those witnessing the event than to the actual patient themselves.*

His head lolled to the side, eyes half-slits behind round, historically accurate spectacles.

For an instant, all I could picture was his utter delight when Moira had returned from the Edinburgh optician after picking up his new frames.

"Doug?" I shook him gently. The muscles had gone slack now and so, so still. A white-hot panic spiraled up my spine and shot out to every nerve ending. I grabbed his lapels and shook him so hard the glasses dropped to the floor. "Doug!"

My dad's family were charter members of our tiny town's only country club. Before my mom decided she'd had her fill of my grandmother's prejudice against anyone not born with a certain skin color and bloodline, we'd often joined them in the eighties-era dining room for Saturday brunch. From my spot near the huge smoked-glass wall, I used to watch the other kids splash in the turquoise swimming pool.

I—of course—had never been allowed to touch toe to the cool water, though. Just the sight of those other kids roughhousing had caused my mom to decide it was imperative I become certified in CPR.

Why? I'd asked. *Am I going to drown in a mud puddle?*

Now, I sent up a prayer of gratitude as I ripped open Doug's white shirt and—kneeling at his side—began performing chest compressions.

I ignored the crowd's mutterings as I made the sharp downward thrusts.

One, two, three, four, five . . . fifteen.

When I pinched his nostrils closed, tilted his head back, and sealed my mouth over his, discust and objections rang out through the hotel lobby.

"What in God's name . . . ?" "Dear Lord! She's kissing him. She's kissing that dead boy!" "She must be mad!"

I ignored them as I heaved two long breaths into Doug's lungs. I watched his chest rise, then fall with each exhalation.

Come on. Come on.

Nothing.

I started again. Over and over.

Fifteen compressions. Two breaths. Fifteen and two. Fifteen and two. That's it. You've got it, Walton. Keep going. Don't stop.

By the sixth or seventh round, the muscles in my arms were trembling. I was out of breath. I could no longer press down hard enough. Tears blinded me until all I could hear was the susurration of the crowd around me. They sounded confused. Angry.

Wake. The. Hell. Up!

As I bent to pinch his nostrils one last time, I felt someone grab my shoulders and try to haul me back. "That's enough, girl, you're shaming yourself."

"No!" Ragged and desperate, I jerked out of the anonymous grip and struck out blindly, connecting with something soft. I heard an "Oof" as I crawled forward and jammed my fingers under Doug's now-pliant jawline.

Wait. Is . . . is that a pulse?

Before I could feel it again, two sets of hands dragged me back. This time, no matter how much I fought, I couldn't get away. I scratched and twisted, snarling, "Let go of me. I need—"

"Make way!" a deep voice boomed. "Let me through. I'm a doctor."

Still held back by strangers, I nearly sobbed with relief as a handsome older man came bustling through the ring of onlookers. Dressed in black and carrying a leather satchel, the man's long salt-and-pepper hair pulled straight back and tied at the nape of his neck. I could hear his knees pop as he eased himself down beside Doug and peered through the spectacles that rested on the tip of his long nose. A uniformed assistant knelt at the doctor's side.

"I am Dr. Carson. And if I may ask, how long has the young man been unconscious?" The doctor's voice was calm and soothing as he picked up Doug's limp arm and placed two fingers to his wrist.

"He stopped breathing." I yanked loose from the men who had been holding me, and still on my knees, crawled closer. "His heart stopped too," I said. "And so I—"

The doctor's brows rose patiently as I stammered. "He . . . I—I was . . ."

How to explain CPR to a nineteenth-century physician?

But Carson only nodded, as if he understood completely. He rummaged in his bag, pulled out a rudimentary stethoscope, and placed the belled rubber end against my friend's chest.

A small movement caught my eye. I looked down just as Doug's chest rose slightly. I tensed as it fell. When it rose again, and again, pure joy erupted through me.

Though Doug's eyes didn't open, a labored snoring rattled from his throat. He twitched, lips turned down, as if suffering a nightmare.

"How long has the lad experienced these episodes?" the doctor asked quietly.

"Since he was seven. Head injury from a car acc—" I stopped, gulped. "A *carriage* accident."

"I see," Carson said as he laid the stethoscope aside and began to run long, gnarled fingers over the bones of Doug's skull. "Well, I believe the boy will live. But I need to get him over to my hospital to further evaluate his condition."

That was so not a good idea. Medical treatments during this age were still primitive. Besides, we weren't going anywhere until Mac, Phoebe, and Collum returned.

I shook my head. "That's not necessary. He's had these fits before. I think he just needs to rest. Can someone help me get him up to my room?"

The doctor opened his mouth to answer but closed it as

the assistant leaned over to whisper urgently in the doctor's ear. As he did, his knee bumped the doctor's black bag. It tipped over, and the contents spilled out across the floor.

A small rubber hammer. A flared silver tube. Several brown, glass vials of stoppered, hand-labeled medicine.

And a half-empty metallic syringe, the attached needle dark with dried blood. As I knelt next to my afflicted friend, one of the vials rolled and came to rest against my skirts.

My eyes trailed across the label's fancy script. *Tincture of Coca. 80 percent.*

I picked up the vial.

The contracted pupils. The rapid breathing. And that spot of blood on Doug's neck.

I got slowly to my feet. My mouth moved, though at first no words would come as my gaze wandered from the syringe to the puncture wound, finally settling on Dr. Carson.

"What did you do to him?"

CHAPTER 23

THE DOCTOR DIDN'T SPEAK. HIS KNEES SNAPPED AS HE got to his feet. A thickset man whose florid jowls overlapped his tabbed collar pushed his way to Carson's side. His hoarse drawl sounded like humidity and cicadas and cotton fields baking in the sun. "This girl here went and *kissed* that mulatto, Doc. Just kissed him. Right here in front of God and everyone."

"It's true," someone else in the crowd confirmed. "Saw it with my own eyes, Doc Carson. Kissed that darkie right on his black lips."

"Despicable." One of the snide women who'd been slamming her friend in the Ladies' Reception room held a lace hanky to her mouth. "Shameful. She must be mad to carry on so."

A murmur of agreement from the crowd at that.

A toothy young dandy in cravat and lace sleeves made a crude remark.

"Shut up," I snapped. "You have no idea what you're talking about."

A malevolent mood burgeoned amid the thickening mass of spectators. They shoved in closer. My chest tightened as their criticisms grew increasingly vulgar. The tide of revulsion and hatred began to build as it swept through the crowd.

"Call the constable," someone suggested, with a response of general approval.

"Hold it," Dr. Carson called out. "Hold on now. Do not judge the girl too harshly. She has but lost her sensibilities and become overwrought. I believe, however, that I can help her." He raised his voice. "Dupree! Josephson!"

Two men in flat caps and navy tunics moved into the circle. Brass buttons gleamed as they laid a canvas stretcher beside Doug's nearly still form. One grunted as they leaned down to grasp his feet and shoulders. "He's a big 'un."

"Don't touch him." Ignoring me completely, the two men lifted Doug and laid him on the litter. I took a step toward them, but as I did, I saw the doctor gesture to the attendant standing at Doug's head.

"Just come quietly now, miss." The man spoke through a mouthful of brown teeth as he stepped toward me. "No one needs to get hurt here."

Panic had begun to seep from my pores. *Ambush. Ambush. Ambush.*

The word pulsed through my brain. This "doctor" had—

for reasons I couldn't begin to fathom—injected my friend with cocaine. Enough to bring on seizures. Enough to stop his heart. If I hadn't been here . . .

But. Why?

"Please." Desperate for the slightest twitch of sympathy, I looked from face to face. I might as well have been begging the marble pillars. Tiny, icy fingernails of dread clawed their way up my back.

With a practiced movement, the attendant snatched my elbows and whipped me around, pinning them behind me. Pain shot through my shoulders as my arms were practically wrenched from their sockets.

"Now, now," Carson spoke softly, palms raised as though I were a raging animal who would go after him with teeth and nails. "There's no need for all this. We're here to help you. You'll feel better soon, I assure you."

He dug around in his bag. Soft light from the chandelier glinted off a syringe.

I went perfectly still in the attendant's grip. "No."

"Hold out her arm."

A second, beefy attendant joined the first. Thick fingers dug into the flesh at my elbow and wrist as he wrenched my arm from the other man's grip and held it straight. The sea of spectators blurred as Carson wrapped a short leather belt around my bicep and cinched it tight.

"Don't do this," I spoke quietly. Sanely. "There's no need. I was only trying to save his life."

Humming under his breath, the doctor only thumped

the tender inside of my elbow. Like a traitor, the antecubital vein rose, blue and pulsing beneath the surface of my skin.

Only a couple of the transfixed onlookers would meet my eye. Several were laughing. Apparently, this had become the day's entertainment. A circus, with Doug and me as performers in the center ring.

The doctor filled the syringe and tapped the glass to rid it of bubbles.

James, the bellhop who'd brought our meager bags up to the suite, jostled through to the front of the crowd.

"Doc Carson," he said. "Perhaps we should wait for Miss Randolph's people—"

"Not to worry, James." The doctor smiled as he cut the man off. "We shall, of course, send word once we get these two settled at Greenwood."

Though James nodded, a frown crinkled the skin between his graying eyebrows.

"Wait!" I called after him. But he'd already disappeared into the crowd.

Carson oozed concern as he stroked my hair. "Oh, you poor, poor dear. What a burden it must be to be female. Ruled by emotion." He sighed. "Thank the stars God, in His infinite wisdom, has given man dominion over you. To censure you—gently, as one would a beloved child, of course—when tender feelings overcome reason. Not to worry, though. I am here. I will help you." With no warning, he jammed the large-bore needle through my skin, piercing the vein. I screamed through clenched teeth.

When I felt the sting of the drug, I went crazy. Pins flew from my hair, pinging on the marble as I flailed like a trapped rabbit. When I lunged a kick at Carson, the goon behind me shifted. His hand clamped down on a muscle at the right side of my neck. From shoulder to fingertips, my arm went numb, and a red line of agony shot up my neck and into my head.

"Whatcha giving her, Doc?" one man called. "If it shuts her up, I might take a batch home for the missus."

Several men snickered in agreement.

"This," Carson lectured as he emptied the contents of the syringe into my arm, "is a brand-new derivative of morphia, only recently discovered. Called 'heroin,' when administered intravenously in the proper dosage, I've found it quite effective at bringing on a state of euphoric quietude."

Carson withdrew the needle. A line of blood streamed from the hole to *pat-pat-pat* upon the clean white marble.

As a melty, delicious calm filled my chest and began to roll through my limbs, an article I'd once read flickered from the files inside my mind.

Heroin (diacetylmorphine) was first synthesized in 1874 by the English researcher C.R. Wright. The drug went unstudied and unused until 1895, when Heinrich Dreser, working for the Bayer Company of Germany, found that diluting morphine with acetyls produced a drug without the common morphine side effects. Heroin was touted to doctors as stronger than morphine and safer than codeine. It was

*thought to be nonaddictive, and even thought to be a cure for
morphine addiction or for relieving morphine withdrawal
symptoms. Because of its supposed great potential, Dreser
derived his name for the new drug from the German word
for "heroic."*

There was a question I meant to ask. Something important. But my lips had started to go tingly. I tried to focus. *There's something I need to do.*

Suddenly, I couldn't quite bring myself to care. As the effects of the drug slipped down my legs and back up into my head, my knees turned into rubber bands.

"Rubber bands," I said to no one in particular. "Rubber. That's a fun word. Rubbery rubber."

Is that me? Am I talking? I wondered. "Another fun word is numb. Num-bah." I looked over at an old lady with hunched shoulders who was sneering at me with disgust.

"You kind of look like a turtle," I told her. "But I like turtles, so thass okay."

The doctor's face appeared before me. Huge. Blearing in and out.

"Naughty." I tried to cluck my tongue at him, but it had swelled inside my mouth.

The attendant's arm slinked around my torso as my legs gave. Two attendants grunted as they lifted the stretcher and began to carry Doug from the lobby. I reached out toward them, knowing somehow that it was a very bad idea for them to take him away. But with the drug dragging on my limbs and eyelids, I couldn't really remember why. After all, Doug was lying down. And lying down sounded like a really great idea.

A nap. Yep. A nap would be awesome right about now.

Dr. Carson nodded to someone behind me. I was lifted off my feet, hoisted into someone's arms. Whoever was carrying me began to push through the crowd toward the open door of the lobby. Though it felt great not having to use my legs anymore, a little voice inside me spoke up, telling me not to leave with these people.

"Wait," is what I wanted to say. But the hunk of meat inside my mouth wasn't cooperating and all I could manage was a soft "W-w-w-w."

We emerged through the brass doors into the brisk late afternoon. Sunshine slanted across the buildings, leaving our side of the street in shadow. We crossed the sidewalk and I was deposited inside a spacious carriage. My jelly spine no longer wanting to hold me upright, I slumped sideways. Wind streamed through the open windows, carrying a faint scent of smoke and frying meat. The doctor climbed in after me and ordered the driver to take us to Greenwood Institute.

My head bounced against the velvet interior as we began to move. Out the window, I saw the people who'd followed our little drama to this point begin to disperse.

I struggled to sit upright. *Hold on. This isn't right.*

Half a block from the hotel, I saw two familiar, red-haired figures hurrying down the sidewalk. Gripping the door handle, I dragged myself over until my chin rested on the bottom of the open window. The figures stopped dead in their tracks. Both their faces crinkled with confusion.

The last thing I recall as the coach sped by and the darkness pressed in is Collum's voice fading into the distance as he shouted my name.

CHAPTER 24

THE BOY HELD TIGHT TO THE GIRL'S HAND AS THEY RAN.

He'd promised her grandfather that he'd take care of her until her Poppy came for her. But when the other children veered away toward the forest root cellar, the boy had circled around to the back side of the huts.

"Stay here," he said as he concealed her behind a large holly bush. "I have to go back and help my mum."

"No!" She'd grabbed at his hand, but he was already running.

The girl wasn't sure how long she'd knelt there, behind the bush. But at the sound of shouts, she jumped to her feet. She wanted to flee. But she knew not in which direction safety lay. And besides, her grandfather . . .

She stole up to the rear of one of the wattle and daub huts. When she peered around the corner, she saw the large Spaniard on his horse, looming over the boy's mother. The boy was trying to wedge himself between her and the rider. Just as the woman pushed the boy behind her, a flash of silver.

Red droplets arced into the air, glittering like rubies in the winter sun. They boy cried out as his mother went to her knees, then toppled into the dirt. He covered her body with his own.

"Poppy. Poppy. Poppy." The girl whispered the name over and over, but did not see him.

"Search every hut," the Spaniard called to his men as he wiped the dripping sword on his sleeve. "Then burn it. Burn it all down."

The other riders dismounted. Naked swords gleamed, torches flamed as they began to kick in doors.

The old man with the staff shambled forward. The Spaniard jerked his head and one of his men cut the old man down with one stroke. Women screamed. Smoke choked the air. At the center of it all, she thought she saw her grandfather, his little-used sword raised as he charged toward the Spaniard.

The girl crumpled. Tears and tears and more tears. She saw the boy kneel beside his mother. She watched him brush the hair back from her blood-streaked face. A final bow of his head, and then his quick hands removed something from her neck.

The boy stood very still amid the chaos. His eyes roamed over his ruined, burning village until they finally met the girl's.

Much later, she kept slipping on frost-tinged leaves that littered the forest floor, but the boy never let her fall. When night crept in, he told her they'd better not build a fire for fear the bad men who killed his mother might find them. The boy covered them both in branches and leaves. They huddled together. And sometime during that long and terrible night, he must've *wrapped his skinny arms around her. For when she woke in a pink and gold dawn that glittered through the treetops, the boy was holding her.*

Though I fought to hold on to it, the memory receded in a whirl of white. Still half in that other world, I whispered to the boy. "Oh, Bran. Oh, I'm so sorry."

"Ah." A man's voice, close to my ear. "You're awake. Delightful."

One of my lids was peeled open. A candle flame thrust close to my eye. A drop of hot wax dripped onto my cheek and scalding a trail toward my ear. I wanted to recoil from that tiny blaze that seared through my addled mind, but I was too tired to move.

I think I groaned as the candle passed back and forth, back and forth, the finger peeling back my other lid and performing the same routine.

"Nice," the voice said. "I believe our patient shall be back with us very shortly."

Nearby, a woman spoke quietly. I swallowed, my throat so dry my tongue stuck to the roof of my mouth.

"Mom?" I croaked.

Silence. My nose was itching something fierce. When I went to raise my hand to scratch it, something stopped the movement. I tried the other hand, but the same thing happened. When I shifted my legs, I felt something wrapped around my ankles, holding them in place.

I tried again, struggling weakly against the bonds.

My breath started to come faster then. A snake of iron wrapped itself around my ribs, squeezing, squeezing as I fought against the force that tried to pull me back under. *I'm tied down. Why am I tied down? Oh, no. No no no! This is … No. Trapped! Help!* My eyes shot open as I wheezed for breath. Above me, a huge, primitive light bulb dangled from a white ceiling. I squinted against the incandescent glow as the socket swayed on its cloth-covered cord.

"Wha?" My tongue still refused to form words. "Who …"

"Good evening." The voice preceded the middle-aged woman's face by only an instant. Her head moved into my field of vision, blocking the light as she stared down at me. "Welcome to Greenwood Institute, Miss Randolph."

Panic began building, building inside me as I took in the woman's poofy, upswept hair. The tiny white nurse's cap. A spotless apron covering her dark, high-necked gown.

Deep lines bracketed either side of her small mouth as she said, "I am the hospital matron, Mrs. Harp. Follow the rules and there shall be no problems. Do you understand?"

Recent events began to click into place, one after the other, with a rapidity that choked me.

Doug, on his back in the hotel lobby. Not breathing. The needle, plunged into my arm by someone … the doctor …

I tried to jolt upright as I remembered. Carson. He drugged me. Oh God, he drugged me and took me away. And now …

I twisted against the restraints. The back of my head banged once, twice against the hard, cold surface beneath me.

"Let me go," I demanded through gritted teeth. "Let. Me. Go!"

"Now, now," Dr. Carson spoke. "Calm yourself or I shall have to sedate you again."

"Where's Doug?" Carson's pseudo-concerned face appeared to my left. "Where is my fr—" My brain snapped the right words in before I could completely mess up. "Where is my servant? Why am I here?"

"Miss Randolph." The matron was too close. When her stale breath washed over my cheeks I turned my head away. She grasped my chin and jerked me back to face her. Her saccharine tone made shivers roll up my spine. "The poor dear doesn't even remember having the episode, Doctor."

"I didn't have an episode!" I shouted into her face, causing her to recoil out of my line of sight. "Let me go. Let me out of here!"

As I bucked against the four-point restraints, Dr. Carson loomed over me. "Young lady," he snapped. "If you cannot manage to calm yourself, not only will I administer the full contents of this . . ." He held up a metallic and glass syringe like the ones I'd seen at the Waldorf. "But we shall also be forced to put you in a more secure restraining device. I believe you may have heard it called a straitjacket?"

I froze. Angry tears pooled at my hairline. My teeth ground together so hard I was sure the enamel would shatter.

Cool it, Walton. Just calm the freak down. 'Cause that? That would be bad. That would be like dying. Worse than dying.

"Good girl," Carson said. "Much better."

I wanted to slap the smugness off his face. I wanted to tear that syringe out of his hand and jam it into his eye.

"Where is Doug?" I said, jaw clenched against the rage and fear that pounded through my blood. "Is—is he all right?"

"The young man is resting comfortably," Carson said. "He is no longer in any danger."

My body relaxed minutely as I released a long breath. *Thank God. Thank God.*

"When can we leave? You see I'm supposed to travel to—"

"I'm well aware of your travel plans, Miss Randolph. Very aware indeed."

My eyes shot to his. Something about the way he'd spoken the word . . . *travel* . . . made my already uneasy gut turn in a slow revolution. He patted my shoulder and disappeared from my sight.

Several of what must have been Thomas Edison's early bulbs dangled at intervals, illuminating the small room. Turning my head as far as it would go, I could just make out the top of a rapidly darkening window.

How long was I out? Had to have been hours. I remember . . . what? Those men carrying Doug out. Being manhandled into a carriage. And then . . . something else, but what?

Come on, Walton. Think!

As I made myself relax against the restraints, I realized the drug was dissipating. I was sore, stiff from lying here so long. A nagging ache scratched behind my eyes. But my brain was beginning to clear.

Collum! He and Mac, there on the sidewalk. Just before sleep pulled me under, they had seen me being hauled away in the doctor's carriage. Surely they'd followed.

Surely.

"Miss Randolph." Dr. Carson's face appeared above me as he spoke. "If you can remain calm, we shall remove your restraints and have you escorted to the ladies' ward, where you will remain until it is time for your evaluation. If you cannot remain calm, we shall bring in the other device I mentioned. You shall be placed in an isolation cell for twenty-four hours. For your own safety, of course," he said. "Do I make myself clear?"

Biting my lip so hard I felt the edge of my teeth pierce the skin, I nodded.

"Good girl."

CHAPTER 25

I DON'T KNOW EXACTLY WHAT I WAS EXPECTING OF Greenwood Institute.

Something out of a horror movie, maybe, with crazed, wild-haired patients chained to the walls. Darkness. Filth. Wraiths in white gowns, shrieking and ripping out their own eyeballs.

I was pleasantly surprised.

At first.

I mean, *academically* I knew that by the end of the Victorian era, changes had begun to take place in mental health care, particularly in America. When wrestling with some of my own "issues" I'd come across plenty of material about this innovation, the private asylum. Generally administered by nonmedical personnel and set up for wealthy, cash-paying patients, these "clinics" boasted elegant lodgings, pastoral settings, light and air and decent food. More spa than nightmare, these substitutes for the horrific, overcrowded public asylums actually did a lot to reform treatment of the so-called deranged.

If you were rich, that is.

But I'd also read plenty about the atrocities that often took place at these private institutions. With no governing council to keep a sadistic owner in check, the people inside fell under his complete control. Trapped behind wrought-iron gates and green lawns and lovely brick walls, the helpless patients were subjected to cruelty, experimentation, and unspeakable, indescribable barbarity.

After giving the order to release me, Dr. Carson bustled from the room, followed by the matron, who murmured something about a Mrs. Caldecott and surgery. A broad-backed guard in a quasi-police uniform of dark blue cloth, epaulets, and gold buttons unlocked the leather bonds at my wrists and ankles.

A young nurse rolled in a primitive wooden wheelchair. "Name's Hannah, if'n it please you, miss." She maneuvered the bulky conveyance close and patted the seat. "Now take your time. Don't want you goin' all muzzy-headed afore me and Sergeant Peters can get you settled."

I started to refuse the chair, hoping if I walked . . . maybe I'd get a chance to run. But the instant I sat up, my vision went splotchy. I felt as though every drop of blood in my head had suddenly surged down into my gut. I gagged.

Thankfully my stomach was empty and I only dry-heaved into the metallic pan the girl hastily retrieved.

Cheery and chirpy, Nurse Hannah's voice drilled into the back of my sore head as she wrinkled a pert little nose. "Forgive me, miss," she said. "But you look like someone's painted your skin with lead, like in those old queen days. And I bet ye're powerful thirsty. Most of 'em are, comin' off of the new drug."

New drug. I recalled, then, Carson's bragging. He'd dosed me with heroin. Freaking heroin.

Hannah hurried back with a metal cup of lukewarm water that smelled and tasted of dirt and the pipes it had traveled through. I downed it in three slugs. It was so delicious, I moaned.

A veil draped from the girl's white cap, covering the back of her upswept, dirty-blond hair to the shoulders of her black dress. A high collar and full apron were bleached a brilliant white and starched crisp as a potato chip. When Hannah gave me a reassuring smile, her apple cheeks gleamed from a recent scrubbing.

The guard leading, our group of three wheeled out of the room. I craned my neck around to look up at the girl.

"Um . . . Nurse Hannah?" I figured polite was the way to go here. "Excuse me, but do you know what happened to my . . . servant? The boy who was brought in with me? Tall fellow with glass—with spectacles? His name is Douglas, and—"

"Wouldn't know, miss," the girl cut in. "Men are taken to

D and E wings, they are. We nurses aren't allowed over on that side. And I'd never break the doctor's rules. No, never that."

Her gaze slid from mine to skitter across the carpeted floor and floral-papered walls. The round cheeks flushed to crimson.

She's lying. Why would she lie about that?

No clue. But Doug was here, somewhere. I just had to find him . . . somehow . . . and get us the hell out.

In the corridor, electric sconces lined the walls, interspaced with soothing paintings of country meadows and flower gardens. The air smelled sweet. Too sweet, as if the myriad bouquets that topped a series of narrow tables barely concealed a whiff of decay.

As we rolled along, Sergeant Peters didn't say a word, though Nurse Perky sure kept up her end of the conversational stream.

"Yer awful lucky to be here, miss," she said. "Some of the other hospitals . . . Oh, you don't even want ter know. Had an aunt what was in Bellevue. That were a horrible place." She patted my shoulder in what I assumed was meant to be reassuring. "Not to worry, though. Our Dr. Carson's a right genius, he is. Here at Greenwood, we treat our patients like human beings. The doctor insists on all the most modern treatments. Some of the other docs in town even come here to study his methods. And he's come up with so many new ways to help all these poor souls . . ."

Hannah waxed on about the amazing Dr. Carson as

we passed bright, elegantly appointed rooms lit by electric chandeliers. Marble fireplaces, plush carpets, and luxurious furniture filled each space. And the people who populated them appeared well dressed and calm, as if they'd just popped in for a little chat.

But there are bars on the windows, I noted. And as we neared another doorway, I heard sobbing. Hannah sped up, but I caught a glimpse of an older woman kneeling in the center of an oriental carpet. Ignored by the others in her area, the woman rocked back and forth, hands pressed to her temples as she wailed incoherently.

The cries quickly faded as we crossed the brick-lined breezeway that led into the next wing. I squinted at the darkened, expansive lawn. Strewn across grass still brown with winter were groupings of ornate iron benches and tables. An evening breeze blew by, bringing with it the sweet scents of daffodil and narcissus and freedom.

"See how nice it is here?" Hannah went on. "It's a far cry from where I live, I can tell yer that. Me and my Freddie's building? Smells like sauerkraut and soiled nappies most 'er the time. Course we ain't been blessed with one o' our own yet. See, my Freddie, he's gone out on the fishin' boats for weeks and . . ."

Hannah droned on as the mute Peters removed a ring of jangling keys from his belt. As he unlocked the door to the next wing, I gnawed at a cuticle, hiding a frown. *Locked. Dammit.*

This corridor was identical to the last, though here, the

doors were all shut. Hannah trailed off as two nurses and a man in surgical whites pushed a covered gurney down the hall toward us. Beneath the rattling of metallic wheels, I could hear a woman's soft, slurred cries.

"No," she moaned. "Please! Do not do this to me. Where is Albert? Where is my husband? I demand you get him at once!" Her head rose from the flat pillow. *"Albert!"* I winced as the desperate cry echoed off the scalloped ceiling. Sobbing, babbling, begging, she cried, "Please. Wait. Just . . . just wait. I'll be good, I swear it! I shouldn't have spoken out. I know that now. Please, allow me to speak with my husband. Please."

The nurse at the head of the gurney leaned down and whispered something in her ear. The sheet writhed and twisted. I saw, then, the leather bonds strapped at wrist and ankle. Loose curls the color of autumn leaves cascaded over the sides of the gurney as the woman whipped her head back and forth.

"Mrs. Caldecott," the nurse snapped. "Control yourself. Your husband has, in fact, given his full approval for the procedure. Signed the papers this very morning, he did."

Hannah wedged my chair against the wall as the other group approached. Mrs. Caldecott had gone limp. She looked to be in her late twenties, with lovely pale skin and delicate bones. As they squeezed by in the narrow hallway, her hand shot out. Dark green eyes bleary with terror locked with mine as her fingernails dug into my arm.

"Help me. Please." The words dropped hopeless and limp

from her chapped lips. "I am not deranged. Do not let them do this to me."

I sucked in a breath. I wanted to say something . . . anything . . . but before I could force out a word, Hannah wrestled her away. I flinched as Mrs. Caldecott's nails scored five desperate lines into my skin.

"No-o-o-o-o." The cry cut off abruptly as the outer door slammed shut behind them.

I am not deranged.

Snippets I'd read about Victorian asylums flapped open inside my mind. The most haunting had been penned in 1879 by the wealthy writer and attorney Herman Charles Merivale. *My Experience in a Lunatic Asylum by a Sane Patient* was a first-person narrative of the author's own entrapment inside a private mental institution.

> *If the readers of this true history will imagine for themselves*
> *a number of hospitals for typhus fever, where any one of*
> *them, man or woman may, upon the first symptoms of a cold*
> *in the head, be shut up among the worst cases—with moral,*
> *social, and physical consequences beyond man's power of*
> *description—they will know something of the meaning of*
> *private lunatic asylums.*

I remember thinking, at the time, how terrible it must be to feel so helpless. So caged.

Mrs. Caldecott's eyes haunted me as I pressed my back hard against the wooden slats of the wheelchair.

"Miss?" Nurse Hannah started, but I interrupted.

"What—?" I had to stop, to swallow down a diamond-hard nugget of fear. "What are they doing to her?"

"Aw now, miss," Hannah said, her chipmunk voice unaffected. "Don't you worry none about Mrs. Caldecott. She's been here a long time, she has."

We moved ahead toward a wide set of double doors. A brass plate mounted beside them read GREENWOOD LADIES' WARD B.

"What's Ward B mean?" I asked, though I kept careful watch as the guard removed the ring of skeleton keys from his belt again and rattled through them.

Okay. Locks from the outside. Sergeant Peters has keys. Check.

"We just passed through Ward A, see?" Hannah was explaining. "Most of the patients on that ward either have very minor *problems*"—she whispered the last word as if it were something obscene—"or they've been here long enough, and are responding well to treatment. They may have earned special rights and privileges, see."

"Can they leave here if they want?"

Hannah chuckled. "Oh no, miss. No one leaves Greenwood but what the doctor releases them. I mean to say they are allowed additional freedom within the hospital. They may have visitors whenever they wish. Go outside on the lawn when it suits them. Walk the gallery. All Ward A patients are allowed to attend the special entertainments. Things such as that."

"What special entertainments?"

"Oh!" Hannah cried. "We have the loveliest performances here. Just last week, we had an entire orchestra. We've had a magician, an opera singer. Dr. Carson spares no expense."

As the guard continued to sort through the keys, Hannah tucked a stray strand of hair behind my ear. "Aw, don't look look so glum, miss. You'll be reassigned to Ward A a'fore you know it. Dr. Carson will know what's best for you." Eyes alight with hero worship, she said, "He'll fix you right up. The doctor can fix anyone."

Peters gave a loud cough, then grumbled about keys and locks. I looked up as he raised the jangling ring up to the light of a nearby wall sconce. Metal sang on metal as he slid one key after the other slowly around the brass circlet, lips moving as he silently counted.

He made a selection, then held the key aloft as if examining it for nicks. I could smell pipe tobacco and starch on the navy wool of his coat as his eyes flicked sideways to mine.

Seven, I noted as he slowly turned to insert the key into the lock. *Seven keys in all. And the one for this door is right in the middle, three on either side. Did . . . Did he just show me that on purpose?*

"What in blazes is taking so long, Sergeant Peters?" Hannah whined. "It's nearly time for my shift to end, and I've still Miss Randolph to get settled."

Peters nodded as he reattached the ring to his belt and opened the double doors. As Hannah pushed past, I risked a glance up at him. One side of his bushy mustache twitched at the edges before he turned to lock the doors behind us.

Another set of keys opened the brass doors of a small elevator that juddered us up two flights.

"Welcome to Ward B, miss," Hannah said as she wheeled me out of the elevator and into a corridor that stretched out so far, I couldn't see the end. "This is the main ward. Ain't much different from A, 'ceptin' there's just a few more restrictions is all. Ain't that so, Sergeant Peters?"

The nurse leaned down and whispered in my ear as the wheels bumped along the wooden floor. "Just be glad Dr. Carson didn't assign you to Ward C. I hate seeing new patients get sent there straightaway."

Before I could ask what went on in Ward C, we stopped before a door of dark, glossy wood. A guard with a weedy goatee stood sentinel. "Gotcher self another victim, eh, Nurse?"

"What are you doing here, Dupree?" The sergeant snapped, an edge to his rumbly voice. "Your shift ended two hours ago. Where's O'Connell?"

Dupree grinned, his narrow jaw and protruding yellow teeth giving him a distinctly rat-like appearance. "Had to go. Wife's birthin' their next brat. That's six for him." He poked the older man in the shoulder. "Ole O'Connell must be gettin' it pretty regular to get that many pups out of her, eh? Course, they're papist, and you know how they are. Breed like rabbits they do."

Sergeant Peters stiffened. The muscles in his neck went rigid as he stared at Dupree. "I'll hear no more bawdy talk in front of the patients. We clear on that, Dupree?"

"Take it easy, *Eldon*," Dupree replied, palms out in a conciliatory gesture. "I'm just talkin'." His tiny black eyes roved toward me, then glided down my body until I felt like I'd been slimed. "Well, well," he said. "Doc sent us a looker this time, didn't he?"

Peters moved so that his bulky form blocked me from the other guard's line of sight. "Open the door, Dupree," he said. "Then go. I'll take the rest of your shift."

"But—"

"You are dismissed."

Sergeant Peters's tone brooked no argument. Dupree sneered as he wrenched the lock open, then elbowed past Peters. Pausing, he bent until his face was inches from mine. Dupree's nostrils quivered as he inhaled slowly through his nose.

"Ohh . . . you'll be a fine addition to Ward B, miss." I hid a shudder as the tip of a pale tongue darted out to wet his lips. "A fine addition indeed."

CHAPTER 26

"She's back!"

We'd barley crossed that threshold when a sturdy older woman, dressed in at least a dozen yards of heavy black silk, stormed us. Tall black feathers protruded from her snow-white hair. They wobbled when she stopped abruptly and glared down at me.

For some reason, I didn't want the sergeant to leave. I twisted in my chair to look at him, but the door was already closing, and he was on the other side. The lock clicked. There was a finality in the sound that tugged my stomach up into my chest.

The elderly woman's strident voice pulled me back around. Punctuating each word with a thrust of her folded fan, she said, "This. Is. Not. Mrs. Caldecott. Where is she? Where is Louisa? Tell us at once! Where did they take her?"

"Now, now, Mrs. Forbes," Hannah said soothingly. "You know we ain't to discuss 'nother patient's treatment with—"

"Treatment?" Mrs. Forbes's voice sliced through Hannah's

speech like a light saber through butter. "Ha!" The woman turned to address the two ladies perched in the ornate seating behind her. "*Treatment,* she calls it. You have the unmitigated nerve to call it *treatment?*" She scowled at Hannah. "If that *doctor* scrambles her brains like he did poor Miss Allen's over there . . ."

The slender young woman Mrs. Forbes indicated was seated in a wing chair, a kitten sprawled on the lap of her frilled pink gown. Paying no attention to the shouts, the girl smiled blandly at the tabby as it batted one of the ribbons that threaded through her cascade of white-blond ringlets.

"Oh, do stop playing with that blasted cat, Annabelle, and pay attention."

When Annabelle Allen looked up, I realized there was something deeply wrong with her. Though pretty, with doll-like features, the girl's vacant smile never altered. Her huge, hazel eyes looked vapid, empty, fixed on nothing as she stroked the cat.

"Whatever is the matter, Mrs. Forbes?" Annabelle said. "Bootsie and I have come up with the most marvelous game."

Mrs. Forbes stared at the girl, her large baggy eyes softening before she whipped back in our direction.

"Mrs. Forbes." Hannah spoke up before the woman could start her tirade again. "This here's Miss Randolph. Maggie is supposed to be bringing clothes from the community wardrobe, as the dear ain't got a stitch with her but what she has on. Please make her feel at home, won't you?"

Mrs. Forbes merely snorted.

Hannah ignored her as she removed the blanket from my lap and helped me stand. My legs wobbled as the other women watched silently.

"Dinner in a half hour," the nurse said to me. "Maggie is the chambermaid—though where she is at the moment, I couldn't say. I will find her. She's to help you dress, do your hair, and such. Which, if you'll forgive me, miss, looks like a bird's nest after the cat's gotten to it."

As I automatically lifted a hand to the back of my hair, a spike of fear jammed me between the ribs. Though I still wore the teal gown the seamstress had dressed me in only hours earlier, the neckline was loose. The tiny buttons on the back of the high collar gaped open.

When I patted the embroidered fabric over my chest, all I could feel was my heart hammering beneath.

My lodestone. Gone.

I wheeled on Hannah. The sudden movement, combined with the remnants of the drug, made me sway. I gritted my teeth, forcing my voice to sound calm and reasonable. "Nurse Hannah, where is my pendant?"

When she didn't answer, I grabbed her. "The necklace I was wearing when I was brought in. Where is it?"

Hannah snatched her arm away. "You just calm yourself right down, Miss Randolph, or I will call the guard. Your necklace is safe. The doctor, he don't let folks go to Ward B with nothing that can be used to harm others."

"Harm . . ."

"She means," Mrs. Forbes explained, "that it was removed, in case you become inclined to choke someone with the chain."

As Hannah marched off, muttering under her breath about lazy maids, I tried to calm myself. This wasn't like last time. Mac had two extra lodestones tucked away in his case. Still, the black opal pendant had been in the Carlyle family for generations, and I couldn't help but feel even more violated.

"Don't think to get the jewel back, either," Mrs. Forbes murmured, sending a fish-eye glare after Hannah. "I think Carson sells them. I've been asking after my emerald hairpins for seven months now."

As I stood beside the wheelchair, the other women—aside from Annabelle Allen—all stared at me. Even Bootsie seemed intrigued by my bedraggled hair and creased, rumpled gown.

After what felt like an eternity, Mrs. Forbes released a sigh that made her perfect posture slump. "You might as well come sit, child." Taking my arm in her firm grip, she led me toward a divan upholstered in rich burgundy velvet. "That slattern Maggie isn't worth two red cents. The nurse will probably find her taking a nap in one of our beds. Why," Mrs. Forbes went on, "if the girl were in my employ, I'd—"

"But she isn't in your employ, is she, Dorothy?" A curvaceous, striking woman in her thirties interrupted Mrs. Forbes. With tawny skin and upswept hair the color of rose gold, the woman lounged against an arm of the opposing couch. "In fact, since your perfect son took over that moldy old mansion of yours, all the servants are *his* now, aren't they?" She shook her head in mock sorrow. "I hear he and his cow of a wife are living it up, spending all your lovely money. While you rot here in the madhouse, just like the rest of us. You can pretend otherwise," she added. "But you know it's true."

Dorothy Forbes's upper lip quivered in outrage. "Don't you dare speak of my son, Lila Jamesson. You know nothing. M-my Wilbur just wished me to recover my nerves, is all. Why, I can leave any time I want." Dorothy was shaking, bits of spittle gathering in the corners of her mouth as she turned an alarming shade of fuchsia. "And as for you. We all know why *you're* here." She stomped off to plop down at the grand piano on the far side of the room. But not before we all heard the hissed word. "Unnatural."

"Yes. Yes," she called to the older woman. "We all know how little you approve of my tastes, Dorothy." Green-gold eyes and lips that tilted up at the corners gave Lila Jamesson a feline appearance. With a boneless, slinky grace that matched her looks, Lila slid from the sofa's arm and glided across the oriental carpet to settle herself at my side.

"Oh, I'll admit, when my husband discovered—in a very compromising manner, I might add—that I enjoy the company of women, he was a bit . . . put out. Imprisoned me here so that the good doctor could rid me of my 'aberrant inclination.' But I won't stay long. Not near as long as her, anyway."

Hannah strode back into the room, followed by a maid and a young girl in a pearlescent evening gown. "Miss Rittenhouse," she said, "this here's Miss Randolph. Let's make her welcome." The nurse tilted her head toward the girl. "Miss Rittenhouse is eighteen, close to your own age, miss. I imagine you two will become fast friends, ain't that right, Miss Rittenhouse?"

The girl didn't answer. Only stared down at the carpet with her arms crossed, hands covering the exposed skin between her long white gloves and capped sleeves.

"Our Priscilla's quite the sight, isn't she?" Lila Jamesson leaned close, pressing a shoulder against mine as she whispered. "You know, I've often wondered why her mother bothers sending all those marvelous clothes, when they shall only become stained with blood." Raising her voice, Lila called out, "Evening, Priscilla, lovely gown. New, is it?"

Priscilla didn't speak and gave no indication that she'd heard Lila's snide tone.

I felt my smile fading, but forced it back into place as the girl looked at me.

Priscilla Rittenhouse's cheeks, forehead, even her exposed chest, were pitted with deep acne scars. One side of her mouth sneered up, tugged by a dreadful scar that zagged from her upper lip across her cheek and into her hairline. Another scar sliced down the opposite side from her temple to just below her cheekbone.

The girl's hands dropped to her sides as she fidgeted with her gown, and I bit back a moan.

In the few inches of visible skin, dozens of sets of parallel scars ranged up both arms. I tried to count, but there were so many. Priscilla noticed my regard and her close-set eyes narrowed. Whipping about, she snatched a matching wrap from the maid's arm and stomped past to the dining room.

"Did that to her face when she was fourteen." Lila didn't bother to whisper this time. "You see, her parents come from two of the great Philadelphia families. Her mother was— and still is, actually—a celebrated beauty who married the handsomest boy in Pennsylvania. Everyone claimed that any child they produced was bound to be the most beautiful creature imaginable." Lila pivoted toward where Priscilla waited near the long dining table, picking at her arms. "You can imagine their disappointment."

"I'm here, I'm here," called a woman dressed in mossy green and dripping with diamonds as she rushed from the short hallway that led to the private bedrooms. I stood, but before I could blink, she was reaching for my hands, squeezing them between her own. "A new girl!" She smiled and nodded so effusively, a few strands of mousy hair escaped from the pearl-covered snood. "Oh, how marvelous! It is so wonderful to see a new face, and you have not even met them yet, have you? Oh, what jolly fun."

Lila Jamesson groaned.

Releasing me from her clammy grip, the woman reached into a beaded handbag and brought out a photograph. She thrust the thick paper at me, leaving me no choice but to take it.

"Aren't they beautiful? I simply cannot wait to finish up my holiday so that I may be with them again. I do hope they haven't been troubling the new nanny." She giggled, the sound manic and eerie. "Especially my Lionel. He is such a scamp." Her fingernail tap, tap, tapped the photo in my hands. "Look. Look. Doesn't he have his father's eyes?"

I refocused on the sepia tones. Her children ranged from a boy of about ten to an infant in a frilly white gown, cradled in the seated father's arms. It looked much like every other Victorian photo I'd seen. A girl in a huge hair bow and a toddler in short pants. Then I looked closer, and a chill started creeping up my legs.

"Quite so, quite so," the mother was saying. "Nan acts the little mother to the younger ones. And Billy ... well, he looks so much like my side of the family. The baby is teething, which can be such a trial, but ..."

As she babbled on about how the new nanny had been a bit difficult, the back of my throat began to ache. I swallowed, forcing myself to take a closer look at the picture.

The woman's face was slightly blurred. Only hers. The rest of her family—every last one of them—was absolutely, perfectly clear.

Victorian photographs took a long time. Each exposure was nearly a minute long. There was nearly always some blurring, caused by even the tiniest of movements. Children especially had a difficult time holding still. These children had not moved a muscle. They hadn't moved, because they couldn't. Every one in this photo, except for the woman standing before me now, was dead.

"It was the new nanny." Lila's whisper brushed across the back of my neck, making me shiver. "Amelia's husband got the girl in trouble. A fairly common occurrence, of course, and generally handled with a letter of reference and a tidy sum. But the girl got angry. When Mortimer Langdon refused to acknowledge the child, the girl took a jar of arsenic and poisoned the lot of them. Even the servants. She then stabbed herself in the stomach and bled out right there at the dinner table, seated in Amelia's place and wearing one of her gowns. When poor Amelia came home the next morning from visiting her sister, she found them there."

I nodded, but it was all I could do to keep from curling up in a tight ball right then and there. I wanted to lie down and cry myself to sleep.

"Immediately after the photographer left," said Lila— and I heard actual emotion in her husky voice—"Amelia locked up the house. She refused to let anyone inside. She stayed there for days, with her family rotting around her, until her sister had the authorities break in. When they found her, she . . ." Lila's breath hitched. "She was trying to nurse the baby. By the time her sister had her brought here, her mind had snapped."

Amelia Langdon hugged the photo to her chest, eyes closed as she whispered, "I must remember to buy Lionel a new pair of shoes. He grows out of them so quickly."

She wandered off, muttering to herself, and I turned to Lila. "I—I don't even . . ."

"Yes," she said, all flippancy gone from her voice. "I know."

The nurse clapped her hands, startling me. "Maggie, you slattern. Take Miss Randolph to her room at once, and help her dress. We don't want to delay dinner, now do we ladies?"

Over at the mirror, Priscilla was mumbling to herself. "Ugly, ugly, ugly."

"Oh Lord." Lila rolled her eyes. "She's doing it again, Nurse."

The nurse shot Lila a look and led Pricilla away from the looking glass.

"She'll be next to go under the knife. Unless . . ." Lila peered deep into my eyes, her gaze keen as she asked, "What did you do?"

CHAPTER 27

AFTER THE MAID STRIPPED AND STUFFED ME, UN-
ceremoniously, into an ocher gown that smelled of its former owner's rose perfume, I sat to a formal dinner with the
rest of my little group.

Seven courses, served on bone-thin china by two uniformed footmen, as if we were visiting some great estate.
Consommé, followed by cold lobster salad with bitter
greens. A roasted game bird called a plover. Roast beef in
mushroom sauce. Potatoes and carrots and buttered peas.
Two kinds of pillowy rolls. All of it interspersed with tart
sherbet served in tiny frosted bowls.

This, I thought, staring down at the bowl of glistening,
honey-glazed fruit that had just been set before me, *this is
insanity.* How can they just sit here, eating like kings, pre-
tending they're out at some fancy dinner party?

Throughout the meal, Amelia Langdon chattered in-
cessantly about which dishes were her kids' favorites and
who among her "darlings" couldn't tolerate fish or refused

to eat carrots. Toward the end of the meal, she tugged on the sleeve of one of the servers and quietly asked him to have a box of the diminutive iced cakes delivered to her "silly brood."

"And be sure to sign the card 'From your loving Mummy,'" she called as he walked away. Spearing a slice of pear, she smiled over at me. "I'm sure my babes miss me terribly. Such a long holiday this is. I should think of heading home soon." She chuckled. "Until I can make arrangements, the cakes shall be a sweet reminder that their mummy thinks of them always and—"

Annabelle Allen's little-girl voice cut in. "Begging your pardon, dear Mrs. Langdon." The girl's head turned in odd, bird-like increments toward the older woman. She smiled sweetly, patting Mrs. Langdon's arm. "Perhaps I am mistaken," she said. "But I thought your children were all dead. Yes, yes. I'm quite certain I remember hearing that. All of them. Dead. I believe it was Bootsie who said as much?" She looked down at the kitten in her lap. "Didn't you, Bootsie? Dreary, dreary. Dead. Dead. Dead."

Mrs. Forbes gasped as Annabelle Allen began rocking her kitten, crooning to it in a high, childish soprano: *"Rock-a-bye baby, in the treetop. When the wind blows, the cradle will rock. When the bough breaks, the cradle will fall. And down will come ba—"*

"Stop!" Lila Jamesson shot to her feet, lips peeled in fury. "Stop this instant, you stupid girl. Can't you see what you're doing to Amelia?"

Annabelle only looked puzzled, as if someone had just asked her to solve a complex math equation.

I felt like someone was pinching my heart between giant fingers as Mrs. Langdon slowly got to her feet. The photograph still clenched in one hand, she began to back away. "I —I believe I shall lie down for a spell. The, um." She licked her lips. "The children. They . . . They need their mummy well rested."

Mrs. Forbes pushed her plate of half-eaten food away, and buried her face in her hands. Lila Jamesson stormed off without another word. A terrible sadness washed over me as I realized that fancy food or no, the women were all prisoners trapped inside a pretty box.

Coffee was served in the sitting room. I downed it, thinking it might help stave off the exhaustion.

"What happened to her? To Annabelle, I mean?"

Suspicion narrowed Lila's gaze as it sharpened on me. "How could you not know? It was in all the papers. Everyone knows about Annabelle Allen."

"I—"

"Then again, your accent reveals your Southern origins, yes?" At my hurried agreement, she sneered. "Your ignorance, then, is not at all surprising. In fact, I would wager very little of importance makes it through that region's filters of bigotry and narrow-minded provincialism."

I opened my mouth in defense, then let it close.

"One night, seven years ago," Lila said, "when Annabelle was but thirteen, she went down to the kitchen. Took a butcher's knife from the rack. Crept into her father's bedroom. And with the help of two young serving girls, stabbed him to death in his own bed."

My hand flew to my mouth. Like icy pebbles of sleet, horror pinged me in a thousand places. "Why?" I croaked, unable to reconcile the odd, child-like young woman with her cat and her blank eyes with cold-blooded patricide.

"Why do you think?" Lila spat. "Why else would a thirteen-year-old girl murder her own father? He'd been 'bothering' her since she was a child. The serving girls too. Annabelle has a younger sister, only seven at the time. When that *degenerate* began turning his eye on the sister, Annabelle had finally had enough."

"What about her mother?"

"The mother," Lila scoffed. "She knew. She must have known. I believe it was her own guilt that caused her to hire the best lawyers. They fought to have Annabelle committed, rather than sent to prison for life. The woman did that much, at least, before disowning Annabelle and fleeing the continent with the other daughter."

"She was different before." Lila and I both jumped when Mrs. Forbes spoke from just behind us. "I was here. I knew her prior to the doctor's . . ." She waved a hand. "Intervention. The girl was kind to me. Troubled, yes, but smart as a whip. Most of the time, she was fine. But on occasion, she would suddenly blurt out the most awful things." Chin quivering,

Mrs. Forbes whispered, "Lewd, intimate things. Or she would remove her clothing and go running around in the altogether. Then one day, a guard got familiar with one of the younger girls. Annabelle drove a hat pin through his eye. They removed her to Ward C and two months later, she was returned to us with parts of her hair shaven away and horrific scars on each temple. From that day until this, she has been as you see. An imbecilic shell."

Psychosurgery? But . . . But that can't be right? Surgical intervention for psychiatric purposes didn't begin until sometime in the 1930s. It makes no sense.

Sick, furious, and utterly confused, I followed Mrs. Forbes's gaze. Annabelle Allen noticed us watching and gave a brilliant smile that set my teeth on edge.

CHAPTER 28

WHILE EVERYONE BUT ANNABELLE CHATTERED OVER needlepoint and mending, I roamed the area, searching for any possible escape route.

There were only two doors. One to a short hallway that housed our six bedrooms and single lavatory. The other to the main hall outside. That one was firmly locked. And —I deduced from the male voices and occasional phlegmy cough—constantly guarded.

The window was out, too. No bars, but with Ward B's third-floor location that didn't much matter. With no handy trellis or opportune rain gutter, shimmying down the red-brick wall was not an option.

Heartsore and exhausted, I rested my forehead against the thick, cold glass. Thunder rumbled in the distance. Lightning flashed behind an ominous roiling cloud bank. Heavy raindrops smacked against the panes.

As the storm raged toward us, the muffled booms intensified, turning to cracks that beat at my eardrums like a battery of gunfire. The scent of ozone suffused the air as bolt after sizzling bolt slammed to earth. Then came a lengthy flash that momentarily destroyed night's concealing shadow, and I jerked suddenly upright, certain I was seeing things.

I mashed my nose against the glass as if I could push right through it and into the rain-soaked darkness.

Come on. Come on.

Flash. *Crack.*

There it was again. It hadn't been my imagination, or even wishful thinking. It was real. *He* was real.

A slim, solitary figure stood just outside the black spikes of the clinic's treacherous fence. His hands gripped the bars as if he wanted to tear them down with his bare hands. Head tilted up, he stared toward the upper floors.

With lamplight behind me, I knew that anyone watching from the outside could see me. Raising my hand high above my head, I laid my palm against the cold glass. The storm was passing. The intensity of the lightning dimmed, but I still saw it when the figure outside raised his own hand toward mine.

I'd know that shape anywhere. And even as the storm acceded the night back to darkness, I never took my eyes off the spot where I knew Bran Cameron waited for me.

There was no mirror to expand the tiny, tiled bathroom. As I pulled the chain on the overhead tank and washed my hands and face with frigid water and silky, lavender-scented soap, the walls began to close in on me. The large clock on the sitting room mantel bonged nine times. I added up the hours. Fifty-nine. Only fifty-nine hours left before the Dim returned to take us home.

Nope. I commanded my rapidly escalating pulse to slow. *No. No, you are not going to freak out right now. You just need a plan. Think, Walton. How would Bran get himself out of this?*

His name passed through my thoughts like a soothing balm. My heartbeat calmed. I could breathe again.

"Bran's here," I whispered. My hands relaxed their grip on the pillar sink. *And by now, he's contacted the others.*

Bran and Collum may not like each other much, but they'd work together to get us out. And I knew my best friend. Phoebe and Mac would tear down heaven itself to save Doug and me.

I was still smiling when I plopped down in one of the wing chairs near the fireplace. When I looked up, the others were all watching me. I tried to hold on to the comfort I'd wrapped around myself, but like a sunbeam on a cold and cloudy day, it was fleeting. The warmth dissipated. I felt my chin start to wobble as the faces around me blurred to pale ovals. I nipped hard on a snag of cuticle and stared down at the jumping flames.

I will not cry. I won't. I won't—

Annabelle Allen rose from her spot on the floor. Smiling, she laid the sleeping kitten in my lap. "Here," she said. "Bootsie will make it all better. Feel how soft she is?" She picked up my limp hand and laid it on the warm, purring body.

An image flashed. Hecty the menace, strands of doll hair snagged in her whiskers. The scene of home made me think of Moira and Lucinda. Of Mom.

The tears fell.

"Thank you," I choked out. "Thank you, Annabelle."

I must've dozed off. When the hallway door suddenly opened, I jerked forward, wrenching my neck. Everyone went stiff and silent as Dr. Carson strolled in. Nurse Hannah and the matron were on his heels, both toting silver trays covered with white cloths.

"Evening medication, ladies." Dr. Carson smiled, nodding at each person in turn. His gaze held on me. "I thought I would drop by personally. See how our new patient is settling in."

When no one responded, his affected grin began to wilt. "I see," he sniffed. "Well? What are you waiting for?" Snapping his fingers twice at the nurses, he said, "Get on with it."

"Yes, Dr. Carson." Nurse Hannah quickly began handing out pills, drafts in glass tubes, and small tin cups of water.

Mrs. Forbes, who had been noticeably silent since dinner, stared down at the pills in her hand. "Where is Louisa Caldecott?" The older woman jutted a chin at Hannah. "I asked *that* one earlier, but she wouldn't say a word."

"As is correct, Mrs. Forbes," the doctor replied. "You know we do not discuss—"

"Will she return to us a drooling, cat-petting ninny like Miss Allen over there?" The volume of the older woman's voice rose as she stood.

"I do not believe I care for your tone, Mrs. Forbes," Dr. Carson said. "Sit down."

All the other patients began to study the cups in their hands. To my surprise, however, Lila Jamesson stood and moved to take Mrs. Forbes's elbow. "Don't mind her, Dr. Carson. Dorothy is tired, that's all. It has been an exhausting day, what with Louisa and the new girl."

"I do not appreciate having my methods questioned, Mrs. Forbes." The doctor's nostrils flared as he studied the older woman. "Perhaps it is time for another ice bath to cool your humors?"

Mrs. Forbes's eyes went wide. "N-no," she stuttered. "No. I—I apologize, Doctor. I didn't mean—"

"Yes, yes." Ignoring the woman's protests, Dr. Carson gestured to the matron, who set down her tray and went to the door. "I believe cold hydrotherapy is just the thing to put you in order."

Two attendants I'd never seen before entered the room. Mrs. Forbes's haughty manner had disappeared completely as she begged and pleaded. It did no good. The burly attendants shoved the now-pale Lila Jamesson aside. Each gripping Mrs. Forbes by an arm, they began to drag her from the room.

I jumped to my feet. "What are you doing?" I demanded. "Let her go! She's an old woman, for God's sake."

Before I could say another word, Carson's thugs had the sobbing Mrs. Forbes out in the hall. The matron followed and slammed the door shut behind her.

Carson's steely eyes locked on mine. And though every impulse told me to shut the hell up, I didn't shrink. "Where are you taking her?"

"Mrs. Forbes will be taken to the hydrotherapy chamber and given twenty minutes in an ice bath, followed by ten more with the cold hose. I've found a generous cold water treatment wonderful at cooling the temper." Apparently done with our little exchange, Carson then rounded on Lila. "Mrs. Jamesson, you have become very forward again. Perhaps it is time to schedule a few more rounds of manipulation?"

Lila paled and took a step back. "No. Not that, please."

Seeing fear, horror, and disgust mingle on Lila's lovely face, my skin crawled.

It can't be what I think. I'm wrong. God, please let me be wrong.

Because I had a terrible suspicion I knew what Carson meant by "manipulation." I'd read about it only recently, and it had made me want to throw up. A Victorian method, administered by male doctors to cure "hysteria" in women. It was intimate, intensely personal, and amounted to nothing more than sexual abuse. For a woman like Lila Jamesson . . .

"Then," Carson was saying, "I suggest you keep your thoughts to yourself."

Lila nodded. A tear dropped to the carpet at her feet.

Upon the doctor's barked order, each patient obediently swallowed down pills or liquid or both as Hannah checked them off on her list.

The nurse came to me last, holding out a palm-size tray with two ivory pills and a glass vial filled with a dark, oily substance.

I picked up the tablets, palming them as I pretended to pop them in my mouth. The bitter liquid I held under my tongue as I fake-swallowed and gave the nurse a closed-mouth smile.

Carson snorted and exchanged a knowing look with Nurse Hannah. "That's very nice, Miss Randolph," he said. "But I believe we'll need for you to open your mouth, please."

I tried to do it. To open my mouth without dribbling the noxious fluid. But the acrid taste had flooded my mouth with so much saliva I knew I'd be outed if I cracked the seal even a little.

Dr. Carson sighed. Before I could blink he was on me, smashing my head against the sofa's firm back. One hand came down hard over my mouth while the other pinched my nostrils closed. I flailed, fighting for breath. My ragged nails raked down his wrists. He hissed, cursing under his breath.

I had no choice. I swallowed in reflex. Satisfied, the doctor abruptly released me. When I fell to my knees, coughing and gagging, the pills rolled out of my hand.

Watching the entire exchange closely, Lila Jamesson's sharp eyes tracked the pills' progress across the floral carpet. With a subtle twitch of her skirts, she concealed the wayward meds beneath the folds of amber silk.

Eyes still watering, I looked up at her. She gave an infinitesimal shake of her head, then glanced pointedly away.

"And now, ladies," Carson said, straightening his lapels, "I believe it is time for you to retire. Nurse Hannah, if you will kindly show the ladies to their quarters."

"Yes, Alexander." The nurse's eyes went wide as Carson wheeled on her, his irritation plain. "I—" Her cheeks blazed with color as she babbled. "That is to say—of course, *Doctor*. Right away, sir."

The nurse scurried off like a scalded cat. Like a clutch of automatons, the patients stood and began to follow her from the room in an orderly line. Lila's needlepoint dropped from her hand. Carson glanced her way but said nothing as she bent down to scoop it up. When she passed I glanced down at the carpet. The pills were gone. Rising, I made to follow, but Carson held out an arm, blocking my path.

"Sit, Miss Randolph."

When I refused to comply, he only shrugged and straightened his lapels again. "Do not think I enjoy manhandling my patients. I'm a doctor, not a monster. Everything I do is in the name of scientific advancement. But I expect full cooperation from those in my charge. Do you understand?"

When I wouldn't even look at him, he sighed and ran his gaze over the raised welts my nails had left behind. "Please do not force me to modify my initial treatment plan for you," he said. "Which I can assure you is quite mild."

The doctor took two steps until his face was inches from mine. Jaw tight, I refused to flinch as he leaned in to whisper, "Of course, I'd prefer to treat most of my patients with a daily regime of Prozac and Zoloft, with a side of Xanax or Haldol. But when in Rome, eh?"

When he stepped back, a smarmy smile tugging at his lips, I couldn't help it. I gaped at him, stunned to my core.

It can't be. That's . . . that's impossible. He winked as if we shared some delicious secret.

The floor beneath my feet went spongy. Dots appeared at the corners of my sight.

Alexander, Hannah had called him. Until then, I hadn't known his first name. *Dr. Alexander Carson.* A fairly common name. But he . . . he wasn't common, was he?

For years, my mom had begged me to go with her on her world lecture tours. A renowned history professor, author, and speaker, my mom was in high demand. Every year, she begged, promising to show me the world. I— coward that I was—always refused, breaking her heart time and again.

At fourteen, I became obsessed with finding a way to manage the anxiety disorders and phobias that ruled my life. Our small town's library was minuscule, but I scrounged the

Internet for anything I could find about or relating to the study of psychiatry.

As I stared at Dr. Alexander Carson now, a single article, short and green-tinged, appeared before my eyes, half obscuring his face.

Bellevue Psychiatrist, Facing Indictment for Unethical Practices, Disappears

By TERENCE JONES

NY Times, May 13, 1983 — Dr. Alexander Carson, 43, of Manhattan, scheduled to appear in court last Monday to face indictment on 23 counts of unethical practice, has apparently disappeared from his Eighth Avenue home. When police arrived at Carson's apartment yesterday to take him into custody, he was not in residence. After a thorough investigation, police report no signs of forced entry or foul play. Also, the presence of Carson's passport and belongings make the possibility that he fled the country less likely. Anyone known to harbor or assist Carson can and will be charged as an accessory.

This morning, NYPD Detective Antony Donato issued the following statement: "We are investigating every avenue of Dr. Carson's disappearance. An APB has been issued and I have no doubt he will be found and justice served for the heinous acts committed against the patients whose trust Dr. Carson has betrayed."

There had been no picture, and I remember being only

slightly intrigued, wondering what types of "heinous acts" the doctor had committed. The hospital had apparently closed ranks when a 1985 class-action lawsuit had been filed against it, citing inability to pursue further action against the absent Dr. Carson, himself.

Absent didn't begin to describe it. The missing psychiatrist from 1983 was standing before me now, in the year 1895.

The drug must have begun to take effect about then, because my sight went bleary. My lips felt numb, and my knees wobbled, forcing me to sit. Or fall.

"I see you understand. That's good," Carson said. "As long as you cause no trouble here, I believe we will get along just fine."

CHAPTER 29

I BARELY REMEMBER UNDRESSING AND CLIMBING BETWEEN crisp sheets. At breakfast the next morning, the drug's after-effects left me shaken and queasy. I couldn't even look at the silver tureens of scrambled eggs and piping hot sausages laid out buffet-style on a sideboard in the dining room.

At least I was back in my own gown, brushed clean and pressed by the maid. Barely picking at the triangle of toast the server had placed on my plate, I forced myself to down a glass of apple juice and two steaming cups of creamed coffee.

I was standing by the only window in the sitting room, staring out at the deserted lawn, when I saw them. I noticed Collum first, in his workman's clothes, sandy hair covered by the flat cap. Then Phoebe appeared in my field of view, followed by Mac and another man, tall and dressed in black. His face was shaded by a bowler hat, and I couldn't make out his features. My three friends turned, hands raised to shield their eyes from the slant of morning sun as they scanned the windows.

My heart slammed into my throat as I waved frantically. *Here! I'm here!*

When they didn't respond, I pounded on the thick panes. Phoebe turned to Mac. As her mouth moved, Mac shook his head. Collum's fist banged down into his palm, obviously furious.

"What are you doing?" Lila hissed as she jerked at my arm, trying to tug me away from the glass. "Are you insane in earnest? You'll bring every attendant in the place down upon us."

"Those are my friends down there," I said, yanking away from her grip. "I have to let them know where I am."

I heaved at the sash, but it was either nailed or painted shut. The group on the lawn turned and began to march away toward the cast-iron gate.

"No!" Desperately I scanned the room, plans firing off in my head. I raced over to the piano, snatched up the small bench that sat before it, and ran with it back to the window.

"Miss Randolph, no!" Lila shouted. But it was too late.

With a grunt, I swung the bench as hard as I could into the window. The shattering sound was as loud as a car crash. Splintered wood and shards of glass rained down on the lawn. I dropped the shattered remains of the bench on the carpet and leaned out the ruined window. Mac, Collum, and Phoebe stopped in their tracks and whipped back around as I screamed, "I'm here! Collum! Phoebe! I'm here!"

Phoebe saw me first. Snatching up her long skirts, she raced across the lawn until she was standing just below.

"Hope! Oh, Jesus! We tried to get in to see you, but they turned us away! Have you seen Doug? Are you both okay?"

"I haven't seen him since they took us—"

Strong arms wrapped around my waist and lifted me off my feet, hauling me backwards. Kicking, I fought against my captor. "No! Let me go!" I cried. "Phoebe! Collum! Help!"

"Be quiet, miss," a low voice growled in my ear as a beefy hand clapped over my mouth. "It's Sergeant Peters. I want to help you, girl. But if you don't keep quiet, you'll bring down every guard in the place. Or Carson himself will come, and trust me, that's the last thing you want."

From the window I could hear shouts. Phoebe screeched my name, then Collum bellowed as other voices joined theirs. Men shouted, ordering them to leave the premises at once.

"If I let you go, do you promise to be quiet?" Tears of frustration burned my eyes as I nodded.

Peters's hand left my mouth. He set me down gently, took my elbow, and tugged me to the far side of the room next to the now-benchless piano. His coarse face serious, he began speaking, low and urgently. "Listen to me. I want to help you get out of here, Miss Walton."

My eyes went wide at that. Peters only nodded solemnly as he went on. "I been working here goin' on four years now, and I seen things that ... well ... that no true Christian should see." Peters drew out a handkerchief and swiped at his forehead. "I always try to do right and protect the poor patients best I can. But I can only do so much. It wears on a man, witnessing that kind of evil day after day, do you take my meaning, miss?"

I nodded. "Yes!"

"Last night, after they brung you in, I was making my rounds at the fence. Your people stopped me and offered more coin than I could make in ten years' time if I got you out." Sergeant Peters flushed to the roots of his iron-gray hair as he mumbled. "I'd a done it for free. Carson, he does the devil's work and that's the truth of it." Bleary brown eyes rose to meet mine. "Only . . . it ain't easy for a man of my years to get a job these days. The landlord just went and upped the rent. And I'm still payin' on my Selma's burial and . . ."

Peters went on but I barely heard. A feeling like helium mixed with sunshine had begun to fill me. I gripped the side of the piano to keep from flying up to bump the ceiling.

"Please, Sergeant Peters," I told him. "You don't have to explain. Take the money. Trust me, they have plenty. But what about my friend Douglas? We have to get him out, too."

"Yes. The both of you. The lad's in Ward D on the men's side. He's the only occupant as that's new construction. It must be soon 'cause Doc Carson, he—" Peters shifted and cast an uneasy look at the door, then at the cluster of women who watched from across the room. They stared back. Only Annabelle seemed oblivious that something unusual was happening.

"He said he'd convinced the head doctor at Bellevue to

come watch him perform some *'procedure.'* Said it was like what he did to that poor Miss Allen. But that he wouldn't have to cut through the skull no more."

A shiver skimmed across my shoulders as every piece of research and information I'd shoved back the night before roared into my head. Articles and pictures and reports. Flashing and flashing.

He's talking about the transorbital lobotomy. That's it, isn't it? Oh dear God.

They'd called it a miracle cure. Almost a fad. The young field of psychiatry had blown up and been ablaze with the news of the new phenomenon.

Tens of thousands of the procedures had been performed.

The inventor was even considered for the Nobel freaking Peace Prize.

People with haunted eyes lined up in a hallway, awaiting their turn.

Black-and-white image of a supine patient. Men in old-fashioned suits gather around, watching as a surgeon prepares to drive his mallet down onto the slender steel protruding from the patient's eye socket.

A magazine cover, upon which an aproned wife with rose-painted cheeks serves pie to her family, the ad inside promising a permanent cure for "moodiness," "female maladies," and "disobedience."

Close-up of a twelve-year-old boy, his eyes blackened and swollen shut, his mouth stretched wide in a scream.

But I knew, I *knew* that the procedure was not due to be invented for another fifty years. *Fifty years.*

Suddenly everything began to lock into place.

Snap. Snap. Snap.

The needle mark in Doug's neck. Carson's insistence on taking the two of us with him. Locking us up.

He was one of them. A Timeslipper. Or . . . at least involved with them in some way. Had he been here this whole time? If—once contact is made—time runs on parallel lines, from 1983 to the present was more than thirty years.

And now he was . . . what? Stealing credit for what would one day be a banned and barbaric procedure, fifty years before its true creation?

Of course he is, I realized. *Because it will make him famous. It will make him rich.*

"Time's running short, Miss Walton. We should be going."

I looked up at Sergeant Peters's lined, earnest face. I tried to swallow, but my throat had gone dry as bone. "Of course," I managed. "Let's go."

Lila was watching me. I could see the hurt and betrayal forming in her eyes, and I knew I couldn't just leave them here to fend for themselves against that monster. I hurried to her and whispered quickly. "Listen, I'm going to find a way to get you out of here," I told her. "All of you. Who can I contact? Tell me, please."

Lila looked away. "Just go," she snapped. "You don't know us. You owe us nothing. Just leave."

The other women turned their backs on me, making me feel like slime scraped from the bottom of their shoes. Only Annabelle smiled as she hugged her kitten to her chest.

Then Peters was gripping my arm, tugging me toward the door, talking low and fast. "Boy's in D-14. I'll bring you up there. There's a laundry chute at the end of the hallway. You two'll slide down while I run around and meet you in the laundry and unlock the back door. Your people will be waiting for you there, but we must go quick-like. Carson, he won't put up with no trouble in his establishment. Once he hears about this—" He waved a hand at the broken window. "No tellin' what he'll do to you, miss. He—"

"What"—a deep voice boomed through the room— "in the name of all that is holy is going on here?"

Dr. Alexander Carson strode in, his sharp eyes missing nothing. The shattered glass. The discarded, broken piano bench. Peters's grip on my arm.

"Good man, Peters," Carson said. "Take Miss Randolph to the isolation cell. It appears she has become violent. Which means we shall have to reevaluate her treatment plan, after all."

"Yes, sir." Peters's eyes bored into mine. "Come along quietly now, miss."

I shot a look at the other patients, praying they'd go along with our desperate little farce.

Priscilla and Mrs. Langdon looked away. Lila Jamesson's troubled gaze locked on mine. For an instant, I thought she might give me up. But as I passed, she gave a quick nod of acceptance. Sorrow struck me then at leaving them. But my mission was clear. Get Doug. Get out.

Then I'd try to find a way to help them, before Carson started carving up their brains.

I went along, acting cowed as Peters marched me across the room. We were nearly to the door when Annabelle Allen suddenly piped up.

"Oh, Dr. Carson," she said in an eerie little-girl singsong. "Sergeant Peters is taking Miss Randolph outside. He's taking her from your lovely hospital to meet her friends. I think he is being awfully naughty to disobey you like that. Don't you agree?"

Carson spun toward us. His eyes narrowed in suspicion as they darted back and forth between Peters and me.

I froze, but Peters didn't miss a beat. "Oh, what notions these patients come up with, eh, Doc? It's enough to put you off your feed."

Chuckling, shaking his head in amusement at the insanity he had to deal with every day, he continued herding me toward the door.

The doctor held up a hand. "Hold a moment, Sergeant."

Though the command was quiet, the threat was clear enough. The other guards stepped into the room. I tried not to flinch as Peters dug his fingertips deeper into my arm.

Carson knelt before Annabelle. "My dear Miss Allen," he asked, sweetly. "Is this true? What you said about Sergeant Peters helping Miss Randolph to leave?"

She nodded ardently, baby-doll ringlets bouncing against her shoulders. "Oh yes, oh yes! He said he would take her away from here, just like you do when my kitties get too sleepy." Annabelle raised the small tabby for the doctor's inspection. It drooped, limp and lifeless, from her fist. "I hugged her and hugged her, but she will not wake. May I have another, please?"

Carson blinked, hesitating for an instant. "And how many kitties will this be for you, since you've been here, Miss Allen?"

"I think . . ." The girl frowned in concentration. Then she beamed at the doctor. "Sixteen!" she told him. "This is kitty number sixteen."

Behind me, I heard Lila Jamesson gasp.

"And do not forget," said Annabelle, wagging a finger at Carson. "She must have yellow stripes and a gentle face. She must look exactly like my first sweet Bootsie. Naughty Papa, taking her from me like that and twisting her little head so that she became so tired. I was quite put out with him."

Annabelle cuddled the dead kitten to her chest, rocking it back and forth as she crooned, "Pretty kitty. Sleepy kitty."

My stomach squeezed tight against my spine as the doctor smiled at Annabelle. He patted her knee as he stood. "Well, then," he said. "Number seventeen it shall be."

CHAPTER 30

THE LITTLE GIRL COULD NOT WALK ANOTHER STEP. HOW COULD her feet pain her and feel numb at the same time? She'd not eaten all day, unless one counted the bitter acorns that had made her stomach rebel.

She thought longingly of the scant bites of stringy, half-grown rabbit the boy had trapped the day before. He'd cut himself skinning the small creature. The girl had ripped off a piece of her petticoat and tied it around his injured hand.

He'd worked so hard to sear the meager meal. But the wind that roared through the forest kept rushing down from the tree-tops to snuff out their pitiful fire. The boy was patient, starting over again and again, but the flames had barely licked at the dripping chunks skewered on a green twig before another cruel gust would undo his endeavors.

Now she could no longer feel the tips of her fingers or the end of her nose. Night was closing in, in shades of silver and gray. When she slumped onto a fallen log, her doll clasped in her arms, the boy perched beside her.

"*I think we shall soon find my uncle's village,*" *he told her.* "*And he will help us.*"

Though the boy sounded certain, she'd seen his face as he searched the ground and the trees overhead. Though he never admitted it, she knew they were lost. When he heard howls moving closer the night before, he'd woken her and made her run. Stumbling through the darkness, he hadn't allowed her to slow until they'd left the savage sounds far behind. Finally, he'd helped her into a tree and secured her to a thick branch with his own hempen belt before settling in beside her.

When dawn broke through the icy treetops, they climbed down together. He held her hand as they walked, chattering of his uncle's warm hearth and his aunt's rich squirrel stew. Her mouth watered when he spoke of the butter and soft cheese his aunt would smear on piping hot bread. How they would soon be tucked under quilts beside a roaring fire.

He hadn't stopped talking all throughout the short day. But now the sun was setting again and he'd gone silent when no village appeared.

More snow was falling. And though the thick trees blocked the worst of it, flakes still snagged in the girl's hair and collected in her lap where she huddled against a great tree. When her stomach twisted and growled with hunger, she curled in over the pain.

"*You are hungry,*" *he said, slanting a glance toward her.* "*And—*" *His head bowed.* "*I—I lost the flint when we fled the wolves.*"

The little girl's heart sank as she thought of spending another cold and dark night without a fire. Though he'd tried to encourage a blaze by rubbing a stick between his palms until they bled, the wood was too damp to take spark.

When the boy's head bowed again in defeat, she wanted to weep. But she forced her shoulders straight. Was she not the granddaughter of the great Dr. John Dee? Had she herself not had audience with the mightiest queen in Christendom? Small she might be, but weak she was not. She raised her chin, and though her voice was raspy from the cold, she said, "Do not worry. We shall survive this. All will be well."

"No!" The boy shoved to his feet, twisted about, and dropped to his knees before her. "We are lost. And I shall pretend no longer. I —I am sorry, milady. I have failed you."

When the troubled boy looked up at her with eyes of lake-water and summer grass, something seemed to crack open inside the little girl's heart. She reached out and placed a cold palm against his cheek. "No," she said. "Never that."

A grating sound tugged me awake. My eyes popped open. At first, I couldn't move. Adrenaline spiked through me, making electricity dance across the back of my tongue. I realized I was lying face-down on a hardwood floor, my arms trapped beneath me. Groaning, I heaved myself to my side, and tried to shake some feeling back into my numb arms.

A cold spear of pure and utter panic tore through me when they wouldn't move. Slowly, reluctantly, I angled my head down to see the canvas contraption that encased me from hips to throat.

No. I closed my eyes, breath coming faster. *Oh, no. No no no no.* This is just another nightmare. Just a dream.

A scream began to build deep in my throat as I struggled to rip my arms loose, but the straitjacket that held them wrapped around my body was too tight.

Wrenching and jerking, I somehow managed to pull myself to a sitting position. Beneath the coarse material I was still wearing my own teal and silver gown, which a sullen maid had dressed me in that morning. The whalebone corset—combined with the straitjacket—constricted my chest. Beneath my skin, it felt as though each rib was collapsing in on itself. I could almost hear the slim bones giving way, piercing my lungs with their jagged ends. *Crack. Crack. Crack.*

All was white inside the spartan isolation room. Walls. Ceiling. Floor, though that painted surface was now scratched and dull. Sets of iron rings were bolted to the wall, and a slop bucket sat in one corner of the windowless cell. A single bulb dangled on a frayed cord above my head. When it crackled I shoved with my feet, until my back hit the wall.

What . . . ?

It all came back in a nauseating rush. My friends on the lawn. The broken window. Sergeant Peters, who had tried to help. Annabelle Allen and her poor murdered kittens. I'd panicked and rushed for the door.

Stupid. So stupid.

My knees ached from being slammed to the ground,

one side of my neck felt swollen from the bolus of sedative Carson had plunged there.

Afterward, there had been nothing. Until now. Until this.

Can't move my arms. Can't breathe. Can't . . . Can't . . .

My scalp prickled.

Oh God, what day is it? What time? No window. Is it day or night? How long was I out? What if it's too late? What if they had to go back without me? What if they had no choice but to leave me here? What if . . . What if . . . What if . . .

A shrieking dread took hold of me. Blinded by it, I bucked and reared, trying to get loose. I rolled from one side of the room to the other, fighting the canvas. But it was no use. I couldn't get free. My throat closed up. Darkness edged in as I sobbed and gagged. A black square marked the closed peephole in the center of the only door. I scrabbled over to it on my knees.

"Please . . ." I wheezed, but with empty lungs my words were barely audible. "Let . . . me out."

Every cell in my brain was screaming that the oxygen couldn't last. Not in this sealed room that was filling with carbon dioxide every time I exhaled.

"Let me out!"

"Shut yer trap." A muffled male voice came from the other side. "You'll get yours soon enough."

Slumped against the door, I slammed the back of my head against the unforgiving wood, again and again. Pain shot across my skull and down my spine as tears squeezed from my closed lids. "Please . . ."

The only answer was a scathing laugh. Like scalding acid dripped onto flesh, the claustrophobia I'd suffered since childhood began to corrode my reason.

My spine gave. I toppled over. More black dots appeared with each blink. Splinters from the rough planks raked my cheek as my chest struggled to draw in one last breath.

Bran. Help. Wh–where are you?

The light bulb fizzed, snapped, and went out. The darkness was instantaneous and complete. My ravaged brain tried to grasp for some reason, any reason not to just give up. I brought up a single image. Bran Cameron's eyes.

Green and Blue. Grass and Sky. Lake and Ocean. Leaves and Water. Yes. That's a nice thing to think about as you die, isn't it?

A blast of freezing water crashed across my face and chest. I retched and struggled to sit up. Spluttering, drowning, I swiped an arm across my . . .

Wait? My arm? My arms! They're free!

My eyes shot open. As water streamed from my sodden hair, I looked down at my hands in amazement. *My hands. I can see my hands.*

Someone grabbed my wrists, wrenching me to my feet. Water blurred my vision and before I could even view my attacker, he twisted both arms behind me and dragged me backwards until my aching arms and back were pressed up against him. Though I couldn't see the man, I smelled him. Body odor and hair pomade.

"Just you be quiet now, miss." I recognized the voice. The sleazy guard, Dupree. The rodent-faced man Sergeant Peters had ordered away from the ladies' door. Dupree's rancid breath wreathed around my ear. "Doc's comin', so you better behave, or you won't like what's next."

The door was open. It was open! I dragged in the blessed air that was swarming into the room. I licked at the water still dripping from my hair, trying to wet my parched mouth.

"Thanks to you," Dupree whispered, "that nosy nelly Peters got hisself canned, he did. Now that I'm in charge, I believe I'll call on Miss Allen. It's been a while."

I shuddered as I thought of the child-like Annabelle and her string of dead kittens.

"Now you . . ." Dupree pulled me close, pressing the entire length of his body against my back. I struggled, but he only wrenched my arms back until a ripping pain shot through my shoulders. His breath came faster as he jeered, "Bet you wouldn't lay there all still and cold, would you, now? No, not you. You got fire in you, girl-o. Little wildcat you are."

Horror, disgust, and raw animal fear spiraled through me, but then Phoebe's voice sounded in my head.

If they grab you from behind, Hope, just stomp down hard on their instep, aye? They'll let go quick enough. That's when you turn and kick them in their wobblies.

Slowly, I raised my knee.

"You may release the patient now, Dupree," Dr. Carson called from the doorway. In his hands he held the stiff canvas contraption that had been around me. I froze as its iron buckles jangled and its obscenely long sleeves dripped to the ground. I eased my foot to the floor. "You won't be any trouble, will you, Miss Walton?"

I cringed, the idea of being put back into the straitjacket making me curl in on myself. *No. Please don't put me back. I can't do it. I—*

My head snapped up. My jaw unhinged as I stared at Carson.

He *knew*. He knew my real name.

He smiled. "You must understand, Miss *Walton*. I did not wish to restrain you, but your behavior left me with little choice." His eyes flicked toward the guard. "Dupree," he said. "Have you made the proper arrangements with Patient Smith?"

"Yeah, Doc," Dupree said. "Man's trussed like a Christmas goose."

"Hurry along, then. I don't have all day."

We stopped before a door just like my own. Another guard stood watch, a leather-wrapped cudgel in his fist.

"Quiet today, Doc," the thick-necked guard said, keying the door open. He stuck his head inside and shouted, "Ain't gonna cause no trouble, are ya, you mad bastard?"

Carson frowned at the guard. "This, Mr. Malloy, is a fashionable establishment. I'll thank you to keep the obscenities to yourself." He waved a hand at the guards, who both stared at me with avid faces. "Leave us. Wait at the end of the hallway. I'll call for you when we are done."

Something shifted within the darkened room. A shuffling. The clink of chains. I had to cover my nose and mouth to keep from gagging at the malignant odor that oozed from inside.

My feet didn't want to move, but Carson pulled me forward through the doorway. Without letting go of my arm, he reached out. A click, and the giant bulb that dangled overhead sparked into life, exposing smeared and dingy walls. Green spots danced in my vision and I had to blink a few times to clear it.

At first, I wasn't sure what I was looking at. A pile of rags. A scarecrow crouched in a far corner. Heavy chains looped through iron wall rings and ran down to manacles that wrapped around stick-thin wrists and ankles.

"What is this?" I whispered.

The huddled creature raised its head. A pair of red-rimmed eyes met mine. And it felt like every particle of the room's foul air flooded into my lungs all at once.

The last time I'd seen him he'd been dressed in chain mail and tunic, not some torn and filthy smock. The white-blond hair was long now, tangled and greasy, except for two oddly shaved areas on either temple. His face had aged tremendously, but there was no mistaking the man's identity.

A line of drool stretched from one corner of his shrunken mouth, leaving a dark circle on a food-encrusted smock.

"No." I tried to back up, but the doctor blocked me. "Impossible. He's ... He's ..."

"You know this man?" The doctor grunted in genuine surprise. "How fascinating. I'd no idea. I only wanted the two of you to meet, as I believe Patient Smith has much in common with you and I.

"The man was already a patient at Bellevue when I arrived here nigh on thirty years ago. The physician over his case had given up on treatment. I convinced him to let me take over Smith's care, and when I built this hospital, I brought him with me. But how could *you* possibly know—"

I could no longer hear Carson. The room had begun to spin in a swirl of white on white, until all I could focus on was the revenant of the human being I'd met only months before.

Chains clinked as the now-old man raised his arm, pointed a long, yellowed nail directly at me. *"Wiiiitch."*

I flinched as the gravelly sound of his voice skittered across my skin like a thousand roaches.

Eustace Clarkson.

Lackey. Brute. Would-be rapist. Guard of the London City Watch, in the year of our Lord, 1154.

It wasn't as if I'd had a choice. He'd already knocked Bran unconscious, and would have killed us both. But not before he'd done much, much worse to me.

The entrance to the chasm had been right there and the man had been strong, yes. But also stupid.

I learned then that killing someone is surprisingly easy when you have no other option. I shoved. He fell. And Eustace Clarkson had disappeared into the Dim, where no final thud ended his horrible screams.

I still hear him sometimes when I wake in the night.

"It's impossible," I whispered. "He's dead. I saw him fall. I —"

Eustace lunged at me. Broken, blackened teeth bared, fingers curled into claws. Rage and madness and fury. I leapt back, slammed into the wall. The chains arrested his advance, jerking him backwards like a rabid dog.

He slammed to his knees, muttering to himself as he signed the cross over and over. "Demons. Demons. Demons everywhere. Lightning in my head. Witch girl in my room. Kill her. Kill the lightning man."

Carson cast a hand out at the pitiful scrap that once had been Eustace Clarkson. "A year or two before I arrived, the police found him in an alley in Five Points, beaten near to death. The constables brought him to Bellevue, where he claimed to be a knight brought back from Hades." The doctor swallowed. "Having made that particular journey myself, I must say I understood the sentiment."

I was suddenly exhausted. Too bone-tired to pretend anymore as I watched Eustace lunge against his chains again and again, each time growing weaker as he rasped, "Kill the demon witch. Kill the lightning man. Kill them. Kill them all."

"He's from London," I said. "Twelfth century. But he was no knight."

Carson shook his head. "Incredible. As you can see, the man is no conversationalist, and I admit there've been times I've longed to speak to someone who truly understands my circumstance. I only wish you and I had more time to chat of that world we left behind. Unfortunately, I've had to make other arrangements for you." He sighed. "A shame, really."

"Arrangements?" I asked, my gaze straying to the shaved —and now that I looked closer—scorched areas on Eustace's temples.

He'd called Carson "lightning man."

"I must, of course, be wary of drawing too much attention too quickly. You've no idea how difficult it's been to wait decades on appropriate modernization. Patient Smith was the only one I dared experiment on. But brain surgery has been in practice in some form or another since the ancient Egyptians. It was not too huge a leap for me to introduce its utilization in psychiatric medicine."

And the old shall be made new again.

Carson withdrew a small leather notebook. Scribbling, he asked, "What year, exactly, did you come from? I—for instance—am originally from 1983."

"I know."

"Do you?" He looked at me curiously. "How did you come to cross over?"

"Probably the same way you did."

Carson laughed. "I do hope it didn't cost you as much as it did me."

"How much *did* you pay the Timeslippers? That's what happened, right? They hid you so you wouldn't go to jail."

For an instant, the doctor looked impressed, and then he raised one lazy shoulder. "I'd seen the writing on the wall. I knew I would likely go to prison for a long time. I could have fled the country, of course. But where to? And simply leaving would likely mean I could never again practice medicine. I must admit, I despaired."

When I snorted, he flashed me a warning frown. "Can you even begin to imagine my joy at learning there was another way? A place where I would never be found and ..." He lifted a finger. "Could continue my practice, my experiments, with little or no restriction? No nosy review boards to censure what could have been groundbreaking work in the world of psychosurgery. No litigious family members. No federal investigations." Carson's bitter tone softened as he cocked his head to look at me. "Here, my dear girl, I may do as I please."

"Yeah, I noticed," I said. "Which makes you a sick—"

Carson slapped me. A backhanded blow that sent me stumbling across the room. Blood welled from a cut inside my cheek as I crashed to my knees, and Eustace Clarkson made his move.

He snatched me by the hair and dragged me toward him. My heels scrabbled against the filthy floor as Carson shrieked for the guards.

Eustace was old and weak, but I was still no match against the cumulative decades of rage and hate. He drove me to the floor. Hands closed around my neck, squeezing . . . squeezing.

Witch Demon. Witch Demon.

Dupree and Malloy burst into the room, clubs already raised. Blows rained down on Eustace's shoulders and back, but he wouldn't stop. As I clawed and kicked, the doctor appeared, rolling some kind of massive device.

"Hold him," he told the guards. "Hold him now!"

With his hands still choking the life from me, a guard took Eustace in a headlock. A gray film had begun to bleed over my vision. But I saw the doctor slap something that resembled oversize headphones over Eustace's head and secure the strap beneath his chin.

Eustace's grip on me loosened as he screamed and tried to rip off the ersatz helmet. I sucked in wisps of air while more guards rushed in. One grabbed my hands and hauled me out from beneath the foaming madman.

At least six guards held Eustace Clarkson while Dr. Carson fiddled with the dials on the now-attached machine.

"Ready!" Carson shouted. "On my signal, let go and do not touch him, understood?"

A hum of electricity. Eustace howling. Blood pounded in my ears as I tried to get my bruised throat to function.

"Now!" Carson yelled. "Clear!"

The guards fell away, leaving Eustace on his knees alone. The doctor flipped a switch, sending volts of electricity crackling through his emaciated form. The room filled with the stench of singed hair and charred flesh. Eustace quivered and juddered, his body now little more than a mass of cooking meat.

The guards, entranced by the sight, had forgotten my existence. One of them, in his haste to let go before the electricity zapped him, had fallen to his side only inches away from me. An iron key ring hung half in and half out of his pocket.

Normally I calculated the odds and evaluated all possible scenarios.

Screw that. That sadistic bastard isn't going to touch me ever, ever again. Hell. No. I'm getting out of this Victorian loony bin. Tonight.

While smoke drifted from the top of Eustace's head, I reached out, snatched the guard's key ring, and slipped it into my bodice.

CHAPTER 31

I HAD NO IDEA WHAT TIME IT WAS. BUT MY STOMACH wouldn't stop rumbling, which meant lunch and dinner had likely passed. They hadn't brought food. But then they wouldn't, would they?

NPO, nil per os, the Latin term for withholding food and fluids. Well, of course. Nothing to eat or drink twelve hours prior to surgery. Don't want anyone vomiting on the surgeon, now do we?

Carson himself had marched me back to my room. Furious, he'd flung me inside.

"Do you know," he said, his mouth curled into a cruel sneer, "I actually considered postponement. I thought perhaps it might be interesting to speak with a fellow traveler. But you are a disruption, Miss Walton." He smoothed a hand over his hair. "In the morning, I shall unveil the world's first transorbital lobotomy. It will astonish the medical community and secure my spot as the leading psychiatrist of the age. And you . . . you will have the distinct honor of being its first recipient. Good evening, Miss Walton."

After he left, I paced the perimeter of my cell for what felt like a dozen lifetimes. Periodically, I'd hear the *clip-clop* of footsteps, and would press my ear to the door, certain it was the hapless guard come to search for his missing key ring. But either he hadn't noticed its absence, or was afraid of admitting he'd lost it, because each time, the footsteps passed me by. Once, my heart all but stopped when the clang of a gurney approached, and I thought I'd left it too late, that they'd come for me before I could make my escape.

The claustrophobia still rushed in like a vicious dog to nip at my sanity. Several times throughout that long, long night, I had to lie flat on the floor, forehead pressed against the dingy, splintered wood to fight off crescendoing waves of panic. When everything had fallen into an ominous silence, the voice inside told me it was time. That if I had any expectation of getting out of here with my brain intact, I had to go. Now.

Just get on with it, Walton. If you're gonna do this thing, then freaking do it already.

I drew the key ring from my bodice, but my hands shook so badly, I couldn't even fit the right key into the lock. I paused, ignoring the walls that I swore were closing in again, and began to count my breaths like Mom had taught me so long ago.

In . . . two, three. Out . . . two, three.

Insert. Turn. *Click.*

To my surprise and great (silent) whoops of relief, the door snicked open. I peeked out into the darkened, empty hallway, pulse throbbing so hard I could feel it behind my eyeballs.

The boy is in the East Wing, Peters had whispered to me just before Carson had finished with Annabelle and had both of us dragged away. *Room 14 in Men's Ward D. There's a laundry chute at the north end of the hallway. I'll send you both down that way, then come around and unlock the laundry door. Your people will be waiting outside. That's your way out.*

With no idea which way I should go, I turned and headed for an open doorway at the far end of the left corridor. There, a darkened set of steps led up. A stair creaked so loudly beneath my weight that it echoed off the walls. Sure that the sound had alerted every freaking guard in the place, I plastered myself against the wall and waited for my inevitable capture.

It took a while to convince my body to unclench. I'd been in tight spots—literally—in London. But I'd always had someone with me. Collum and Phoebe. Rachel and William.

Bran.

This time, no one could help me. Peters had done as much as he could and had paid a heavy price. If I failed, I would do it alone, and the consequences for me, for Doug, for my entire family would be catastrophic.

I prayed under my breath as I climbed the rest of the way

up. At the top, I pressed my ear against the door. Hearing nothing, I tried the crystal knob. Unlocked.

The next corridor was stuffy and windowless, housing a series of closets and storerooms. At the last door on the right, I struck gold. The room was small, plain, with a flagstone floor. As I peered through the gloom, I saw a huge metallic bin seated against the left wall. It emitted the distinct aroma of dirty sheets and musty towels. A draft filtered in from the crack beneath a door on the far wall that I figured must lead up to the outside. Above the bin, one lone sheet draped from the lip of a laundry chute, like a ghost too tired to make the final leap.

The rest of my stealthy journey through Greenwood Institute consisted of a series of wrong turns, backtracking, and gut-churning close calls. By the time I reached the set of double doors labeled GREENWOOD MEN'S WARD D, I was wound so tight a mouse fart would have sent me right over the edge.

Deep within the confines of the mental asylum, a clock bonged the hour. One. Two. Three. Four.

Four a.m. Shift change. You got this, Walton.

From the floor below came a muffled wail that was soon taken up by others throughout the building. One after another, patients cried out in pain or loneliness.

Back home, before it all went to crap, Mom, Dad, and I

would sometimes sit on the front porch to watch the fireflies gather. In the balmy, deep summer silence a train would pass, or a car alarm would go off, and it would begin.

It always started with one dog. Then the entire canine population of our small town would join in, filling the night with a chorus of creepy howls.

These were not dogs. They were human beings, whose combined pain oozed up the walls, bled across the floors, and dripped from the ceiling of what should have been a place of healing.

Men's Ward D was still undecorated, the floor gritty with plaster dust. Wires protruded from unfinished walls and ceiling, awaiting electrical fixtures. The only light in the long corridor came from two oil lamps set on the floor at either end. The far lamp guttered, but I grinned as its light revealed the square outline of a laundry chute, just as Sergeant Peters had promised.

Bare soles skidding in the powdery dust, I approached room 14. My pulse jumped thirty beats at a movement that turned out to be dust bunnies scampering in a shadowed corner.

I swiped damp palms over the velvet day gown, and selected a key from the iron ring. As no alarm had yet been raised, I assumed the guard had decided not to reveal his carelessness. Not yet. But my luck wouldn't last forever. We had to get out.

Fast. Before the doctor's surgical team arrived at my room and realized "patient zero" had decided against having her brain split in two.

Relief washed me head to toe as I keyed myself into room 14, and saw the big form huddled beneath a blanket.

Tiptoeing so as not to alarm him, I whispered, "Doug? Doug, are you awake? It's me. Can you—?"

The shove caught me flat in the chest. I flew back and slammed hard into the wall. My vision flashed to white as the back of my head smacked into solid wood.

"Get the fuck away from me, you sick bastards!"

I crumpled to my knees. "Doug," I managed to croak. "'S Hope."

The floor vibrated when Doug thumped to his knees beside me.

"Oh, bloody damn," he cried. "Hope! What are you *doing* here? Jesus, I'm sorry, lass. Are you a'right, then? I thought you were one of them. That nurse, she told me they were going to take me to . . . to surgery today." Doug shuddered. "Jesus, I'm sorry. Did I hurt you?"

Doug snatched his glasses from the small table and squinted through the smeary glass. "Shit. Oh, shit. You're bleeding." He plucked a wadded handkerchief from the dresser and pressed it to the back of my head.

"Ow."

He flinched as I yelped. Spots of red dotted the white cloth. I gingerly touched the lump that was erupting on my scalp. But my head was clearing and there was no time to worry about it now anyway.

"I'm fine." Doug's image doubled, but fortunately the two worried faces quickly merged back into one. "Seriously. But what about you? Are you okay?"

He nodded, though I recognized the strain of fear and isolation. I knew it all too well. He reached for me and wrapped me in his muscular arms.

"Jesus," he said as he hugged me tight. "I was terrified I'd never see any of you again. I tried to escape. Tried to kick the bloody door down. But the wankers kept drugging me."

"Me too," I told him. "Ass wipes."

He pulled back and I grinned up at his dear, sweet face. "What now?" he asked.

"Now we get the hell out of here."

Doug nodded and scrambled to his feet, giving me a hand up. Though the room wobbled, there wasn't time to let it steady.

"What's the plan?" he said.

I laid it out for him. "But it will all be for nothing if we don't get out before daylight."

"Then let's roll, aye?"

My hands shook, and for a horrifying instant, the small key wouldn't turn in the laundry chute lock. "Oh God. Oh no. No no no."

"Let me try."

I stepped aside, gladly. With a slight jiggle, the lock dis-engaged and the chute clicked open.

"Awesome," I said. "Now go."

We'd worked out that if, by unlucky chance, anyone hap-pened to be in the laundry room when we emerged, Doug had a much better shot at kicking their ass.

Something creaked behind me. I whipped around, eyes on the double doors at the far end. "Take the keys so you can unlock the door to the outside."

Doug nodded and hugged me hard. "Hope," he said. "I can never thank you enough. You could have snuck out. You didn't have to come after me."

"Are you kidding?" I told him. "If I left here without you, Phoebe would take those knives of hers and use me for tar-get practice."

Doug grinned, then maneuvered his head and broad shoulders through the opening. It was barely wide enough. He wormed inside until only his legs protruded. His voice echoed back to me. "Looks like a fairly steep drop-off here."

The lock at the far end of the ward clicked, loud as a shotgun in the quiet. Doug froze, but I shoved him as hard as I could until, cursing, he dropped away.

The chute snapped shut on its tight hinge. I whipped around just in time to see the ward door open. The stunned look on Dupree's weasel face was almost, *almost* worth it.

"Well, well. Ain't this a pip." Hands on his hips, he bared his rodent teeth. "Whatcha doin' up here, girlie?"

Without turning, I eased the chute door down until it mawed open behind me.

"Don't. You. Dare," he warned, then turned and shouted, "She's here! I got her!"

Boots pounded on the wooden floorboards as I turned and thrust myself headlong into the dark opening.

Go! Go! Go!

Far below, I heard the rustle and soft "Oof" of Doug's landing. I scrambled forward, hands grappling for the spot where the rough wooden boards veered off into the vertical descent that would take me to safety.

There! Flat on my belly I squirmed, hands outstretched. My upper body tilted downward at a sharp angle. Gravity was winning. I began to slide. *Yes. Yes. Yes!*

Hands closed around my ankles, ripping me backwards. My already sore head cracked against the lip of the entrance as Dupree dragged me from the chute. I hit the floor flat on my stomach. Air exploded from my lungs.

With one twist he flipped me over onto my back. His greasy hair hanging down on either side of my face, he fell on top of me. Yellow teeth showed in a leer as he pressed down. I tried. I tried to shove him off, but I was too weak.

Always too weak.

"Knew you'd be a hellcat," he grunted, grappling for my wrists. "We are going to have us all kinds of fun. With Peters gone, I'm in charge, and oh . . . I'll be seeing *you* on the regular."

Light from oil lamps bounced off the ceiling. Dread and terror mixed and swirled inside my head as Dr. Alexander Carson stormed down the hall, trailed by the matron, two guards, and Nurse Hannah.

"Caught her, Doc," Dupree panted as he rolled off me and jerked me to my knees. "I was just about to—"

"Thank you, Dupree," Carson interrupted with a hale clap to the wiry guard's shoulder. "You'll make a fine sergeant."

"Yeah," I snarled. "You two make a perfect match."

"The rest of you," Carson said, ignoring me as Dupree and another guard hauled me to my feet. "Bring Miss Walton straight to the surgery suite. We proceed at once."

CHAPTER 32

DRIFTING . . . DRIFTING . . .

Am I dead?

I thought the words, then decided to test my theory by speaking them aloud.

"Excuse me," I said politely to the white-capped figures bustling around me. "Am I dead?"

When no one answered, or even acknowledged my existence, I decided it was a distinct possibility.

They'd strapped me to the table in the operating theater. Of course, since they'd forced some vile black liquid down my throat, nothing had really bothered me much.

A sharp jab in my arm. Fire flowed into my veins. Just like that—the muzzy, comfortable state vanished.

I'm not dead, I realized as everything that had ever happened to me pulled itself into strident focus in my mind. I remembered everything. Everything I'd ever read, seen, heard blew into my brain all at once.

I'm not dead. I'm not dead. But oh God, I wish I was.

I felt it all now. The operating table a block of ice beneath my back. My hands and feet cinched tight. Leather restraint buckled across my forehead, and a thin sheet covering the shapeless hospital smock. The stringent odor of rubbing alcohol rose around me, making my eyes water as a series of uncontrollable shudders racked me from head to toe.

Whatever the doctor had just pushed into my arm began to sing through my veins. My pulse raced faster and faster until it roared with an unnatural speed. And I was suddenly and utterly wide awake. My eyes popped open.

"Ah." Carson's face loomed over mine. "I see you're back with us. Apologies for the abrupt awakening, but I've found I get better results when the patient is hyper-alert. Cocaine works fine for now, though I am fiddling with other concoctions."

Above my head, six huge Edison bulbs blazed to life inside a metallic hood. The brilliant lights blinded as the drug inside me made my muscles twitch and shake.

The surgical doors opened and a red-faced, uniformed guard dashed up to the table. The man's jowls waggled as he gave his report.

"The mulatto boy got away, Doc," he huffed. "Found the door to the laundry room wide open and tracks leading to the fence. The gate was locked, so he must've climbed over. But he had help, that's for sure."

Doug got away? Oh, thank God.

I beamed up at the now-livid Carson.

"Yeah," I said. "Sorry about that."

I felt Carson's fists twist in the sheet that covered me. His jaw tightened as he glared at the guard. "That," he said, "is disappointing, Mr. O'Neill. Quite disappointing."

O'Neill's mouth opened and closed. "I am sorry, sir. I don't know how—"

"Just go," Carson snipped. "You are contaminating my environment."

The guard slunk out of my field of view. Carson stared after him. Then his gaze slipped down to meet mine. "The boy was incidental to the arrangement, and therefore of no consequence."

It was the second time he'd mentioned an arrangement. One I assumed Celia had ordered her goon squad to set up. I wondered if Bran knew yet about his mother's involvement.

Instruments clanked against metal trays as the doctor and his team set up. When Carson appeared again, he didn't meet my eyes. My teeth chattered. From cold. From terror. From the drugs.

"Look." I tried to take a deep breath, but the claustrophobia and clink of metallic instruments held my lungs in a vise. "Don't do this. We have money. Lots of money. We can give you all you want. Please, just let me go."

Carson spoke to the man across from him, his face set in counterfeit sincerity. "Poor thing. She doesn't realize we're only trying to help her."

I heard a scrape as he selected an instrument. I struggled and fought against my bonds, but it did no good. I was trapped like a rabbit in a snare. And unlike the rabbit, with my head strapped in place, I couldn't even gnaw off my own foot to get away.

"Dr. Perkins," he said to the young bearded assistant on my other side. "Cover the right half of the patient's face."

A cloth came down, covering my right eye. When I screamed and tried to squirm, Carson nodded to his assistant, who jammed a leather bite plate into my mouth, flooding it with the taste of tannin. I ground down, weeping at the familiar smell of the stable. Of saddles and stirrups and freedom.

No. No! Please. Please, God help me!

Fat overhead bulbs glinted on the silver instrument as Carson's hand came into view. An ice pick. Sharp. Lethal. Permanent.

My stomach lurched. Nausea rolled up. I was going to puke. I was going to choke on it and die right here before he could ever touch me.

Terror as pure and undiluted as glacial ice surged beneath my skin. I screamed through my gag, clamping my eyes hard shut, as if that would protect them.

"Hold her!" Carson commanded. "I cannot work this way!"

"Doctor," the assistant said. "Perhaps sedation would be prudent for—"

"No," Carson snapped. "Nurse. Hold her head."

Rough hands came down on either side of my face.

Thumbs dug into my cheekbones, stretching the flesh of my face so tight it felt as if it would split in two. With the back of my head pressed to the table, another set of callused fingers pried open my left eyelid. Carson took a breath and brought the pick closer. When cold steel touched the inside of my eye, next to my nose, I howled behind the chunk of leather.

His other hand appeared, clutching a small wooden mallet. Helpless, furious tears streamed down to soak my temple as cold metal pricked the tender inner corner of my eye socket. Carson nudged the eyeball away to fit the tip firmly into place.

Pressure. Burning.

No.

The doctor's jaw flexed. The hammer rose. Higher. Higher, as he prepared to slam it down and drive a splinter of sharpened steel up through my sinus cavity and into my brain.

Let me die. Let me die. Just let me —

Boom! Pop! Crack-crack-crack!

The hand holding the ice pick faltered. It jerked, scoring a path down the side of my nose as one after the other, the massive light bulbs above Carson's head erupted in a shower of sparks and shattered glass.

The room plunged into blackness. Ozone choked the air. A nurse screamed. Chunks and slivers of burning glass rained down on my thin covering, tinkling on metallic trays and scalding me in a hundred places. For an instant, I wasn't sure if all this was only my imagination. If even now, Carson's ice pick was severing the connection between the two halves of my brain. If the darkness was only my mind's way of checking out.

"What in the hell is going on here?" Dr. Carson shouted. "Someone fire up a lamp. I will not be delayed."

The nurse's coarse hands retreated from my face. "Must be the fuses again, Doctor," she said. "I'll send someone over to look—"

Shouts from outside the door. Thumps. Bangs. A muffled scream.

A blue flash licked up from the tray nearest my head, the sparks igniting a metallic bowl filled with rubbing alcohol. A nightmare's worth of masked faces bloomed around me before someone threw a damp cloth over the dancing flame, snuffing it out.

In the darkness, everything went very, very still.

"Did you hear that?" Carson's assistant whispered, just as something heavy bashed through the surgery door.

"Hope?" a voice yelled. "Hope! Are you in here, lass?"

CHAPTER 33

Joy, strong and bright as the sun, blazed to life inside me when I heard Collum MacPherson's hoarse shout. I screamed his name through the gag.

"What is the meaning of this?" the doctor yelled. "How dare you interrupt an ongoing surgical procedure? Remove yourself!"

"This is it!" Collum called to someone outside the room. "She's here!"

A concentrated beam of white cut a swath through the darkness, illuminating the perturbed faces of the medical team. It snapped off. Three long seconds passed before it flashed again.

Off. On. Off. On. The light ruptured the darkness in short strobes, until it landed on my face, blinding me.

"Jesus, Mary, and St. Bride!"

The wonderful sound of Phoebe's voice renewed my struggles. My back arched against the table. Phoebe rushed to my side as the light faded.

SPARKS OF LIGHT

When it flashed again, the bright beam glinted off Phoebe's knife as she jabbed it toward the enraged Carson. "Get away from her with that thing, you slagging monster," she snarled as she felt down my legs and sliced through the bonds around my ankles. "You touch my friend again and I'll carve you up like a bloody Easter ham."

Before the light faded again, she'd sawed through the thick strap holding my head in place. Behind her, light blazed from a hole cut into the side of a wooden box that Collum cradled under one arm. My mind pinged, matching the object with a science-journal article on Nikola Tesla, and the diagram of a primitive flashlight.

Collum's other hand clasped a brutal leather-wrapped club. My throat closed as the afterimage burning inside my lids revealed the comforting sight of Mac's outline next to Collum.

Flash.

Mac moved to cover Phoebe, a pistol aimed at the doctor's crew.

"Hope," said his gravelly voice in the dark. "Are ye hurt, lass?"

I felt the strap give. As Phoebe freed my hands, I ripped the gag from my mouth and scrubbed the taste of leather from my lips.

"I—I'm okay." I tried to sound brave, but my teeth were chattering, chopping the words into micro-bits.

Phoebe's nimble hands roamed my face. I heard a growl

as her fingertips slid in the blood that was oozing from the scratch near my nose.

"Oh, Hope." Her voice was low, scared.

With the drug still shrilling through my veins, I started babbling. "I'm okay. You got here just in time. He just scratched me. God, I'm so glad to see you. Did Doug get out? Please tell me he did. And can you get me the freaking hell out of here?"

"Doug's fine. He's out—"

Screams. The pound of fists and footsteps. Shouts that seemed to come from everywhere.

"Sir!" I turned as the red-haired O'Neill threw open the door at the rear of the room. Uplit by the oil lantern in his fist, there was no mistaking the fear on his dour features. "Doc Carson! Something's happened. The prisoners—I mean, the patients—they're free. Running the halls, they are. And someone's set a fire. It's chaos out there, sir. What should we—"

The rest of the guard's words died in his throat as his mouth dropped open into a dark oval. A confused expression squinched his eyes. One hand rose to wipe away the blood that suddenly trickled from the corner of his lips. He dropped to his knees, the oil lamp slipping from his fingers and rocking on its base as he slumped face first to the floor. I saw it, then. A knife that protruded from the back of his neck.

The lamp uplit the macabre figure that loomed behind him. Terror sunk icy claws into the muscles around the base of my spine as the blank, empty eyes surveyed the room.

On the opposite side of the table, his back to us, Dr. Carson had gone very, very still.

Blood rimmed Eustace Clarkson's mouth. It dripped from his chin, staining the chest of his hospital smock. I had no idea whose it was, but when he swiped a careless arm across his face, I knew it likely wasn't his own.

"Holy Mother, save us." Phoebe reflexively crossed herself. "Is that—?"

"Yeah." I eased off the table, never taking my eyes from the crazed man as I slid into a crouch and pulled Phoebe down beside me. "It is."

"But I thought he was—"

I shook my head as we peered over the edge of the table. Eustace leaned down and jerked the serrated kitchen knife from the guard's neck. When he stood, strands of lank white hair stuck to the gore on his cheeks. One of the assistants approached him, but backed up fast when Eustace's arm rose, wraith-like, to point the knife at him.

Behind us, Collum and Mac were fending off more guards, but I couldn't look away.

"Lightning. Lightning. Lightning in my head," Eustace was singing, the words tuneless as he advanced into the room. "And it burns. Oh, doesn't it just."

Alexander Carson made a sudden, scuttling move to escape, but Eustace's head snapped in an oddly reptilian gesture. His sunken eyes fixed on his tormentor.

"Mr. Smith." Carson tried to sound authoritative, but the whine in his voice undercut the words. "G-get back to your cell at once."

"I knew this place for hell." Eustace spoke without affect, eyes never leaving the doctor's. "Oh yes. Soon as I arrived, I knew it. The air, you see? It smelled of burning. Burning souls. Where dragons steam their foul breath upon the water and the fires, they burn all night to cast their greasy soot into the sky. Mountains of brick and stone and oh . . . I knew then I'd been cast down to the fiery lake." He pointed the knife at Carson. "And I knew you, devil. I knew you."

Tears rolled down the creature's ravaged face, tracing two clear paths through the red. "But the lightning. Over and over and over, the lightning and the smell, it never leaves me and my own flesh, it burns away, bit by bit."

The old man who'd once been Eustace Clarkson picked up the guard's lantern by the handle. He held it out before him, then pressed the other palm against the scalding glass. In seconds the stench of burning meat drifted to us.

"All those years," Eustace said as he advanced slowly toward the frozen Carson. "You and all your demons sticking me, sticking me with your devil thorns and I tried . . . I tried to beg God's forgiveness for my sins." His head shook violently back and forth. "No use. No use. Then the wires and the lightning and the *burning,* ohhh . . . the burning was the worst of all."

From the other side of the table, we heard an odd crackling. Phoebe gagged and I realized the noise was the sizzle of

Eustace's hand as it cooked down to bone and sinew. Barely seeming to notice, he stopped only a yard from the terrified Dr. Carson. Emaciated cheeks pulled back from gory teeth in an eerie, almost child-like smile. "But I think this time, it is you who shall burn."

With a motion so fast I could hardly follow it, Eustace Clarkson raised the oil lantern high and slammed it to the ground at the doctor's feet. It shattered in an explosion of glass and kerosene and flame. Alexander Carson writhed, screaming as lines of fire began to race up his body. Nurse Hannah ducked beneath the table, her eyes squeezed shut as she shrieked the doctor's name over and over.

She buried her face in her hands, and I caught the glint of a silver chain around her neck.

Nope.

Staying low, I crawled to her.

"What are you doing?" Phoebe hissed, though she stayed glued to my side.

"She has my lodestone," I whispered. "I'm getting it back."

Phoebe gave a sharp nod. "Damn straight. Let's grab it and get the bloody hell out of here."

While Nurse Hannah wailed, I reached over and grabbed the chain. She whirled on me, eyes and mouth black holes in a pale oval as I clutched the jewel in my fist and yanked.

The damn chain didn't break, and like a demented feline, Nurse Hannah raked her nails down my arms. When I refused to let go, she grabbed a fistful of my hair and tried to rip it out. I slapped at her with my other hand.

Phoebe loosed an agitated huff. "Cheese 'n rice, we've no time for a bloody catfight. There's a madman on the loose."

She whirled and landed a kick on the side of Hannah's head. The nurse went limp and I yanked the chain off her.

"Phee," Collum called over his shoulder while bludgeoning someone I couldn't see. "That mad bastard is coming your way!"

She nodded at her brother, then leaned up to peek over the tabletop. I followed, and wished I hadn't.

Pinned between sporadic gunfire on one side and a knife-wielding lunatic on the other, we didn't have a lot of options.

Phoebe slid her slim, steel throwing knives from her boot. Blowing out a breath, she leapt up and tossed all three in quick succession. *Thwack. Thwack. Thwack.*

Eustace grunted loudly.

"Oh, sweet Moses." Phoebe dropped down. "That's not good. I've think I've but pissed him off."

We peeked. Three knives protruded from Eustace's torso. He did not seem to notice. Flames had begun to skim along trails of alcohol spilled across the floor, casting a golden light that shivered across walls and ceiling.

"Witch girl," he called, taking one shambling step toward us. "Where are you? Thou shall not suffer a witch to—"

Flash and bang from Collum's pistol and a precipitous black hole that appeared in the center of Eustace's forehead. For a long and very strange moment he did not react. Orange flames glinted, demonic, in his eyes as his arm rose, index finger pointing at me.

Then, like a diseased tree succumbing to the rot inside, Eustace toppled over onto Dr. Carson's flaming corpse. Sparks blasted up. In seconds, the flames consuming Carson had found a new fuel source to feed upon.

Collum was holding the pistol that had finally ended Eustace Clarkson for good.

Collum gestured with the gun. "This way."

"They're getting away," someone shouted down the hall as we ran.

Phoebe grabbed my hand and pulled me behind her. A shot blasted. We ducked as plaster rained down on us from above.

"That was a warning, aye?" Mac's authoritative voice carried over the shrieks and laughter of mental patients running through the halls. "Dark or no dark, anyone comes after us gets it in the chest."

We moved through the shadows as a unit. Collum beside me. Phoebe and Mac guarding us front and rear. Midway down an inky corridor, I skidded to a halt.

"Come on," Phoebe urged. "This way. We have to—"

"I can't leave them here," I told them. "We have to get them out."

"Who, Hope?" Mac panted.

"My friends."

With audible groans, they followed as I veered off toward

Ladies' Ward B. But when we arrived, the door was ajar, the rooms beyond, empty.

No time to wonder if they'd escaped or simply been evacuated as gunshots sounded from the vicinity of the front entrance. We turned back the way we'd come. The weak beam from the boxy flashlight flickered. One last, brilliant, white-hot beam, and the flashlight emitted an explosive *pop-pop*. Smoke began to leak from the hole cut into the wooden box.

"Uh, Collum?"

He cursed and let the box drop to the floor.

"Take a right here, lad," Mac instructed as Collum, leading our little expedition now, paused and hooked a right. "Less than twenty paces. Here we are."

We ran across gray stone, through scents of bleach and lye toward the open back door. Beyond it lay the diffuse light of a cloudy dawn.

Phoebe's grin wrapped me like a toasty quilt on an icy afternoon. "Wait till you see the surprise."

I faltered for an instant before I realized what she must mean. Or rather . . . who. And since I hadn't seen him during the rescue mission, it had to mean he was waiting just beyond, acting as watchman, perhaps, or fighting off guards to clear our escape route.

I beamed at her, my feet propelling me faster toward the boy I knew was waiting for me outside.

Phoebe stopped me.

I never had friends before coming to Scotland. My life had been a solitary existence of books and study and mind-deadening routine. I'd only recently learned about the very real existence of "best friend ESP."

"Oh-h." Phoebe's eyes went soft with compassion. "Oh, I'm that sorry, Hope. The surprise isn't . . . I mean . . . it isn't Bran. He's not here."

Though I tried to hold it, I could feel the smile slipping from my face. "Oh. That's okay."

Phoebe leaned close, keeping the conversation private as she said, "Now you listen to me. That boy loves you, and no mistake. Don't you worry a bit on that score. He wanted to be here, believe me. It's only that some complications arose. But he'll be meeting us, soon as he can."

"You've seen him?" I asked, pulling back so I could look at her. "He's okay?"

"Oh, aye," she said. "Tell you all about it, later. But let's get the hell out o' this horror movie first."

"You have no idea."

From the doorway, Collum signaled for us to hurry. After ascertaining that the coast was clear, Phoebe dashed out. I started to follow, but Collum stayed my movement.

I turned to search the shadowy laundry room behind us. "What? You hear something?"

Collum's steady hazel eyes searched my face as he shook his head. "No, no. I, uh, I'm just glad you still have all your nuts about you is all." He smiled down at me, and the melancholic stab I'd felt at Phoebe's news faded, a bit.

I felt like a piece of meat thrust through a grinder. Physically, emotionally, mentally. But I was back with my friends now. My family. And as Collum jerked his chin for me to precede him, I felt all the gummy little pieces of myself begin to mold back together.

"Me too," I told him. "Me too."

CHAPTER 34

CRISPY, FROST-TINGED GRASS BURNED THE SOLES OF MY feet as I darted across the side yard toward the narrow servant's gate.

"So . . . ?" I cocked my head at a guard slumped against a nearby tree.

"Just a wee doze," Collum said. "Come on."

The wrought-iron fence jutted skyward, spiked and imposing. I passed through the gate, then turned to look back. In the milky dawn, I could just make out the knots of people gathering on either side of the gilt-inlaid front gate. Carriages had begun to pull up on the street side. Enraged family members bundled out, shouting at the guards to open the damn gate.

The tall figure of Lila Jamesson appeared from behind the brick edifice, the others trailing behind her. Priscilla. Mrs. Langdon. Mrs. Forbes, only slightly bowed, tugged a wide-eyed Annabelle Allen along behind her. Lila approached the fence slowly. On the other side, a squat, balding man stepped forward. For a long moment he only stared at her. Then his mouth moved, and though I could not hear the words, Lila threw her head back and laughed. He reached a hand through the bars. After only a brief hesitation, she took it. The man nodded, let go, and moved to the gate.

He bellowed at the gatekeepers, "Open this gate immediately, I say!"

As if she felt my eyes on her, Lila turned. When she saw me standing at the rear gate, she smiled and dropped her chin in a graceful farewell.

On the cobbled street, a glossy black carriage waited to spirit us away. Harnesses jingling, two magnificent black horses stamped and huffed. They looked as anxious to get away from this hellhole as I was.

"Where's Doug? And whose carriage is—?"

The door swung open, and it took me only an instant to process the identity of the man who stepped out.

"Ta da," Phoebe sang quietly. "Listen. Be mindful what you say. He knows who we are and generally from where and when and all that. I'll tell you later how it all happened. But for now, he's made it very clear that he wants to know nothing of his own fate or that of his family, aye? Nothing. He made us swear."

Our eyes met and I saw the sorrow and indecision that pinched her freckled features.

"But ..." I began, then Collum stepped into my line of sight.

"Not a word," he warned. "It's not your place or mine. The decision was his to make, and he's made it."

Irritated, I nodded in acknowledgment. But this was *not* over. Based on Phoebe's expression, I was pretty sure she didn't think so, either.

In a speckled gray suit and greatcoat, the man whose portrait I had seen every day in the library at Christopher Manor approached. Top hat tucked under one arm, he dropped into a respectful bow. "Miss Walton. I am Jonathan Buchanan Carlyle, at your service. And if I may be so bold, I believe you and I are relations. Of a sort?"

In March of 1895, Jonathan Carlyle was close to thirty. He'd been married to Julia Alvarez for a few years now, and their only son, Henry, was due in late summer.

"How—how do you do?"

In only three months, this kind, intelligent man would witness the gruesome, Dim-related death of his friend and brother-in-law. And in fourteen years, his precious little girls would die because of an innocent mistake made while on a voyage to his own past. A mistake that would forever cement the war between the families Carlyle and Alvarez.

He deserved to know.

Jonathan's face crumpled with compassion. Reaching into his pocket, he retrieved a clean, folded handkerchief, and pressed it into my hand. "If you will forgive me, Miss

Walton, you look as if you might weep. Of course, you've been through a terrible ordeal. One that would cause anyone to become undone. Please, allow my carriage to transport you to a place of safety."

When Jonathan offered his arm, I took it gladly.

"You!" Three guards rounded the side of the building. "Stop right there!"

"Damn!" Collum hustled me into the carriage. He, Phoebe, and Mac jumped in after, slammed the door shut, and yelled at the driver to move it. We took off at a run, and in moments had left the nightmare of Greenwood Institute far behind.

The buggy was luxurious, if a bit tight. We crammed in, shoulder to shoulder on the creamy leather seats. Me, Phoebe, and Mac on one side. And opposite, Collum sat next to a smiling Jonathan Carlyle.

When we turned off the bumpy side road onto a main thoroughfare, the ride smoothed out and the carriage picked up speed on the macadam road. A row of three- and four-story brick townhouses lined the street in this quiet, wealthy neighborhood. Bundled against the morning chill, people hurried along the tree-lined sidewalks or popped in and out of the tidy shops. I hugged myself as wind whipped in through the open windows, blowing my loose hair everywhere.

Collum shrugged off his overcoat and handed it to me. "Here. You're shivering."

"Thanks."

I thrust my arms backwards into the coat and nestled into the warmed wool. The homey scent of lanolin and soot and boot polish reminded me of Christopher Manor. I struggled not to burst out in hysterical sobs.

Mac squeezed the back of my hand. "Good to have you back, lass."

Things had been so crazy up till now. Getting Doug out. Dupree. Getting caught and waking up on the surgery table. Eustace. Everything had happened so fast, I hadn't had time to think. To process.

But now, in the quiet of the carriage, it swarmed over me.

"Is your eye paining you, Miss Walton?" Jonathan asked. "You keep rubbing it. I pray you were not injured?"

I smiled, shook my head, and ordered my hand to stop. Just stop. But I could feel the kiss of cold steel against my nose, the tip of the lethal ice pick as it pricked the inside of my eye. My hand rose to my face, again and again and again. The remnants of the drug cocktail I'd been injected with jittered through my nerve endings. And every time I tried to close my eyes I could see Carson hovering above me, the mallet raised to strike.

I rubbed and rubbed and rubbed.

Shaking. Not just from the chill. Jonathan was talking about how very much he wished his Julia had come along on this journey. How the pregnancy had been difficult, but that had she known about our presence, she would have braved anything to be able to meet us as well. Upon learning that the woman who'd appeared at his home only months before was only posing as friend, Jonathan's kind hazel eyes went flinty with indignation.

"The lady was a charming creature, to be sure," Jonathan admitted. "And yet I confess to some trepidation. My wife felt no such compunction where our visitor was concerned, particularly upon hearing her to be a blood relative. She will be sorely disappointed."

When he spoke of Nikola Tesla, his brow creased in remorse.

"I deeply regret my own naiveté," he explained. "Had I not handed over the plans the lady gave to me. Had I listened to my heart and not my head, he would not now be closeted with his assistants, refusing entry to anyone, until the innovation is complete."

"He won't let anyone in?" I asked. "Not even you?"

"I'm afraid not," Jonathan said. "It has always been Niko's way to withdraw from society when a new idea strikes."

"But he'll attend the party at the Vanderbilts' tonight," Phoebe said. "At least we believe so."

Jonathan frowned. "As you have said, and yet I am not certain. Niko can be a stubborn creature when it comes to his experiments. I do, however, hope to convince him of the necessity of his appearance."

As they chatted of our plans for the next twenty-six hours I tried to listen, tried to nod at the appropriate times. But their voices faded in and out, going smeary and warped.

Delayed shock, I realized, as I brought up a series of facts and figures, letting them roll through my vision in the hope that logic might counteract the cascade of symptoms. *A common reaction to emotional or psychological trauma.*

Heightened perception. Check. My skin felt too tight. And what the hell was that smell drifting in the window?

The aftereffects of excess adrenaline, which can bring on extreme fatigue or nervousness. Check. A burned, metallic taste on the back of my tongue. Muscles sore from exertion. So, so tired.

Shallow breathing. Difficulty concentrating. Trembling. Check. Check. Check.

I shifted, trying to make a bit more space. But with Phoebe on one side and Mac on the other, there was little room. *Too tight. Too tight. Got to breathe. Need air.*

Oh, and nausea, I realized. *That's a symptom we can add to Wikipedia.*

"Hope?" Collum's eyes narrowed on me. "What's wrong?"

"N-nothing."

Jonathan was watching me, his expression soft with concern. "Stop the coach!" he called. "At once."

The carriage jerked to a shuddering halt and I bolted, crawling over Mac and stumbling down the steps to the sidewalk.

Phoebe hopped down beside me as I doubled over, retching. "It's all right. Just breathe. You're doing fine."

Mac, Collum, and Jonathan stepped out and without a word, made a ring around us, using their bodies as a shield from passersby.

The sickness was subsiding. I cleared my throat, hacking and spitting in a most unladylike manner, one that probably alarmed the gentlemanly Jonathan to the core, though he said nothing.

I couldn't seem to stop the tears. I didn't know if it was from the dry heaves or just a profound relief at *not* having had a steel instrument jammed into my eyeball. At *not* becoming another Annabelle Allen.

Yeah, that was probably it.

Without a word, Phoebe wrapped her arms around me. We held on for a long time, both of us aware of how bad it could have been. Finally, snotty and hoarse, we told the boys we were ready to go.

The closer I got to stepping back into the carriage, the more my pulse raced. The thought of being crammed up in that small space for even one block sent my gut into another rebellion.

"I, uh, think I'm going to walk for a bit."

Collum started to protest, but something in my face stopped him. Sighing, he snatched his coat from the carriage floor where I'd dropped it, and draped it over my shoulders.

"Wrap this around you," he asked. "Don't want you catching pneumonia before they've invented penicillin, aye?"

CHAPTER 35

BY THE TIME WE'D GONE A COUPLE OF BLOCKS, I WAS starting to regret the whole "walking barefoot through New York City" plan. The icy March wind—a mere annoyance while we were inside the carriage—now seemed dead set on bowling me over. A freezing mist floated from the narrow strip of sky overhead and clung to every inch of exposed skin, turning my bare feet into meaty hunks of ice.

But I could breathe again, and ... I was free. A little frostbite? *Meh*.

I tried to hide it when I started limping.

Something was happening down the block. Angry shouts erupted and carried toward us. At the corner, we saw traffic come to a screeching halt. A buggy slewed to the left, causing the wagon driver behind it to haul on the reins to avoid T-boning the smaller vehicle.

Barrels rolled from the wagon bed and burst upon the macadam. The scent of vinegar wafted toward us as a hundred green, tubular objects rolled into the street.

A horse in the same smoky shade as the sky careened around the corner. Its rider was leaning low over the animal's back, a slouch hat shading his face as he dashed in and around the wagons and buggies, never slowing as he twined his way through the gridlock. Pedestrians scurried for the sidewalk. The rumble of irritation rose. Police whistles shrilled. People cursed and hurled produce at the rider. Something smacked him in the chest and splattered. He ducked the vegetative missiles until he reached the clear strip of road that ran between the backlog of wagons. The horse broke into a dead run.

And I turned to stone, because I knew that rider. No one on this earth moved with the same graceful fluidity.

"Bran."

Phoebe squeezed my arm and bounced on her toes beside me. "Told you he'd be here soon."

Collum muttered under his breath.

A few yards from our little group, two enterprising newsboys darted out between a couple of the wagons and dropped to their knees, snatching up handfuls of the stray pickles that had rolled down the street toward us.

"Dammit!" Collum cried, already running as he shouted. "Stop!"

Collum bolted down the narrow alley between the stalled conveyances. Bran's mouth dropped open when he saw the oblivious kids directly in his path. Collum reached the boys and grabbed the backs of their jackets to haul them aside.

But the boys scratched and spat, unwilling to let the brawny stranger manhandle them away from their prize.

It was too late anyway. The spirited horse had no intention of slowing. Collum and Bran had time to exchange one look before Collum yanked the boys against his chest and dropped to his knees, curling his body over them both.

Bran's gaze skipped left and right, but there was no way out. Only feet away, he jerked up hard on the reins. The gray responded with exquisite execution and soared up and over the huddled threesome.

"My God," Jonathan breathed. "Magnificent."

Phoebe gasped. "Whoa."

Bran shot a look over his shoulder. Collum rose, and while the newsboys dashed off, cursing him, Bran's head dropped in obvious relief.

Jonathan turned to Mac in alarm as Bran cleared the wagons and steered the horse toward us. "I say, is that man intending to run us down?"

Mac chuckled. "Not us." He jutted a chin in my direction as he and Jonathan scooted to the inner edge of the sidewalk. "Just her."

The dusky animal threw up its head, barely skidding to a halt before Bran was off its back. Eyes wild, cheeks red with cold and exertion, he gripped my shoulders.

"Hope!" Panic hoarsened his voice. "Are you all right? Were you hurt? Why is there blood on your face? God's sake, someone talk to me, please!"

Shaking, my chin quivering like a kid who'd lost her mom at the mall, I looked up at him.

"Hey, Bran," I managed. "You've got some gunk on your cheek."

He stared down at me, his gaze unwavering as he swiped at his face and rubbed thumb and fingers together. "Hothouse tomatoes, if I'm not mistaken. Shame, really. Tomatoes are quite costly this time of year."

"Yeah. Shame."

My voice cracked, and with a moan, Bran crushed me to his chest. I could barely breathe, but this confinement I did not mind. Wool scratched against my cheek as I burrowed into him, breathing the spice of a cedar chest and damp wool and a citrusy bite of some nineteenth-century soap. But beneath all that lingered a hint of apple and the fresh, cold aroma of an icy forest.

His heart was in jackhammer mode beneath my ear. Despite the cold and fog and passersby who clucked their tongues, I could have stayed that way for the rest of my life.

When Bran eventually let go and stepped back, I became suddenly and acutely aware that beneath Collum's coat I wore only a shabby smock. My hair looked—as Nurse Hannah had once declared—like cats had been clawing at it, and my frozen feet were caked in filth. I hadn't bathed in two days and . . . Oh God, I needed a toothbrush.

That slow grin appeared, and I wanted to sink beneath the crust of the earth. As an unfortunate blusher—no graceful rose-tinged cheeks for this girl—my face and neck heated up and I knew that now, adding to the entire Hope Walton wreckage, my face was turning into an appalling patchwork of red and white blotches.

"Okay," I said. "You can stop staring. And I know it's bad, so you don't have to lie."

"All right." Bran's head tilted as if giving my appearance a thorough inspection. He spoke very seriously, but his eyes were gleaming like sunlight through stained glass as he said, "Hmm. While I do admit you look a bit like something my dog once dragged from the shrubbery . . . I believe I can bear it."

He kissed me then, and if it had been dark, the stars would have fallen from the sky to shower us in their silvery light.

Behind us, someone groaned. Pretty sure it was Collum.

"So-o," Phoebe said. "This is sweet and all, but could we maybe get out of the rain sometime today?"

She was right. In the last few seconds the mist had thickened into a drizzle. Funny. I hadn't even noticed.

Collum gave Bran a guy chin bob. "Nice jump."

Bran nodded. "Thanks. And I appreciate the intervention. Murdering innocent children was definitely not on today's agenda."

Mac clamped Bran's shoulder as he and Jonathan hurried

past, collars raised against the dampness. "Good show, son," he said.

Phoebe bussed Bran's cheek and trotted after them. I started to follow, but my feet—apparently having decided to abstain from any kind of forward motion—stayed in place. I toppled forward.

Bran caught me before I could face-plant into the pavement.

"Thanks," I said, trying to coax my now thoroughly numb feet to just *move* already.

"Begging your pardon, milady."

In a perfect imitation of a medieval nobleman, he scooped me up and deposited me on the horse's back. I was shuddering now with wet and cold and okay, the fact that Bran was *here*.

He leapt up behind me, unbuttoned his wool greatcoat, and wrapped it around me on top of Collum's. I nestled against his chest, luxuriating in the combined warmth.

"All things considered," he said, "I generally find the horse a more expedient mode of transportation than crawling down the sidewalk." As we trotted off through the slowly clearing traffic, I felt his chuckle rumble against my back. "Except when on a boneheaded mare who decides she is the one in charge." Pressing against me, he called over my shoulder, "Run loose like that again, you mad beast, and it's straight to the glue factory for you. And trust me when I say in this age that is no idle threat."

The horse turned her huge head and eyeballed him as if to say, *Sure, dude.*

Bran sighed theatrically. "Women."

As we trotted through the streets of late Victorian New York City, Bran's arm tight about my waist, I began to relax. Though I could no longer feel my feet and lower legs, the rest of my body grew toasty as he cuddled me close.

The shakes subsided, and my blood began to race as his fingers traced along my waistline through the thin material.

"I'm sorry," he said quietly near my ear.

"Hmm?"

"I should have been there."

"Oh," I muttered, sleepy. "'S oka—"

"No," he interrupted. "It is not. And I swear that if I hadn't known you were in the best of hands I would never have . . . Well, it's difficult to explain. You see, Gabriella and I had to . . ."

I stiffened, and my body twitched away from his. The coat dropped to puddle at my waist.

"Oh, no. No," Bran hastened to add. "God, no! Don't —don't pull away. It isn't like that at all. Please, allow me to explain."

After a moment, I let him settle the coat around me again, though the blissful warmth had faded and I was now wide awake.

But the truth was, I didn't want to be *that* girl. Jealous. Spiteful. Despising the only person who watched Bran's back when Celia was around. Gabriella had covered for him so he could spend time with me. And she hated Celia almost as much as I did. I shoved the green-eyed monster way, way down and let myself relax back against him.

Bran started to speak, but had to pull up short to avoid running down three children, dressed to the eyeballs in expensive school uniforms, who darted out into the road before us. Their frazzled nanny trotted in their wake, pushing an old-fashioned perambulator. When I saw a baby's chubby fists wave up from inside her snug conveyance, I was surprised at the sudden and fierce longing for my sister.

I miss you, Ellie.

I cleared the obstruction from my throat as Bran put his heels to the horse. "So," I said. "What happened today?"

What was more important than rescuing me?

"We were preparing to leave for the institute when I received a message from Gabriella that said Blasi was looking for me. I didn't want to leave, Hope. But Mac and Phoebe convinced me I had to maintain my cover. God, you don't know how hard it was not to storm in there after you."

No, I thought. You *don't know how hard it was.*

"I had to pretend I'd been holed up in a . . . in a brothel," he said. "It was the only thing I could say that Blasi would believe."

We rounded the corner. The carriage was parked just this side of the Waldorf near a service alley. As they spotted us, the others climbed out and gestured for us to turn in there.

Bran trotted the gray swiftly toward a servant's entrance and hopped down before the others reached us.

"I want you to know that I've never been so afraid in my entire life," Bran said, his eyes locked on mine. "I couldn't survive it, Hope. If something had happened to you, I—" He shook his head, for once unable to summon the right words.

From my perch on the horse's back, I stared down into the face of the boy I'd loved since I was four years old. All his native cockiness had vanished, leaving only guilt and misery in its wake.

"Please forgive me," he whispered.

In answer, I jumped down into his arms. He held me so tight. As the others bustled down the alley, I pulled back. Searching the blue and green eyes I knew so well, I decided to shove the last, niggling seeds of doubt far beneath the surface of my mind. I would allow them no light, no air. I would let them suffocate and fade forever from my mind.

Whatever happened, he's here now. We're together, and that's all that matters, right?

CHAPTER 36

Oscar Tschirky met us at the door.

"Mr. MacPherson," he cried, and quickly escorted us out of the rain and through a humid, bleach-scented laundry to the service elevator. "Oh, I cannot tell you of my relief upon receiving your message just now. I only pray you can forgive me for asking you to enter this way, instead of welcoming you in the lobby proper. I was, of course, only thinking of Miss Randolph's comfort."

The Waldorf's employees were so well trained, the young elevator operator didn't so much as flinch when I entered wearing little more than a man's coat. With my bare feet and sodden, stringy hair, I must've looked exactly like what I was, an escaped mental patient.

"Oh, my dear Miss Randolph." The little maître d'hôtel bowed low before me. "I was so grateful to hear of your recent, ah ... liberation. Of course, the news of Dr. Carson's criminalities had already begun to spread even before this morning's events. Several of New York's best have gone to retrieve their beloved family members, whom they entrusted into the doctor's care in good faith." Oscar Tschirky tsked. "I do hope the fiend is punished to the full extent of the law."

Bran wrapped an arm around me while Mac put in, "Please excuse Miss Randolph, as she's feeling a bit peaked just the now."

Oscar nodded, obviously dying to know what exactly had occurred, but entirely too polite—or good at his job—to press any further.

At the door to our suite, Bran tugged me a few feet away. "Listen," he said. "You need to know that there's something else going on. Something to do with Blasi. I don't believe my mother or Flint was aware of it before they sent us, and I've no proof as of yet, but something feels off."

From my bedraggled hair to my stinging feet, exhaustion sang inside me. The hotel's long, carpeted hallway seemed to expand and contract, and I was struck suddenly with the oddest certainty that we were all inside the belly of a great ship. Outside these walls, a mighty storm bore down upon us, intensifying with every second. Waves slammed the hull again and again and again, and I knew there was no way we'd ever outrun the deluge. I closed my eyes as the seemingly solid floor beneath my feet began to dip and sway.

Waves and waves and more waves slammed into me on a rip tide of exhaustion.

I keeled to the side, and Bran caught me, his brows low . . . worried . . . as I snorted. "My luck it's the freaking *Titanic*."

"Hope?"

I waved it off. "Nothing. Just tired."

"What are you talking about, Cameron?"

My eyes shot open. Collum stood to one side, his voice raspy as he asked, "What feels off?"

To his credit, Bran didn't hedge. "I'm not certain. Not yet anyway. All I know is that Blasi has been acting very strange. Very secretive."

"And?" Collum asked.

"Your guess is as good as mine at this point, mate."

An itchy, uncomfortable silence stretched between the three of us.

It was Bran who had the willingness to break it. "I have to go," he said. "As I'm supposedly debauching myself at some seedy underground gaming establishment in Hell's Kitchen at the moment, it wouldn't do for one of Blasi's people to step off the lift on the wrong floor and see me going in or out of this suite. According to Oscar, no one knows or will know that you have returned. Still, I can't imagine it will take much for word to spread."

"Yeah." I glanced over at the open door where, bless Oscar's heart, it looked as if half the Waldorf staff was lined up preparing to wait on us. "I bet the whole hotel will know soon enough."

Collum's steady hazel eyes bored into Bran. "You'll be attending the soiree tonight, I understand?"

Bran nodded. "Yes. Blasi managed to secure an invitation, though I do not know how. He's hoping to get Tesla alone."

"Then we'll just have to make sure he doesn't."

Collum stalked off into the suite. Shaking his head, Bran watched him go. "I've said it before and I'll say it again." He looked down at me, smiling. "The old boy does grow on you, doesn't he? Like a fungus. Or a particularly mealy wart."

A chuckle whuffed from my lungs. "He does."

Bran's eyes crinkled at the corners, and I blinked as a wisp of memory floated up.

After slipping his mother's medallion over his head, the little boy had taken her hand. He never cried as they ran deeper and deeper into the forest. But his blue and green eyes had looked so sad. After hours in the cold, the little girl wanted to comfort him. When she saw a cluster of snowdrops near the log they huddled beside, she had plucked one and handed it to him. The little boy had gazed down at the delicate white blossom for a long time. And when he looked up at her, his eyes had crinkled at the corners as he gave her a tremulous smile.

"Bran?"

"Hmm?"

"I'm ... I'm sorry about your mother." My voice broke. "Your real mother. In the institute, I—I remembered what happened to her. I remember when you took this from her."

I slid a finger beneath the leather cord and tugged it free of his shirtfront. The worn silver medallion felt warm against my palm as I clutched it tight. "I'm so sorry," I repeated. "If my grandfather and I had never come to your village—"

Bran tilted his forehead against mine. "Shh," he whispered. "None of that matters now. And if you'd never come, I would be nothing but dust in some forest grave. Your bones would lie in some ancient churchyard. We never would have met. Don't look back, Hope. Never wonder. That path is closed to us now. But this one is just beginning."

His breath warm against my lips, he whispered, "Now get some rest. I will see you tonight, no matter what. And Hope, promise me you'll be careful, all right?"

Trying to be flippant, and failing miserably, I said, "You too."

Bran's fingers slid into my hair as he kissed me. It was a soft, sweet kiss that was over way too soon. Though not so soon that I didn't feel the hunger waken and stretch inside me. Not so soon that I missed the growly moan that rumbled through Bran's chest where it pressed me against the wall. Panting, he cursed under his breath as his hands trailed down my arms. He pulled away. In his absence, cold rushed in. By the time my eyes fluttered open, he was gone.

Inside our suite, a phalanx of servants waited to cater to our every need. The moment we entered I was draped in thick, warmed towels and whisked off to the elaborate bathroom. Before I knew it, I was stripped and immersed up to my chin in a clawfoot tub full of scented, steaming water.

While one maid worked lather into my ratty hair, rinsing it with cool rose water, another worked on my scraped and battered feet.

After helping me into an embroidered dressing gown

and matching slippers, Lida, a round-faced, Prussian girl sat me in a low chair and combed sweet almond oil through my tangles. Lethargy dragged at me. In a half-fugue state, I drifted in and out as warmth from the fire soaked into my bones. Every once in a while, the image of Carson's ice pick would glint over me and I would jerk upright, a scream trapped behind my teeth.

On a stool behind me, the sturdy Lida hummed quietly as she combed and twisted, combed and twisted, drying my hair into gleaming ringlets that flowed down my back like twirls of obsidian. With a final murmur of satisfaction, she arranged the mass of it on top of my head and secured it with a few jeweled pins. She passed me a silvered hand mirror. "Does miss like?"

Curls she'd artfully left unpinned brushed my cheek and tumbled down my back. I smiled, barely recognizing myself. "Yes, thank you, Lida."

She picked up my filthy hospital smock with thumb and forefinger. "Is miss to be wishing this is washed?"

"No," I told her. "Miss is to be wishing that is burned."

Lida nodded. "Yes, this I would be wishing too."

Mac had dismissed all the servants by the time I entered the living room.

"How can you even *think* of not telling the man?" Phoebe, ensconced in a robe of heavy silk the color of aged ivory, perched sideways on the couch with her feet tucked beneath Doug's thigh. But her face was hot with anger as she snapped at the freshly shaved Collum.

"If your children were going to die because of some stupid mistake you could easily prevent, wouldn't you want to know of it?"

Collum's tight lips opened as he started to respond. Then he saw me and swallowed back whatever he'd been about to say.

"It's not as simple as that, Phee," Mac responded in a calm, reasonable voice. "Jonathan wants to know absolutely nothing of his own future or that of his family. You heard him say so yourself."

"Aye, but you can't seriously believe that extends to the accidental murder of his own babes, can you?"

Wearing black tuxedo pants and undershirts, Mac and Collum were ransacking a buffet, balancing china plates piled with crustless sandwich triangles and petite pastries.

Phoebe saw me. "Here," she said. "Hope agrees with me, don't you?"

"Of course I do. We have to find some way to tell him. We can't just let it happen."

While Phoebe graced her brother and grandfather with a triumphant *see-I-told-you-so* look, I was smiling at Doug, who grinned back so big, his cheeks lifted the wire spectacles. He started to get up but I waved him back.

"Don't get up."

I leaned down and gave him a fierce hug. Doug's liquid brown eyes looked huge behind the magnified lenses as he shook his head. "Gah, Hope. I was that scared when you didn't come down the chute after me. Then I heard you scream, and I tried to climb back up. But the damn chute was too steep. I—I'm sorry for leaving you there."

His face, guilt-ridden and miserable, tore at my heart.

"Douglas Eugene Carlyle." I gave my best Aunt Lucinda impression, earning a smile from him and a massive, grateful grin from Phoebe. "I would have murdered you twice over if you'd come back for me. Besides," I said, dropping the awful accent, "they would have gotten you too, and who knows what might've happened. I'd say we're both pretty lucky."

"Agreed." Mac spoke through a mouthful of pastry. "We're all here. We're all safe now. And that's the end of that. Now it's time to discuss what comes next. We have"—he glanced at the intricate clock on the mantel—"seventeen hours and thirty-eight minutes until we must be back inside that dreadful cattle tunnel. And we haven't even spoken with Tesla yet, much less convinced him to destroy the device. So let's start—"

A knock on the door interrupted him. Collum, whose keen eyes hadn't left me since I'd entered, gulped down the rest of his lemonade and went to answer it.

Sniffing the air, I moaned. "Is that coffee?"

Phoebe started to get up. "You sit. I'll get it."

"Och. Oh, no ye dinna." In my most outrageous burr, I said, "You'll be a-stayin' right where ye are then, lassie. I'll be fetchin' a cup o' the bean fer meeself, ye ken?"

She and Doug exchanged a look before bursting into

roars of laughter. "Wh-what?" Phoebe wheezed. "What in blazes was that?"

I tried to look insulted. "Um, that was *Moira?* Hello?"

Mac—whose laugh reminded me of the sound my horse makes when she has a gas pain—bent, hands on his knees. "Oh, my sweet girl," he said, shaking his head. "I love you dearly, but ye sound more like a leprechaun with tonsillitis than my darling Moira."

I scrunched my face at them, but I was grinning when I turned to pour the rich coffee into my cup. As I watched the cream swirl and disperse, I felt my energy begin to return.

"You gotta admit," I said, plopping in a few sugar cubes, "I'm getting better, right?"

By the time they quit laughing, I was snugged down on the opposite sofa, slippered feet tucked beneath me as I sipped.

Collum returned from the small foyer, laden to his chin with a variety of white, ribbon-tied boxes and a stack of creamy envelopes clamped between his teeth.

"No, no. Don't mind me. Stay. Enjoy your comedy hour. I've got it," he grumbled through the mouthful of ivory paper, then bent and let the envelopes drop to a table.

"Ooh! What's all this, then?" Phoebe jumped up and began pawing at the packages, causing Collum to juggle and stumble or face dropping the whole lot.

"Dammit, Phee," he grunted at his sister. "Hold your water." He dumped the boxes on the sofa beside me. "Here.

Have at it, you animal. The boy who delivered them said it came from Madame Belisle."

Phoebe began mauling the lovely heavy cardboard, shop paper, and painted teakwood boxes, snarling the ice-blue ribbons into hopeless knots.

Collum looked over at his sister, shaking his head, though I thought I saw his features soften with fondness. "She's always been like this," he told me. "I remember one year, couple of days before Christmas, there were all these presents under the tree, aye? Phoebe was just a wee thing, but she kept sneaking in to unwrap them, even after Gram took a wooden spoon to her."

Across the room, Mac nodded, grin widening with the memory as Collum went on.

"Well, we got up Christmas morn to find that she'd woken during the night. Gone downstairs. And unwrapped every single one. Knowing she'd have her hide tanned again once Gram found out, she tried to rewrap them so we wouldn't know." Collum barked a laugh that pulled wide grins from everyone in the room. "Da had to cut the tape out of her hair."

Phoebe looked up at her brother, a scrap of the brown shop paper stuck to her chin. "I remember that," she said. "Took months for my bangs to grow back out. But I got an Easy-Bake Oven. Gram wanted to make me wait to play with it, but Da only laughed and said that if I was that determined, then it wouldn't matter where they hid it, I'd only find it and end up burning the house down around our ears."

Doug chuckled. "I was still in Edinburgh when that crime was committed," he said. "Though I do recall my first Christmas at the manor when a certain redhead *somehow* convinced me to spend the night hiding behind the drapes because she'd decided to find out if Santa Claus was real."

Mac's shoulders shook as he laughed. "Aye, and as I remember it, the two of you fell asleep. When we couldn't find you the next morning, we spent hours tearing the house clean apart searching for you. Moira got herself all worked up, convinced you had somehow gotten down into the Dim's cavern and been whisked back in time, never to be seen again."

The four of them exchanged more comical, nostalgic stories. And though I smiled along, I squirmed at the sharp little ache that pinched at me, wondering what my life would've been like had Mom brought me to Christopher Manor to live, instead of marrying my dad and moving to America. If instead of sedate Christmas mornings with my new books ... always books ... I had been one of those hiding in the drapes, or having my bangs snipped to the scalp.

That's a twisty path, I realized. *Your what-if road is too freaking crooked, Walton; better step off. If you let yourself follow it, you'll start thinking things like ... What if Mom had never found me? What if she hadn't brought me back with her to this time?*

What if I'd never been taken from the sixteenth century? What if I'd spent all my Christmases with the man and woman who'd given me life? What if I was now nothing more than a bit of dust and bone, beneath a crumbling headstone in some old parish churchyard, like Bran said? What if. What if. What if? No. That is a path I do not want to tread.

Mac passed out the envelopes. "One for each of us, looks like."

I hefted the thick vellum. Inside the envelope was a stiff card, embossed at the top with a swirling *V.* The gilt-engraved invitation read:

The company of Miss Hope Randolph is requested to attend a soiree at the home of William K. Vanderbilt, on the evening of Wednesday, 13th of March, current year.
8 o'clock p.m.

Number 660 5th Avenue,
New York City, New York.

At the bottom, scrawled in a childish hand: *I do so hope you will come. Consuelo V.*

Phoebe whooped as she ripped hers open. "You did it, Hope! We're in! You must've made an impression on Connie."

"Yeah." I smiled through the pang of guilt. "Yeah."

I knew I'd had no choice, and besides, what I'd told Connie Vanderbilt hadn't been a complete falsehood, had it? I wasn't being shipped off to Scotland to marry some guy I barely knew, of course. But the rest of it? That I understood.

There was an expression for it. In my own time, casual overuse had stolen away most of its original meaning, leaving it flabby and worn as an old sock.

But for Connie, the condition of being "hopelessly in love" existed within a very literal context. Like most women from time immemorial, she had no choice. No hope. Her history was already written, and she would never, *ever* end up with the man she truly loved.

Would a future Viator one day look upon me with the same pity I felt for her, knowing that—for Bran and me —the phrase fit all too well?

My hands were shaking as I turned to the packages beside me and began ripping into them, hiding my face from the others as I emulated Phoebe's careless abandon.

"Whoa." Fabric whispered in the sudden quiet as Phoebe tugged out a shimmering ball gown of frothy azure tulle. She held the exquisite garment up against herself. "Gotta give it to old Frenchie," she said. "She might've been a hateful old bird, but she knows her way around a needle and thread."

CHAPTER 37

MY OWN MADAME BELISLE CREATION DID A PRETTY
damn good job of disputing that assertion.

I spread the gown across the couch and stepped back,
thinking some distance might make it look a bit less re-
pulsive.

Yeah. No.

"The bloody thing looks like a strawberry and kiwi
smoothie left out to spoil in the sun," Collum commented.

"Thanks," I said, with a face-melting glare. "That helps."

"Boy, Hope, you must've slagged off that old bat but
good," Doug said, and I was pretty sure he wasn't joking.

"We could switch?" Phoebe offered. "I'd just need to cut
the length off that one and add it to mine and—"

"That's okay," I told her. "I'll survive. Who cares?"

I did. I cared. I knew I shouldn't. I couldn't stop staring,
though the taffeta skirt's riotous floral pattern seemed specifically designed to scorch the retinas. Silk, in the approximate
shade of an overchewed piece of bubblegum, made up the

bodice. Added to that, the wads of white and magenta lace that capped each sleeve looked like bandages crusted in old blood.

I averted my eyes. Told myself to stop being ridiculous.

Bigger fish to fry, Walton. Way more balls in the air, or some other worn-out metaphor.

But I was going to a ball.

A freaking ball.

And . . . maybe I just wanted to look pretty? For once.

Phoebe's eyes had narrowed. They flicked from the gown to me and back again. Hands on her hips, she shook her head.

"No."

"No what?"

"Just . . . no." She stood, walked over, and snatched the gown in one hand and yanked me up off the sofa with the other. "No dawdling, Hope, we've work to do. Thatta girl. Hurry now. Rock and roll."

"What exactly are we doing?" I asked as I stumbled along behind her.

"I," she said, "am playing fairy godmother. And you, my love, are Cinda—bloody—rella." At the door to my bedroom, she stopped and yelled over her shoulder at the guys, "Scissors, stat!"

She made me put it on. When I stepped out from behind the patterned screen, she blew out a long breath.

"Jesus wept." She covered her mouth in mock—or maybe real—dismay.

"Right?" I answered. "But can you really fix it? We don't have much time."

She whistled. "What *did* you do to that stuck-up old croissant, anyway?"

I could only shrug as I moved in front of the full-length mirror. "Oh God, it looks like a wound infection."

"Hmm."

My head shot up. I knew that "Hmm." Phoebe was studying the dress, teeth sunk into her bottom lip. I'd been blown away by my friend's capabilities under pressure more than a few times.

"The sleeves. They go first."

I hugged her so tight, she squeaked. "All right, all right. Where are my blasted scissors?"

We ignored Collum's irritated knocks and Doug's sporadic time checks. The whole thing took less than thirty minutes. By the time Mac intervened, we were both ready.

Phoebe threw open the bedroom door. "Come in, then, and tell me what you think."

"It's a dress, Phee," Collum snapped as he stalked through. "I don't give a . . ."

He looked in my direction, and did not finish the thought.

"So it looks okay?" I asked. "She hasn't let me see it yet."

Bobbing his head up and down, Collum said, "Aye, you'll do."

"Thanks." I said it with sarcasm, but I didn't really care. I knew it was better. Anything was better.

"Voilà!" Phoebe pulled off the sheet that she had placed over the mirror.

I blinked at the transformation.

"Whoa," I said. "You. You are amazing."

Phoebe had first ripped off the sleeves. At her direction, I'd then removed the topmost petticoat so she could strip off a layer of crinoline. The ivory now swirled in drapes over the flattened skirt, muting the migraine-inducing pattern. After shearing away every thread of lace and extraneous ribbon, only dainty silk now held up the much-lowered bodice.

The design was fresh and delicate. Instead of being over-whelmed by the gaudy ornamentation, my pale skin and dark hair emerged. Ribbons encrusted with seed pearls were threaded through my gathered hair. I turned from side to side, enjoying the tickle as stray curls brushed my now-bare shoulders.

Phoebe smushed in beside me. Her reflection grinning at mine.

"You," she said, "are going to send the lads to their knees."

"Not once they get a look at you."

I wasn't lying, either. In shimmering tulle that matched her eyes, Phoebe was simply stunning. Auburn hair curled and was swept back with jeweled combs. Silver threads glinted, showing off her curves. She was so vibrant that if anyone thought too hard about it, they'd realize she was playing dress-up. Phoebe MacPherson simply burned too bright for the staid Victorian age.

"Jesus, Coll," she called as she saw her brother still gaping at me. "Close your mouth, aye? You'll catch a fly."

The sun was well set by the time Jonathan Carlyle returned.

"What did you find out, Mr. Carlyle?" Collum asked, before the man had even removed his gloves and shiny top hat.

Jonathan dropped his things on a tabletop and tilted his head at the crystal decanters of liquor grouped on a table nearby. "May I?"

After pouring two fingers' worth and taking a significant slug, he turned back to us.

"My dear friend Tesla, being of a somewhat recalcitrant nature even at the best of times, was in a state of agitation I have rarely witnessed. He initially refused to be disturbed in any way, barring even *my* entrance. When he finally allowed me in, I—I tried to explain how I'd changed my mind about the enhancement. How I'd been deceived as to the motives of the people who brought me the plans. How I regretted having brought them to his notice."

Jonathan winced. "We, ah ... we very nearly came to blows over the matter. This, from a man I've known for fifteen years. Niko was quite vexed and—upon my arrival —was behaving in a manner that could be considered odd, even for him. I do not yet know the source of this distress. The good news, however, is that he shall be in attendance at the ball tonight. Even Nikola Tesla cannot so insult his benefactors as to withdraw from the occasion." Jonathan shot back the rest of the whiskey. "I have, at least, persuaded him to ride with us, where you shall speak with him at your leisure. He awaits us now."

Jonathan set the glass down on a small table next to me. From the remains of the drink rose a sharp alcoholic scent. But beneath the sting lay more subtle notes. Peat and smoke and heather. The scent of the Highlands. The back of my throat ached suddenly with missing it . . . with missing home.

"Are all the security measures we set still in place?" Mac asked.

Jonathan nodded. "Yes. Men front and back. Sergeant Peters was grateful to add his skills to the crew we hired. They've been apprised only that there is a chance of vandalism, but they are ready for any sort of approach. Though I employed them, even I had difficulty in getting past."

"And what did you tell him of us?"

Jonathan sighed. His head seemed to sink down into his shoulders, and I could tell that lying to his friend had cost him. "Only that you were old and dear family friends. People I trust beyond measure. And that you are aware of our . . . situation." Jonathan Carlyle pressed his lips together, obviously reluctant to speak, but unable to stop himself. "But I feel I must ask . . . The fire? All of Niko's work destroyed? Is it . . . is it truly inevitable? I admit, it pains me greatly to know this and yet be unable to stop it, or even warn my friend."

Mac bowed his head. Collum stared out the window.

Doug, who'd so longed to visit Tesla and his lab, looked devastated. Tonight, his great hero would lose everything he'd ever worked for. "Jonathan," he said. "I am as sick about Professor Tesla's lab as anyone can be. You'll know that in the time from which we come, I am the caretaker of his . . . y-your . . . *our* device. I've studied the man and his inventions my whole life. And while I want more than anything to preserve his life's work, the fire tonight is one of those things we call a sentinel event. A historical incident too well documented for there to be any kind of alteration."

Phoebe rose to her feet and took Jonathan's hands between her own. "I wish we could tell you a different tale. You've no idea how much. But as we explained in the beginning, it is from you, yourself, that we've learned the rules on how this all works, aye?"

Collum and Mac exchanged a glance. Mac stood first. "You'll remember, Jon, the fragments from your own journal we showed you when first we met?"

Jonathan nodded, a smile tugging his lips.

Mac nodded. "Just so."

We'd thought long and hard about how best to convince Jonathan of our authenticity. In the end, it had been my mother's suggestion to let the man's own words do our talking for us. After careful consideration, we'd selected several journal entries, cutting and pasting to ensure none could cause any sort of ripple.

And though two had specifically mentioned how certain events in history could be neither changed nor altered, Phoebe told me that when they'd revealed the pages to him, it was the last entry that had caused the greatest impact.

Jonathan Carlyle reached into the breast pocket of his tuxedo jacket and quickly scanned the entry. I couldn't read the words from where I stood, but I knew which one he'd kept.

My son is born! I have a son! Today is the most glorious day that any man has ever lived! He is hale, with a cry fit to rattle the windows. I admit here that I wept when I first beheld the sight of my Julia, lying there in a measure beyond beauty as she handed our child into my arms.

"I know we thought, were the child a boy," Julia said to me, "that we would call him Mordecai, after your great-uncle. But he does not look like a Mordecai, does he, darling?"

Gazing down at the squirming bundle, I laughed and told her, "No, beloved. He most assuredly does not. In fact, he looks to me as if his name should be . . ."

We'd cut the last word, not wanting to influence the baby's name any further. It didn't really bother any of us that we'd nixed the name Mordecai. We figured Henry Luis Carlyle owed us for that one.

Jonathan brushed a finger over the page, his gaze wistful and very far away.

"Henry." He looked up and grinned broadly. "He'll be called Henry, though I shall be careful not to speak the name until this very moment."

Jonathan said nothing for a while as he examined each of our carefully blank expressions. He sighed. "You're certain of Niko's safety? There was ... shall be ... no injury to his person or that of anyone else?"

"No one will be hurt," Mac answered. "Of that, you can rest assured."

CHAPTER 38

THANKFULLY, IT WAS JUST A FEW BLOCKS TO TESLA'S. As Doug and Mac stepped down onto the sidewalk, two figures emerged from the shadows.

"State your business," declared a gruff voice.

"Stand down, Peters," Jonathan ordered as he disembarked. "These men are with me, and shall join you on your watch tonight. Has there yet been any sign of trouble?"

Sergeant Peters stepped out beneath the streetlight. He no longer wore the navy uniform of the Greenwood security, but the pea coat and flat cap of a civilian. "Seen the same carriage ride by three times within an hour. It was covered, and they changed out the driver. But I marked it." He cocked his chin at Mac and Doug. "You gents armed?"

Mac grinned as he eased his jacket back, revealing two large revolvers that hung from his belt. "Good to see you again, Sergeant." He gave Peters a crisp nod, then repeated the gesture for the burly blonde at his side.

The Vanderbilts' Petit Chateau occupied the entire corner of Fifth Avenue and Fifty-Second Street. A five-story behemoth of pale stone, peaked shale roofs, and small balconies, the mansion would've looked more at home on a sunny hill in the French countryside. Like bony witches' fingers, slim medieval turrets protruded skyward. And seated atop the main construction lay a high-pitched gable with three odd, porthole-type windows.

As the carriages queued up to disgorge their silk-and-satin-clad guests through the decadent front gate, I suddenly got why the snobby Caroline Astor had declared the house a "monstrosity of extravagance."

"Crap on a cracker," Phoebe whispered when we took our spot behind the long line of glossy black coaches. "This place is insane. Like one of those movies where they keep the murderous aunt locked up in the attic."

"Or a Daphne du Maurier novel come to life."

Nikola Tesla sat across from me. His knees bounced. He rocked back and forth. He shifted, and the fingers of one hand tapped a constant cadence on the other wrist. He seemed in a state of perpetual motion. When Tesla had emerged from the building and, without comment, climbed into the carriage, his gray-brown eyes had barely grazed over us. And yet, I knew in that single glance he'd forever memorized each and every one of our features.

Of course he did.

Just because we both possessed an eidetic memory doesn't mean that we processed that data at the same level. The man was beyond genius. My own "gifts" weren't even near the same ballpark. I may store all those massive skeins of information, but unlike myself, Nikola Tesla used every single strand.

I'd seen so many pictures of Tesla. Had basically papered my room with the man during a brief but intense preadolescent crush. And as I snuck glances, I saw that he looked much like the images I'd collected. Tall. Lanky. Handsome, with a slim mustache and spare, hawkish features. His clothes were immaculate, his posture perfect. But the pictures couldn't possibly capture the odd charisma or the frenetic energy that seemed to radiate from him.

Collum had wasted no time. "Mr. Tesla. We need to speak about the enhancement you—"

Ignoring him completely, Tesla scooted forward on his seat, leaning in almost too close to me, as though he didn't understand the logistics of personal space. Speaking in the sibilant accent of his Serbian birthplace, he said, "Jonathan says that you are like me, yes?"

Starstruck, I managed to nod. "I . . . yes. Yes, sir. I'm Hope Walton. My friends and I are all so honored to meet you, Professor—"

Apparently done with his version of the niceties, Tesla pounded on the roof. "Let us away," he called to the driver. Not even glancing in Collum's direction, he said, "There shall be no more talk of the device business until we are done here. I stay only long enough to speak with Vanderbilt and Astor. Then I must immediately return to my lab. There is much to do. At that time, you may state your case. This is my final word."

"Our Nikola," Phoebe whispered. "Quite the charmer, isn't he?"

Above our heads, every one of the mansion's myriad windows glowed with diffuse golden light. Music and the muffled sounds of laughter penetrated the stone walls. I secured my wrap around my bare shoulders, shivering beneath its heavy ivory silk as the five of us stepped from the carriage.

Phoebe tugged at her low neckline. "Ugh. Sure as sunset, this thing's gonna slip and show my girls. I should have taken it up an inch or so. And who are all those people watching us?"

The spectators, mostly middle-class, were obviously keen for a glimpse of New York's wealthiest and most prestigious inhabitants. A cadre of uniformed policemen held back the crowd as we funneled through the portal and into the Vanderbilts' fenced yard. Though I knew little about Hollywood, I had a feeling this was as close as I'd ever get to walking the red carpet.

"Speaking to that ..." Collum hurried after Tesla, who moved rudely past the queued guests, too impatient to wait his turn. A brilliant flash boomed from the portico just ahead where the host was posing for a photo with each guest in turn.

Tesla bounded up the steps, neatly cutting off a man with enormous sideburns and his affronted, bejeweled wife. "I say!" the man exclaimed.

"You say?" Tesla rounded on the man. "You say what?"

When the flummoxed man only opened and closed his mouth, Tesla scoffed and turned away. "Never understood that phrase. If you have words that need to be spoken, simply speak them and be done, yes?"

"Why, look here, Mina," cried a voice from the line. "It's our own little Niko!" A man stepped out of the queue and strode over to plant a hearty slap on Tesla's back.

Short and stubby, hair already going famously white, Mr. Thomas Alva Edison—creator of the light bulb and the direct current, holder of more than a hundred patents, and Tesla's most despised rival—grinned up at Tesla. A much younger woman in lavender ruffles tripped along as she hurried to join them. Bow tie askew, tuxedo coat misbuttoned and frayed at the hem, the nearly fifty-year-old inventor may've looked like someone's rumpled old uncle, but I noticed his leering smile did not reach his eyes.

Straightening his immaculate greatcoat, Tesla responded to his former employer in a voice flat as a sheet of paper. "Edison."

"I must say, Niko." Edison raised his voice just enough so that it carried past the fence and into the first few rows of spectators. "It's right unusual to see you keeping company with a . . . *female*."

Edison's emphasis on the word didn't go unnoticed by the avid crowd. The aging inventor paused, letting their whispered speculations spread.

"And here I thought you eschewed the company of ladies . . ." Another sly, deliberate pause. ". . . so you could pursue those little notions of yours."

Without a word of warning or the slightest hesitation, Nikola Tesla snaked his arm through mine, nearly yanking me off my feet when he hauled me up the steps to meet the host.

William Kissam Vanderbilt's buggy eyes tracked the inventor. "Why, Professor, I am honored. Welcome to my home."

Vanderbilt extended a hand in greeting. Tesla recoiled, though he quickly recovered. I felt a shudder run through him as he took a deep breath, then placed his gloved hand into Vanderbilt's. Their handshake was odd, and seemed to go on a bit too long. When it was done, Tesla spoke with a barely concealed grimace. "Even providing the relative safety of the glove," he said, "the touching of hands can often lead to illness. I would suggest—when next we gather—we propose an alternative greeting for members."

All the guests within earshot tittered. If Tesla noticed, he didn't react. But William Vanderbilt did. Baring his teeth, he spoke through them. "This is not the place for such a private discussion, Professor." Vanderbilt then reached up with his right hand and patted his lapel three times. Standing in front of him, I caught the tip of something gold sticking out from beneath the black cloth as he eyed Tesla. "Are we clear?"

Tesla's jaw tightened, though he quickly agreed. Then he repeated Vanderbilt's distinct gesture. *Pat. Pat. Pat.*

Puzzled, I slid my eyes sideways. There, over Tesla's heart, his lapel covered a lump that looked suspiciously similar to Vanderbilt's.

What the hell?

"Now." Something in the tycoon's false bonhomie set my teeth on edge. "Let's get that photograph taken, shall we?"

"Yes," Tesla murmured, eyes still fixed on Vanderbilt's lapel. "As you say."

Though I doubt he was aware of it, Tesla's grip on my arm had tightened to the point that—putting aside the option of creating a huge scene—I had no choice but to follow.

Of course, by then it was much, much too late. As we positioned ourselves beside the host, I turned to peer at Collum and Phoebe. From the looks on their faces, I could see that they, too, realized what was about to happen.

What do I do? I mouthed.

Phoebe opened her mouth, closed it. Collum, looking slightly pole-axed, only shrugged.

The photographer disappeared beneath the black cloth of

his enormous camera. The lighting assistant measured out his flash powder.

The photographer yelled, "Hold!" And I did the only thing I could think of. I ducked out, angling my body as far to the side as was possible without ripping Tesla's arm clean out of its socket. Unless fate had gotten even weirder than usual . . . the only part of me that would appear in the 1895 newspaper photo that Moira, Phoebe, and I would find in the year 2016 would be my gloved arm and one recently altered sleeve.

Inside the vaulted foyer, male and female attendants took wraps and coats and furs. I motioned to Collum and Phoebe and sketched out the details of the strange exchange between Tesla and Vanderbilt. Collum frowned. "Any idea what it means?"

I shook my head.

"Great," Phoebe snapped, her tone uncharacteristically sharp as she handed her wrap to one of the attendants. "One more damn mystery to add to the pile."

I glanced over at her and saw the troubled look she was working so hard to hide.

"Hey," I said, tucking an arm into hers. "They're fine. If I know Doug, he's having the time of his life in that lab."

"I know," she said. "Plus, Mac's there and all the other men. It's only . . . Did you see his face? He barely got to see

Tesla, much less speak to the man. I know he must be so disappointed."

That was the plan, of course. While we watched Tesla's back, Jonathan would convince him of the danger of ever constructing another device. And with Peters and his security force protecting the lab's perimeter, Mac and Doug's mission was to locate and destroy the already built enhancement, making sure it wouldn't survive the fateful fire.

For Doug it would be as dreadful and agonizing as drowning puppies in a river.

She was watching her brother as he moved into bodyguard position behind Tesla. "And it's not just that. Collum's right. Think what we might do with the enhancement, if we could bring it back with us."

"Yeah," I said. "I really thought Aunt Lucinda would change her mind about that."

"Collum and Doug went to her before we left, you know." Phoebe's wide, mobile mouth turned down, the frown unnatural on her normally cheery face. "Tried one last time to persuade her. Apparently, she refused to even discuss it. I'd never seen Coll look so downcast."

"I know," I said. "Well, do you think Doug might, um—?"

She shook her head. "No. Doug will do his duty. They've probably already destroyed the little bugger. It's not fair, though. It might've been our only real shot at finally locating Da."

Servants gestured for people to move out of the foyer

and make their way into the entrance proper, and I gave my friend's arm a tight squeeze, letting her know that no matter what happened, I was here for her. Always.

CHAPTER 39

WE WALKED FROM THE FOYER AND INTO THE *ARABIAN Nights*.

Everything was shimmering, jewel-toned, and luscious with silk. It rippled from the walls. Draped from chandeliers. Dangled from the two-story ceiling in great swags of color. Our low-heeled boots immediately sunk into Turkish carpets that covered the vast expanse of marble.

Above our heads a Capuchin monkey in green vest and fez rode a minuscule bicycle calmly across a hair-thin wire.

"You've got to be kidding me," I whispered.

Bare-chested men in turbans and gold balloon pants wove among the guests offering trays of jeweled goblets and bite-size delicacies. In a parlor just off the main hall, tuxedo-clad gentlemen lounged on silken pillows, ogling a gyrating belly dancer.

Phoebe wrinkled her nose. "Ugh. Smells like a weed shop on going-out-of-business day."

I nodded as the smell of pungent incense filled my nose.

"It looks like the inside of a freaking genie's—" I stopped suddenly. "Um . . . And how exactly would *you* know what a weed shop smells like?"

She rolled her eyes. "Stumbled into it, one day while me and Doug were out shopping for Mac's birthday." Her teeth flashed, a relief of white in the sumptuous, over-colored room. "Almost bought my own grandda a dragon-shaped bong before we figured it out."

"Nikola, darling. You came!"

Though I'd seen her in person only days earlier, without my very specific memory, I would never have connected this woman with Consuelo Vanderbilt's frumpy, uptight mother.

She glided up to take Tesla's hands in hers. Though the same protruding pale eyes and snub nose turned up to simper at Tesla, clothed as she was in a too-revealing gown of eye-watering gold silk, Alva Vanderbilt looked like a someone had tried to pass a potato off as a Christmas gift.

Tesla managed a fleeting smile, though I could see his jaw muscles flex with a desire to wipe off his hands. "Mrs. Vanderbilt."

"Please, do call me Alva, won't you?"

When she moved in to kiss Tesla's cheek, he recoiled, gaze pinned to the woman's very ample chest.

Affronted, Mrs. Vanderbilt stood there with her mouth open. "Why, I nev—"

"Pearls," Tesla choked out. "You—you are wearing pearls. I cannot abide the sight of them."

She blinked at him, the anger on her face gradually morphing to pity. "Oh, you poor dear," she said, fingering the strand of huge matched pearls that disappeared down her bodice. "Yes, I'd heard of your strange sensibilities, but I'd quite forgotten. I shall ring for my maid and have her take them away, posthaste."

"Do not trouble yourself so. In all honesty, we shall be here for a short time only. To meet with Mr. Vanderbilt and John Jacob Astor. Has Mr. Astor arrived?"

Mrs. Vanderbilt pouted and I wanted to puke. "Yes, and he will be delighted to see you," she said, her voice flattened. "He's been sick with concern that you would not attend. I don't believe I've ever seen him or my husband worry so over a guest." She made a little moue of distaste. "William is still greeting our guests, of course. But JJ is somewhere about. I could . . ." The woman's voice trailed off as her bulging eyes skimmed past Phoebe and me, and landed on Collum. "Nikola," she purred. "Won't you introduce me to your lovely young friends here?"

Gilded peacock feathers wobbled from Alva Belmont Vanderbilt's upswept hair as she breezed past Phoebe and me to plant herself directly in front of Collum. "My, what a handsome boy you are."

As I watched, Collum's face turned the color of the burgundy swath dangling just above his head. I bit back a snort as Mrs. Vanderbilt wiggled closer, practically propping those enormous boobs of hers right on his chest.

"I do not mean to appear brusque, Mrs. Vanderbilt." Tesla gestured toward the staircase. "But I believe we should go and find Astor, yes?"

Alva Vanderbilt, champion of the women's suffrage movement and one of the wealthiest and most powerful women of the late nineteenth and early twentieth centuries, whined, "Must you take this one?" She tucked her arm into Collum's. "He is quite delicious. Let me keep him for a while, won't you?"

Since I'd known him, I'd seen Collum MacPherson single-handedly fend off two chain-mail-clad, sword-wielding brutes. I'd watched him have his shoulder sliced open to the bone and seared back together with a white-hot poker. But I had never, ever known him to look as scared as he did when Alva Vanderbilt tried to drag him away with her.

"I—I—I," Collum stuttered.

"Sadly," Jonathan said, appearing from nowhere to rescue Collum, "I am afraid Professor Tesla and I have need of a strong young man tonight."

"Don't we all?" Mrs. Vanderbilt muttered beneath her breath, making Collum squirm even more. "Good evening, Jonathan," Mrs. Vanderbilt said without interest. "How is Julia?"

"My wife is well, thank you. She shall bear our first child in—"

Alva interrupted. "Yes. Yes. How lovely. Well, I shan't detain you any longer." Rising on tiptoe she leaned in, her lips brushing Collum's ear as she spoke to him sotto voce. "I shall be waiting anxiously for your return. Oh!" Her gaze hardened. "Consuelo."

I wheeled around to see that the timid girl I'd met at the Waldorf was smiling as she looked at me. "Miss Randolph," she said. "I'm so delighted you came."

My mouth split into a huge grin. "Miss Vanderbilt," I replied. "Thank *you* so much for your gracious invitation."

In a sparkling gown of white chiffon, and with her hair piled on top of her head, Consuelo Vanderbilt was beyond lovely. After a quick round of introductions, Mrs. Vanderbilt sauntered off, calling greetings to her guests. Collum stared after her, looking like he'd just swallowed a spider.

Consuelo tugged me to a quiet spot next to the steps. Away from her mother's watchful eye, her smile vanished. "Mother found out," she said. "She would not allow my . . . my friend to attend and has sworn to lock me in my room after tonight. I fear I shall never see him again." Her voice trembled as she pulled me close. She looked up at me with damp eyes. "He has asked me to run away with him," she said. "Do you—do you think I should?"

My mouth fell open. "Why would you ask *me* that?" I said, eventually. "We've only just met, and—"

"But you are the only one who understands," she begged. "You, too, are being forced into a loveless marriage. Would you not do the same? Would you not give up everything to be with the one who holds your heart?"

Oh God, I thought, as I took in a deep breath. *What do I do?*

My Aunt Lucinda's recurrent lecture blasted through my head.

Viators hold an awesome and terrible responsibility. As interlopers we must — above all — hold tight to our knowledge of future events, particularly from those whom we encounter in the past. Even though it might seem callous . . . even cruel . . . the one thing that we must never, ever do, is interfere with the happenings of things yet to come. One wrong word and we could ruin lives and events beyond imagining.

I looked at Consuelo's hopeful face, and swallowed down the painful knot that formed beneath my sternum. I smiled, though it felt like a scarecrow's grimace as I tried to mimic what Aunt Lucinda would say in this kind of situation.

"I think," I said, "that we cannot easily step off the path that the future has laid before us."

"This way," Tesla was calling as he slipped into the stream of guests who were heading up the two arcing staircases that led to the open second-story landing.

"I see," Consuelo choked. "Yes, I'm sure you are right, Miss Randolph. I suppose that path you speak of is the only one open to me now. Thank you. I — I bid you a good evening."

Consuelo Vanderbilt bowed and slipped quietly away.

But not before I saw the tears that crested her eyelashes roll silently down her cheeks.

Silks in purples and reds and golds flowed down the banisters. As we climbed, I let my hand glide over the slick, cool surface. Next to me, Collum stared straight ahead, his face as grim as I felt.

"What was that all about?" Phoebe asked.

"I think I just ruined that poor girl's life," I said, miserably. "She wanted me to tell her it was okay to run away. But that's not what happened . . . will happen."

"You didn't have a choice, Hope." She wrapped a soothing hand around my waist and squeezed. "It's okay. It's part of the job, you know?"

"A sucky, sucky part."

"Aye," she agreed. "It is that."

"You did what you had to do, Hope. Sometimes that is not an easy task," Collum said.

"Then why do I feel like utter and complete crap?"

Collum took hold of my shoulders and looked at me with that serious, steadfast gaze that always made me feel safe. "Feeling like crap," he said, "is just a hazard of the job, one we never get used to."

In the shadowy rear of the wide second-floor landing, an older gypsy woman sat behind a table. A group of young people gathered around to watch a muscular guy cluck like a chicken.

"Come, come," said Tesla, moving toward a set of tall open doors with the rest of the crowd.

As we walked away, the gypsy called after us. "You! Little one." Phoebe turned back. "Me?"

"Yes." She nodded, the huge hoops in her ears waggling as she crooked a finger. "I sense something about you, child. A greatness that is as yet undiscovered. You are a creature of moonlight and magic. Come and allow me to set it free."

"Oh, no you don't," Collum said as Phoebe swayed toward the woman. "No time for that weirdness. God knows what she'll make you do. Come on."

Phoebe groaned, but trudged after him. As we approached the wide entrance, I tripped, catching myself on Collum's sleeve.

"The hell?" he said, startled.

"Oh no-o," I moaned.

Phoebe grimaced. "Damn. I was afraid of that."

The sheer overlay she'd whipstitched to the waist of my skirt had come free and was dragging. The toe of my shoe must have caught it, and ripped the entire front section loose.

"Oh, miss!" A maid standing sentinel near the door rushed over to bob a curtsy. "Come with me. We have a seamstress on hand for just such emergencies."

Collum cursed as Tesla moved off, unaware, and obviously unconcerned with such trivialities as torn skirts.

"Well, go on with you then," Phoebe told her brother, Moira incarnate as she waved him on. "Go and do what you came to do. We'll be right along."

The maid deposited us in an exquisite pocket parlor, loaded with all kinds of Chinese tchotchkes, which — based on the myriad photographs that covered walls and tables alike — the Vanderbilts had acquired on a recent trip to the Orient.

Phoebe stood. "Might as well make for the loo, while we've a moment. Be right back."

The elderly seamstress took her time getting there, but once she started in with her needle, the repairs took only moments. By the time she'd helped me back into the gown, and taken off, Phoebe still hadn't returned.

"Where is that girl?" I muttered under my breath as I reached for the crystal doorknob.

The door opened suddenly inward, startling me so that I had to hop back.

"Ready, Phe . . . ?"

My voice died.

Because there she stood. In all her perfectly polished elegance. In all her stupid, heiress glory. For what felt like eons, neither of us moved or spoke. I don't think either of us blinked as Gabriella de Roca and I stared at each other.

Then she closed her eyes and murmured, "Oh, gracias a Dios!"

Darting an uneasy look over her shoulder, she rushed in

and closed the door behind her, muting the sounds of a ball in full play.

Before my lips could remember how to form words, Gabriella was hugging me. Squeezing until my bones creaked. "Thank God I have found you in time."

I lost my tongue. Like . . . it seemed to have literally absconded from the inside of my oral cavity.

"Please," she said, stepping back. "We must to speak. Please."

It was that second "please" that did it. That, and the bruises on the pale underside of her arm. Four of them. Dark. Long. Parallel. The exact size and shape of human fingers.

"You have no reason to trust me," she said in an accent that made me think of bullfights and ornate cathedrals and plazas baking under the hot sun. "But I had to try. Brandon is in much danger. And though I have told him this as well, I think he is not willing to take it seriously. This is why I have come to you."

I wanted to make a rude noise, but instead found myself asking, "What kind of danger?"

Gabriella sighed. Her perfume, honeysuckle and tuberose, clashed against the delicate pear-scented eau de toilette I'd dabbed behind my own ears. The sickly sweet mélange assaulted my senses as I stepped back.

Next to her, I felt knobby and wooden, a crudely made puppet conversing with a creature of mist and water.

Her deep green eyes seared into mine. "Blasi, he is watching me always, so I have only a moment. Before we came to this place, Celia told him I am not to be trusted. The woman does not care for me, and I do not blame her for this, as the feeling is . . ."

I could almost see the wheels inside her head turning as she searched for the right word in English.

"Mutual?"

She nodded. "I despise her." She said it so simply and sincerely that I felt the smallest crack open in my defenses.

"Yeah. Join the club."

The sleek bun at the nape of Gabriella's neck didn't allow even one strand to fall as she nodded. "Sí, sí. I would join this club. But as much as I wish to place the blame on that *bruja*, I do not believe she knows all of what he has planned."

"Of what *who* has planned?"

"Blasi." For a second, I thought she might spit on the floor. "You know this man?"

"Only by reputation."

"He works for Brandon's mother and grandmother. This you know, yes?"

I nodded.

"And that he has been ordered to bring back this . . . this *thing* of Tesla's. This also is no surprise to you?"

Yeah, well, good luck with that. Besides Mac and Doug, he'll have to get past Peters and his six guards.

When I refused to acknowledge the question, Gabriella

waved it off, as if my answer was of no concern anyway. "You have men there, guarding the lab. This Blasi knows."

I tried not to react, but something in my face must have alerted her.

"Sí," she said. "What you do not know," she added, "is that Blasi has more. Many, many more. More than eight men were deployed from the future. Blasi has hired many others from this time. And he has a spy in Tesla's employ, an assistant of Tesla's named Jacobo. For much money, this assistant tells Blasi everything Tesla has done. According to Jacobo, the professor tried to create the enhancement from Blasi's design many times, only to fail. He sent three men through the machine he created, along with this new element. Two returned after three days, as is usual. The third man was never seen again. Only days ago did one of the enhancements—taken into the past by a man named Emil Stefanovic—succeed. Emil was gone for a total of six days, nineteen hours, and forty-three minutes. This prototype is the only one that works. And according to Jacobo, Tesla trusts no one with its location. Only he knows where it is hidden. Blasi," she said. "He knows this. And he will use whatever means necessary to get it."

Frigid tidal waves of dread began to swell inside me.

"I have to go," I said, skirting around her.

"¡Espere! Por favor, tengo algo más!"

"What?" I snapped, eyes on the door. "What is it?"

"I need your help," she said, green eyes locking with mine. "Blasi . . . Blasi va a matar a Brandon."

I was nobody's physical threat. My normal means of causing people injury generally involved me tripping and falling on them. Though once, I'd accidentally impaled Collum's hand with a seventeenth-century dinner fork. But though I was shorter than the dancer by more than a head, I had blind, seething panic on my side. Before I knew it, I had her shoved up against the wall. Behind her lay wallpaper covered in watercolor renditions of Chinese characters. A likely priceless geisha figurine fell from a table and shattered.

I didn't care.

"Did you just say," I snarled, "that Blasi is going to kill Bran?"

Eyes glittering with tears, Gabriella nodded.

"Talk."

She tried, but my forearm was still pressed against her throat. I swallowed. Made myself let go. Stepped back.

"I—I'm sorry," I said. "It's just—"

"No. No. This is understandable. I am glad of your fear, because Brandon has none. I told him all this, but he is a man who believes nothing can ever truly harm him. You know this about him?"

"Unfortunately yes."

"Blasi has spoken to Doña Maria of taking Celia's place as leader of the Timeslippers. He has convinced her that her granddaughter has become desequilibrada ... loca. That she uses resources unwisely, concerned only with the rescue of

Michael MacPherson. Maria is old and tired, yes, but she is not blind. She ... She told Blasi that if he succeeds in this mission, she will honor his request. Brandon will try to block him, and Blasi will not let that happen. I may despise Celia Alvarez, but Blasi? He frightens me. I think, should this thing come to pass, none of us will be safe. Blasi must be stopped."

"How do you know all this?" I asked, as my mind tried to decipher what this could mean for all of us.

She wouldn't look at me as she shrugged in that way only European women can pull off. "He believes I am with him."

"Why would he think that, Gabriella?"

Throwing back her shoulders, raising her chin high, she said, "I am doing what I must to protect mi familia. Would you not do the same in my place?"

She turned away before I could utter a word, but I saw it when her hand rose to swipe at her cheek. My mind began to fill in the gaps, and my stomach rolled over.

Because I was pretty sure I knew what she had to do to gain Blasi's trust.

"Gabriella, I —"

She shook her head without turning. "No," she said, her voice hoarse. "I have known Brandon for a very long time. He is like the brother to me." She took in a shaky breath. "I think he should go back with you to *your* home, *para siempre.* It will never be safe for him to return to the Timeslippers now."

For an instant I let the idea consume me.

Bran at Christopher Manor. The two of us, together every day. Mornings in the library, tucked up, debating literature and history and travel. Lazy horseback afternoons on the moors. Sunsets by the river. In the evening we could smile at each other across the dinner table.

And the nights . . .

We both startled as someone rattled the doorknob. The maid who'd helped me peeked around the door. "Pardon me, miss. Is everything all right?"

Gabriella's voice lowered to a bare husk as she slipped away. "Brandon is in Blasi's way, Hope, and he will stop at nothing. Help him. This is all I ask of you."

I found Phoebe seated at the fortuneteller's table. Her eyes looked bleary, but at my approach she stood.

"Sorry," she said. "I've never been able to resist having my fortune told and . . ." She trailed off when she noticed my expression. "What is it? What's the matter?"

I shot a look at the gray-haired gypsy, who was counting stacks of coins. I took Phoebe's arm and led her away, quickly filling her in.

"But?" she said when I was done. "Why should we trust a word that dancing Delilah has to say?"

"You didn't see her, Phee," I said. "I—I think I believe her."

"Hmmph. All right, then. Let's go find Coll and the other lads. We'll tell them. See what they think, aye? And we'll need to speak to Bran, too. Is he here yet? Did whatsername say?"

I shook my head, though I knew he must be. I was already feeling lighter from sharing the burden. As we strolled toward the ballroom door, I glanced over at Phoebe. "Oh," I asked. "So, what was your fortune?"

"Bah." She waved a hand dismissively. "Waste of money. Just the same old claptrap. 'You'll fall in love with a tall, dark stranger.' Did that when I was seven, didn't I? Do me a favor though, and don't tell Collum, aye? I hate it when he gives me *that look*."

CHAPTER 40

THE DECORATIONS IN THE BALLROOM WERE VASTLY different from those in the rest of the manor. It was as though we'd passed through Aladdin's cave and entered a fairy forest. Above our heads hung garlands of white and pink flowers, twined with ivy and sparkling ribbon. Barefoot girls in gauzy dresses floated between guests, passing out flutes of champagne. A rain of petals drifted down onto bejeweled hair and black-clad shoulders.

We scanned the crowd.

"I don't see . . . Ah!" Phoebe said. "There they are."

To the right of the steps, Tesla was embroiled in a conversation with William Vanderbilt and another man whose face I could not see. Collum and Jonathan stood close by, watching their charge closely.

"You go find lover boy," Phoebe said. "Then I'll grab our lads and meet you in that far corner behind the ice sculpture of the goat man. I'll take my time so you can have a few minutes alone with him."

"Thanks," I said, grinning. "And ... I think that's supposed to be Pan."

She raised an eyebrow.

"The ice sculpture. Pan's the god of nature. Son of Dionysus, god of wine?"

"Looks like a bloody goat man to me," she said, and struck out through the crowd.

From a far corner of the room, I let my gaze roam over every face I could see, but it was so crowded and the partygoers were constantly shifting. Panic began to squeeze my chest.

Too many people. Too many. I'll never find him. Getting hard to breathe.

As I stood beneath one of the cherry trees that dotted the ballroom, pink petals fell over me in a constant flutter. I cupped my palms, filling them with the velvety blossoms. Then, eyes closed, I raised them to my face and forced myself to breathe in the sweet, tantalizing fragrance.

Slowly, I exhaled. I looked up, and straight into a familiar pair of blue and green eyes a stone's throw away. For a long instant, everything and everyone else blurred around us.

We had so many obstacles. So many scary things that had to be discussed.

But it *was* my first, maybe my only, ball. And the boy I loved was standing only twenty yards away.

You're killing me, he mouthed.

I tried for a casual *oh-well* shrug, but as he wove through the crowd toward me, the thrill that had begun to thrum through my nerve endings was making it really hard to pull off.

"There you are," I said as he approached.

"And there *you* are."

The tabbed collar and white tie contrasted with his tanned face and neck. A tailed black jacket fit snugly across his shoulders. All the way to the shiny black shoes, Bran looked at ease and natural in his nineteenth-century garb.

His eyes took on that sleepy look I knew well, and a slow, sideways smile began to emerge as he held out a hand. "May I have the pleasure, Miss Walton?"

I glanced across the ballroom. Collum's and Jonathan's heads were tilted toward Phoebe. Tesla's attention was fixed on the tall man standing beside Vanderbilt.

Soon they'd all be here, and my one chance to dance with Bran would be over.

"But Tesla and Collum will be here in a—"

"Hang Tesla and definitely hang MacPherson," he said. "I think we deserve this, don't you?"

I paused, but only for an instant. "I would be honored, Mr. Cameron."

"Not here, though," he said. "If Blasi notices ..."

"Where?"

He grinned, and I was lost. "Come with me."

The room we stepped into was a gallery, lit only by silver moonlight that streamed through three tall windows. At any other time, the historian in me would have stopped to examine the dozens of portraits that lined the long room. But I knew we had only moments, and after that, who could say what would happen?

Bran took my hand and led me into a patch of lustrous light. As we stood there I let my gaze drift down over the arched brows, past high cheekbones, over the too-long nose, to his lips.

As he moved closer, his scent sparked something inside me. I knew—from reading, of course—that people often confuse love with what is actually just a chemical reaction that sometimes occurs between two individuals. Was that all this was? Hormones that interacted with and complemented each other?

Then I looked up into his eyes, the blue and green washed in light until they were all but indistinguishable from each other.

And I remembered the first time I'd seen those eyes under the shimmer of the moon.

Bran held out his arms. The grin faded as he spoke in a smoky voice that made my stomach tighten. "Dance with me, Hope."

The orchestra began the opening strains of the leisurely, somehow sensuous "Beautiful Dreamer," by Stephen Foster. The music seeped through the walls. The vibrations of violin and cello rumbled through the floor and up my legs.

I stepped into Bran's arms. His palm settled warmly at my waist. Taking my other hand in his, he slowly began to move me backwards across the room.

Having no clue how to waltz, and with my natural klutziness in full sway, I lost count of the times I stumbled or stepped on his toes. But his movements were patient and measured. As he counted quietly under his breath, I eventually caught the rhythm.

I don't know how long we spun around the gallery. Time had decelerated into an adagio of shadows and light and heat. On every revolution Bran drew me in closer, until his arm was wrapped around my waist and our bodies were pressed together.

We eased to a stop in the center of the room, bodies half in and half out of shadow as we stared at each other, breathing hard. My head tilted back as he pulled me hard against him. I could feel the flat stomach and the firm muscles of his long legs pressed against me as he leaned down and kissed me.

Soft and unhurried, the kiss soon deepened until we were panting not from dance, but with need. His lips found mine again and we surged together, the heat building until I didn't even know my own name.

Outside the empty tree trunk, the little girl shivered, even though the little boy had long since removed his own meager cloak to wrap around her thin shoulders.

As he stood next to her, the wind riffled the boy's tunic, making him shiver.

"You are cold," the girl said. "Take your cloak with you. You need it."

The little boy shook his head as he knelt in front of her. "You need it more than I, milady. Come, I will carry you. Wait for me inside the tree, where you will be safe. You shall have your Elizabeth for company and I shall return soon. When I do, I will have a nice fat rabbit for us to share."

He had picked her up then, though he could not have weighed much more than she herself. When he set her down inside the great tree, he stared at her upturned face. Without warning, he leaned in and pressed his cold lips to hers.

"I will return to you," he said in a voice she barely heard above the roar through the treetops. "This is my vow, milady Hope. I shall always, always return to you."

I stepped backwards out of the circle of his arms.

"What?" he said, noticing my expression. "What is it?"

"Nothing," I said. "Well, everything. But I just realized that you really do keep your promises, don't you?" I grabbed his hand and towed him toward the door.

Our hands still linked, he tugged me back to face him. "To you? Always."

I smiled up at him. "I mean, except for that one."

Slim eyebrows met over his nose as he frowned, quizzically.

"You promised me a rabbit when we were in the tree. I never got that rabbit," I told him. "Just one measly old apple."

He threw his head back. Our laughter twined together, bright as moonlight and light as helium as it floated toward the gallery's high ceiling.

As we opened the door and stepped back into the ballroom, I said, "Bran, I talked to Gabriella. She told me all about Blasi."

"Hello, Bran," a voice said. "Been looking all over for you. And this must be the lovely Hope Walton. I'm curious, Hope. Given how you ladies love to chat, I'd be very interested to know what—exactly—my sweet Gabi had to say about me?"

Bran's grin had vanished. My pulse began to speed for an entirely different reason. I recognized the man Gabriella was so afraid of, standing only feet away, head tilted as he smiled at Bran and me.

CHAPTER 41

WE'D RESEARCHED THE MAN PLENTY AFTER BRAN'S revelation at the Highland games. Young. Swiss. Secretive. By the age of twenty-three Gunnar Blasi held doctorates in three different physics fields. Considered a prodigy, he was recruited straight out of school by CERN. He'd worked for the international organization only a year before his employment was suddenly and inexplicably terminated. Even with Doug and Moira's investigatory skills, we could only find rumors and speculation about his abrupt dismissal.

The few photos we'd managed to locate—including one that showed his CERN ID badge—portrayed a nondescript bearded guy with frameless glasses and stringy hair pulled back in a man bun.

The guy watching us now was anything but nondescript. Fit and trim. Handsome, with the blond Nordic features of his homeland. Blasi's once-ratty hair was now cut fashionably short. He was clean-shaven, and the glasses—if they'd ever been anything but an affectation—were gone.

And though he maintained an almost friendly grin, as he approached, his impenetrable black eyes held all the warmth and charm of a cobra coiled to strike.

Bran positioned himself between us. "Blasi," he said. "I've been looking for you too. If we might have a word, I can—"

The man walked right past him. "Hope." He had only the barest accent. "I'm glad we're having this chance. You see, I always enjoy knowing my competition. It makes winning so much more pleasurable. Don't you agree?"

"I—"

"Blasi," Bran said again. "I've already told you, I'm handling this."

Gunnar Blasi glanced down at Bran's hand on his sleeve. "Yes, you did say that."

My eyes skittered frantically over the crowd, but I couldn't see any of my people.

Where are you, Collum? Where are you, dammit?

Then my gaze snagged on Tesla, just emerging from a narrow doorway, followed by two men. The first was William Vanderbilt. The second I immediately recognized. John Jacob "JJ" Astor IV, then the richest man in the world, and the most famous passenger to die when—in seventeen years' time—the RMS *Titanic* would sink beneath the icy waves of the North Atlantic.

Finally I spotted Collum, Phoebe, and Jonathan moving

near the wall as Tesla chatted with the two tycoons. He kept touching his lapel as the men bowed and left.

Skirting the dance floor, Collum, Phoebe, Tesla, and Jonathan headed in our direction. An instant later a group of strangers intercepted them. *Ringed* them. Collum went stiff as one of them leaned in and spoke a few words. Phoebe's head jerked toward the spot where she knew I was waiting. Our eyes met. After only a few seconds' conversation, the group began to march across the ballroom and down the steps to the main entrance. At the top of the stairs, Collum pivoted, gaze skimming the crowd. I wanted to wave my arms, jump up and down, scream, "Where the hell are you *going?*"

Then I saw a metallic flash, as one of the strangers quietly and casually pushed the tip of a half-concealed pistol into the small of Collum's back.

The guests, wrapped up in their drinking and dancing and socializing, hadn't noticed a thing.

"Well, that went even smoother than I predicted." Blasi, too, had been watching the scene at the top of the stairs. "Of course, my men probably warned yours that if they didn't go along quietly, they'd just start shooting people. They'd have done it too. Barbarians have no clue about timelines." He tsked.

His eyes fixed on something over my shoulder. "Ah, here comes my little dancing queen."

377

"Gunnar." Gabriella de Roca didn't look at me as she limped past. "Did you see? That went well, did it not?"

"Hello, darling." Blasi took hold of her shoulders and planted a lingering kiss on her lips. With his face only an inch from hers, he whispered, "So, what did you tell them?"

Gabriella smiled, but she was blinking furiously. "Tell who? I—I do not know what it is that you mean?"

"Sure you do. You opened your pretty little mouth, didn't you?" Blasi tapped Gabriella on the tip of her slim nose and the skin on my back prickled with a sense of danger despite the man's jovial tone.

"You had to go and get all gossipy on me, Gabi. What a shame. I should've known, I guess." Blasi's expression was open and pleasant, as if conversing about a favorite book. "But you were so good at . . ." He chuckled to himself. "Well, you know what you're good at, don't you? *So* good, in fact, that I didn't even realize what a lying little whore you are until right now."

"No." Gabriella's voice shook. "Please, Gunnar, te equiv-ocas."

"No, I don't think I am mistaken, darling. I think it's *you* who are mistaken."

Bran had been growing increasingly tense up to this point, but now his hands fisted. His nostrils flared. His shoulders knotted, and I knew then that this was going to get very, very messy. His hand inched toward the gun I'd felt against my ribs when we danced.

Two men strolled up. Big. Balding. Almost interchangeable. "Everything okay here, Dr. Blasi?"

"Yeah," he replied. "Any trouble at the lab? Got that all wrapped up?"

The men nodded.

"Good. Time to go join them, I guess. Though I am having a marvelous time here. These Victorians really knew how to throw a party." He sighed. "Let's go get the professor and have him show me where he hid that damn enhancement. Then I want to watch while he and all the rest of you burn to a crisp in that fire." Blasi clapped Bran on the shoulder. "Sorry about that, friend."

He'd said it all so casually, so . . . pleasantly . . . that for a second I thought I had misheard.

Bran's fingers found mine.

"Gunnar." Gabriella cozied up to him, trying to drape her sinewy body over his.

He shoved her away. She stumbled on her bad leg and nearly fell before Blasi's men caught her. "You know what? I think I'm done with her, too. She can join the rest. Make it easier to clean house when we get back."

Another of Blasi's men appeared at a nod from his boss and bundled Gabriella away before we could even process what was happening.

"You," Bran said to Blasi in a mild, conversational tone, "are a psychotic fuck. Oh, and Hope . . . ?" he went on. "Run!"

We shoved through the door back into the gallery.

Gritting his teeth, Bran held on to the door handles as Blasi and his men tried to ram their way in.

"Grab that fireplace poker!" Bran yelled.

I snatched it up and he ran it through the handles, buying us a few precious seconds. The glamour of the manor vanished as we darted into a service corridor. Here, the plaster walls were unadorned. Dust skimmed the baseboards of the scratched wooden floors. No expensive electricity for the servants. In this normally invisible part of the house, old-fashioned gas wall sconces flickered as we raced through pools of the dull yellow light.

A greasy-haired man in white cap and stained apron stepped around a corner in front of us, toting a tray of dirty dishes. We swerved around him, a lit cigarette dropping out of his mouth as we ran past and down the stairs.

At the end of a short hallway, a door to the outside had been left propped open with a chunk of broken brick. The scent of damp concrete and cigarette smoke drifted in. All I could see of the dark alley beyond was the blank wall of the next building.

Shouts rang out behind us. The cobblestones were slick, and I skidded as we pounded across them toward the street. Bran yanked me upright as we made for the sidewalk.

On the street outside the Vanderbilt manor, Bran hauled a dozing carriage driver down off his seat. When the man saw

Bran's pistol, he did not hesitate. "Take it, then. It ain't mine, what er I care?"

Gunnar Blasi's men burst through the door we had escaped through just as Bran whipped the team of horses into a full-bore run.

In the thin layer of silk, I was shaking from the cold. From shock. From fear of what might happen to my friends. Bran grasped the reins with one hand and yanked off his coat with the other. I draped it over my shoulders and clutched tightly to him as we careened around corners. We pounded down empty streets, and I saw the stars begin to fade above us.

"He's got them, Bran. All of them. And you heard what he said . . . he wants to watch them burn."

His concentration fixed on urging the horses faster and faster, he called, "Not going to happen. We know where he's headed. He's a sadistic bastard, but he's arrogant. We can use that."

We jounced and jolted through street after street until at last we pulled up to the rear of Tesla's building. We jumped down from the carriage, secured it, and quietly rounded the corner. Something moved near the front of the building. Two crouched figures. I took off running.

"Wait!" Bran hissed, but I ignored him, because I knew who I'd just seen. He ran to catch up.

On the shadowy New York sidewalk, Phoebe's blade glinted in the latent glare from the new electric streetlights.

"Ready?" she was saying to someone as we approached.

"And I swear by Saint Mary and Saint Bride, if they've touched a single hair on any of their heads, I'll—"

"Hey."

Phoebe and Collum wheeled, weapons raised. I held up my hands. "Whoa. Hold on. It's just us."

"Hope!" Phoebe threw herself at me. I didn't dare move, not wanting her—in her exuberance—to accidentally stab me in the back.

"What happened?" I asked. "They took you and then you—"

"Got away," Collum said. "As they were forcing us into the carriage. They took Jonathan and Tesla, but we ran. Stole some horses to get here. They marched them both into the building a couple of minutes ago."

"We haven't seen Peters or any of the other men," said Phoebe. "But Doug and Mac are up there too." She was breathing hard. "We—we have to go get them."

Collum leaned out to peer around. He turned back to us and whispered, "There's blood on the sidewalk."

CHAPTER 42

WE DIDN'T HESITATE AS WE ROUNDED THE CORNER TO the front of the building. I barely registered the splatter of dark crimson that painted the bricks just outside the half-open door as we shoved through it and charged into the darkness of the narrow stairwell.

On the second step, my foot skidded in something wet. I thrust my bare hand out to break my fall. It landed on something soft, pliant, and sticky. With a stifled cry, I jerked back just as Collum stepped down the steps to shove the door the rest of the way open. He was cursing under his breath, but stopped when the streetlight revealed the first body.

The man was lying face-up, features half-shadowed, but I recognized him immediately.

"Oh, no."

Even though I hadn't known him well, grief washed over me. Inside the horror show that was Greenwood Institute, only one person had tried to watch over me. Sergeant Peters had been my guardian angel there, and he'd looked out for the other girls, too, as much as he could. I hated to think what worse things might've happened without his restraining hand.

He looked at peace now, eyes closed, his face unlined. I sent up a prayer that he and the wife he had so loved were reunited at last.

"Shot in the back," Bran muttered. He gestured toward the gleam of dark liquid that sheeted the front of the sergeant's jacket and trailed down the steps to pool just inside the front stoop.

A little way up, a second body was shoved against the wall. Bran leaned down and pressed his fingers against the man's neck. It wasn't necessary. The young man's sandy hair was dark with blood. Light brown eyes stared, glassy and empty.

While Bran closed the man's eyes, Collum slammed a fist against his knee. "Bastards." Blowing out a long breath, he visibly steadied himself.

"Listen carefully." Collum spoke quietly, hazel gaze trained on his sister's face. "We don't know what we're going to find up there. But we have to keep it together, no matter what, aye?"

I understood what he was implying, though it felt like a punch to the diaphragm. If Blasi's people had killed these men in cold blood, there was no telling what they'd done to the others.

It took Phoebe another second. But when the realiza-

SPARKS OF LIGHT

tion hit, all the color drained out from behind her freckles. Without a word, she whirled and started to dash up the stairs. Collum snatched her back.

"No." He swore as she kicked, catching him in the thigh with the pointed tip of her boot. "We can't just go barreling up there with no—"

Far above our heads, a door slammed. We froze as heavy footsteps echoed down the stairwell.

"That big mulatto done knocked out one of my goddamn teeth." The muffled complaint bounced off the walls and rolled toward us. "I swear I'ma kill that somebitch."

"Yeah, well," another voice replied. "Once the Swede shows up I'm gone peel me a few pieces off that old Scotchman. Bugger sliced my arm up good and proper 'fore I got him tied up."

They're still alive! The thought screamed jubilantly inside my head.

In the dusk of the stairwell, my gaze shot to Phoebe. Her eyes had gone wide, frightened but relieved.

Alarm shot through me as a rough laugh rolled down the stairs. Another voice shushed the first two. "Shoot anyone that ain't got the code word."

"Come on," Collum whispered. "We'll have to find another way in."

When Phoebe only stared up toward the nearing footsteps, Collum jerked on her arm. "Phee!"

My friend whipped around. Her normally open, friendly features had tightened into a look I'd only seen once before.

Unadulterated fury. "Fine," she spat. "But how are we supposed to get in there?"

Before we left home, I'd glanced over the historic blueprints of Tesla's Fifth Avenue building, along with those of other structures along the street. I closed my eyes and let the images flow across my vision.

"I, uh . . . think I know a way," I told them. "But we have to hurry. Let's go!"

Without another word, I stepped out onto the sidewalk and took off down the street. I ignored their hushed cries as I prayed I was right, and that they'd trust me enough to follow.

Breaking into the building two down from Tesla's was no challenge for Bran's lock-picking ability. In moments, we'd climbed up to the roof and stepped over its lip to the flat top of the building next door.

But now, as Bran, Phoebe, and I stood on the edge of the rooftop staring across at Tesla's building, I realized my brilliant idea had encountered a bit of a snag.

"So." Phoebe gave me a sidelong look. "The alley . . ."

I looked down, down, down to the passageway bisecting the two buildings. "Yeah."

"How wide?" Collum, keeping well back from the edge, called.

Phoebe squinted. "Seven, eight feet, at least."

Collum made a strangled noise that—coming from

anyone else on earth—I would've termed a panicked mewl. He had one arm wrapped tight around a sturdy chimney, and his broad, freckled face looked paler than the moonshot clouds above his head.

But Collum was Collum. He wasn't going to let a little thing like crippling fear get in the way of duty.

"Well, we'd better figure something out soon," he called, after a quick look at his pocket watch. "We've thirty-eight minutes until fire takes the building."

Already, a faint scent of smoke was filtering up from below. According to the research, the basement fire had taken its time to spread.

Initially.

But once the flames ate their way up through the oil-encrusted floor of the ground level machine shop, the conflagration exploded, taking only moments to engulf the entire structure.

Even now, we might ... *might* ... have been able to stop the fire. To save a priceless accumulation of incalculable genius.

But days before we'd left on our journey to the past, it'd been Tesla's own number-one fanboy who'd nixed the idea for good.

"Much as it pains me, we're going to have to let it happen, aye?" Doug told us, around a mouthful of Moira's "parrich." "With such a well-known event, any intervention won't succeed, and in fact, we might make it worse. As a verra wise man once said, 'Life breaks free, it expands to new territories and crashes through barriers, painfully, maybe even danger-ously. Life, uh . . . finds a way.'"

"That's beautiful, Doug. Really profound," I said to the suddenly and curiously hushed group around the table. "Who said that? Was it Sir Wa—"

Phoebe laughed so hard she fell off the bench. Collum was choking on a spoonful of inhaled oats, and I didn't think it was a damn bit funny when I learned the "poetry" that had touched my heart came from a blockbuster hit about freaking dinosaurs.

"I'm sorry, you guys," I said as I stared down at the alley far, far below. "I thought we could just step across. I had no clue."

"Well," Bran said, "suppose it's plan B then."

The relief on Collum's face dropped away when Bran hurried over to the first building's roof and disappeared in-side the door we'd left propped open. He returned moments later, carrying a long, narrow plank, a thick coil of rope, and several iron crowbars. He propped the beam up onto the lip of the roof, and carefully slid it across until it created a bridge between the building we were on and Tesla's.

"Problem solved." Bran clapped once. "But please. Mind the gap."

Phoebe smacked a palm to her forehead. "Gawd. Tell me you did not just say that."

At that moment, with his fiendish grin and wind-disheveled hair, Bran looked like some debauched lordling out for a night on the town. Everything inside me clenched as he turned and stepped out onto the board.

"It's good solid oak," he said, edging toward the open air between the buildings. "Not that processed trash they use in our time. Lucky, that."

"You," I said, "have lost your mind."

"Do you have any other ideas in that miraculous brain of yours? No? Then we go this way."

He hurried back and hopped off the plank. "Good luck for us they were renovating, yeah?"

Humming under his breath, he secured one end of the rope around the nearest chimney. Hoisting the coil onto his shoulder, he stepped onto the plank again and began to dash across to the other side.

The plank wobbled.

I made a noise as Bran froze. But then he smiled. "No worries, dove."

Without another word, he began inching out until he was standing dead center over the drop between the two buildings.

"See?"

My heart had crawled so far up my throat, I was gagging on it. Beside me, Phoebe stifled a yelp as Bran gave a little hop. The wood bowed the tiniest bit under his weight, but didn't break. "I'll just tie the other end of the rope over there, to use as a safety line and voilà! Simple as pie."

As Bran scampered the rest of the way across the beam, I looked back at Collum. He stood in the very center of the roof, as far from any edge as he could possibly get. One arm was wrapped firmly around a chimney. The other was pressed against his stomach. Bran began gathering up the slack in the rope. When the line went taut with a snap, Collum flinched.

I nudged Phoebe. Her small blue eyes went all soft as she looked at her brother. "He fell off a cliff once, see?" she said quietly. "When we were kids. Gram and Mac had taken us on holiday and Collum snuck off with some local lads to go cliff climbing. Gram was livid when she couldn't find him. Then we got the call."

They'd rushed to the emergency room to find Collum already in surgery with a broken femur.

"He told me about it once," she said. "Halfway up, his crampon had come unmoored from the rock. Ever since, well . . ."

I nodded. No one understood the power that phobias could have over a person better than me. I wasn't a huge fan of high places, either. But they didn't ruin me the way enclosed places did.

Bran crossed back over the beam, gripping the now-taut rope that stretched a foot or so above his head as he went. When he hopped off on our side, his face looked grim.

"Sorry, but we need to go," he said. "I heard shouting down below. I think we'd best hurry."

Phoebe scowled. "If this thing breaks, I'll haunt you for the rest of your days, Cameron."

"I've missed you too, Phoebe." Neatly avoiding the punch Phoebe jabbed in his direction, Bran called out to Collum, "Ready, big guy?"

Collum looked as unsure as I've ever seen him. Phoebe sighed. "I'll go first. Show him it's safe."

She stepped onto the beam. My best friend possessed both a natural athleticism and a spine of steel. Even with all those gifts on board, I could still hear her muttering death curses at Bran as she reached up to grab the rope. One hand and one foot at a time, she inched her way across the wobbly beam to the other side.

"It's not that bad," she called as she stepped down onto Tesla's building. "Just don't look down, that's the trick."

Bran gave her a thumbs-up, then motioned to Collum, "Okay, sunshine. You're up."

When Collum only stared down at his feet, Bran frowned. "What's wrong with — ohh."

Hands stuffed in his pockets, Bran strolled casually over to where Collum stood. I watched, waiting for Collum to tell Bran to go to hell. When Bran's hand rose to grip Collum's shoulder, I thought, *Mm-hmm. Here we go. You're just begging to get punched, aren't you?*

I couldn't quite hear their exchange, but even from where I stood, I saw it. The instant when Collum's careful stone-faced façade began to crumble. His stiff posture drooped. His gaze slowly rose to meet Bran's.

No. Way.

My mouth dropped open in complete and utter astonishment as Bran pulled Collum in for a back-slapping guy hug. Collum nodded, and—shoulders back—walked with Bran to the beam.

Collum's hands scrubbed back through bristly, sandy-colored hair in a gesture I knew all too well. *Stubbornness.*

He stepped onto the beam. Near the edge of Tesla's building, Phoebe gaped at her brother, then spread her hands in a question I had no idea how to answer. I shook my head. *No freaking clue.*

"All right." Bran spoke quietly to Collum. "You got this, mate. Just like we discussed. No fear."

The rope shimmied as Collum's shaking hands reached up to grip it. He paused to take in a deep, deep breath, then began inching his way across.

Frozen, I could only stare as Bran called out words of encouragement. "Doing great, mate. Past halfway. Almost there. Yes!"

When Collum stepped down off the beam onto the other side, Phoebe threw her arms around her brother's waist. Collum shoved her off and stumbled a few feet away, where he dropped to his knees and began to retch.

"Good man," Bran murmured, before turning back to me. "You ready?"

His arm came around my waist. My heart gave a little *zing.* "As I'll ever be, I suppose."

I stepped onto the beam and grabbed the rope. The wind

blew, molding my skirts against my legs and whipping my hair out behind me.

"Slow and steady," Bran said.

"I got it."

One foot after the other, hand over hand, I moved out over open space. I stared straight ahead, forcing myself not to look down at the hard ground six stories below.

My heart was pounding so hard my eyeballs pulsed in rhythm.

Not far. Not far. Keep going.

Halfway across, the wind changed abruptly, until it seemed to gust straight up from the deep crevice below. It belled my skirts out around me, the wind filling them like a hot air balloon that lifted me to my toes.

As I tried to force my heels down, I wobbled precariously on the narrow plank. "Oh crap. Oh crap."

Bran was already running along the plank toward me. I steadied myself, but when he staggered to a quick halt, he pitched forward. I grabbed one pinwheeling arm and yanked it up. He grabbed the rope, breathing hard.

"Thanks for that."

"Payback for Westminster," I said. "Now we're even."

CHAPTER 43

From below, deep inside the bowels of the building, came a series of soft *whoomphs*. We felt the brick and mortar and wood structure quiver beneath the soles of our feet.

"The hell?" Collum squinted down at the flat surface as if he could see past the bird droppings and pebbles and six stories to the basement furnace far, far below.

An image flashed in my head, of a wall hanging I'd seen in medieval London. A ship full of sailors preparing themselves for death as a monstrous leviathan ascended to consume their doomed ship.

"That can't be good," Phoebe said as she wobbled her way across the roof.

"Nope." As I watched, wisps of black smoke rolled up from the side of the building and dissipated in the starless sky.

A rusted, metal trapdoor opened up onto the unoccupied sixth floor. Collum yanked it aside as if it weighed nothing, and climbed down the ladder without a word. Before I could blink, Phoebe followed.

"Hey." Bran, poised on the top rung of the ladder, grinned at me. "Plus side: no blasted tunnels this time."

Just as he disappeared I heard the jingle of tack, the *clop-squeak* of a carriage arriving at full clip.

Ignoring Bran's call, I darted across the roof. On the sidewalk some eighty feet below, the two guards from the ballroom had already stepped out of the carriage. A mist of thin smoke haloed the nearby street lamp. Blasi's blond hair glowed near white as he exited the carriage. Gabriella got out next.

In the darkest part of the night, even the starlight had faded. The city of New York, barely a toddler in this age before skyscrapers, slept on in dreams and shadows. I was exhausted and scared out of my mind. And though I couldn't be completely, one hundred percent certain, Blasi didn't look like a guy who was planning to kill his girlfriend and roast her body in a house fire.

Something else was bothering me. But Bran had already hoisted himself halfway back onto the roof and was gesturing for me to hurry.

"The stairway's clear," he said. "Come on, I'll guide you."

He disappeared back into the dark rectangle. I descended and let him lead me through the dusty, cluttered rooms to the stairwell.

Just before we eased out onto the top landing where

Collum and Phoebe were waiting for us, Bran spun. His arms slid around my waist. His lips found mine, warm and soft and too quick.

"Sorry," he whispered into my hair. "Couldn't be helped."

"I forgive you," I said, but I held on to him, needing this . . . needing us . . . for just one more second.

"Blasi's here," Phoebe whispered as we scurried over to join them. "He and Gabriella and the other two guards just went inside."

The door to Tesla's lab must've been left open because I could just make out Bran's features as they clenched. "If he hurt her—"

"I don't think so," I told them. "In fact—"

"Nikola Tesla!" Blasi's voice boomed up the stairway. "It is such an honor to finally meet you. I've admired your work all my life."

"Illogical," we heard Tesla reply. "You could not be many years behind me in age, and therefore what you term as 'my work' is not something for which someone like you could have a lifelong admiration. Leaving that aside, I ask you what kind of esteem is it that lends itself to abduction? Speak plainly. What it is that you want?"

The sound of a door snapping shut, and the stairway went black.

"Hope," Collum whispered. "You stay here while we go take care of the guards in the stairwell." He turned to

Phoebe and Bran before I could open my mouth to protest. "We do this fast and quiet. No shots."

Bran snapped a two-fingered salute. "Pardon," he said. "Bit of clarification. Are we snapping necks or bashing brains today? Your call."

Collum, whose sarcasm meter had never been very finely tuned, didn't blink as he handed out the crowbars Bran had scavenged from the construction site next door. "Disable and disarm only. We have tactical advantage here, so a solid blow to the back of the neck should do it. We are not murderers."

God, I so did not want to stay up here all alone. But I had no illusions as to my combat abilities. I knelt at the top of the staircase as the other three crept down.

Thuds. A couple of grunts. Silence.

Taking too long. Way, way too long. Where are they? Oh God, what if—

Phoebe rounded the landing, grinning as she loped up the steps, the boys just behind her. They were barely out of breath.

"Didn't even see us coming," she told me. "Left them trussed up and snoring on the second landing."

"So," Collum rasped. "There are still three guards inside, plus Blasi. We go in hard. Cameron, you cover the right. I take the left. Phee, you come in behind. We'll cover while you locate Mac and Doug, aye? By then, Cameron and I should have cleared, but I'll still feel better when Mac's free. Hit knees, hips, torso. No kill shots unless absolutely necessary."

"Speak for yourself," Phoebe muttered.

"What about me?"

They shared a look I didn't like. At all. Collum's eyes skated over me, assessing. He frowned when he saw me clutching my one measly dagger. Between the three of them, they carried a veritable arsenal.

Phoebe reached into her bag and retrieved a small silver revolver about the size of my palm. "What about this?"

"She hasn't trained with guns," Collum argued. "Much less a derringer."

"Aye, but we can hardly let her go unarmed, now can we?"

"What about the Colt?" Bran said.

Collum shook his head, which made me want to slap that serious *I'm-in-charge* look off his face as he said, "Hope isn't going in at all. Not until I give the word."

"Just stop it!" I snapped. "Okay? Stop talking about me like I'm not even here. I know I'm no warrior, but those are my people too. Just give me a freaking gun, Collum."

Collum peered at me for a long moment. I knew he was probably thinking: *Can we really trust her not to shoot off her own foot?*

I glared right back, letting my rage and determination show. I knew Collum and Phoebe—Bran, too, for that matter—thought they were protecting me. But I was not helpless, and I was sick and tired of other people deciding *my* fate.

I'm a Viator too, dammit. And I can decide what I'm capable of, thank you very much.

Before anyone could stop me, I snatched the Lilliputian gun from Phoebe's hand and moved to the steps. "Ready when you are."

CHAPTER 44

IT ALL HAPPENED SO FAST. LATER, I WOULD TRY TO re-create it in my head, but even with my abilities, there were simply too many elements to follow.

Kneeling outside the door, through which came the sounds of crashes and shattering glass, the slam of heavy objects being overturned.

A sharp crack. A muffled cry.

Then Collum and Bran were blasting through the door. Shouts and ear-numbing shots. Bangs and more glass shattering. The caustic mixture of gunpowder and burning oil and frying electricity. Smoke everywhere. A shot at the ceiling that made the bulbs flicker and go out.

After that, everything seemed to happen in a series of flashes. Lit only by the crackle of electricity overhead, my brain was unable to decipher the utter and complete destruction of what once had been Nikola Tesla's lab. Blasi's men had ripped the place apart.

"Holy. Friggin'. Hell."

"Took the words right out of my mouth," Bran said as he shoved me down behind an overturned table.

Golden and crimson sparks danced and popped from dangling wires. Chunks of machinery and other, unidentifiable objects lay strewn across the floor in a jumble of glass and twisted metal. A six-foot tower, one of two that were identical to those that lay beneath Christopher Manor, was on its side. Half of what might have been an intricate web of black yarn was still tacked to the wall. The rest hung in a limp tangle.

"Doug! Mac!" Phoebe shouted in triumph as she wrenched open a small utility closet and the two men tumbled out.

Collum scrabbled over a pile of detritus to the spot where Jonathan and Tesla sat on the floor, hands and wrists bound. Tesla's eye was swelling. As Collum struggled to free them, I saw one of the guards take aim. I didn't think. I just raised my gun and fired. I missed, of course. The bullet ricocheted toward me, spraying me with shards of brick before splintering one of the tall windows. The building itself seemed to inhale. A draft of dark smoke streamed in to thicken the already dense air. The shot was off, sure, but when the guy ducked, Bran dove on top of him. They went down in a flurry of fists.

I couldn't see Blasi or Gabriella anywhere.

Coughing. Coughing. Everyone coughing now.

Collum fired. A yelp of pain answered.

"Screw this." A spotty-faced guard with a beard stepped

out and tossed his gun aside. He sidestepped toward the door, clutching his wounded shoulder as blood drenched the arm of his tuxedo jacket. "Don't shoot," he said. "I'm out of here."

He ran. Sleeves covering their mouths and noses, the other two took off after him.

Ropes still dangled from Mac's wrists as he hobbled over to pull Tesla to his feet. I helped Phoebe saw through the sinewy ropes that secured Doug and Jonathan. The instant Doug was free, Phoebe threw herself on him. Eyes screwed shut, he kissed her fiercely on the top of the head. Jonathan Carlyle rubbed at his wrists, his face a mask of sorrow as he surveyed the wreckage.

"Stop!" Blasi's shout echoed off the ceiling. "Stop! Don't fucking move or I swear to God, I'll kill her."

Gunnar Blasi edged out from behind the untoppled tower, pistol jammed into the soft flesh beneath Gabriella's chin. Her hands were clasped together, begging. Her red-rimmed eyes were huge with terror.

"Where is my enhancement, Tesla?" Blasi coughed and spat on the floor. "Where is it?" He screamed this last part, like a furious toddler denied his animal crackers.

"Gone." Mac, hoarse but utterly composed, stepped forward. "I told your men, but they wouldna listen. Douglas and I, we found the professor's hiding place and destroyed the thing. See for yourself, 'tis over there, smashed to nothing." He wheezed in a breath. Tilted his head toward a dark opening in the wall where several bricks had been removed.

On the counter lay a smashed and mangled metallic tube. Tangled wires and electrical guts and small piles of what looked like minerals were strewn around close by. "The thing is done, lad. So let the girl go. Let's all leave while we still can."

Blasi laughed. He *laughed.* "Whoo!" Hacking, he wiped his eyes with the back of his gun hand. "That's not good. Oh, that is not good at all. You have no idea what you've done."

No warning as Bran made his move. In a lightning-fast sprint, he shoved Gabriella out of the way and slammed Blasi to the floor. Gabriella stumbled. Her bad leg crumpled beneath her. She cried out as she went down hard on hands and knees. Bran's attention wavered for only an instant, but it was enough for Blasi to wrench his hand free and slam the gun into Bran's temple. As Bran teetered, Blasi thrust him aside and bolted for the door.

Phoebe made to run after him but Collum grabbed her. "What do you plan to do, then? Kill the man? Take him back and turn him over to the authorities?"

Bran got to his feet and moved toward where his cousin was kneeling in the center of the floor. Gabriella de Roca lifted her head and wheezed through a silky curtain of hair. "Is this true, Professor Tesla?" She inhaled, coughed. "The enhancement device, it is destroyed?"

And I knew then what had bothered me when I saw

Gabriella emerge from the carriage. Knew what I had not seen when she hopped down and strolled across the sidewalk with Gunnar Blasi.

"Yes."Tesla—nineteenth-century gentleman that he was —took a step, hands out to aid the poor, helpless girl. "Do not concern yourself with that anymore, miss. I shall never again—"

"Look out!" I tried to scream the warning, but my throat was ripped from coughing.

Bran looked at me like I'd gone crazy as he reached Gabriella's side. "Hope?"

Only Mac and Collum reacted. Mac was closer.

Just as Gabriella leapt to her feet with an uncanny— and undamaged—dancer's grace, Mac raced forward and knocked Bran aside.

The bullet meant for Bran took Mac in the chest, spinning him to the side.

"Mac!"

I think it was Phoebe who screamed the name, or maybe it came from me. Everything was smoke and heat and blood and nothing . . . nothing was real anymore.

From his spot on the floor, Bran could only gape up as Gabriella aimed once more. She pulled the trigger, but the gun either misfired or was empty. She chucked it away in disgust just as Blasi burst back into the room and grabbed her hand.

Bran knelt in the center of the room, staring at the girl . . . the friend . . . he'd grown up with. His face held no expression, though he looked suddenly like the little boy from the forest.

I wondered why no one was moving. Why weren't they moving? Then I saw the reason. Such a small thing. It fit into Blasi's hand like a miniature black pineapple. He'd already pulled the grenade's pin, though he clamped down hard on the trigger as he and Gabriella backed toward the doorway.

Blasi smiled broadly as he hugged Gabriella tight to him.

She looked at Bran. "I am sorry, Brandon. Truly. Gunnar and I both wanted to keep you with us, but Doña Maria would not have it. I warned *her*"—she waved a casual hand in my direction—"to keep you out of this. To take you back to her home, where you would be safer."

"You were like a sister to me, Gabi," Bran told her in a flat, emotionless voice. "All those times I protected you from Celia. Every time your mother abandoned you, I was there."

Gabriella at least had the decency to look ashamed as she glanced away.

"Yeah," Blasi said. "Shame. We could have used you. And while I may not be all into Maria's whole 'Restoring the True Faith to its former glory' rhetoric, as long as she lets me loot and plunder while we hunt for the Nonius Stone . . . I'll do whatever the fuck she says."

Jonathan and Doug were speaking quietly to Mac as they knelt over his prone form. Collum and Phoebe stood nearby, but their attention was glued on Blasi and Gabriella.

Gabriella's eyes watered, though whether from tears or smoke I couldn't tell. "Gunnar may not be a believer,

Bran, but I am. I—I had to make a choice." Coughing, she wheezed out, "Do you remember the day last winter when it snowed? Bishop Mendez and Father Pietro were there. They spoke with us in the sculpture garden. Do you recall what they told us?"

Bran's head tilted, unsure. Then his jaw dropped as the memory returned. "Wait," he said. "You . . . you can't be serious?"

"Trust me," Blasi said. "They aren't kid—"

Moving with a synchronicity only those trained together since childhood could manage, Collum, Doug, and Phoebe charged.

CHAPTER 45

TOO FAR. TOO LATE.

My friends wouldn't shoot. If they did, Blasi might drop the grenade. With Collum in the rear, Doug and Phoebe would swing out to flank the pair. Capturing Blasi and Gabriella, however, was only the diversion. The true mission lay in Collum's hands. Literally. While Phoebe and Doug drew the others' attention to themselves, Collum would pounce. Blasi was a smallish guy. If Collum could reach him in time, he could easily envelop Blasi's fist with one of his own. With Blasi unable to let go or drop the explosive, they could reinsert the pin. It wasn't a terrible plan. But Blasi and Gabriella were already running backwards.

My vision pulsed a hard and fast warning as Collum hit the door an instant after Gabriella slammed it shut. Something heavy clunked onto the landing. Two sets of footsteps pounded down.

"Back!" Collum yelled. "Everyone get ba—!"

Boom.

The door saved them. Built in a time when people still cared about craftsmanship, the door only buckled inward. By the time Collum and Doug wrenched it open and saw that most of the landing and the first few stairs were missing, Blasi and Gabriella were long gone.

I counted limbs, saw they were all more or less intact, then shoved the overturned table off me and raced to Mac's side. Kneeling, I pressed my palm against the floorboards. They'd grown almost uncomfortably warm. Outside the window, the night was obscured by a veil of smoke.

Jonathan Carlyle still knelt behind Mac, propping him up. I looked up at Tesla. "The time! What is the time!"

With jerky and robotic movements, Tesla checked his pocket watch. "It is three forty-eight in the morning of the thirteenth of March."

Twelve minutes until the alarm is sounded, until people begin gathering outside on the street. Until they begin evacuating the buildings on either side of us. At four twenty-three a.m., the unfortunately ineffective fire brigade will arrive. And eleven minutes after that, the entire building will be engulfed in flames.

Gotta hurry. Gotta hurry.

Mac's dear, careworn face was covered in soot and filmed in an oily sweat. So pale he looked like a wax effigy. His lips peeled back as the breath hissed between red-rimmed teeth. The humor lines around his eyes had deepened into grooves of agony.

"Mac." I tried to keep my voice calm and steady, but it

quaked as I told him I needed to check the wound. There was barely any blood, which at first I took for a good sign.

Bran knelt beside me and between us, we ripped away Mac's blood-stained shirt. Bran worked without speaking. A blank sheet of copy paper held more expression.

Phoebe whimpered as she slid in across from me. Collum followed an instant later.

Here, near the floor, the air was somewhat better. But the haze around us was growing denser as oxygen was replaced with the stench of scorched wood and fried electricity and the burnt greasy tang of motor oil.

Overhead, only one wire—damaged when Blasi's men searched the place—still fizzed and snapped. As we gathered a beneath the amber shower, each spark of light reflected inside the smoke like the Fourth of July on a foggy night.

Phoebe took Mac's knobby, leathery hand and clutched it to her chest, and I had to squeeze my eyes shut so, so tight to keep the tears at bay.

Mac reached up to touch his granddaughter's face. "'S a'right, mo ghràdh," he wheezed. "Right . . ." Wheeze. "Rain."

"Mac, please!"

"Shh." Even barely able to draw breath, Mac was still Mac, offering comfort, as he'd always done.

Then, he coughed. A red mist fanned through the air. When a bloody froth oozed from his lips, I felt my heart wither.

Bad. This is bad.

We gently rolled him to the side, to check for an exit wound. The older man's pale, freckled back was smooth, which meant the bullet was still lodged inside. Bright, oxygen-rich blood bubbled from the neat hole in his chest.

"Roll him back. Roll him back." Frantically, I searched my memory for anything, everything regarding gunshot wounds. There was but little. My brain was packed with the useless and ridiculous minutia of historical facts and figures. Battlefield medicine had never been at the top of my list.

It was Jonathan who got it.

"I believe his lung has collapsed."

I sat back on my heels.

Tension hemopneumothorax (or collapsed lung) is a life-threatening condition produced by either blunt or penetrating chest or thoracoabdominal trauma. Signs of tension hemopneumothorax include: Difficulty breathing. Lack of breath sounds on the affected side. Hemoptysis, or blood in the sputum, often with a foamy appearance. As the affected side fills with blood, the lung will collapse down to the size of a fist. At this point, the patient will be unable to breathe.

Frantically, I searched the wreckage around us. "Hurry. Get me a cloth or something. We have to stop this bleeding."

"Hope?" I didn't answer. Collum spoke my name again, this time like a firecracker thrown at my feet. "Hope!"

I looked at him and Phoebe across their grandfather's

wide chest. Everyone was coughing now. Eyes streaming. Sweating and squinting through the smog.

Mac inhaled, the rattle growing weaker. A spasm rocked him. Jonathan held on as Mac writhed in his struggle for oxygen.

"We need to get him out of here," I said. "To clean air. To a hospital."

"Can we get him down those stairs?" Jonathan asked Collum.

Collum stared into his grandfather's face, the fearless, indomitable leader replaced momentarily by a lost little boy. "I don't . . . I'm not sure."

Bran pressed his ear to Mac's chest. "His heartbeat is erratic. And I cannot hear any breath sounds."

Mac reared up in a violent spasm. His hands fisted as he went rigid. His chest heaved, but hardly any air moved between his dusky lips. After several agonizing seconds, he went mercifully limp.

"Here." Tesla bent toward me, holding out a wad of raw cotton. "I use it to pack my more delicate instruments."

I grabbed it, tore off a large piece of the white fluff, and pressed it to the wound.

No flinch. No groan. Mac's features remained slack and empty as his breath still wheezed and the cotton wicked up the blood. The wad grew heavy. I tossed it aside, but the same thing happened with the next handful and the next. With every inhalation, Mac's chest moved a bit less.

Sweat trickled down my back. The room was heating up

quickly. Tendrils of smoke had begun to ooze up the inner walls.

Jonathan put an ear to Mac's mouth. "The breathing has become more strained."

"I know," I snapped. "Just give me a second."

I took a deep breath, and let drawings and images of the human anatomy ... any article, any vague reference ... roll through my brain.

When my eyes opened, I knew what had to be done.

The gold standard for treatment is thoracotomy—a tube inserted between the ribs and into the chest cavity—to release the pressure.

Without this immediate intervention, this condition is, in every case, fatal.

"I need tubing. Glass or—or rubber if you have it. And a small, sharp knife."

Doug's bleak gaze met mine. He nodded in understanding. "Can you do it?"

"I don't ... I don't know."

My hands were shaking as I pressed a fresh wad of cotton to the wound. But I now knew, without a doubt, what was happening.

Mac's lung had been punctured by the bullet. With no exit wound, the bullet had likely been slowed by a rib. Shards of bone fragments had severed arteries and veins, and now his right lung and chest cavity were filling with air and blood. If we couldn't drain it off, he would suffocate.

Tesla's long face looked ravaged as he stared around at what had once been the center of his universe.

"It will burn," he said. "All of it, gone."

"Professor!" I shouted. "Please. Listen."

Tesla's expression cleared as I explained what we needed. "Oh. Y-yes. I see. Of course."

While the professor and Doug searched the rubble, Phoebe smoothed back her grandfather's thinning hair.

"Tell me he's going to be okay, Hope. Tell me."

"I don't . . ." I hesitated. Stalling, I pressed the heel of my hands hard between my eyes. I mumbled, "This should work. In . . . In theory, this should work."

Mac stirred. His eyelids fluttered. Bleary blue eyes focused on Phoebe and he tried to smile, but his too-pale brow furrowed as he struggled for breath. "Kids—" *Wheeze.* "Where?" *Wheeze.*

"Shhh," Phoebe told him. "It's all right, Mac. We're here. And all of us, right as rain." Her lips trembled as she held tight to her grandfather's hand. My throat constricted as Mac squeezed his eyes shut, a tear rolling down each side to dampen his faded red hair. His lips barely moved as he murmured a Gaelic prayer.

"Aye," Phoebe choked. "But you rest now. Because you're going to be fine. Just fine."

I had to look away, unable to bear it as she laid her small head on her grandfather's chest. Mac's hand rose and stroked her hair. His gaze roamed until it found his grandson. "Proud . . ." he wheezed. "Of you . . ."

Collum's Adam's apple bobbed convulsively. He leaned down and kissed his grandfather on the forehead. "I know, Mac," he managed. "You tell me every day."

Exhausted, Mac looked at me, the words escaping on a sigh. "Hope. Our precious . . . lamb."

Mac—the first person I'd met when I arrived in Scotland, the first person to make me feel like maybe I didn't have to be all alone in the world—smiled at me. "Tell Moira . . . I'll wait . . . by . . . picnic ta . . ."

His eyes drifted shut as he passed back into unconsciousness.

Everyone gathered around once the supplies were ready. Mac's lips were blue and his fingernails dark. His chest barely moved now. As Collum handed me a tiny knife, my hands shook so hard my fingers wouldn't work.

"I . . ." I couldn't see past the tears. "I can't . . ."

Collum nodded, clasped the knife. "Guide me."

Bran put a hand on his shoulder, his eyes filled with sorrow. "I can do it if—"

"No." Collum shook his head. "No. I've got it. Hope?"

I bore down, focusing a needle-sharp light on everything I had ever seen, read, heard about the procedure for evacuating a collapsed lung.

Coughing and coughing. Sweating and coughing again. Finally, I nodded.

"Pour the alcohol over everything. His skin. The knife. Over and through that glass tubing."

The room filled with the eye-watering aroma of whiskey from a silver flask.

Mac's breathing suddenly stuttered. His back arched as his mouth opened, struggling for air. His cells were starving for oxygen. He was drowning in his own blood now, the fluid inside the collapsed lung shoving its way across his chest cavity to smother the one good lung he still had.

"Hope!" Phoebe cried. "What's happening?"

"Hold him down! Okay, Collum," I said. "Right there!"

I touched a fingertip to the space just between the fifth and sixth ribs. With a thrust, Collum slit open the skin. "Deeper," I said. I held back the skin as Collum sunk the knife through the tough cartilage. "That's good," I said. "Here."

He took the glass tube from me and pushed it carefully through the cut. "More," I urged. "More."

I was choking on smoke and tears now as Collum pushed the tube in farther still. Something popped deep inside. Blood gushed from the end of the tube and splattered across the floor. Air hissed out after.

"That's it!" I cried. "You did it! You did it!"

Collum turned to me, beaming.

We waited.

"Mac?" I said, when nothing happened. "Mac, you . . . you have to breathe, now. Please. Just breathe. Please!" But my pleas did no good, because we were too late. Phoebe was lying across her grandfather's still, still chest, clutching him. Wailing. And Doug was leaning over her, holding her so tight. And Bran was looking at Collum and me, and his eyes looked sad. So very, very sad.

He spoke the words gently. "I'm sorry, Collum." And I knew then that it was over, because I had never, ever heard Bran call Collum by his real name. "You tried. You tried so hard."

CHAPTER 46

Across the street from Nikola Tesla's lab, we watched the fire consume the building and everything inside. The inferno seemed appropriate somehow. Ruin and devastation and loss. We'd made it down the stairs with Mac's limp and lifeless form only seconds before the fire and the smoke would have made escape impossible.

As Collum and Doug laid Mac carefully across the carriage seat, Nikola Tesla sat next to me on a stoop with his head in his hands.

The structure shimmied, as if its bones had become porous, like an elderly woman's fragile spine. Fire shot up from the roof in puffs of orange. Muffled bangs shook the ground beneath us.

"That would be the gas reserve in the basement." Bran, leaning against the brick wall on my other side, spoke in a rasp. "If I had to guess."

Our voyage from Tesla's lab to the street below had been nothing short of hellish. Hellish in the most literal sense. Though Blasi's grenade had badly damaged the fourth-floor landing, Bran, Doug, Tesla, and Jonathan bridged the gap using ropes and tabletops. They braced the makeshift staircase with the only object sturdy enough to support our weight . . . the single intact tower. Dismantling the mushroom top had taken Tesla only seconds. But he'd flinched when the others hoisted it through the door and dropped it down onto the next level.

Like Charon escorting souls across the river Styx, Collum —ignoring any offer of assistance—carried his grandfather's body through the flames.

"I'm sorry, Professor," I told Tesla. "I wish there was something we could have done."

Tesla raised his head, and it might have been only the reflection of the flames . . . but there was a peculiar, almost unearthly luminosity in his eyes as he turned to look at me.

"God has spoken," he said. "And has set his judgment against this venture. I am finished. For many years, I spent my time searching for an object that I now know will ever elude me.

He cupped his hands. Let them drop.

I glanced over at Bran. Just after we'd made it to street level, he showed me what he'd collected seconds before we ran. His pockets had been stuffed with dozens . . . no, hundreds . . . of scribbled notes, newspaper clippings, pages torn from books. A few pieces even looked like bits of ancient parchment.

Though the items were from completely different eras, each and every one mentioned a single thing.

The Nonius Stone.

Tesla was fiddling with his jacket. He held out his palm, and the firelight glinted off the pin he'd hidden beneath his lapel.

Ah. So that's what all that business with Astor and Vanderbilt was about.

Tesla's gaze rose to the ruin of his life's work. "I only entered the brotherhood as a means to further my search. What good will this do me now?"

He let the pin drop onto the sidewalk between us.

"I believe I shall travel," he said. "I have long wished to see the West of this nation. But hold one moment, if you please. I—I have something for you. Please, take it. But do not open it until you are far from this place. Do I have your word?"

When I nodded, Tesla reached for a shoebox-size bundle at his feet. Wrapped in burlap and tied with twine, it smelled like smoke and regret.

"Thank you," I told him.

"You may not say that once you have opened it."

He took my hand in his. "Goodbye, Miss Walton. Go with God," he said. "And remember, every man is but a spark of light in an infinite darkness; soon extinguished but might and brilliant all the same."

And then Tesla, the greatest mind of his age, turned around and walked away.

Collum trudged over to us, head hanging. "It's time."

From down the street, alarm bells rang. A horse-drawn fire truck raced toward us.

Doug led Phoebe to the carriage. She looked like someone who'd been scourged from the inside out. Face swollen with tears, she started to climb up. Her head turned as she spied Jonathan Carlyle. After a quick consultation with Doug, she kissed him and walked over to Jonathan.

"May I speak with you for a moment?" she said.

"Of course," Jonathan replied, taking her arm.

It didn't take long. Jonathan drew back in horror at whatever she said. Collum watched them, and I thought he might try to intervene. But he turned away and climbed up beside his grandfather's body without a word.

At the riverbank, the low tide had left a gravel strip along the water's edge just large enough for us to enter the cattle tunnel. Dawn had broken, though the sun was hidden by low clouds. The city around us was mist and smoke and everywhere ... everywhere ... everywhere gray.

Moira MacPherson was a Scot. Her eyes were dry when they lowered her husband into the earth beside his ancestors in the small graveyard near the manor. As the piper's song spread out over the moors and mountains, Moira lifted her eyes to the Scottish Highlands as if she could see Mac there, waiting for her.

I'd paused to retie my shoe as the rest of the family passed out of the fenced graveyard, and so was the only one to hear Moira's quiet voice as she placed a hand on the granite headstone. "Fare thee well, my only love. Fare thee well a while ..."

So many people came to the wake. I served punch in the library, with Bran at my side.

"It's so strange to see them here," I said.

"Who?"

I tilted my head toward the fireplace, where painting of a young woman and her large brood now shared space with Jonathan Carlyle's family portraits. The other daughter—Penelope—had been taken by a flu epidemic, only a year after she would have perished beneath the ice.

Destiny, I supposed. Fate. Something like that.

But there were many photos and paintings of the older girl, Catherine. As a pretty teenager. A wedding photo alongside her smiling husband. Elderly, surrounded by her children, and her children's children.

Phoebe had done it without hesitation or remorse. She'd simply told Jonathan Carlyle the truth. As far as we could tell, there'd been no global disaster as a result. No mass murderer in the family tree. And apparently no one of that branch had joined the "family business" either, though we would have a lot to explain to Lu once things settled.

A young man had brought his wife and twin boys to the wake. He stood now, looking up at the portrait of his great-great-grandmother, pointing her out to his squirming sons.

"Can you take her?" My mother walked up, my wailing sister on her shoulder. "She's colicky, and I want to take some tea up to Moira. She's resting."

"Of course," I said. "Come here, chubs." I took Ellie, but she squirmed and grunted in my arms, clearly unhappy with life at the moment.

"Hang on. I know a little trick." Bran hustled over to the broom closet. The real one, not the hidden entrance to a world of risk and danger and glory that most of these people would never know existed.

Bran came back pushing a vacuum cleaner. "All right," he said over the noise. "Give that little dove to me. This will work. Plus, all babies love me."

Ellie did love him. Of course she did, which irritated me no end.

It also made every muscle in my body go gooey as

warmed caramel, watching Bran Cameron run the vacuum while crooning softly to my baby sister.

When he turned it off, Ellie was sound asleep.

"I—I used to do this for Tony," he said. "He was such a horrid little thing. I was the only one who could quiet him."

Bran had a long and private talk with Aunt Lucinda. Neither one had yet revealed what was said. But I had seen the stunned look on Lucinda's face when the door to her office opened. Whatever Bran told her . . . it wasn't good. I'd eventually get it out of Bran, though I had a feeling it had to do with Blasi's and Gabriella's statements about the restoration of the True Faith and whatever the two priests had told.

We'd had little time alone in the few days since our return. Mac's death had ripped a piece of all our souls away, leaving aching, empty space behind. Watching Phoebe grieve and Collum shoulder the blame had made it ten times worse.

"Go for a ride later?"

My breath caught at the soft, husky tone. I looked up at Bran, and heat fired to life from some new place deep inside me, rising . . . rising to color my face.

He saw it, and that cocky grin began to spread across his lips. Blue and green eyes went sleepy and heavy-lidded. At the promise I saw in those eyes . . . at the intensity . . . the heat inside me went from a soft simmer to a roiling boil.

"Um, yeah," I said. "If Ethel's not too mad at me."

"She *can* get a bit surly when she's not paid enough attention." He rocked Ellie in his arms. "I wonder who she gets that from?"

I kicked him under the table. He yelped, startling the baby.

"Now look what you've done," he said, but he was grinning at me in that Bran way that made me want to smack him and kiss him and roll around in the heather with him all at the same time.

"Who's got a surly sister?" he cooed to Ellie. "You've got a surly sister, yes you do."

"This would be one of those *stop talking* moments, Bran."

"Then I stick by my statement," he said. "Surly."

He looked down into my sister's chubby face. She grasped his finger and his smile wavered. "I'm going to get my brother out of there, you know."

I swallowed. Nodded. Felt my own smile fade. "I know."

After the initial storm passed, Aunt Lucinda met with Collum, Phoebe, Doug, and me privately. "I've spoken with Brandon," she told us. "And I've agreed to let him stay here for the time being."

Aunt Lucinda met each of our eyes in turn. She was looking better. More color in her cheeks, despite the pain etched permanently around her eyes. Mom had mentioned that the treatments were going well.

Curled up beside Doug on the aged leather, Phoebe appeared shrunken. She wore baggy shorts and a loose tee. Most disturbing was her hair, still the same demure auburn she'd chosen before we left, to better match the wig.

Back in his usual gold-framed glasses, Doug was watching the girl he loved. He looked different too. Older. Some of the gentleness siphoned away.

"From the information Hope and Brandon have shared," Lucinda said, "I believe we are now dealing with an entirely new threat. Gunnar Blasi and Gabriella de Roca have their own agenda. We must be on our guard at all times."

Lucinda sighed and selected one of two objects from the table beside her. After we'd returned to Christopher Manor, alone in my room, I had unwrapped the bundle Nikola Tesla had given me. When I saw what was inside, I stared down at it for a long, long time. Then I gave it to Lucinda. Though gifted to me, the contents affected us all.

My aunt's faded-denim eyes skimmed over the words inscribed on the piece of yellowed parchment, sealed between two thick panes of glass.

"Nikola Tesla told Hope that he located this several years ago in his research on the Nonius Stone," she told us.

She laid the glass on the table. Everyone leaned forward to read the elaborate script. Everyone but me. I didn't need to read it again.

To my most noble Friend,

A development has come to light on the Objecte dear to both our hearts. I shall first share with you the history I have so recently uncovered.

From ancient times, a clandestine Order of nuns, said to be endowed with Holy mystical knowledge, kept the Objecte in strictest secrecy. Only one per generation was trusted with its location, passing the secret on to a younger, worthy Sister upon the old one's impending death.

This I have traced back over four hundred years to the last person known to possess this information. A close confidante of Queen Eleanor of Aquitaine herself, it seems. Unfortunately, the good Sister died before she could pass the secret to her successor. The secret, then, died with her. Or so I believed.

I admit, I was faire perplexed. The trail gone cold, I was not certain where to turn. But oh, dear Lady, I impart to you the most joyous of news. As you know, I have consulted the stars often of late, and they have been disturbingly vague. But at last, noble Friend. At long last.

Today, I received an unexpected visit

from an old acquaintance. Edward Kelly
is a brilliant man. One with whom, until
recently, I held a close friendship. I had
not seen him in some months, not since our
disharmonious parting in Prague. He came
to beg my forgiveness for events which I
shall not mention to one so pure as your
great Self.

Kelly knew I sought the stone. Burdened
by guilt and shame, he revealed that he located the Objecte nigh on two years ago, and
hid the fact from me. Now, out of sorry recom-
pense he . . .

But I digress. His words are of no
matter against what he brought with him!
The Objecte, Lady! Oh, and it is the true
Objecte. My assistant Michael, a bright
and promising young Scot, is also familiar
with the Objecte's lore, and has seconded my
initial verification. As he transcribes this
letter for me now, I see him nodding his
agreement.

Great Lady, I shall soon travel to
London, and lay in your hands that which
has so long eluded us.

Written from Mortlake, this Saturday,
the xvi of July, year of our Lord, 1588.

*As always, I remain your most constant
and humble servant,*

$\overline{OO|}$

I leaned in then, and touched a finger to the glass,
tracing the familiar signature. Memories of my kind, gentle grandfather surged up from the shadowy back part of
my memory.

I hadn't shown anyone the pin that Nikola Tesla cast off
on the night his lab burned. I could feel its shape through
the front pocket of my jeans. I'd known what it stood for the
second I picked it up.

The rosy cross seated on a pyramid. The symbol of a very
old, very powerful, and supposedly very archaic organization.

The Hermetic Order of the Golden Dawn.

*A mystical order, akin to modern-day Masons, who arose out
of the Rosicrucian movement of the sixteenth century. A movement, by the way, whose society had been at least partially based
on the occultish writings of none other than Dr. John Dee.*

*A laundry list of secret societies had formed, one after the oth-
er, following Dee's death. Once considered the greatest mind of
his age, in Dee's later years, he'd become obsessed with the occult.
Had believed his friend Edward Kelly could speak with angels,
and had been convinced that he — and only he — could translate
this celestial language.*

When I thought of Dr. John Dee, of my Poppy, it left

me oddly hollow. As if a surgeon had carved away a piece of something small but vital.

"But," Phoebe said. "The letter ... Dee's talking about Da, isn't he?"

Aunt Lucinda studied each of our faces before speaking. "Yes," she said at last. "Yes, I believe so. The timing works, and it actually makes a lot of sense. I can see how it would be very like Michael to position himself in this way. Now," she went on. "As to this."

She held up the second item. Lucinda and Moira had found it in Mac's pocket, shortly after we brought his body home.

Lucinda held the tubular metallic object across her flattened palm. "Moira and I have discussed this," she said. "Mac MacPherson was one of the wisest people I've ever known. If he believed this enhancement was important enough to save, then we will—one day—consider its use. I say *consider*, only." She raised a finger. "In the meantime, we must ensure it never falls into the wrong hands."

Lucinda set the enhancement down with a clink. Collum's eyes never strayed from it as Aunt Lucinda straightened. "And one other thing." She paused until everyone's attention—including Collum's—was focused solely on her.

My aunt's thin upper lip pulled back from her teeth.

Shock thrummed through me at the raw savagery in her voice.

"Everyone rest. For two weeks we honor and mourn our fallen brother. But after that, we shall begin to form a plan." Lucinda's words, fueled by grief and rage, scalded us like steam. "We now know Michael's most likely location. And I swear to you . . . *they* may have taken away my dearest friend's husband . . ." She stood, and I could feel my heart hammering harder and harder as she spoke through clenched teeth.

"But by *God* we are going to give her back her son!"

CHAPTER 47

"Here you are, my lamb. It took some doing, but she looks just as good as new, if I do say it myself."

Moira's apple cheeks didn't rise high enough to squish her small gray eyes when she smiled anymore. And when she handed me the newly repaired doll, I could see the empty space behind them.

"Thank you so much." I turned the delicate, priceless poppet over, examining her. "Wow, you can't even tell."

"'Tis fortunate you kept her in your bag at all to get her home. Were I you, I'd put her up somewhere safe. Out of the clutches of that demon creature."

We both looked at the kitten. Hecty was crouched low, calico fur standing on end as she readied to pounce on a sunbeam that danced across my bedroom floor.

Moira turned away from me, voice hoarse as she bent down to scoop up the kitten. "Damn little beastie."

For two days after we'd buried Mac, Hecty would not leave his gravesite. She didn't cry or yowl. Only lay atop the cold earth, her head in the exact spot where Mac's vest pocket would've been.

My lips trembled and I had to nip down hard on a half-healed cuticle. "Moira, I—"

She raised a hand to my cheek. Her palm felt like the cool side of the pillow as she studied me. At the wisdom and the compassion and the strength I saw, my own eyes started to water.

"No, no. None of that, now. There's much to do and more. We've a voyage to be preparin' for, now don't we?"

Letting the cat slide to the floor, Moira stood back up and pulled me into her soft arms for a quick embrace. Then, hands on my shoulders, she spoke.

"Life gives us the path, lamb. But it's our choice whether to creep and crawl along it, or stride out with shoulders back and head held high."

For the first time in the two and a half weeks since we'd lost Mac, I saw the familiar spark of spirit.

"Aye," she said, nodding at my doubtful expression, "I agree. Load of horse malarkey, that is. Mac spouted that same bit off at me when we were new married and I'd burned the rack of lamb. His nasty old besom of a mum was coming for Easter dinner, see, and I was beside my-self." She smiled, her eyes far, far away. "I smacked him with the potholder and told him if he wanted to walk a path so badly, there was the door. Get to steppin'."

A laugh burst out of me. From the other side of the room came a loud sniff.

Phoebe was leaning against the doorjamb, watching us. She looked as forlorn a creature as any I'd ever seen. Of course, she'd been extraordinarily close to Mac. His death had hit her harder than almost anyone.

Moira said nothing, just held out her arms. Phoebe scrubbed a palm up over her nose and raced to her grandmother. With an arm about each of us, Moira strolled to the window. She gave us each a squeeze, then let go and pushed up the sash.

The temperate breeze smelled of rich earth and stone, of animal dung and the sweet, nutty floral of the heather and gorse. It whisked past us, sending the kitty into paroxysms of delight as she gave chase to a swirl of dust bunnies.

Moira squinted at her granddaughter's still-drab hair and shapeless clothes.

"No. No, no. I will not have it. Phoebe Marie MacPherson," she said, in her sternest Gram-speak. "For the love of Mary and Saint Bride, take yourself down to Fiona's salon straightaway. I don't want to see you again until that hair of yours is some shade of color one cannot find in nature."

The grin that slowly split my best friend's face was the most beautiful thing I've ever seen.

"Oh, but your grandda loved this place with all his heart," Moira went on, looking out at the vista below.

"He did at that, Gram," Phoebe choked out. "He did at that."

Outside, the Highlands were a riot of green and purple, yellow and white. And always, always the gray granite peaks of the mountains. Gnarled and knowing and eternal, they watched over the pastures and townships below.

"And just *what* is it you all find so interesting?"

We turned to find Aunt Lucinda in a pair of flowy linen pants and curiously bright floral top.

"Just admiring the view, love," Moira said, her keen gaze taking in Lucinda's short, now wigless strawberry blond hair and coral lipstick. "And where might you be off to, then?"

"She's going out with Greta," my mom teased as she slipped past her sister and entered the room. "Aren't you, Lu?"

Aunt Lucinda scoffed, though her cheeks pinked. "For heaven's sake, Sarah, could you possibly act a bit less juvenile?"

"I understand it's what little sisters were placed on this earth for, or don't you remember?"

My heart glowed to see a new lightness around my mother's eyes as she winked at us. Tucking a white strand of hair behind her ear, Mom leaned up and bussed Lucinda on the cheek. "You deserve this, darling. I mean that. I'm happy for you," she said. "Now, shall Ellie and I walk you out?"

In the field below, two knobby old rams crashed horns, while a group of ewes looked on in bland amusement.

I realized I'd been hearing something else too, for a while. The metallic *clink, clink* of sword strikes. The groans and grunts of athletic effort. Male shouts.

I had to lean out a bit to see them. In the stable training

yard, Bran and Collum were sparring with swords while Doug twirled his oak staff, ready to join the melee.

Collum stayed low, heavy gladiator sword barely moving as his steady gaze tracked Bran's whirling, fluid motions.

"Earth and fire. Water and air."

I hadn't realized I'd said it aloud, until Phoebe snorted. "Oh bother. Hope's going all poetic on us now."

I shoved her, and when she laughed, my heart nearly burst.

The boys tumbled to the ground in a heap of steel and muscles. Across the field, the rams slammed together again.

"Males," Moira said, chuckling, as she walked away. "All the same and no mind the species."

THE END

ACKNOWLEDGMENTS

There's no way I can ever thank all the people who helped make this book into a real, live thing. But I'm sure going to try!

First and always, thank you to my husband, Phil. We fell in love when we were seventeen, which only proves that young love is real and can last forever. After all these years, I still get butterflies when you walk in the room. Since the day I strolled through the house after having a shower epiphany and told you I was going to write a book, you've been my biggest fan, my alpha reader, and the only one who keeps me from walking into trees. I love you, baby. This book belongs to both of us! 45888.

My heart belongs to our strong, handsome, brilliant sons, Phillip and Parker. We're a proudly nerdy family— we love to read, and we laugh every day. Trust me when I say . . . it's the best way to live! I love you both more than you will ever know.

I dedicated *Sparks of Light* to my mom, Nena Butler, my second alpha reader, and the person I want to be when I grow up. I inherited my love of books from you, and it's still the best gift I've ever received. To my sweet daddy, Duck, who's so very proud of me; and to my brave, beautiful sister, Jennifer, and my smart and lovely nieces, Hannah, Kayley, and Ava (who let me use her middle name for my main character).

Thank you to my friend, my fierce and brilliant agent, Mollie Glick. Mollie, you're my shield in this scary new world of publishing and I'm forever grateful to have you on my side! Thanks also to her wonderful assistant, Joy Fowlkes, whom I bug endlessly, and who fits her name so beautifully.

Thank you to my fantastic Houghton Mifflin Harcourt editor, Sarah Landis. Sarah helped me lead Hope and the gang through this new adventure in ways I never dreamed, and I absolutely adore you. So, SO many thanks to my awesome new publicist, Michelle Triant, for loving these books and wanting to get them out in front of you all! And thanks again to Ann Dye and Lisa DiSarro, my phenomenal marketing team! And all my gratitude to the rest of the lovely folks at HMH Kids for believing in Hope's story.

Thanks always to the author Heather Webb, my critique partner and writing BFF . . . and to my real-life BFF since Mrs. Irby's third-grade classroom, Kelley Riggs Nichols.

Love to all my Arkansas friends, including Linda Gayton, Yolanda Longley, and Lynette Place (whose talent made my author picture look halfway decent). Michelle Buchanan and her brilliant daughter Marlee, thank you for being my beta readers. And to Phil and Deb Palludan for being the bravest people I've ever known!

A huge thanks to my new "posse," the Sweet 16s. I couldn't get through the day without WAY too many texts, IMs, emails, and frantic phone calls flying between me and Marisa Reichardt, Shea Olsen, Shannon Parker, Catherine Lo, and Kathryn Purdie. And thank you so much to all my "big sister" authors, who've helped mentor me through this crazy writing world: Jenny Martin, Joelle Charbonneau, Lee Kelly, Rysa Walker, Leigh Bardugo, Brenda Drake, CJ Redwine, Lisa Maxwell, and Erica Chapman.

All the love and gratitude in the land to the phenomenal YA blogging community, especially my precious "assistant" Miranda Eduardo ♥ (@TBF & @mirandareads), Rachel (@yaperfectionist), Kris—My Friends Are Fiction (@Kris10MFAF), Jamie (@RockstarBkTours & @arnoldjamie13), Brittany (@BBookrambles), and all the lovelies at @YAReads, plus so many more. You guys make this journey exponentially more fun!

And as always, I'm forever grateful to Diana Gabaldon, for making historical time travel totally and completely badass.